The Redemption of a Good Girl Gone Bad Part 2

By M.J.Brown

Love
M J Brown

1

Dedication:

To everyone that still DREAMS

Special THANKS:

To my Future Family THANK YOU. I pray that you will understand why Mommy did this and forgive me, Jesus made me Do it for you for the Future, I pray for you daily. My Husband, Thank you Baby.
My Angel's, even the dark ones, you inspire me. Always my Heavenly Father, and ME.

Thank you:

Always, my Mom and Dad, I LOVE YOU both. To my family thank you for your understanding. Thank you for always telling me you're proud of me.

Word of Scripture: Psalms 107:2

Let the Redeemed of the Lord say so,

JOY

to the World Productions presents:
"The Redemption of a Good Girl Gone Bad 2"

07/20/09

Heart Break

This is a Heartbreak
It was one that ached
Heartbreak
A Heart that was in bondage screaming
to be set free
Heartbreak
Every depth of feeling it.
Scratch then ripped finally shattered.
Heartbreak
Many ask why But I....try to mend in many different
ways
Talk to my heart, teach my heart, discipline my heart
Most importantly pray to Jesus to make a way for my
heart
I ask to forgive every mishap from me and them.
Keep it clear – My Heart
I also ask the Lord out of curiosity what if an operator
can remove it and give me another one.
Will it work, A New Work?
My Heart put together AGAIN.

m.j. brown

Isiah 53

A.K.A – TIN WOMAN

03/07/07

My Plans

I try not to think of the negativity
that surrounds me and reflect
on the positivity in me and let
it shine to see.
I always say things could be worst.
Don't reflect on the pain or hurts.
Things could be a lot worst.

Wait to you share your purpose
I have a Great life with happiness
and a little strife. That's been life.
If you look in my book, Please read
the words to deeply understand me.
I take nothing for granted every
since the day I was planted. I took everything
I could stand because it was part of the plan.

M.J. Brown

Raising a Family
(La Familia)

The most important thing in life to
me
What I think is the most valuable key.
Is building a family
A foundation that stands strong
Especially when things go wrong

When Man and Woman are join
With their new found source which is
Love
To whom is it given from?
Its suppose to be the one up above
A Beautiful covenant if it's Real Love

Remember don't step on his toes
Only one can be in Control
Lady's if you like to drive, let him be
on the passenger side.
Please!!! Have a gentle side

When children come into play
That's when it's vital to stay
home and raise a Familay.

m.j.brown

Chapter 1

Making It Happen

I woke up this morning ...pulling up my eye mask
that hides my pupils from the beaming sun coming from
my double sided windows in my bedroom. Opening my
eyes slowly, I then sat up to have a good arm stretch for the
morning. First things first I thank God for waking me up.
Instantly after that, I thought about the most awful dream I
had. I can't believe the horrible things that I went through
in this dream. Running my fingers through my long hair
with heavy thoughts remembering what occurred in this
dream. I thought: *That would have been a nightmare to
have scars on my face.* As I sat up and touched my smooth
skin on my face wiping the cold out my eye.

I then focused on my newly bought Michael Amini
canopy bedroom set – It's a Monte Carlo collection with a
light brown finish. Actress/ Singer Solange Knowles had
the very same bedroom set but grey on MTV Cribs. You
would ooh at the sight. It was internationally shipped here.
It's amazing how my bed had to have a specialist come and
build my queen sized bed up to perfection to fit me. I had to
step back and admire my taste. It was my first big purchase

that I'm proud of. I took my time getting out of the bed putting my French pedicure feet in my Scooby doo slippers. In the back of my mind I kept thinking of that horrible dream. Getting in my hall way where my art deco is placed I went in my dark bathroom to do the second thing that comes natural and that's use the toilet. I rub my soft face to make sure it was just a dream. My Co Co brown skin felt smooth and well taken care of. I got up. Getting my tooth brush out of the vanity mirror to brush my teeth, to confirm this belief I turned on the light switch of the bathroom. I closed the mirror back looking up to the mirror and BAM! Scars on my face in the same place.

My heart and mind felt assured knowing it was just a horrible dream I had this whole time. My mind played a very bad trick on me. The dream felt so real. After a few years reality hadn't sunk in that I have these marks on my face. In the dream I replayed that whole traumatic experience all over in just hours of sleep. At the end of the dream I woke up feeling like this thought is so refreshed in my mind that it was just a bad dream... my face is fine.

Having that kind of dream for the first time feeling like it was so real. "It's time to get ready for the day," I said out loud to myself. I have an eleven o' clock and a 1 o'clock class today.

The fall semester is going great I enrolled in fifteen hours and all the classes I can handle. This time in school I advised myself only taking two concentrated courses that were at junior level. I had approximately four more semesters to go.

Real Love is happening with my relationship with Aaron still. We're together now in a good understanding relationship. Even though I have my situation with Javontae it's not the same as my situation with Aaron. See Javontae is my best friend turn fiancé. Javontae and I have never been intimate. We hardly spoke on the phone not even having time to see one another with him being only three hours away in New York.

With me living in Maryland, Aaron and I saw each other every other day. He made sure we took time to go out to eat and talking – having movie nights was a regular thing for us. Sometimes I even cooked. He made sure we spent time between my hectic schedules even coming up to my job. He's falling in love with me and I'm starting to feel the same way. Aaron's actions showed it the most. How he held me or his deep looks into my eyes when I talked to him.

He finally found a job that accepted his background. It's a construction company but work. He had to pay a little debt to society that made it hard for him to find a better one. He did a little bit of time for a drug traffic charge back in California where he lived. That lifestyle was something he's trying to stay away from. That's why he moved up here to Maryland. I went into some of the drama I too got away from in Oklahoma. So that's how we really connected. He once had a baller's lifestyle with bread but now he's dealing with crumbs. He was saving up to get a car and stop driving his mother's gold 99'Honda Accord.

Things started to change for me and the mindset on how to choose a companion. Not just finding someone that's accomplished however one that has a kind heart too. Aaron knew that that's what I was looking for, a man established. He knew I had expensive taste by the looks of my apartment. Out the blue he said to me once: "I can't buy you those expensive things right now but I can do things that come from the heart... things that will make you smile."

Aaron did have a way of touching my heart, like walks on the harbor, sitting in my car or his home sharing funny stories, learning situations that occurred in each other's lives. He also had a goofy side.

It wasn't always about sex with him however he always showed a deep passion for me as if we had met before in a past life. Just the way Aaron looked into my eyes touching my hair or body, holding me with care.

Aaron wanted me to be his girl and be the only one he was with. When we first met I had pre warned him that I have a situation with Javontae. Aaron never really showed much concern to it especially knowing the details of how it's not going anywhere. No communication, No hugs and No Love. Javontae and me hardly even kissed let alone have sex.

One thing about Javontae, he's getting his future in order going to Columbia University for a master's degree in communications. He had confidence that he's going places and wanted me under his arm to show off even more. I liked the sound of picking out a big city to live in where he started his career in broadcasting. He made it sound even juicier in the conversations we did have about building a home from the ground up.

Javontae's a very distinguished looking guy with fair skin and kept nicely groomed. His nickname is Monkey which gives you an idea of how he looks. One thing about Javontae he's in his prime of getting his goals intact. Aaron was not, he's older in his early thirties. I'm still in my early twenties. Even though Aaron would sometimes get braggadocios about being an extra in some movies and doing some modeling in California.

He's so fine that sometimes I would even mess with his ego and tell him he wasn't all that. I had a problem with him living with his mother at thirty-two. Even though her house is very nice in a ritzy area in Maryland, that's what made it okay. Plus she's running a business out of her home taking care of the elderly. Aaron helped when she went to stay overnight somewhere else. I would sneak over on those nights he had to keep Ms. Tyler.

Ms. Tyler is a ninety – two year old woman that's so sweet. She lived with them needing full time assistance. He would put her in the bed and we would go watch television in their costly looking family room connected to his room being perfect for us. It's the bottom floor in the three story brick row house.

It's sort of amazing that out of the girl's Aaron had seen at the clubs he picked me to be with. And yes he's that fine he could choose any girl in those clubs to be with by his looks alone. Sometimes I even thought: *Wow! He's really with me.* Aaron is Indian and Black, tall, dark caramel tone with coal black wavy long hair he kept braided in a pony tail that went to the middle of his back. He looked like something right off of the Last Mohicans to be specific Hawkeye's brother. He had a body exactly like Tyson Beckford but without all the tattoos and also his sexy street appeal. One thing Aaron loved to do is workout. The one thing I wished I could do for him is braid, but I didn't know how.

He would hold me close and look in my eyes while I looked into his just sitting on my couch. Sometimes he even laid his head on my stomach while we held each other. To me that's special. Since I didn't have a television in my apartment we would listen to music. We both are fans of Jay-Z analyzing his lyrics listening. He loved when we would be listening to the radio and Alicia Keys song "A Woman's Worth" would play. He would kiss me somewhere telling me this is the song he thinks of me. He even bought me the CD and we made love to the whole thing once. It's was beautiful. A REAL good feeling to feel but guilt is in the back of my mind.

12

One thing I was trying to focus on is school. It's my junior and almost senior year, meaning I was taking junior and senior level courses. This time I had to give it my all. After my 1 o'clock class was over. I went to the mall to fill out applications at the high end retail stores like Nordstrom's. When I was in Macy's I bought some Fashion Fair make up. I walked past the Outline store where they sell high end clothing. I saw the most different looking dress I've ever seen that had a message on the long form fitting dress. It caught my eye because being orange on one side and white on the other. The message is on the white side in black letters saying in a nutshell that it is good for change in your life. Make a journey to get out into a new positive environment, see the world. At the end of the message it said don't forget your toothbrush. It made me laugh out loud. I had to buy the item, looking inside the dress to get the price off the high end looking tag saying Moschino $230 dollar's. I knew I had it on my debit card. I tried on the medium then the small, the small fit me perfect not too fitting but form fitting. It's the last one and I had to get it because it was the whole meaning of me being there, change. I purchased it feeling so happy about it. I added to the sale by getting Aaron some nice boxers and socks. I have to save though because I'm trying to buy me a nice size screen T.V.

My friend Ty that use to walk me to my car works for Best Buy. Off his discount he was going to buy it for me. He goes to Howard University in D.C. but has a condo in B-More, that's short for Baltimore.

I have to get a job that is not fast money lifestyle. Since I had a little bit saved up it was a good start to help me. Less than three thousand dollar's which I thought is aaight for a college student on her grind for only a month.

13

Working some where I had no previous experience in. I had a new goal. But I had to cash out soon and say goodbye.

When I got home I had a message from my brother Martin calling me. He wanted me to call him back as soon as I could. I called... Martin is always the one that spreads any family breaking news. He let me know that our father just got laid off from his job. My Mom and Dad just moved on the nicer south side of Tulsa, Oklahoma. In a new house that my Mother is going to have to now take over paying for everything. I was frozen in my steps of not knowing what to say. I know my mother is helping me plus trying to settle into a south side home which was newly bought and furnished. I felt bad so I called my Mom's up, she said she's going to believe by faith that everything was going to be alright. I told her I would send some money to her. I told her I'm planning to send money to her after I got off the phone. She thanked me over and over. She quickly switched to saying was I for sure I could give her the money? I told her I was saving it and then some. I didn't want it to seem like I had big money. To them all they knew of my job is that I'm a hostess at a Friday's. I know I'm riding on a lie but that's the only profession decent to tell my job description. She explained that I might have to take over the car payments for the 2000 modeled silver neon I had. She would continue to pay for the insurance. I told her I could start for the next month. Getting off the phone thinking: *Now what am I gonna do?* I'm in deep thought of my father's situation.

By this time a lot of girls hated me at Diamonds however kept it friendly, they had no choice I never had a nasty attitude towards them, like they had sometimes, especially a dancer named Icy. She's cool at first but showed her fake side early. If her money wasn't going right it would show on her hard looking face that had a lot of

14

acne. Icy wouldn't converse like she usually does if her money was right. She had this perfect toned chocolate body with small breat and an onion shaped butt but a face from hell. Her body is smooth and flawless. I guess we sort of had that in common but my face is pretty it's these scars that are from hell. ☺ I know I'm still beautiful and I know I'm bad in a good way. But it was still something sexy about Icy too. Her tracks were glued in by her. The tracks you could see under her real short length hair.

Like me, she didn't sport a whole lot of make up just eyeliner and lip gloss. I knew she hated the fact that I'm taking all her customer's. Icy and the other girl's knew they saw my talent of beauty shine, scars and all. Being that five to eight girls working during the day which is not a lot. They knew that I could have just a genuine conversation with guys that come in the club. I wasn't in to doing dirty things on the side like me sucking, f-ing or getting poked. Just dance and talk. Cage is the bartender. I also had Cage in my corner, every time he worked he racked in customers for me. Cage adored my physique that he'd witnessed for going on the fourth week. I'm tall with beautiful long legs. My tone is a dark brown. My hair is long and I had a part in the middle.

Drew is this older white dancer that had dark roots but blond long wavy hair she looked washed up and drugged up all the time with her eyes real low and talked real slow. She is very attractive however something was wrong with her, even though she didn't drink alcohol. She had a decent body and most of the time Drew wore a cheerleading suit, she let Icy stay at her apartment. They also did a little tricking on the side

I didn't want to be label as a girl that makes her money by having sex for money. I didn't want to be labeled anything but a person trying her best to survive. I didn't survive how Icy and many other dancers had to survive. I've witnessed her selling herself. Me, being nice taking her to her destinations at motels to do you know what. Me, I've never had to be put in that predicament.

The strip club life I learned is different from the ones on the movies. I know it sure didn't look it. Imagine a bar, behind the bar is a low stage with two polls and a walled mirror. We had a juke box that had some of the latest music and some oldies.

I felt fortunate to have made the money I made so far. A lot of those girls didn't even have a car. They would catch a cab and get a tab at the bar to pay their cab fair. Like Dee, she even took the bus with another dancer named Holly that's Caucasian. At this point I didn't know what to do with how to make a means to an end for living. I've been filling out applications for a month now and one call back however their hourly wage is eight dollars.

Calculating that up every month part time is not enough for the cost of living. I would have to get a roommate or quit school and get a full time job which is out the question. I really wasn't complaining about my job as a dancer. It's the right hours and good pay that I did honestly without going home feeling dirty. I kept my moral standards, values, intelligence and education in sight for people to see. I carried myself like a lady. The only complaint is the bitches that did whatever to make a dollar to do a little extra to steal customers. Or the guy that comes to see me, I don't like to say customer about the guy's I sit with. That feels like too much of selling myself to them, I'm not a hoe(whore) or a trick. I'm just surrounded by them. I got a lot of sense running through my bones. I sell my personality or at least the one I made up. I told people I'm from Texas and never told my real name that's Jordyn. My stage name is Lonnie. I kept it business never personal.

I got along with a selected few. Dee, well Fantasy, her stage name in the club is working day still but wandered to other clubs because she wasn't making enough ends at Diamonds. To me Dee is very attractive in a Brandy Norwood kind of look. They look like they could be twins with those same slanted eyes however Dee is a dark ebony kind of color. She's wearing a boy cut mini afro but wore a wig to work. We both dreaded night shift however that shift made more money.

One thing I loved about Dee is when another dancer talked about another dancer and they weren't present. She would call them out saying: You shouldn't talk about that person when they're not present. I always kept my mouth shut and did the best thing and listen in this environment.

It's going lovely for me well for Lonnie at Diamonds however it's all in the summer's heat that's soon coming to an end. I had regular's but my daily money is changing. From almost four hundred a day to two hundred a day, the owner's even gave me a bigger bonus too.

Night is starting to look like a way to make more money. We had to gain as many twenty dollar drinks as possible. The club also has sixty and one hundred dollar lap dances. How the club hustled the girls where on a twenty dollar drink, we only get five dollars off of it. Can you believe that? We get more off the lap dances however dancers could also gain more money by asking for tips when we danced or gave a private dance. Everybody's base pay is different. Mine being a hush hush one hundred and fifty, most girls start out with fifty. Plus a bonus after five twenty dollar drinks I get ten dollar's instead of five off of my drinks.

I called Steve; one of the owners to Diamond's and told him that I wanted to move to some nights. He had no problem with it. Matthew or Matt, one of my regular's that

I gross most of my money with told me how faster it is. He doesn't come down at night. Matthew is a family man that really loves to come down to talk and clown around laughing at life. I like that about him. He dressed like a casual clean bum however owned a piece of a marketing firm. What's so cool he hung around some down brothas. The three of them would come in and clown around buying drink after drinks. He didn't care how many. They all agreed that there were two girls on the block that had the best ass and I'm one of them.

Roderick Boyd the doctor would still try to visit on his lunch however he's planning to make a health clinic in D.C. for people to go to. He's really busy on that end finding other doctor's to join in. He would take me to lunch too that where harmless. Before Aaron and I, Roderick bought me out for an hour to spend time outside of the club environment just to have lunch. We would go to exclusive restaurants in Baltimore that had an upscale taste, like Ruth Crisp and our favorite McCormick's & Schmick's.

He looked like an older brown skin Jay-Z wearing glasses. Roderick is in his early fifties. Married and lives in D.C. That's what kept boundaries around our relationship moving forward. He's one of my best regular's beside Matt. However he sat on top price lap dances. He was generous with tips ranging from one hundred to two hundred dollars. Roderick became tired of giving the club money and then big tipping me. He started giving me money sometimes just on general purposes like a tip just for going to lunch with him instead of being in that club environment. Of course I would meet him and talk. I think he felt sorry for me because I shared some of my pain, including my rape experience finally. He's the very first person that told me that it was a five year grace period of someone reporting rape and it had only been two. He's a

18

good person to talk to because he encouraged me on how strong I was. It's very therapeutic to talk him. He saw me in a different category than any other dancer he's sat with before. Every once in a while at lunch he would ask me to ride with him. For a few hours while he goes to a meeting. He'd drop me off in his newly bought Lexus at Arundel Mall to shop depending on how long he would take. I would mainly get house stuff with some nice walking shoes. I would pocket some to save but look like I shopped because he wanted to see everything I bought. One thing about Roderick he loved to shop. For a gift for my place he bought me a piece of furniture, a curio. Once we had a field day at Best Buy buying me a futuristic stereo, CD's to listen to and an expensive telephone. Once I got in my relationship of knowing Aaron. I then told Roderick about it. Then his visits became less.

I told Aaron how much of a big spender Roderick is. I promised Aaron that I wasn't sleeping with Roderick. However Aaron didn't know Roderick is taking me to lunch or shopping.

When any of my regular's would come in while a booster is there for a tip I would ask them to buy me whatever had my style. Even if it came down to behaving like a five year old I would do it. And it would work every time. I'm also a good tipper to the runner's that run to get our food or an item we might need like thongs from the Gayety store. I know that some of the daytime girl's hated that I splurged, especially Icy. She's only mad because I took some of her regular's too. She had to understand that we're in the same category being Black with a nice body.

Just because we had friction wasn't the reason I'm going to night shift. I really didn't know any dancer's that work night but Icy. Plus I would see this blond haired Black female that always came in with an attitude. Being a night girl she would come in early on the day shift for some reason I would be the one on stage and she would always stare at me as she switched to the dressing room.

For night I knew money might be better. I had a goal of getting a 320 Benz. I knew I could do it, just save. I play by the rules and didn't want to step on anybody's toes but get in where I fit in for my income to grow.

I chilled out for the rest of the night with Aaron coming over. We lay on my couch holding each other I told him about my move. He wanted me to be sure about it. Saying the same, it's much faster. His ex-girlfriend was in the same business as me before us in Cali. They broke up because she started selling her body having sex. He never wanted me to go that route. He told me to be straight up and tell him. I swore to him I wouldn't sell my body for sex. If it got that bad I would ask my family for money. But it was like I'm making money just like a drug hustler. Maybe not big time but enough to keep my bills up to date, food in my cabinets and refrigerator, plus getting my care products from Victoria Secret and high end department store's. From fragrances to nice looking panties. I had a real good lifestyle. Having all I needed lavish living. I didn't splurge on clothes but wore nice walking shoes to school. I always dressed comfortable at school. My wants where satisfied as much as me needs. I'm comfortable however riding on a guilty conscious. I had one class tomorrow but it's going to be my first night working at Diamonds.

Chapter 2

Use What God Gave You

School is going great, starting out at a smooth pace. I decided to take some classes in designing. So I took a clothing construction class to learn more of the technique of sewing and designing clothes. Getting into class session the instructor's name is Professor Celeste. She just started as I walked in talking about the basic things to remember when you're beginning to sew and do design work.

Professor Celeste is a petite older woman with long light brown (dred) locs. She has a face like a light brown owl. I quietly pulled out my notes for an exciting beginning of one of my niches. Minutes later a punk rock looking beautiful Black chic came in. She's fair skinned and was very pretty. After she sat the instructor said someone smells like smoke and it had to be her because she just walked in. Everybody drew their attention to the odd dressed pretty girl. Then I said: "It might be me I don't smoke but I was in the car with someone that was smoking a black n mild."

Then everybody gave me their attention for a moment. I fibbed just to get the attention off of her. After class she came over to introduce herself and to thank me for taking the attention off of her. Her name is Dawn. She even favored the singer Aaliyah but her hair was cut in a neck length bob. We were walking to our car's together learning that we stayed close to each other off of Moravia. Her father just bought her this house and she invited me to come over. I went for a while to talk. As we sat Dawn took off her hair. To my surprised discovering it's a wig. Her hair was two times longer than her wig she's rocking, which made her look even more like Aaliyah. She told me she's Black and White. She liked to smoke cigarettes, even weed. She asked if I wanted to smoke a blunt. I quickly said no thanks. I'm proud of myself for not accepting a chance to smoke. We had a nice short visit of thirty minutes. I went home to prepare for the night.

At work day shift I never drunk with alcohol in my drinks, I always felt like it's a night thing. When I got to work at 7:40 p.m. I walked in this tiny dressing room full of bitches. It wasn't hardly any room but I found a space in the corner so my back would be facing it. I'm already made up in the face I just needed to get dress. The same blond haired Black female with an attitude is doing her usual staring. As she walked in she said: "WHO GOT ON MY SCENT?   WHO'S Wearing Love Spell?"

As soon as she said Love Spell I looked up and didn't have a problem telling her it's probably me. She rolled her eyes getting out of her make up.

Guys said she had the best body at Diamond's until I came. A lot of ignorant loud weave wearing female's where talking in the dressing room. I could always tell a girl from Baltimore when they say do they pronounce it dew or to it sounds like tew. There's another brown skin girl my color that's quiet keeping to herself, like me.

The day crew came in from there shift making it worst with capacity. I had to hurry up and get out of there. Icy's drunk self came in stumbling by and locked her arms around the blond haired fair skin female saying:

"LUSCIOUS GIRRRL…I'M FV<KED UP." Icy said with an irritating laugh. Luscious had a thing for Icy but the only thing stopping Luscious is she already had a girlfriend. Icy started clowning around with this other dancer named Chocolate. Chocolate is a combination of Puerto Rican and Black. She's attractive with a dark chocolate tone, cheerleader petite frame with coal silky black shoulder length hair that's hers. I could tell she had a wild side about her, a live wire too. She wasn't a hater either.

I put on what I call my Prince outfit. Its lavender purple and white, stripe lacey Victorian dress that's short only showing a little of my booty cheeks that tied up twice at the chest, like a corset and the rest just flowed to the side with a matching thong. I had this cute bridal guarder belt to go with it. As I walked out to go to the floor Chocolate said out loud to me: "DAM YOU GOT ASS GIRL. HER ASS ID BEAUTIFUL…LOOK," Getting the other dancer's attention to look at my booty.

I looked down at it saying thanks shyly to her. I went to the bar to order something with vodka in it. I only like clear liquor. It didn't take long for the money to start rolling in. I got started early which I learned during the day. Get right on it. I sat down to have a quick drink but soon got up when guy's started coming in. There's mirror's all around this bar so you could see every angle. You could see whose scoring and see whose getting turned down for you to get ready to make your move. It's a faster pace with lesser time than day which is good. Money is faster to get with you spending less time. I danced to mostly Crazy Town's song Butterfly, Jill Scott, a group called Foreigner an old rock tune - Cold as Ice, Mariah and much more. Usually we dance to two songs, one fully clothed and the other take off something… optional. Most of the females at night took their thongs off only a few kept their thongs on the whole dance set. I kept my thongs on…you know leave something for the imagination.

I met that other quiet girl like me. Her name is Carmen and she would remind you of a young Dorothy Dandridge with her hair long, in the middle of her back. She appeared to be a good girl with a fair Diva game like me. I also met this tall Amazon looking dancer named Vondalee. I found out through her that Luscious is a tinee bopper still being in her teens. Vondalee and I were around the same age but she was older. I could tell she had a sincere heart. She is a believer in Jesus Christ too. In conversation Vondalee spoke openly on how good God has been to her. That's how we began to relate and converse. She knew the bible inside out that left me amazed how she's just quoting scriptures. I told her that I stopped going to church because I'm ashamed. She looked me dead in the eye and said: "Don't stop going to church just because of being in this circumstance, Don't. Go back, it's Okay go… it builds your faith up." I told her that I would.

On the other hand I had real live lipstick'lizbo's trying to holler at me for real. Some girl name Xstasy is really trying to tell me how I would love it. Her offer is going in my ear right out the other. I laughed off her attempts however kept repeating how crazy she is. I detected that Chocolate, Carmen and Luscious were the night money makers. But they had to move over and make room for me. Like me, Chocolate is loved by the older rich white men. I guess it's her mysterious color wearing a bright beautiful orange. I observed the night time clientele taking notice of me. In Chocolate's face I couldn't tell if she didn't have a problem inviting me over at the male's request. She had a sense of humor introducing my booty first.

24

I started taking myself back to New Shiloh. Last year a classmate named Rose invited me to New Shiloh. It's a beautiful big church. I sat in the balcony but wanted to bump into my older friend Rose. I got some good word to strengthen me through my walk, Lord knows I need it.

In Baltimore at some place called the Pavilion Jay-Z is coming to perform with his Roca Fella crew promoting his anticipated Blueprint album. He is my favorite rapper plus I admired him and his style of doing things. I'm so hyped that he's coming I wanted to go however I didn't have any one to go with besides Dee who couldn't afford it. Plus I just found out the show is in one more day. So I came up with an idea. I would send him one dozen of roses with a card congratulating him on his Blueprint album, inviting him and his boys to Diamonds with the address. My thoughts were *"Hey ya never know."*

I made sure I saw how the arrangement looked with the flowers and glass vase, got a card that had a champagne bottle on it popping out champagne. No, it was not Cristal but a black and gold bottle. I found the address to the Pavilion and gave it to the delivery guy to ensure a Shawn Carter a.k.a. Jay-Z gets this in his dressing room for tonight. I thought that's impressive but I'm sure that other females have did this same thing. I went to work and every time I danced I played a song that had Jay-Z in it all night long. I kept picturing on every one of my sets he would be walking down those steps. However Jay-Z never showed his face. Maybe too common of a place where there's not many ladies. Even though there were a special one too. I'm still happy with what I did. The next day I called the flower shop to confirm and they said the flowers did get delivered to a Shawn Carter – Jay-Z. And that's what made my week.

I took it as he probably didn't want to be in hot spot with strip clubs all on the block. He has too much of a big name.

The main reason I enjoyed dancing is to dance. I loved being on stage and having all this attention, in the spotlight. The only thing I didn't like is when I sensed hating from the other females working. Not all but some.

My stress reliever is definitely the mall, shopping is a way to relaxation. Specifically home store departments. I invested in the best, from dining ware to furniture pieces, shoes to good quality under ware. Dee is my mall buddy most of the time to ride along or to eat. Dee asked me for a favor in staying with me some nights while her daughter stays with her mother until she could get situated with a stable place. I said sure thinking why not.

Once we went to a matinee movie to see Two Can Play That Game. The movie is an attention getter being funny and clever with wit. An updated movie on real women with independence. Dee and I had a good time being the only ones in the theatre which is cool for us to talk and feel Shante's strategies. By the mall there's a furniture store I like to peak in and see sale things. There was a beautiful Tiger print chair that had a dark wooden finish in the arms and legs. It's my style; I'm doing a safari look in my living room. Its $265 dollar's but I found a scratch on the legs so the salesman got it down to $175 dollar's. I'm just forty dollar's short.

Dee had it until I got home to get in my black velvet box, where my petty cash is located. I appreciated the help in getting the last print like that in the store. Shopping made me happy and content at what I do for a living.

My time for peace is with Aaron. He tried to support me as much as he could like coming to see me at work. Tonight we were having dinner with his mother, Mrs. Carla. I'm very nervous when I got there since it's my 1st

26

time to meet her. His sister happened to be there when I arrived. His Mom and sister have strong Indian features. With his sister we favored and had the same skin tone. His mother is short and a cute size. She had a stern face however pleasant acting giving me a smirk as Aaron introduced us. I had on a plaid preppy looking dress that fit just right for a girlie girl, to my knees and not tight. At dinner with the three us was interesting. Using my manners I sat up straight with Ms. Carla asking about my family and background. Even with her blank expression I knew she's impressed. Her dinner is delicious island cru sine with rice. I also I asked about her roots as well.

After dinner Aaron and I went to see Rush Hour 2. I loved how he held my hand leading me. We had a good laugh. We drove past his house discovering his mother is still there. We had to make another plan. We found a spot in a vacant parking lot. Listening to the radio, we started talking then it would always end up with him starting to kiss me. He even took it to another level in kissing my lips below my face. I wouldn't stop him unless I saw a car coming. I wasn't a car but that's one thing I'm feeling. I started moaning more and then when I start breathing hard I know I'm feeling one getting ready to…..

Instantly Aaron gave me one touch to my right round nipple and that was it. That's one thing I needed and I came. Suddenly the music stopped and the D.J. got on the radio saying:

"May I have your attention… Please… may I get your attention. We've just been informed that Aaliyah has died in a plane crash along with eight other people." The D.J. just started praying.

The mood was shut down. With the feeling I just had it shut down. I started praying along with the Disc

Jockey. I'm in a state of shock, repeating "What" it seemed like a hundred times. "I can't believe that," I said.

"Awe mann, I hope it's not true." Aaron added

"This is not a rumor. This was confirmed at 6:45p.m. In the Bahamas," The D.J. added.

We both just sat there. That's when I started to shed tears for her and the people that were with her. Aaron reached over to massage my neck with his hand. Driving, with the sound of hearing the cars motor, it was complete silence in the car as I took him back around the corner to his house. He kissed my head gently asking am I okay to drive?

"I'll be fine baby," I responded saying. He gave me his adorable smile hearing me call him baby for the first time.

I'm stunned riding home with the radio making it worst by playing her hits. I just can't believe it. Being the same age I grew up with Aaliyah and she's gone physically.

The next day on the radio they made an announcement that they're going to have a candle lighting ceremony on Saturday for Aaliyah and the other decease in front of the radio station downtown. Being a fan of her music and voice I'm definitely going to be there. Since it's Friday, starting off the weekend I decided to go in to Diamonds. Night is faster and in drinks I'm keeping up with the best of them. A very business minded Black guy named Tracy came in regularly and started to visit with me, learning about my aspiring mind. As I sat with Tracy and getting stares from some of the ladies. I pay it no mind but focus all my attention to this guy. And not worry about Luscious and some chick name Fire with vicious eyes. Just know that these mirrors on these walls are the eyes on my back. As I try not to worry about that because hey I'm the one that's getting paid.

But anyway, Tracy is giving me praise on how I carry myself as such a lady. I just remembered to keep it real and tell them this is not a permanent plan but temporary to dance. Going to school is my main pride. And I have to be honest I'm loving how I'm getting by.

Carmen is starting to have problems with Luscious and Chocolate. Both of them being loud mouth talkers of accusing Carmen as taking their customers. Carmen and I sat by each other when we weren't busy. However Carmen kept it cool without even mentioning it to the people she sat with like me and never showed any signs of being scared. I kept close with Vondalee still encouraging me to go hear the word.

One thing I hated about Diamonds is when it gets pack some of the female's have to stand up because the capacity in the bar.

Every time I would be coming and going to work the manager of Oasis next door would try to prove how much of a better club Oasis is to work for. It's starting to sound like a good idea. So Saturday I peak my head in to see the Oasis club. It looked like a long tropical design bar with lime light's and bright rainbow colors. With a huge high rise stage that's the length of the whole wood grained bar with gold trim. I was in aah… of looking at the nice clean huge bar that's ten times bigger than Diamonds. This bar could fit a lot people in it. Plus with the club being two levels, the upstairs is gold everything except the mirrors. It's very classy looking. What sold the club to me is the Las Vegas showgirl's oval shaped dressing room that had vanity mirror's in the middle and a place to sit to put your make-up on with the bubble lights. Lockers went all around the room. When I got back down stairs Mack introduced me to this beautiful Asian and Black daytime entertainer named Egypt the same age and height as me. What we had most in common is going to school. She's going to be a nurse and had the warmest smile. She looked very studious with glasses on. So there were some other nice professional dancer's going to school. I liked this club already. What's really impressive is it's a cleaner and bigger club.

I'm keeping that club in mind. If I'm going to do this type of work do it at the best place. After leaving there I drove closer to the radio station for the candle lighting ceremony. I had to pay my respects to Aaliyah some kind of way. On my way there I'm thinking about moving to Oasis. A dancer named Jen, a girl that got fired for only a moment from Oasis was saying it's the best club to work at on the block. She had that California look blue eyes and blond hair that went to her butt crack, petite bodied. Jen's very stuck on image wearing mostly white and red with thigh high boots. She looked hot and knew it. She knew Chocolate from the Oasis club. Chocolate gave me some insight on that club as well. Chocolate was totally banned from Oasis for some reason I didn't know. Hearing Chocolate in the locker room I was learning her crazy wild side. I knew Oasis is a money making place.

My classmates from back home were calling me to confirm to see if it's really true of me being engage to Javontae. I hadn't told anybody. I confirmed to all the calls of deep concern about our engagement. What's funny that it's mostly guys. I still wanted to try to make it work. But my love is caught up with Aaron. I planned to make a visit to Javontae in the NYC. I would just take the train and stay with my cousins. Next weekend I made those plans. So I had to work hard this week at work to take off for the weekend.

At work the pressure is on. I started to sit with the owner's friend that came in on an every other Friday basis. His name is Reggie. I really like his professional style. He liked my body but impressing him to buy a twenty dollar drink was work. I didn't have to talk sexy or do a move. It's just that he knew the whole set up and the game. But me just being me convinced him that I'm a cool individual. I'm on my fourth drink, which is a low number considering it being 9:40 p.m. with no lap dances and hardly sixty dollar's in tips. I'm always cool never frantic on making money. I have favor. I'm very patient and never show my true feelings like these girl's do when their money ain't flowing in right. But for some reason I got a serious light head ache coming on. Don't know why but I just so happen to have some Tylenol in my bag. So I went to the back to get them plus change and freshen up. I wanted to put on my French maid outfit that none of these bitches have seen. It's so cute with Brazilian cut panties with French ruffles on the booty area, cute. I did it in perfect timing seeing some gangsta gangstas sit down, two of them. That pissed off all of my competition. One of the girls from the loud mouth crew approached the one in the hat. And Carmen is going for the one with the nice dress shirt with a diamond studs in his ears. Which was the one I was checking out he looked like the one with money. Being a full house I had to stand but good looking for the guy's to view. The dude in the hat rejected loud mouth Fire's advance for him. I'm happy however nervous that I might be next as soon as she sat in her bar seat I walked by the guys to go to the front. With a good sign, the guy in the hat grabbed for my hand to come to talk to him. I'm happy on the inside determined to work for a hundred dollar lap dance. Just so happened the guy in the hat wanted the same a lap dance. But for some reason I knew that the dude in the nice shirt had the grip. The guy in

31

the hat leaned over to the other guy asking us to all go to the back; dude is down with having innocent looking Carmen give him a lap dance. As I do most of the time is talk first before I moved up against him to give my special lap dance. I asked him about Norma Jeans and asked does he go there. He told me: "Yeah only on certain occasions because it gets too packed."

His mood kind of changed as he responded with: "So you wanna to work there?"
"No, I just wanted to know if it's an all majority Black club."
"O, Yeah from the females to the people that come to watch. It gets ignorant in there too."
"O No. That's what I'm trying to stay away from. I'm thinking of going next door to Oasis," I said to him.

He nodded his head with his mouth turned down agreeing of good taste then saying: "You have to get all dressed up to get in that club tough."

Then I cut that conversation off and started talking in my PG-13 mack to get my lap dance on. For some reason I always look behind me when performing a lap dance, getting close however watching the distance. After the lap dance it's hard work to convince him to give me a tip however he finally gave in. He also wanted to keep my Brazilian cut panties. My face read my hesitation then he started biding for them twenty to fifty. I gladly went to the locker room to take them off after last call at fifty. Panties sold for fifty dollar's to pay a miscellaneous bill or shop. After they took off that set my night up to stay busy. After my 13th drink I'm feeling enough with liquor in them and told the bar tender to just have juice in my drinks. In fact my headache left however came back an hour later intensified to the highest power. I even felt numb something wasn't right. It's like I'm starting to see white light in the corner of my eyes with the different strobe light. A weird feeling I've never felt. I would go to the back from not wanting anyone to see my hands shake. Finally I called Aaron from the pay phone in the front of the bar. I told him that it's almost time for me to get off and I couldn't drive because I felt so weak. He told me not to drive and he would come get me. He left old little Ms. Tyler home alone sleep.

As we let out for the night the female's got a good look at my fine man picking me up that made them cringe even more with jealousy. I saw Luscious focus her eyes on my prize. He grabbed my bag and led me to his car. I felt dizzy with my focus beading in and out. I left my neon there in a secured garage and drove with Aaron planning to come in the morning to get it. As he parked the car walking to the front door Aaron could tell I was weak with my walking. As soon as I open the front secured entrance door to the apartment building, Aaron grabbed my keys and picked me up to take me the rest of the way. I felt like everything is spinning with a major pain in my brain. I got into my place on the 3rd floor to get right in my bed.

Aaron held me in a way that I had my upper body rested sitting up on some stacked pillows and he's near my stomach resting his head. I'm holding him there gently while he held me. I'm laying there scared to fall asleep. Discovering with him that I took those Tylenol pills before I started drinking. I never wanted to do that again. We left in the early morning when I felt better to drive. I started to love him for things like that. He had my back.

I'm wide awake by 8 a.m. the next morning. I decided to go to work on the day shift today since I didn't have any classes on Tuesday. I'm happy to see Dee there so we could catch up. I hadn't seen her in a week. Another dancer named Paradise is there too to show me more pole tricks. Paradise had skills and was generous with me to show the technique. I always thought having strip teasing and dancing on the pole skills would always keep my future husband pleased more in the bedroom. I wasn't a stranger to the pole just putting a little of my weight on it. I finally mastered the hanging up side down pole trick after that my back felt like I cracked a bone but I played it off very well. It's hurting so bad.

Icy is sitting with this White guy in a black suit and a Black guy is sitting with them that couldn't keep their eyes off me as I danced. As I walked down to get my tips from the other two gentlemen sitting with no girl's.

That is a rule: You can't approach a guy that is already sitting with someone for a tip for seeing you dance, but he kept giving Icy dollars to throw on stage and put on me. So as I walked by the Black guy that looked like his body guard stopped me. The Black guy is named Spider. He wanted to have a drink with me. I also met and thanked the White guy sitting with Icy from England named Neal. He has money, I could tell in the way he talked and how he's groomed. He's astonished by my Black beauty and wouldn't stop staring at me while I converse with Spider. He wasn't paying Icy any attention after I sat with them. Spider let me know he's a bouncer over at Oasis and was trying to sell how it's the best club to make money. We all started conversing as a whole because Neal kept jumping into our conversation. They even offered to take us to Dave and Buster's just for dinner. Icy had a smile on her face to see if I was cool and would consider. I had to decline because I had a bad pain down my spine. The pain is so intense like a knife cutting through my back. I'm hiding it very well I thought, just waiting to get off of work.

The last person I sat with was Matt I loved when he came in to talk. He's so funny with jokes just having a harmless conversation about nothing but the best out of life. He made my night coming in to set me off right when I get paid for today. I kept feeling that my back is going to be a problem. I was telling Dee how it didn't feel right. I left an hour early. As I got to my car and started driving, I had tears going down the side of my face. I just knew I had strained my back when I tried to master that pole trick. I looked up to the sign of Mercy in green letters. Mercy hospital is not too far from the block. So I went to the emergency spot. Thank God I'm still with my mother's medical insurance. I waited and waited, after almost two hours a nurse came to get me I got in the private section. I sat and told her what I had filled out earlier on the questionnaire sheet. She wanted to run some test on me before I met with the doctor. The Doctor is a blond haired lady that wanted me to take a sample of my urine, get my blood pressure and have me breathing while listening to my heartbeat. After five minutes the doctor came back to me and said: "Well you're pregnant. That's causing you back problems."

Thinking in my mind: *Pregnant! O No... It can't be.* I said out loud, "Pregnant."

I didn't want my expression to look like I'm terrified but inside I was. I left but the doctor first got me set up to start coming to see a pediatrician being that I'm just three weeks. I had to sit and get my thoughts together. Leaving the hospital I'm puzzled. I went and took myself to Friday's restaurant around my cousin Lauryn's way in Laurel after visiting with them for a moment. I had a steak dinner but could hardly eat it. I got to talking to the waitress telling her about my news. She immediately started congratulating me and I didn't know what to do. It's the biggest decision I've had to make in my life this far. Do

I keep it or do I do a thing I said I could never do: have an abortion? My mind didn't really know what to do.

I went home to contact Aaron and tell him to come over. He came over quick because I told him it's very important. As soon as he sat down at the table I had this worried look on my face telling him what I'd discovered.
"I'm pregnant."

His face lit up with a smile. But I kept the same expression.
"You want to have it right?............ It's mine...right?" He asked looking at me.
"Yes.....of course it's yours. You're the only one I'm sleeping with. I just don't know what to do." I said laying my head in my hands.
"In the future we can get married, why not have a baby. It's going to be beautiful... with beautiful hair," he said softly rubbing my neck.

I raised my head immediately pushing his arm back saying: "I DON'T CARE ABOUT Good hair and That Kind of Stuff. What ABOUT Money for FOOD, Clothing, Medical and DAYCARE. Those are the things important to me. You can't even hardly take of yourself Aaron let alone a baby and me, we're not ready to get married," I said. I started to shake my head sitting at the dinner table.

"What. You're thinking about having.... an abortion? I don't want you to go through that. A girl I got pregnant had one before and...," Aaron stopped speaking looking down in disappointment.

Then he looked up and said: "I will support whatever you want to do."

But I could tell he thought he still had time to change my mind.

I started to cry saying: "I don't know what to do....... I don't want to go back home. How would I be able to support myself when I start showing? My parents are going to make me come back home and I don't want that. I'm NOT going back home" I said with a determined look of refusing to go back to Tulsa

It's so heavy on my brain that I didn't know what to do. Learning that Aaron wants to keep the baby shocked me. I knew that it would be a beautiful creation made by us two with God but I just didn't know what to do. Then being supposedly engage to someone else. The timing couldn't be worst having plans to go see my fiancé Javontae. I didn't want to break Javontae's heart. The whole thing became bad timing and I started to become hardcore in my decision making.

Aaron couldn't stay the night to comfort me even though he expressed he wanted to but he stayed a while and held me. He had to go back to be there when his mother arrived at home. But I kept imagining how beautiful our son or daughter would be. I started to picture pink things and a beautiful baby girl but smoke poof in front of the image. I made myself stop thinking it.

I decided to call my favorite confidant Yvonne to tell her. Yvonne was a close friend to my family sort of a play cousin. What I loved about talking to Yvonne is that she never held hunches. When I had a problem she always had solutions. She had one more year at Langston. She is very business minded and goal oriented equating up to a future millennium woman. She's a definite no don't have it. Even me breaking down how fine Aaron is and how he's a dynamite package. It's just that he's not financially straight. When I bring a child in this world I want them to have nothing but the best. After hearing some advice from her I called my Twin brother's and told them as well. They're even a definite no don't have it. I told my good friend Ty about it and he said the same that you don't want to mess your career up in having a baby too early in life. I couldn't believe the people I trusted the most with this is giving me a straight up no don't have it.

I called my home girl Yolanda from back home and told her the scenario, she is supportive but didn't have any good words of wisdom however told me she had an experience like this. I even told Dee about it. She's helping me with solutions of trying to keep the baby. She mentioned going to the department of Human Services for assistance. Also her mother is a licensed baby sitter and she would even work with me on a fee. Dee's mom would even baby sit different hours of the night being that Dee's mother knew that she's a dancer. But just Dee along wasn't enough to convince me to have it. I just knew that my parent's would make me come home and I refused to go back to that place where I left behind that hurt. I didn't want to come back being all knocked up the reason for me returning, NO I didn't want that. On the other hand I knew that's a way I could keep a part of Aaron with me forever and I knew the two of our genes put together would make a beautiful child.

Chapter 3

What Could Possibly Go Wrong Next?

New York, New York I love to visit. I feel the busy atmosphere where everybody is on the go. My cousin's where busy hosting some political campaign event tonight at a Harlem Cathedral. Javontae met me there. He hugged me without a kiss. I had a lovely red dress on. He had on a real nice suit to impress my cousin that's on the politic side. She wasn't impressed with him at all. My cousin Bethany didn't like him from the start. She didn't like his arrogant attitude acting as if he's already in the family. When he introduced himself he told her welcome to the family. She immediately corrected him and said: "No I'm already in the family that's what you're trying to do," in her strong New York accent.

Javontae and I found a lovely place in the corner of the terrace overlooking a view. We caught up with each other. I didn't want to go into what's really on my mind so I told him how school and work is going. It's good to see him however I'm still feeling like just a friend. He talked about adjusting to New York and Columbia University. I'm so proud of him and I would tell him that constantly. I didn't know how to come out and tell him that I'm a dancer plus I'm pregnant. He just got over the fact that his cousin

Rico sexually abused me, which hurt Javontae to even discuss. I decided not to discuss what I'd really been doing and what's occurring in my life right now.

He's still drawing this mental picture of how our life is going to be and how stuck up he wanted me to act. What I told him… is that I really wanted to just be myself. I wanted to enjoy this time together because I could really see myself being with him married. I just knew I had to stop seeing Aaron and stand on what I'm drawing closer toward… terminating the pregnancy.

The next day Javontae and I went around Time Square to have lunch and shop. I didn't understand Javontae's affection toward me. He had a hard time showing it. He didn't even know how to reach out to hold my hand. And I felt like it had something to do with Rico.

That Sunday I went back with what I thought was best. I called a few clinics. I called Aaron telling him I needed half of the money sometime this week. I had planned to have it next Monday, so I had Tuesday to just rest. He said he would come up with his part. Aaron told me he would and wanted to be there. I told him maybe in the future when we're better established financially we can do this but in the right way. I just couldn't take that chance now. I shouldn't have said in the bed that I want to have his baby.

My weekly earnings were getting funny and I had to pay my rent, bills plus my monthly car note. I had to be out of work for at least four days.

I went in to work Friday night. It's another tense night where everyone is on their grind trying to get drinks. I'm not feeling it however knew the night wasn't over. After a while business is at a steady pace. I gained eleven drinks and it's only twelve o'clock.

These two guys came in. One is Black the other is White. The Black guy is one of Carmen's regulars. So I approach the White guy before he even ordered a drink. I usually try to wait until customer's get their drinks. But not when I had these fox hounds on the prowl. I kept it real and closely by the ear said that to him. He had a calm quiet spirit with a real low key persona. I asked for a drink to talk to him. He said sure why not. I got an orange juice with a splash of cranberry juice he had a cola. We got to talking and connected on a real cool level. What I liked the most about him is that he didn't try to act or sound Black. He kept his hair in a low cut. Michael is his name and he was starting to attend school. We conversed on school after he learned I attended Morgan. He asked me some computer questions. Our talks started a bond between us to where he came in every day that week. See I never gave people my home number which is the only number to reach me, only my family had that and Aaron. I gave guy's the club phone number. I didn't want to invest in a cell phone. For what? I didn't want to keep up with nobody. So the only way to stay in touch with me is to come to the club. Michael didn't even want me to give him a lap dance when I started to order bigger drinks. He's interesting to talk to.

I also started to help him at the public library. He started to have problems on his English reports. I was happy to help but only if we met at a place I wanted to meet. For helping him, he took me to his spot the ESPN Zone restaurant. You couldn't tell by his looks he had a little bit of drug selling experience however now he had a two year old daughter that made him change completely in that fast lane lifestyle. He adored his daughter that is biracial. His baby's mother is Black. Most of our personal conversations were built around his daughter. I couldn't help but think as we talked: "I wondered was I going to have a daughter or a son."

The weekend is here! I didn't go out. To me work is basically my going out night life. I worked it except Sunday that weekend seemed strange with Aaron not coming around. It's like he's avoiding me. I assumed he hadn't come up with his part. Or maybe he didn't want me to even have the abortion because he has never avoided my calls before. I wanted him to give his part in it like he said he would. This is something I'm going to learn from, start using protection or don't have sex at all. Sunday I basically chilled watching a minister on T.V. and cooking a big dinner. Aaron was invited to come over. But the time he was supposed to arrive he didn't show. I called him at home with no one to answer. My instincts told me that Aaron is up to something. I had to have the money by tonight and he's supposed to drive me home after the procedure is done tomorrow. I called and called. I waited and waited until the moon was at its night time position, high in the sky. I became very upset when no one answered the phone. I had to get it over with so the thought wouldn't fester of keeping the baby. Plus I didn't want to wait too late.

I finally got up and went to Pikesville where he lived. I'm so mad at how Aaron is handling this. Avoiding me isn't making it any better. When I got into the circled community I parked my car so that he wasn't able to see it. His car he bought two weeks ago is there. That really pissed me off but I remained cool. I went to knock on the door which seemed like twenty minutes of just standing there. I left to go to the nearest gas station to call the house phone but no one answered. I called Yolanda and was going off to her about what Aaron is doing. As I explained I started crying for so many reasons and feeling so many different emotions. She told me to get it together because that stress is not good for the baby. I'm thinking heartless: *What baby not after tomorrow it won't even matter.*

I went back over to his place to knock once again and to wait there until someone answered because I knew Aaron's daily schedule and he's supposed to be there. I stayed there until I saw a light from their stair case, its little Ms. Tyler that opened the door. Her old eyes had only seen me once but somehow she remembered. She let me in and in the sweetest voice I asked her where's Aaron.

She said calling out his name so sweetly: "Aaron...I don't know...... I don't know. Aaron..."

Her hands were shaking nervously. I didn't want her nervousness to build up with me asking questions. I wrote a note for Aaron to find down in his room. I went back outside and sat there for another thirty minutes. I just wanted to get this over with.

I went to call Ty from the same pay phone at the gas station. I told him what's going on. He told me to come to his house and he would take me tomorrow. Ty is definitely a friend I could count on. He knew about my relationship with Aaron and he thought its F'd up that Aaron is doing me this way. My mind was full of stress and I had tension all over my body. In my mind set the next morning at 8 a.m. I'm terminating the seed growing inside of me. I attempted one more time to call Aaron. He picked up this time explaining that he was at his sister's trying to get money from her. All he came up with was a hundred dollars. When I got back over to Aaron's house he had the door opened and he had been driving his mother's car that is now parked in the front.

"See, that's one reason why we cannot have this baby because you can't afford it," I said. I didn't have anything else to say but get his part. I'm tired and sleepy.

I'm even scarred about tomorrow. I didn't want any trouble from God on my decision however I knew he's a forgiving God.

The next morning I walked in the waiting room that had at least eight different couples waiting, some mother's with daughters and some with their mate. Some girl-friends with their best friends in support. Ty is there for me at a last minute notice. I filled out the forms. There's total silence with nothing but the T.V. playing. After thirty minutes they came for me to take one last pregnancy test which came up positive. I went to see a counselor to ensure that I'm sure. Everything that woman is saying I made it go right over my head. It didn't even register in my mind because I wouldn't let it. The last thing she asked was I for sure that I wanted to do this. I told her yes... looking her straight in the eyes nodding my head. They made me go back to the waiting room and when they called me again it's time to have the procedure. I wanted to be asleep when they took the seed. I couldn't bear remembering what it felt like for someone to snatch a life out of you. My doctor is Asian and the last thing I remembered was looking into his slanted eyes as I fell asleep. By then it's too late to stop it.

When I woke up I'm out of it feeling an adult diaper around me. I tried not to think about it. When I had enough time to rest Ty pulled my neon around to pick me up. He took me back over to his comfortable condo and put me in his extra king sized bed. He went to go make me some chicken and rice soup. I put on his huge screen television to watch. I sat up to eat my soup after ten minutes of trying to digest it. It wouldn't settle in. And that whole evening I did nothing but throw up. Laying in the bed for thirty minutes then running to Ty's bathroom. I thought God is trying to punish me for the abortion. Ty stayed in his guest room where he had a couch to sleep on. When I was up I thought of Aaron wondering what he's doing, how did he feel? When an image of how our baby would have looked came across my mind I'd block it out immediately. I had to move on quickly. I went back to my apartment and found all these messages with Aaron on my phone. He was there yesterday morning in front of my apartment building. He said he waited and waited. He sounded concern and wanted to hear from me. I had only four days to stop spotting and go back to work. It seemed like this is how I'm going to have to earn my money for the time being.

I'm getting tired of working at Diamonds. Even though I'm starting to be one of the number one money maker's for the night. I was sitting with business owners, hustlers, writers and millionaires… professionals.

As I got up from my last drink with a new guy. I'm walking four steps behind Fire and Luscious. Fire looked behind her to see me some steps behind them. As I glanced in the mirror to check myself I instantly saw Fire take two steps backwards to bump right in to me. She gave me the down and up look with an attitude. Me giving her attitude right back saying: "Excuse YOU" close to her face. I left her in her circle of female's talking sh*t to me that I didn't take the time hear. I went to the locker room to freshen up with those feminine wipes I kept in my care bag. If she wanted to continue talking noise she knew where I was. When I came back out on the floor nothing was said. It's more with the mean looks. As always I paid it no mind. I did a real good job in making a lot of money almost four hundred dollars. Trust me… that's great with at least thirty clubs on Baltimore street with the same system. A lot of other dancer's are checking that out. I'm taking some of their business guy's. They requested to sit with me. And it's a rule that the customer can sit with any one he wants. So I'm gaining enemies anyway. As I predicted at the end of the night I'm going to be approached by the loud mouth crew or at least Fire. As I'm pulling up my capri's Fire came in the locker room at an eight foot distance screaming:

"EXCUSE ME NO I THINK IT'S EXCUSE YOU" She started to point in the air at me saying: "YOU BUMPED INTO ME," Fire yelled. I interrupted and said:

"Whoa…. No I didn't… I stood there and watched you look right at me turn back around to keep walking then took TWO STEPS BACK TO BUMP RIGHT INTO ME"

As I'm saying that she began to get louder so I got louder for her to hear me. I put on my shirt quickly to cover myself. I put my hair band around my hair to let her know: *Hey it's whatever. We can get it on right now.* I was never into talking noise and arguing. So I let her know I wasn't with the talking.

"On the real. It can be whatever. Girl I ain't in to the talking. You need to check your manners" I said standing there immediately dropping my bags. I gave her a stare down with a fierce look on my face.

She starts talking sh*t but not running up saying: "WHO DEW You THINK YOU ARE? You DON'T Want To Go There With Me," she kept saying.

I'm standing there for at least a good three minutes waiting to see if she's going to just shut up and bring it. Every female getting dressed is watching and listening. By this time I gathered my stuff to go get in line to get paid. People in Fire's clique are trying to hold her back now that I'm leaving. With me going to the front to get paid Fire wanted to bring that all out there.

"Look I don't have time for all that… wit chor your loud mouth….. You won't do nothing so shut up" I said out

46

loud. As soon as I said that she dropped her stuff jumping having a fit.

"Now You Wanna Come Out Here And Act All Ignorant Like I Said Girl I Ain't Got Time For This. Watch Where You're Going Next Time." As I was finishing what I had to say Chocolate is leaving the office from getting paid, walking by drunk thinking I'm talking to her.

"WHAT...I KNOW YOU'RE NOT TALKING TO ME" Chocolate said loudly looking all crazy at me. At the same time her big debo acting White home girl stood up and moved Chocolate behind her saying: "Naw. NOW Hold Up."

"See...See all that ain't even necessary. I wasn't even talking to you. You're not the one that I'm having this CHILDISH PROBLEM WITH" I said with an attitude looking straight at Fire. The White girl mumbled something else to say that I paid no attention to because I knew who I was referring to. And that was Fire. She's still yapping her jaws talking about me calling it childish.

I was personally tired of dealing with their sh*t. The snickering, the eyeballing as I talk to my guest, their attitudes and cut throat incidents. Watching my every move, I was starting to get an attitude. And not giving me the respect I show them by staying in my own lane, not trying to F with anybody else's cash flow. Do you.....make your money?

I didn't take it personal however I had enough. Finally Luscious got that loud mouth b*tch to shut up.

I got paid in the office. As I always do count my money in front of the night manager handling the money. I kept track with my number of drinks, my bonus after five drinks and also tipping out the bartender and I'm generous. As I walked to my car I watched my back very carefully. I got some stupid sh*t started with sum silly bitches. But still

47

I paid it no mind and figured out it's time to give Oasis a try. Until then I'll just keep working day shift to get away from the nonsense. That was my last night of child's play. I didn't need any more drama in my life today.

When I got home I always thanked God for making it home safely then counted my money one more time. Stashed some away in my tall black velvet box and then the bigger amount I deposit the next day at the bank. Next thing I always did was make a night snack like a sandwich, BLT or even cereal to eat. Take me a real long bath while listening to the album Songs of a Minor- Alicia Key's track number five on repeat "Troubles." Finish by pampering myself with my aromatherapy products. I would always end up talking and praying to Jesus.

I slept in on my Tuesday I didn't have any classes and I'm just gonna have a day to rest. I laid in my bed until I got a call from back home. It's Tommy, a dude that used to be at skate night on Sunday's back home in Tulsa. He's concerned about me hoping everything's alright since I'm so close to D.C. I'm clueless of what he meant, I sat up and said: "What...What happened."

"You haven't heard. Close by you bombs and some planes crashed into buildings. Turn on your T.V. and look at the news," Tommy said.

"I don't have a T.V," I said. But I immediately turned on my radio. They were talking about a plane in the World Trade Center in New York. The first thing I thought of was that's the building where my guy cousin took me to the top for my 1st visit in New York. That building had a plane crashed in it. I thought of all my love ones there, even Javontae. I told Tommy I'm alright but I need to see if my family is alright. I became worried trying to call them all. I couldn't get any answers. I got up and got dressed quickly getting to Ty's place. As I put on my shoes another plane crashed in to the other building. Once I got there my eyes were glued to Ty's 60'inch screen T.V. I just couldn't believe that America is under attack. I'm sick as can be thinking the world is coming to an end. We even ordered take out with all kinds of flavored hot wings not wanting to bulge from the T.V. It wasn't for entertainment purposes. From 10:00 a.m. to 7:40 p.m. glued to the T.V. I was just getting hungry around 8 o'clock. I'm even nervous to go home. I talked to my family back in Oklahoma and they got in touch with my family and they're fine. I still couldn't get in touch with Javontae.

The next day I did my regular routine of going to class where everybody's talking about it. Each class I had we discussed the whole issue, we didn't even get into the lesson for the day which was A- okay. After the weekend I went to the block to talk to Mack the manager at Oasis. I'm ready to move to a bigger and better club. He said I could start as soon as I wanted to. I made plans for Thursday night. I'm pretty nervous and saw the day competition and they all looked like high fashioned models. I knew I would fit in however it's going to be competitive. I'm up for the challenge and these girls I could tell carried themselves in a classy way.

Aaron came back around with some pink roses on my door step that made me fall for it, plus the money. He took me shopping for a Roca wear velour suit and he got the guy version. He also gave me some extra money to go in with me to finally buy a T.V. and DVD off of Ty's discount. It's a 42'inch that fit right in the entertainment center I had in a layaway. I had to have a T.V. now. What is the world coming to? I'm nervous to know the outcome however I knew we were going to war soon. It saddened me to even think about the whole thing and what those families are going through.

Chapter 4

The Life of a Dancer

I'm in this business going on a month and a half now. I have my place set up like I wanted to. I went with this Safari style decor. I even decorated with some real tropical plants to give it a real safari look. I finally had enough with Diamond's and the BS with those females. Those bitches were evil and cut throat minded just to get that dollar. I knew it wasn't gon change with this new club just enhance in the competition. I planned to take the game I learned from Diamonds and be even more professional. Oasis is a more upscale white collar club than Diamonds. Even Oasis's classy wooden glass door told you there's money flowing in here. It's the best club down on Baltimore Street a.k.a "the Block." Norma Jeans had a name for its self too. I never wanted to step foot in there. Knowing that it's an all Black club steered me away. I knew it had to be DRAMA of all kinds in there. And y'all should know from part 1 that's what I'm trying to stay away from. At Norma Jeans I heard money is there to be made. With Oasis it's a club where White girls are the majority. So it's some drama I know I could handle. Sure there's Black girl's however only a hand full. Then there were other races like West Indian's, Latinas and Biracial girls too, a nice variety of females meaning more competition.

Oasis is a Gentlemen's club highly recommended to tourist, Oriole and Raven fans during their season games. Guy's even came from D.C. to enjoy them selves because D.C. doesn't allow lap dances. Guy's that came into Oasis ranged from the corporate moguls, business owners to big time hustlers to regular Joe's. There's a dress code with no tennis shoes, you had to be twenty-five to get in and you had to buy a drink to stay. The best thing about this club is that you did a strip tease but didn't necessarily have to take all your clothes off. So I plan to take advantage of that by taking my time shedding my clothes making the guy's that came in use their imagination and want more. I wanted them to admire the art form of my body not my kitty K.

Getting dressed at 7:24p.m, the locker room is very clean and nicely built. I made sure for my 1st night that I'm ready to work when the shift started. I put on my beautiful gold metallic two piece tube top and skirt that had gold lace embroidery on the hem. It was tightly fitted. The outfit alone cost me two hundred dollars. The matching dull gold glass sandals is trimmed in that metallic gold lining that went perfectly with my ensemble. I paid one hundred and twenty dollars plus tax. I had plenty of outfits to change in. My favorite is the school girl outfit and my Dallas cowgirl cheerleading out fit I even had pom poms to go with it. I even got creative with regular going out outfits. What got a lot of the other girl's attention- is how I rock'd just a white button down business shirt just the right length to show my thighs. Roll up the sleeves with my glass slippers and a black thong. Sometimes I would wear a tie or my reading glasses. All types of men loved when I wore that. I thought with the six hour's I'm there I should change five times in a night but that's if I'm doing a lot of private dancing.

Being a new girl in a new club I stayed to myself. I knew I had to gain the veterans acceptance. But spoke when I was spoken to. I'm in that zone to get to work and learn their customer's. To the girl's I kept a friendly expression on my face that's approachable. The girl's that had made it in so far were checking me out from head to toe on the low. The night shift started at 8 o' clock. I could tell in their conversation's that they're stuck on themselves.

There's a female that looked like she's from India actually pregnant getting ready to work. I couldn't believe my eyes. She had been working there for a couple of years and I guess she needed to stay on the grind. She's at a full stage of showing but not wearing provocative clothing but a black sheer robe and a short dress. She didn't dance when she got on the floor just sat with her regular's.

I had the same nervous feeling just like the 1st time I started dancing however kept my composure. Walking down this long skinny wooded stairway to get to the 1st level of the club, I put my shield on to cover my nervousness and just perform the way I have. All eyes were on me.

I slipped up and played a song that's not really fit for this crowd or atmosphere but I love the song. When I saw it I instantly picked it. - EnVogue's "Never Gonna Git It" By this time I had a few poll tricks under my belt. I did just the simple ones of lifting myself up to strike a pose or swing around on it. I wanted to first see the other girl's skills. Then show them that I can do some too. I had met one of the bouncer's before at Diamonds named

Spider. He's trying to make me feel too comfortable with his flirtatious ways. Every one that worked as a bar tender, security and the door men wore a white tuxedo shirt, black vest and bow tie with black bottoms.

There's one beautiful Black girl that looked Creole, a face like Vanity and body like a goddess. She wore red to go with her red bone color and had a beautiful personality. Her stage name is Cherry. She's a little older than me but was the first person to speak. To also find out how long I've been dancing and what other club did I work at. Cherry gave me the rundown of Oasis and the rules where basically set up like Diamonds. She told me she comes to work every so often when she needed an extra bill paid or something she wanted material wise like a new bracelet or earrings but she explained not that many girls had it like that. You had to be on a schedule of three to four days to work there. Cherry is cool, I could tell she's the loner type as well. I had to play what I like but made sure it appealed to the audience. I had to put on my acting mode for the majority of the White older men, who seemed to be very attracted to me. With any guy in my age group or close to it, I'm more myself but never got personal in talking.

On stage I gave good eye contact with the customer's in the bar. I just acted like a sex symbol also by putting my favorite male celebrity on their bodies pretending like I'm dancing for guys like Bryce from the R&B group Groove Theory, Usher or music producer Pharrell Williams or even P. Diddy. That's how I picked up business quickly there at Oasis by being a new face. The rules where set up the same but customers weren't allowed to touch the dancer giving them a lap dance, which is excellent. I thought I did okay for my first night on a Thursday. I could have done better leaving out with nine drinks plus one-hundred and twenty-three dollar's in tips after I gave the bouncer's there tips. I'm really pushing trying to get the tenth one. The only bad thing about moving is my base pay had lowered back to fifty dollar's. I'm determined to convince Mack to raise it if he watched how I gain my business with people coming to see me. They're set up the same with the price of drinks starting at twenty dollar's with you getting five dollar's from each drink. Then the lap dance prices started at $60 to $100 dollar's. What's another new seller is Moet champagne starting from $140 to 230.

When it's time to dance we danced to three songs, when it's a lot of girl's we would only dance two songs. You also had to put a dollar in a juke box for songs.

The way I dance is unique since Paradise from Diamonds showed me some poll techniques. I looked like the females straight out of the hip hop videos, the real classy ones. Not opening my legs wide for all the customer's to see inside… that's a no no. I learned a lot from them female's down at Diamonds. My body is already hot my moves blew up the spot. I'm natural born entertainer. Being in my high school band helped me to maintain the stage fright I had inside…that I did well to hide. When it was the weekend that's when the upstairs is open. A lot of my regular's at Diamond's did not like the Oasis club so I had to start over. So I had to really rebuild my regular's back up. I impressed them all with my stage presence I'm something to notice. I just remembered what that older Foxxy Brown looking lady told me to play what the crowd would like to hear. I played R&B, Hip Hop to classic alternative rock. I appealed to the audience.

During the weekend it's steady then it picked up to nonstop business. I went up to the upstairs bathroom, a big thick White girl and this Hispanic & Black looking chick is in the bathroom chiefing out. I quickly close the door to come in however happy to know they smoked here. I wasn't shy to ask if I could hit it one time. I needed something to calm my nerves. The thick White chick looked at the Hispanic chick. The Hispanic chick nodded her head it was cool. Her name is Justice. She reminded me in her looks like Dameeka from back home in Oklahoma only Justice had red hair. She's real petite. The thick White chick is named Ice. She had dark long hair and was aaight in the face. I could tell she is tough acting. I took the two pull rule wiping off any of my mouth print and said thanks. I just needed something to chill me out. When I'm washing my hands a real thin White chick came in with short hair. She's real outgoing, cool personality. Her name is Zoey. She's giving me complements on my body and how I danced with the other two listening. I thanked her and stopped to talk in the nice small unit bathroom.

"What club's did you work at before," Zoey asked.
"I started dancing over at Diamonds a month ago"
"My friend Kelly works over there…. WOW!!
You've been dancing only a month Girl. It looks like you've been dancing longer than that."
"Yep! Just a month, I know Kelly. She's cool…
Well she y'all later, I said smiling keeping it short.
On the weekend I made two-hundred and ten dollar's on Friday and three hundred dollar's on Saturday. Business is going slow the other dancers were all confessing. I could tell I'm going to have to work hard at this club to keep up. I really didn't have to work hard at Diamonds. That kind of money was on my okay days there. I had to set a schedule up in making the money I needed. I couldn't just go splurging every weekend any more. I had to stash some money away for a rainy day.

At school in my clothing construction class we had

55

a project coming up for the end of the year to put on a fashion show. Everyone in the class is so excited however, not as excited as me. Dawn kept her composure to a dull expression about everything. Her style is so far different, kind of hip gothic. Rocking cut off jean jackets with a skirt with tall biker boots. I liked her sense of style punk rock with a girlie twist.

   To start on our projects I went with Dawn to an exclusive fabric store that had all different kinds of material for our sewing pleasure. I wanted to try to make a suit.

   I could tell Dawn had a free spirit by here pattern picks. After looking around I went back over to Dawn's house. This time I decided to chief with her. Since last night I hadn't indulge in chronic smoke in a long time. She got me connected to get some of my own for after work chill time. We chilled talking about everything that came to the brain, school, music and clothes. Dawn decided that it's time to tell me something she's been dying to tell. Dawn is straight up gay and proud. I'm amazed at her coming out and feeling comfortable to share her sexuality. She thought it would end our friendship. I had never had a gay friend before so it's new to me that I didn't know how to react. I just didn't want to judge her. I still thought she could be a good friend. I asked her what I had always wondered: "How did you know you were gay?" She told me she's felt that way since middle school. She even had a girl friend. I let her know that I work around a lot of Gay females. With a lot of curiosity she asked what did I do? I let her know I'm an exotic dancer. Her eyes grew big with excitement of wanting to know more about my job. She wanted to start working down on the block. I gave her every detail I knew on how it works. I told her it went well with my schedule for school. I made sure I got plenty of rest during the day, I took naps. After work I went home and got ready for bed.

Rest is important.

"You just have to be smart. Balance out your health, rest and nutrition with that night life because that night life would leave you tired. I let her know that I didn't drink that much maybe on the weekends, weekdays something light. I let her know it's not that bad. Dawn listened to every word while she smoked on a Newport.

Chapter 5

The Education of Oasis

*I*t was all kind of different characters of females however not that many ghetto chicks in this club. The majority is White females. There's a White girl that complemented me on my body named Alexis. She's trashy but tried to keep it classy. Blond haired with dark roots and a shag cut with some length in the back. In the locker room I learn she's a loud mouth doing rude gestures of burping and cussing like a sailor. She had a square shaped body and played nothing but rock.

The ones that kept it real complemented me on my body, which the majority of them let me know. I always smiled and said thank you but not seeing what they saw. Sure there's a few high classed Diva's that just looked, like this Asian looking petite female.

But Alexis is the main one making a scene of how hot my body is. As I sat at the long bar with mostly the girl's waiting on customer's to come in. A few introduced themselves to me. Alexis sat next to me feeling comfortable with her complementing me upstairs and said:

"So what happen to your face?"

"I was in a car accident."

"Damn! I thought you'd been in a fight." She said smiling with a sigh.

I laughed back saying "No."

"But you're still pretty" Alexis added while getting up to make a move on a customer. I smiled back and said thanks.

Alexis was one of the girl's that kept changing in different outfit's my first night. Her style is mostly wearing white I guess to represent her white trashy ways. She had such a loud mouth that I knew what I said is going to spread throughout the dancer's. She's cool with that thick White girl name Ice. They would constantly talk loud on the other side of the dressing room. Mainly Alexis, talking about her boyfriend Hummer.... break ups and make ups including their fights and him treating her bad.

An attractive Black dancer that seemed to be loved by all, every night she'd hurriedly came through the locker room dress like a bum. Everybody spoke to her. Her name is Nicole. As she got dressed she turned into a Super Diva within an instant. She had beautiful brown skin with a Lola Falana look with hair flowing to the middle of her back with the most voluptuous thick toned figure I've ever seen with double D breast. She mostly wore black tube top dresses to make her figure look like an hour glass. Nicole had the perfect height at 5'8. She had an all around personality. She kept it real with Nicole being her real name. Nicole had been on the "Block" for over ten years when it was ten blocks long. Now being only one block long she knew it blind folded. When she approached me she sat down and said with the most sincere look on her face:

59

"Honey what happen to your face?"

I explained to her as well but in detail with the 101 stitches in my face alone to the fractured nose and femur bone. She went into more depth on how she thought I'm beautiful. Nicole wasn't a hater she spread love with lots of complements. She went on and on about my body and features. Scars within my skin....still with a beautiful grin even with my right eye still a little swollen. Yeah I'm beautiful I had it going on scars and all. She pointed that out to me then adding: "Going through something like that and still be gorgeous is amazing." The word mostly used by her "gorgeous." I almost had her in tears of joy and sorrow that I'm still carrying on and how I believe I could do this kind of job. Scars and all.

You could feel a realness in the way Nicole explained how I'm still attractive better yet gorgeous. I gladly thanked her for it. She told me she had to give credit where credit is due. I knew we were going to be tight. She said she once had a body like mine and was at awe with mine. In my mind I'm wondering why so many people were saying that about me. I thought my own body was aaight. But she's putting my body shape on a pedestal which I couldn't get. With the other girl's I wouldn't admit however with Nicole I let down my guard. With Nicole she has intelligence and sounded highly educated. When she talked she has such glamorous vocabulary, using extravagant wording. She gave me some advice to always go for the gusto, always ask for the highest drink. We bonded from the start. Nicole put me under her wings. She even danced for Madonna in New York City once.

Nicole called the customer's clients. She said she never does private parties and bachelor parties because there's no security for the girls. Everything Nicole said to me I soaked in listening. We talked on a range of topics

60

like the different kind of clients that come in; the girl's having their different cliques and how to be careful in not getting caught up with drugs like so many girls have. She came close to me and said:

"Remember every girl in here has been through something or they have some kind of problem whether it's being molested, on drugs and for majority even physical abuse." She looked around saying: "Every girl has been through something, trust me."

Nicole is an Entertainer. She showed me on the top of the long wall were picture's of White women in bathing suits doing different poises such acrobat poises, I liked.

"Look up there. Do you see any Black women up there?" Nicole said.

"That's funny I don't," I replied.

Nicole gave me a look and said: "It might be a new millennium but some people still discriminate. But with a body like yours it's art and needs to be put up on this wall."

Nicole even filled me in on the owner which is a woman and she's a bossy White lady in her early 50's, attractive. When I say she's bossy I'm not talking about what she said it was mainly her looks. Ms. Kim knew she's the head Bitch in charge. She didn't dress like a rich woman but she had old money, mainly wearing sweat shirts and jeans. Nicole introduced me to Linda the petite bar maid. Linda's a blue eyed bombshell that's a retired dancer. She wore a Chinese bob. Linda settled down married with kids. She's going to Towson University as well.

A dancer named Devine had the bubbliest personality that kept a grin on her face always excited about something, (making money). She introduced herself to me after my third day. She had her clique that looked like they just got out of high school, Bonnie and Destiny. Devine looked Hispanic however was a White girl that just died her long hair to coal black. She kept it twisted up in the front. She had street knowledge as well but still acted like a White girl. She's an average height with small breast. I started to notice for this to be a titti bar small breast were really in here. Like, the Asian looking girl. Nicole told me that's Gi Gi. Nicole even idolized her body and dreaded the nights she had to go up before or after Gi Gi. She came in on my first weekend there. Gi Gi is a size zero Philippine and White combo, 5'3 with blond shoulder length hair. Some thought she favored Christina Aguilera or even the new Pop singer Lady Ga Ga. To me, she did in a way. She's pretty with nice big almond shaped eyes.

Gi Gi is so petite but proportioned like me but hardly had a butt. She's very quiet however the most popular dancer. She's like an acrobat when it came to the pole. She had it mastered. The best poll dancer I'd seen. She did this split on the actual poll while her upper body was flip backwards. She would have this sexy spaced out look on her face moving real slow to mostly rock and a little bit of R&B. All her drinks came to her she hardly moved to make her money and didn't even ask for tips when getting off the stage. She mainly spent her time in the dressing room fixing her self in the mirror. Nonchalant but thinks I'm all that expression seemed unapproachable to speak to. Being the most popular dancer at Oasis, other dancer's pulled her in on their drinks. It seemed like all the girl's wanted to be her friend. All the guy's kept their eyes on her small petite size climbing to the top of the poll looking out at the crowd. Gi Gi's a loner at sometimes however hung tough with Jewel. I'm not gay but Jewel is beautiful. Upstairs in the dressing room she sometimes used foul language to seem down but didn't sound right. She hung with the most stuck up diva dancer's. Jen the dancer I met at Diamonds is a part of that crew wearing their white thigh high platform boots.

I couldn't believe Jewel started a conversation complementing me as we were both going down the stairs around the same time. Breaking the ice saying:

"Dam your ass is phat."

I said "Thanks," Looking weird at the same time with an odd smile.

Later after being busy I sat two chairs down from her. Striking up another conversation Jewel is wondering how long have I danced and where I'm from with my accent. I asked the same and what race is she. Jewel's a West Indian and Black combination with Spanish wavy looking hair past her shoulders. She's from an island named St. Lucas. An Appolonia fair skinned young face being nothing but 5 foot 4 with a butt and more flat chest than me. She could dance very well with a mix of slow grind and shook her booty. She had a cool low key persona, barely out of her teens with a baby and living with her baby's daddy. Chatting every now and then but not really in front of her Diva crew. She admired that I'm in school and wanted to do the same. Most of the girl's during the day go to school she mentioned once when we were conversing.

I'm on a sixty dollar drink that's the shape of the tropical glass just sitting at the bar in a good conversation with this White guy named Morris on diverse topics. Just sitting is a good sign of the guy just wanting to talk. Later this guy in a hat walked in and sat two chairs from us. He's cute and had street appeal with his style. What I noticed, he had a scar on his right side that went all the way up to his jaw like mine but longer. It made me very curious about him. He's also a survivor of something. I made sure I wasn't making it noticeable to the dude I'm now sitting with that I notice this other guy in the mirror. I'm curious to know how he got the scar. He left before I could approach him.

There's this White girl with dark hair to her shoulder's named Tonya she had a banging body. Her butt is just as phat as mine. Since Britney Spear's came out asses on White girls just spread like a new epidemic. I'm guessing she's mixed with Italian. Tonya mostly wore white too and hung with loud mouth Alexis. She kept to herself sometimes. She had a good clientele with Black guys. Tonya could dance too anything and knew how to shake her booty jazzy like me.

I noticed one of the Black girl's that worked there that kept to her self all the time. Everybody's pretty much sociable by now but her. She's very pretty in a natural way without hardly any makeup, my chocolate brown color and had a bombshell body with medium size breast. I would see her come in carrying a Morgan State back pack. I never seen her at Morgan but it's a big campus. I turn to asked her in the dressing room did she go to Morgan she responded yeah. I could tell she was with the short answers so I didn't want to bother her. But when we were on the floor she came up to me and told me she's sitting out this semester.

The bar loops around the club were some people can sit facing the crowd coming in. Best seats to peep the scene. Beginning of the bar in the first seat close to the front door Ms. Kim would sit until about 9:30 looking over her glasses at us trying to work it. That night is going slow. I couldn't believe it, there's no money flow. Mack would get loud and scream at the other girl's in the dressing room. He never screamed at me, he just let me do my thing. I heard he had a thing for Black females.

I had only five drinks and sixty dollars in tips. But I never stressed I kept the faith believing God would always make a way giving me favor. But how these girls have

64

panic attacks you would think they're going to have a nervous breakdown. In the dressing room I heard it all. A lot were inquiring about the amount of drinks each one had. One girl approached me and asked I told her however I didn't feel comfortable. Later I approached the girl that attended Morgan down on the floor she's standing up against the mirrors. Its seats available but I guess she'd rather stand. I asked her how many drinks she had. She told me quick as a flash: "I don't tell people my number of drinks."

"That's understandable," I said. I started saying the same thing to nosy bitches concerned with my money.

Aaron is still being supportive. He came to visit me at the new club sometimes. He sat with me for two drinks one night. He's impressed with the club showing his cute grin. Aaron went to the rest room. He got all the girls attention. Cherry approached me and said: "Oooh… Who is that? Is that your man? Girl he is fine."

I smiled and giggled saying yes.

"Girrrrl, if you all ever wanna do something different….you know… like having fun in the bedroom with someone else wit y'all please let me know." Cherry said with a serious look. Then complementing how fine he was again (laughing).

I'm amazed at this beautiful woman's approach. As she's finishing up what she had to say. Aaron came back and sat back down. She's walking away saying hello to him. I didn't want to tell him so rapidly. But when I told him what she said I had this look on my face to see if he's interested. He looked at me and slightly nodded his head no saying: "Naw…When I'm with someone I'm only with them….I'm not in to that… I just want to be with you." I couldn't believe he passed up a beautiful woman like that.

That's when I truly knew that he's falling for me. See I hadn't been in that many relationships. But I knew and felt this is my first real love. He wanted to have a future with me. I wanted the same in the future when we got financially straight to have a family. He had been married before and could see himself marrying me. I'm caught up in a love triangle, confused. Having a united force with Aaron so strong but having love for my best friend and so called fiancé Javontae. Every time Javontae and I talked on the phone he's always discussing how the wedding is going to be. Instead I would want to talk about how the relationship is going to be. We talked at least one day out the week.

Chapter 6

What's Going On?

$\mathcal{T}$imes were getting tough. September 11th just happened and the media is talking about it nonstop. Not too far from me there's a catastrophe and I'm still on "the Block." It really wasn't talked about at work so much. The guy's that came in there had their own problems let alone worry about America's problem. Then on the other hand a lot of them were thinking it's not the time to go to a strip club. So low and behold down… on the block it became slow. Business wasn't the same for any of the clubs. A lot of girl's from Diamond's moved to Oasis. I lost a good percentage of my regular's from Diamonds, like Matt, Charles and a few others. For some reason a lot of guy's use to say they didn't like going into the Oasis giving them business. Several reasons like the club bouncer's were quick to kick somebody out or some guy's didn't like Mack. I'm use to them not caring how many drinks I had just having a good talk and having fun laughing. I use to make way more at Diamond's. I would rather have the lower base pay to be away from some of them ignorant bitches at Diamonds. I'm still doing good balancing out my bills and real responsibilities. Not having the big purchase luxury anymore. I had to eat and that's my main goal to maintain in the game, eat to grow. I remained trapped in my work situation but it's my survival kit to last.

One night Jewel was on one side and I was on the other side of the vanity. I'm doing my make up and she came in and got on the phone. She was going into how she's never done a threesome and wanted to do one. Then insinuating to the caller of finding someone she didn't really know. To me it was an act of trying to lure me in, but I don't swing that way. I got up after I did what I needed and left out.

The Hispanic chick Justice is cool sometimes to talk to. We were discussing getting nervous in front of big crowds dancing. She gets nervous when a bunch of Black guys come in and I'm the opposite when White guys come in. Justice had a lot of guys come in to see her p popping performance. I started noticing since I stayed around for a week going into the second I'm hanging with them in business, the female's started to warm up to me approaching me as we sat at the bar waiting for business. Justice hung sometimes with a girl named Isis. A Black girl that had a Halle Berry body, not as cute with a gold crown on her tooth to insinuate she's ghetto fabulous. She had an oily long weave that went down to her back bones. She's popular with the old White rich man too.

Ali is another Black girl, this dark chocolate skin colored female with bubble sized eyes. She inquired about my schooling. She's going to school for nursing, Ali told me that while she's puffing on a cigarette. From the start she seemed messy and a big liar. This thick looking biracial chick that could pass for a lot of ethnicities would change

68

the way she talked for guy's all the time. If she's with a White guy she'd put on her White sounding voice, if he's Black she would sound Black. She came up to me trying to sound down, at the same time could not keep eye contact with my eyes instead she would be busy examining my whole face. I got use to it.

One night the second week I'm working and two new faces had started working for Oasis. They were early waiting to work like how I am. One looked Asian or Indian and the other is a fair skinned Black female, both very attractive. The Indian looking chick had Pocahontas long hair that's bone straight to her back. The Black female had an Asian up do with chopsticks in her hair. They're sitting at the bar on the corner by the front door. That's where the dancers mainly sat to be seen by the customer's that came in to the club. I sat one chair down from them. Since I had been there for two weeks now, I knew that they're new. I thought this is a good time to become cool with some other new females that just started. I introduced myself as Lonnie and that broke the ice for us to start a conversation up. The Indian chick is still coming up with a stage name for herself. So we were discussing that. She came up with Butterfly. Misty is the Black chick's name. She's Trina the rapper's kind of thick in her body. Misty is nice and we both agreed she should change it to something else. Misty said:
"I told her she should go by India."
"Yeah, I like India. It goes with your look," I added

The Indian looking chick thought it had a nice ring to it. So she agreed to use that. India explained her roots being a South American from Guyana. India looked just like a China doll. She had features like Aaron's mother. The three of us made an instant bond. We made a means to sit by each other as we got paid out and also walk to the parking lot together. The parking lot they parked at is across the way from Norma Jean's. I started to park in that parking garage instead of the one away from everything. I wanted to walk with more people to be safe with money in my pocket. Every time we walked past Norma Jeans it would be people hanging all outside the door still trying to get in. Yes! Norma Jeans is definitely a hot spot. India and Misty always drove in India's late 90's grey model Toyota Land Cruiser.

Misty is from Baltimore. She had been in some major rap video's India shared with me. But I hadn't seen any of them. India had been in Maryland for a year and a half now. They met at a telemarketing company where Misty told India about Baltimore Street. India's so nervous and has never done this before. I told her I'm fairly new to this as well. I let them know that we were at the best club on the block so I heard. Misty had worked on the block before at Norma Jeans. In between time we talked about Norma Jeans when we weren't busy. Misty let me know that at Norma Jeans you mainly made mad tips. So that's how you made your money. At work when the time started to wind down to wrap up the night that's when every dancer is trying to talk to every guy in the club that's available.

India had this outgoing personality. She could sit and talk to anyone. She didn't mind starting a conversation with one of the girl's. India and Jewel's where born on different Islands but not too far away so they connected. India and I even started to bond as well.

There's also another new fair skinned female that started dancing. Her biggest asset is her chest. She needed to do something with the curly almost fine hair, basically it looked like a dried up thick curl. Her stage name is Dream. She had an attitude on her that stunk from a mile. Most of the girl's caught on to it. She happened to be Ali's family, something like cousin's. Dream couldn't dance to save her life. When Dream talked to any of the girls she had an attitude. So within the next week she got comfortable to ask for tips from guys that were talking with another girl, especially India for some reason. She made a habit of it, even when several females had approached her and said you're not supposed to do that. On that Wednesday almost the end of the night, Alexis is on a drink with one of her regular's. Dream did it again asking for tips. But what she didn't realize is that she did it to the wrong person, Alexis. As Dream is continuing getting her tips Alexis got up and tapped her on the shoulder and told her off about not doing that to her. And Dream's response is "So," and kept stepping.

We got to the dressing room to get dressed after work. Alexis came up the stairs didn't say anything to Dream but just ran up on her and started punching her until she fell to the floor. Dream just curled up in a ball. I saw it all and I was praying that she didn't fall. At her defeat on the ground, Alexi's whole crew came around. Jen, Tonya and Ice started hitting Dream. When Dream fell they started stomping Dream down putting in pounds. I just stood there expression-less with the rest of the spectators laughing it up but what I wanted… is for her to really get up. The bouncer came to Dream's aid and saved her from the ass wiping of the day. Alexis didn't even get fired or in trouble for that. I couldn't believe that Ali just watched it go down and did nothing. I knew right then that she would never have my back if needed. That's the way things go down. What's really going on in this world?

Chapter 7

I Put On

Dawn is ready to go and try the block out to dance. I told Mack in advance that my friend wanted to work. "Lonnie, Is she cute? I don't want any mop rags working at my club," he said smiling.

"Yes she's very attractive Mack. She looks like Aaliyah, she's pretty trust me."

When I bought Dawn in she became extremely nervous to work. At her house she's talking like a pro. Mack is acting slightly impressed. I'm glad I had somebody there I'm cool with to watch each other's back because these girl's be talking about carrying knives and cutting bitches. I wasn't going for that happening to me or anybody I kicked it with. The first night Dawn smoked her whole pack of cigarettes watching the other girl's performing, getting turned on. She gained a crush immediately on Jewel. The veterans were checking her out doing their routine of first day intimidating stares. Her stage name became Flame and I thought it had a nice ring. She picked up a few things to wear mostly black and red. Dawn also loved to rock corn rolls. She's a little stiff when she got up on the stage to work it. I could have been embarrassed for her but I thought it's the White in her. I introduced Flame to India. Flame even gained a secret crush on India. Flame did pretty good that night being a new face that gets the club clientele's attention. She liked it and wanted to come back.

Flame is doing well but she wasn't doing better than me. I tried to give her pointers on how to score in getting a lap dance but after that week she thought she had it down. I was just trying to give her the game that I had to learn on my own. So I let her do her. She wanted her girlfriend to come see her however females were not allowed to come in the bar alone, they had to have a guy companion with them. So her girlfriend got a guy to come with her. Flame's girlfriend is a butch type that looked like a guy with (dred) locks and baggy clothes. For Dawn this job is extra money, her parent's paid her bills. So it's extra shopping money for her. With me I'm saving as I worked each day. I took this job and me doing it as a serious business. I saved every time I got paid, which was day to day. So every morning I would deposit some money in my bank account like businesses do.

The third week I'm upstairs on a drink. Dawn's well now- Flame is starting to get the hang of it. Justice is up on stage dancing. Flame came up stairs seeking at least one more drink for the night. She saw this White guy sitting alone so she approached him. She would always shake the guy's hand first which is a no no for me unless they reach their hand out. You never know what they've been doing. They could have been in another clubs bathroom jacking it off. When Flame stood there talking for like five minutes he bought her a sixty dollar drink. It got Justice's attention on the stage and she said out loud: "HEY, WHAT THE F*<K!!" throwing her hands up in the air. After her dance

set she stormed off the stage. I thought something is going to happened but Justice just went to the dressing room pissed off not putting back on her clothes by the stage. But at this point she can't say anything because that's a rule: If the customer shows interest in another dancer and buys a drink he can do that. When Justice came back out she went up to the guy to see if he wanted to buy her one as well. He turned her down. Flame and the man sat there on the sixty the whole time and talked. So at the end of the night were getting dressed and I knew something is going to be said. Flame's getting dressed by my locker that's in the left corner. Justice's little self came in the dressing room quickly to start telling Flame off yelling: "YO… HEY YOU… STAY AWAY FROM MY MUTHA- FV<KING CUSTOMER'S OKAY… I'm one of nicest bitches here. DON'T FUCK WITH ME," She said loudly. The room is so quiet with everyone paying attention then on the other side some were snickering like the loud mouth Diva group, Alexis's crew.

With a calm sincere look Flame said: "I asked was he sitting with anybody and he said no."

Justice interrupted and said raising her voice caring on even louder: "THAT'S MY CUSTOMER."

That's when I came in and said: "Justice she's new, she didn't know that was your customer."

That's when Justice blew it off still acting pissed off. Flame added holding her hand out: "You can have the money. It's not that serious."

The very next day Dawn came in and Mack fired her. I saw her go to the dressing room coming into work and when she came back she still had her regular clothes on I knew she had been fired. She came over to tell me what happened and she would be checking out Norma Jeans. I

74

told her good luck and Norma Jeans might be better. We would keep in touch at school on her status.

I talked to Mack jokingly about how I thought it was wrong to fire Flame. But he explained that it had nothing to do with what happened the other night. She was in the bottom too many times with not getting out there and working. She was too passive. I noticed the amount of pressure they're starting to put on the dancer's. With a lot of the girl's Mack screamed at and cursed them out at work. But for some reason he never got mad at me or raised his voice. On the other hand Ms. Kim gave the most intimidating and scary looks at me to get to work. What she got pissed off the most is for girl's to just sit while there's available guy's sitting at the bar.

One weekend night I came from upstairs. On the floor I'm walking to the usual spot for the dancers, close to the front door. I notice it's a Black couple with a third female party with them. As I got closer it's the dude with the scar again. I sat down at the bar stool by the door. The guy is dressed in black and he had two females with him. The females are very attractive. One looked like a round the way girl in casual dress clothes and the other is jazzy dressed in big name brands with her hair styled nicely.

The jazzy one is apparently his girl friend because she's giving her man a lap dance right in front of us the whole time. She had a bright smile like my home-girl Ladawna's from back home. Gi Gi is sitting on the right of me across from the couple. Me and Gi Gi caught eyes for the first time and smiled at each other watching the jazzy girl shake it up. The threesome finally left after a couple of drinks. As the guy got up he helped her put on a brown chinchilla coat, that's the baddest coat I've ever seen. I wanted him to come back soon however by himself.

India and I were still cool walking with each other

to our cars. Misty fell off in coming to work. India and I even exchanged numbers and knew each other's real name, her name is Donia. She shared how she was also in a car wreck. Donia showed me her scar on her arm. We had an instant connection and I talk freely about my scars on my face. India knew how to say encouraging complements. Nicole too, she raved about how beautiful I am. Nicole would admit that she wished she had my body and I wished for hers. She made me smile and feel good all the time. Nicole and I had an instant connection too. Sometimes I took her home. I loved Nicole and respected her honesty. Little did she know she use to build up my confidence were I still needed it. She even pulled me in on some lap dance drinks with her.

I had certain guys that are attracted to my look - some Blacks guys from young to old and older white guys. Every so often I sat with a younger White guy. For Nicole she sat with all kinds of races. Her clientele is so diverse. All she had to do is come in for two nights and she's pretty much set for the week.

Since the war is getting ready to pop off a lot of troops were getting shipped to Iraq. Two young white guys came in to have a good time for the night. One chose me to sit with. We started a good conversation, that's when he told me he's a soldier getting ready to go to Iraq. I wished him protection and told him to stay focused over there. On his arm I could see he had a red colored tattoo. It's an actual heart with arteries that had grey bob wire around it. It's dripping with blood. It's the coolest tat I'd ever seen. I interpreted his tat saying: "Someone broke your heart and this bob wire is around it so no one else will do it again." He looked at me and nodded his head yes.

Once I got off doing a double lap dance with Nicole with one of her regular's. I notice this cute business suited

Black guy sitting with India and it wasn't his first time. I saw the scar face dude come in. I went to the dressing room and got freshened up to change clothes. The first thing I'm going to do is approach the scar faced dude to ask what happen. When I got down stairs I'm glad that he wasn't with anyone. I leaned over on the bar stool next to him introducing myself and then said:

"You don't mind me asking. How did you get the scar?" He looked at me and said: "Naw I don't mind. A nigga tried to rob me and I got away."

He pulled back his hoody a little showing the scar that went to his neck to his jaw, where the guy trying to rob him tried to cut his throat. By this time Frank the bar tender approaches to ask if the guy wanted to buy a drink for me. I'm pissed because Frank came up too quickly not giving me a chance to even ask for myself. The guy accepted which made my drink number at twenty which is breaking a new record. The biggest number of drinks I've gotten so far working at Oasis. With my tips and base pay it's a great night. I'm going to enjoy this visit because I felt that he and I had something in common. His name is Jamonos and I liked his style. He started to come to see me regularly after that.

Chapter 8

Final Decision

My heart started eating at me, a feeling I didn't want. I felt like I'm doing Javontae wrong and if I'm going to go through with the engagement. I couldn't keep doing him or Aaron like that even though I grew to love Aaron. I needed to make a decision on who'd to be with. I weighed my pros and cons with the both of them. I wanted to be with Aaron however I knew Javontae is best for me. We were best friends since middle school. When I went through my car accident and got scarred for life. He was there one hundred percent encouraging me. Javontae and I were spending Christmas together at my place and that's where I'm going to lay it all on the table. With what I've been doing for a job and how much I want to try to make our relationship work or is it one.

Christmas is around the corner and I'm going to break the news to Aaron however, I didn't know how and what words to say. I told him that I'm spending Christmas with family so we should celebrate Christmas early. He's cool with that. I'm planning an extravagant week for Javontae and me to get cozy in the Christmas spirit. I bought my decorations for my place from the tree to nice green and red ornaments.

The day that Aaron and I were celebrating I got all my fixings for a nice dinner from The Boston Market. I had shopped for his gifts a long time ago. He came over carrying a big bag. I'm shocked and excited to see what was in there. So we opened our gifts. He also had a small shopping bag from Best Buy that had the DVD, the new version of Planet of the Apes. The big bag I opened and screamed excited to see a nice tiger figurine to go with my safari look. The tiger is in a growl position showing his teeth.

"When I'm not here he'll protect you," Aaron said giving me a smile as I hugged him tight for the gift. We put the tiger right by my door.

My gift is a nice Roca Wear jogging suit with some tennis shoes. His face brightened as he pulled it out of the box. We kissed then ate and watched the movie. In the movie when the General Thande beat those guards to death, the way that he beat them was the same way Wanya beat me in our fight just a year ago. I closed my eyes on the part because it took me back to that incident.

I didn't want to give the news to Aaron on such a nice evening. Instead we made love.

The next morning I'm at a confused state. I knew I could see myself spending my life with either of them. I just knew I'm engage to my wonderful friend. My conscious is also feeling guilty about cheating on Javontae.

After we finished our breakfast we sat in my living room. And that's when I broke the news to Aaron that I couldn't see him any longer. He looked confused and said:

79

"But I thought…………..I thought… you were happy."

"I am but I can't keep doing my fiancé like this by cheating on him. He's my best friend……" There's a big pause for some minutes then Aaron said:

"You're the only reason why I'm still here in Maryland. When I met you I wanted to stay and try to make Maryland work for me."

"I'm sorry Aaron. I still want us to be friends."

Aaron smiled and said: "We will."

I gave him a hug because more than anything I wanted our friendship to continue. He left and I watched him until he got in his car and drove off. I hoped that I didn't make a mistake. Love is a gamble hey I'm willing to act in what I thought was right. Aaron was the first person that was truly in love with me.

Christmas is around the corner and I had plans for Javontae and me. I bought tickets to this play called the Nutcracker. Plus I rented four block buster movies. Javontae wanted me to rent Two Can Play That Game, a movie he said he never seen. I did some heavy grocery shopping with every little snack I could think that Javontae likes. I'm going to have Boston Market for our Christmas Eve dinner. I bought two bottles of Moet champagne to celebrate with strawberries. And I did a shopping spree of three gifts for him and five outfits from Victoria's Secret for everyday this week. To set the mood really off I got two dozen of red roses and stocked up on candles. We had talked for months about how special the week is going to be. It was going to be are 1st sexual encounter. I spent a whole lot making sure that it was going to be extraordinary.

That week Aaron came over to spend some time and watch a movie. He couldn't be in my house long enough without being affectionate. I had to stop him and let him know that I'm very serious about my decision. He let me know that he's leaving before Christmas to move back to California. It's something that I didn't want him to do but I couldn't stop him.

Since I'm on Christmas break I went to work every day that week to catch up with what I spent for this fabulous quality time with Javontae. Mostly everybody that's a veteran in the club is excited and planning their holiday trip. Ms. Kim takes every female that has worked there at least five months at Oasis on an all expensed paid trip to Cancun. I wanted to go but I had only been their two months.

I went to freshen up in the dressing room and caught Jewel crying on the phone because she didn't know if she'd be able to go since she couldn't find someone to keep her son. I thought: *No matter what it is I'm never going to ever show my emotions in the club.*

Early that next morning Aaron came by to give me a long hug and kiss before he left out on his long road trip. I wished him a safe journey and asked him to call when he's there settled. After our kiss I said: "Maybe one day we'll see each other again." He gave me that cute smile and got in his car to drive off. As I watched, tears began to form in my eyes but I didn't cry.

I didn't know how I'm going to tell Javontae that I'm an exotic dancer. I wanted to tell him because I didn't want to keep any secrets from him. A week had past and I'm so excited because Christmas Eve is tomorrow. But that morning I got a call from Javontae saying that his ride had changed plans and would be traveling on Christmas. No big problem I thought, plans had to be adjusted. The couple he's riding with is going to D.C. and since I live

81

down the street from Interstate 95 they could stop at a gas station to meet me to drop him off I suggested. He thought that's a good idea and we planned that.

Christmas day I talked to my family but I hadn't heard from Javontae. Around 3:15 p.m. he called me and told me that the couple wanted him to meet there parent's before taking him to get with me. My mouth dropped of disappointment. I thought: *Why is he putting them before me?*

"We can go over there this weekend. I'll take you," I suggested.

"I want to go now so we can have the rest of the holiday with just us."

I thought that's weird and felt something is up. I'm quiet until he said: They Want to Get to Their Family and They Want to go Straight There.

After another four hour's past Javontae called. He suggested that I come to pick him up at their parent's place. He didn't want to inconvenience them on the holidays. I asked what location where they in. He said the some suburban area of D.C. and from what I've seen of D.C. is far from the suburbs. I didn't know the D.C. area like that but the Capital and tour sites downtown. I'm sitting on my couch like a sad puppy thinking of me spending Christmas alone. I didn't want to argue about it because I just wanted to see him and be with some one on this day. He quickly made an excuse and said that he would call me back.

It's really hard to find things in D.C. and I'm not familiar with the streets. I waited and waited till the sky turned purple. I sat in front of my television eating this picture perfect holiday meal. At 8:46 p.m. The phone rang, it's Javontae. In my mind I wanted to scream at him on how he's doing me. Frustrated however calm I said: "Javontae, What's UP? Y'all just getting there? I Can't

82

Believe what time it is."

Hearing people in the background he said "We got here earlier. Let me give you the directions to come get me."

So he's trying to tell me what someone else is telling him. He finally gave the phone to the person to explain. I wrote every little detail down that he told me because I knew that this is going to be a test on my skill of direction. The guy is visually trying to tell me but confusing himself in the same breath. Javontae got back on the phone, I let him know that I'm forty-five minutes away and I don't have a cell phone. I did have a calling card with fifteen minutes on it so I could call his long distance number from a D.C. pay phone. Once I got to D.C. the directions were going well then I went around this loop and I'm looking for Westchester Lane ended up in the hood.

Since most of D.C. looks like the hood I'm going down a street for five miles and he told me I would see the Lane in two miles of where I was. I finally pulled over and used my calling card and called them. Javontae put the guy back on the phone he said: "O no no… You're way off." He gave me the directions again. Javontae got back on. I suggested that we meet and he said: "They're eating and I don't want to disturb them."

I got back on the expressway and almost ended up at the Chesapeake Bay. I knew that this was not okay. I couldn't believe what Javontae is doing on this day. I'm going out my way and I'm the one that planned for us to have a lovely holiday. This is getting crazy. Its dark I'm alone and a female trying to find him was not in our plans. I pulled over again and found a pay phone at a Seven Eleven. As I put in the digits of my card number a woman's voice said: "I'm sorry you have exceeded your calling card minutes, thank you and goodbye." I stood there in a paralyzed state taking a deep breath and feeling like I failed at my test.

I went in the store to ask the man did he know. He didn't so I just drove back home. I felt like I disappointed Javontae by not finding him. What a waist however in the back of my mind it was getting late. I gave up a half past twelve. When I got back home the first thing I did is grab the phone to call him. No answer but I left a message saying how sorry I am for not finding him. I put it on him to call in the morning so I could try again in finding him. I didn't make it a big deal. I knew he would be in touch soon.

The next morning to the afternoon I didn't hear from him so I took a flight home to Tulsa. I felt so confused. It's kind of good being back. Nobody from my hometown knew about my stripper's ambition story.

At a dinner over my cousin's house I went outside with my youngest of brother's Martin and told him what I had been doing. He gave me dap with a soul sake saying for real…. You be getting paid."

"Yeap. In a way where I don't disrespect myself." I broke down quickly the scenario telling him the game and how it's a classy place.

"That's what's up?" he said. I wanted to at least tell someone close to me in my immediate family. I filled him in on more detailed on my abortion that I tried not to think about. On the other hand my cousin is announcing she's pregnant to the family. It made me sick to my stomach to think I'm not able to share the same news. So I didn't I made it disappear out of my mind quickly.

Of course I wanted to go out so I called my home girl's. Ladawna is in from Houston she's going to stop through the club for a little while too. Yolanda, she's still in Tulsa holding it down getting by. She's now in a

84

relationship with a guy named Bear. Bear is the guy who owned the restaurant that Wanya and I had a fight in. Bear is big friends with Wanya.

Being away for a while I wanted to step in to the latest place to lounge and dance. I create my own look going anywhere. I've always been unsure however felt that I had a famous person's sense of style. That night I looked really Hollywood in my attire but casual dressed in black and grey. Now with these Tulsa Hillbillies I can hang with them in fashion. B-More's another story, their high fashion.

Asking many question's to Yolanda. "How does this look? Is my makeup alright? Help me watch out for my blouse in the club if it pulls up okay, please," I would say. Yolanda rolled her eyes up saying: "Jordyn... you look fine," Yolanda using a tone that signified I'm getting on her nerves. It went over my head however I acted like I didn't see it. I even ask if she would do my eyebrows, when she did she eeewwed at the sight of the hair she had to get rid of, she made facial expression that a real friend wouldn't do. Just an observation.

Yolanda took me to Goodfellas. It's popping all night long. We met up with Ladawnas. Catching up with each other, keeping our ear to the streets. My ex-best friend turned enemy, Mia had moved to Texas. Dre, her baby's daddy she's crazy for got locked up. That's when she became a groupie going to all the concerts waiting for the male artist to choose her. But then she finally got what she dreamed of... marrying a millionaire. He's heavyset and light skinned so it's obvious why she was with him, I know her type. Dameeka got locked up but in Tulsa. Mia's rich husband bailed her out. Dameeka's still into her forte, scheming. Tony even moved to Texas too still with Chip. Teresa's at the club too and we caught up. Teresa's boy friend of three years proposed to her and they got married.

85

She's not a virgin anymore she whispered to me. Tee Tee, (a.k.a Bad Azz) went to college and she's 4.0 student keeping her head in the books. Laila's still in Tulsa and she moving up in her job. Mason and her are still together. Wanya's back and forth in Tulsa and Texas. Wayne did go to jail for a minute then got out and went to a Wielding school. Terrell's still in jail.

Yolanda always has a good time clubbing especially when we all came home. She also told me her relationship problems being the other woman. I listened and really couldn't comment. We've always been down for each other. As we were leaving out, we were holding each others arm up from the laughter we had from inside. We got to the clubs front door lobby we saw Rico and laughed even harder. He took offense to it and approached me saying: "WHAT…What. Wit Ya'll Messy ASSES."

Face to face with someone who had raped me. By this time I said: "YOU Should be THANKING Me… YOU Should Be THANKING Me That Your Ass Is Not In JAIL," I said loud enough looking straight in his eyes through my light tinted shades. At first Yolanda was laughing it off (drunk) but when she saw my serious look she started tugging my arm to go.

He starts flashing his keys to his Expedition parked in the front. I gave him a mean mug saying "What IS THAT FOR? I've Been There and Done That with Vehicles boy, SO WHAT." Yolanda pulled me away from the big circled scene with people all crowded around it.

That's one of the reasons I hate Tulsa. He's one of my bad memories. I'm glad that I'm returning to Baltimore tomorrow. Monday is the first day of school for the spring semester.

Chapter 9

Same Song

The spring semester had started. I enrolled in sixteen credits this semester. Proud that I pulled my G.P.A. back up making a 2.5, the fall semester. Last spring was my 1st year at Morgan State and since then I made some adjustments, study hard life must go on, I had school to think about. I liked my schedule. In the back of my mind not receiving any calls from Javontae disturbed me.

When I came home from the mall and grocery shopping as soon as I walked in the phone started ringing. I put my hand full of groceries down and mall bags to answer in enough time. On the other end a familiar voice said: "Hey…What's up!" It was Aaron.

"You made it," I said with excitement.

"Yeah, I made it…. I miss you."

"I miss you too." We talked briefly. He let me know about his road trip then saying: "Well this is not my phone but when I get situated I will let you know my number. I will write you too…. Okay?"

"Okay," I said with a soft tone.

We told each other I love you and said goodbye.

I'm really missing that guy but tried to hold it deep inside that I already wanted him back. The next time he called I'm going to tell him that even if it meant me moving to Cali.

Work is going great I'm boosting in drinks up to ten to twelve, average. To some of the girls that wasn't enough. Jamonos would come in and he always sat with me. We had good talks getting to know each other on general topics and him telling me in slight detail about B-More. He wasn't in to getting any lap dances however I assumed ol' girl with the chinchilla is giving him enough at home. Even though he told me he wasn't serious with the females that came in with him. Sometimes on our visits I would get up sooner. He would help me out when I'm trying to make a couple of more drinks to reach my goal.

There were some more girls that started; two of them came from Diamond's Autumn and Heather. Autumn is White but a down White chick that still acted White. She's nice and we use to talk over at Diamond's. Autumn had long brown hair down to her back. She wore a part in the middle, hippie style. Autumn hung with crazy Chocolate at Diamonds and when she came to Oasis she hung with Gi Gi and Jewel. I figured they all knew each other outside of here because Autumns first night they automatically walked together to their cars. You can't be apart of that crew so easily.

Another Black female became apart of the Oasis staff to dance. Her name is Lady. I told her that is my mother's nickname to break the ice as I asked her name. Lady's tall, taller than me and thick bone with a face like Cindy's from En Vogue. I wasn't the tallest girl working at Oasis. Day shift majority of them were tall looking like models. Lady and I became cool to exchange conversation. She's danced before, just getting back in to it. She wanted to start saving for a beauty salon, so she started back dancing.

Heather's a money maker in a dirty way, talking that porn talk. Men would wait on her and I always wondered why. What did they see in her for her to rack this kind of business? She's a beat up looking White girl that had an average body that popped out a couple of kids with dull blond hair she kept in a pony tail.

Nicole made a good point saying: "See… some guy's come to sit with girl's that look like there wives but their wives don't talk to them in a way they desire or dress in this way."

Nicole also said that some girl's also did things under the table. Little did the bartender's or Mack know Heather would jack guy's off in the club's lap dance area and plus she had a bad drug problem. All the girls were talking about her even cracking jokes that she's setting up her retirement fund. Alexis…being the ring leader of the jokes in her bully ways.

Nicole pointed out something with Heather also. She would just be sitting there waiting for her customer's. Heather would nod off as if she's tired. But Nicole let me know that's a sign of being on heroin, plus the marks in between her hands and maybe feet. Nicole let me know a lot of the girl's do drugs here coke, heroin, shooting up. I'm determined not to let it affect me. I witness for the first time someone sniffing coke in front of me.

Zoey's having a bad night however needed a fix. I saw the bartender pass something to Zoey and the next minute she put it up to her nose and snorted real hard. *Did she know we could see her*? I looked around like does anybody else see what I'm seeing. I couldn't believe she's that hard up for coke. A dancer told me she used to take twelve E pills a day for two years. I thought immediately-

Poor brain- just imagine what it's going through. It's funny that the whole block is infested with drugs running in and out of the clubs with the police department right next door. That's one thing that slightly made me feel safe walking to my car at night, police were out.

One particular night Spider came to me and said that I had a visitor at the door. It's a female that couldn't come in. I got to the door to my surprise its Dee.

"What's up girl?" I said giving her a hug.

She needed a huge favor to stay at my place. I always told her she's welcome. She wasn't making anything happen with work so she needed to go home early. I didn't have a problem with her going to my place however I only had my one key on me. I gave it to her anyway.

When I got to my place I buzzed up to my apartment however Dee didn't answer it. I waited and waited but no answer. I sat in my car waited… waited and waited till I felt sleepy. I then went to her old spot around my way to see if she's there. For some odd reason of not knowing what to do, I didn't want to go back and wait on my busy street. Cars and people pass by where I park my car. I didn't think I should go to a hotel when I have a place. I thought I'll go some where and park. I went to the nearest church and was so tired that I fell asleep and didn't wake up until the morning.

I couldn't believe where I'm sleeping in my car on Baltimore's dangerous streets. I had to be more careful however knew what it felt like to sleep in a car. When I got home Dee apologized and said she found another club to work at to make her money for the night. I thought it's a careless part on my actions, just trying to help someone in need.

At Oasis… there were independent woman that had a temporary plan to make a mean's to a living and on a

90

mission. It's such a variety of different looks of females wearing a mask not all but majority. I had to keep up because almost all the girl's were guy's favorite, especially Gi Gi. I had to start basically over with regulars. There's this White guy that India started sitting strong with. He would always save her from having a bad night. He's in his late 40's. He could pass for looking like one of the singers in the group The Beatles with their 60's haircut.

India and I were tighter outside of the club. She's two years older than me. We played it cool in the club acting sociable but not letting them see how close we were. She peep me on to doing that at lunch once eating Chinese food. Like me, she loved rice and always ate it with her meal. She let me know that she's having a little static with this Black chick named Isis. Because of the hair styles and figure similarities Isis knew India's competition. I made sure I would watch out for that, India is now my home girl.

India well Donia and I would mainly meet up at Towson, the best mall in Baltimore with four levels. She's married but her husband is in jail. Donia had a daughter that's in Ghana with Donia's mother. India also started to hang with that Indian chick that was pregnant named Melissa. Melissa had her baby and back at work dancing again.

My dance energy is the same being a sight to see exotically. I moved slowly at times and of course fast. Even on fast songs I moved slow. A lot of girls felt like if they didn't give me flattering remarks on my body or dancing skills they're hating. It's like they had to complement me, well some. I got complement's everyday by guys and the female's that worked there. I didn't let it go to my head it just helped my confidence even more. I didn't ever have a chance to study the (music) juke box. I would basically get up there playing any Hip Hop and R&B I would see. One day Ali played an all time anthem especially to native Tulsan's, The Gap Band's song "You Dropped The Bomb On Me." I'm so excited to hear it and went to the juke box as she danced to ensure I knew where to find it when I danced. But I planned to wait and wear my orange color new cowgirl's outfit. I had the same cute style like the Dallas Cowgirl's cheerleading outfit with some white go go boots to my knee. So I waited an hour or two and played it. I couldn't believe Ali's showing much tude. (That's attitude for those who don't know.)

Ali's showing it even when I got on the floor walking by with her buck eye's looking at me. I gave a smirk and kept walking in style, paying her no mind because The Gap Band is from my Hometown. I would see her and her clique giving me salty looks. I know they're talking about it. Why she wanted to beef with me, *I don't know*, me knowing how scary she is. All because we played the same song. I started to notice that's how some of the girl's operate claiming songs every time they danced, Like Ice and Isis. Claiming songs, not me, I like too much of a variety.

I got this new Black guy that would come in and talk my head off with several twenty dollar drinks then top it off with a hundred dollar lap dance. I would always talk him into the lap dance. I would sit up straight using my posture and properness, saying "PLEEZZ."

I liked his company plus he's easy. Just order more drinks for him to get loaded making his credit card get exploded. One thing I couldn't do… is get a Moet bottle from this dude. It's alright though because every time he left I'm counting the kind of money that fold's. Gary is his name and his breath I could not tame. I even held my breath in the conversations. He had a full beard that smelled just like liquor. He would leave there drunk out his mind. I even felt bad at times. I started to play that dominatrix role ordering him to drink some H2O. He liked it and kept coming back for more.

Sure we were in a sex environment however I tried to stay far away from sex talking with guy's that I sat with. Girl's like Ice and Alexis were pros at that gutta butt porn talk. I just couldn't do it.

On breaks I mostly stayed close to Nicole talking on a range of topics besides the club, like traveling, going to wineries to taste wine and cheese to role playing for the guys that came in. Her roles ranged from a lot especially that dominating role. But emphasizing who you could do that to and they love it, mostly White guys.

We both sat with this big timer that had the mentality money ain't a thang. I started to sit with him at Diamonds then discovered Nicole is the girl he sat with at Oasis. Even on my slow nights during the week she would pull me in with her "clients." I would work hard trying to pull her in too. I wouldn't even have to work, with Nicole showing bubbly personality that White guy's love to see and with her triple double D's. I notice she's also starting to catch a cold as we talked. I thought she might need to go to the bathroom because one side of her nostrils is wet on the tip. She played it off well slightly sniffing it right back up in her nose as we converse.

I would help her out sometimes by giving her a ride home to break even. She always encouraged me. That's what I loved about her. I would converse about my traveling experiences and my personal life with her. I started to trust her and she started to do the same.

Some of the dancer's notice Zoey losing more weight. She did look like a bunch of sticks on the stage twirling around the pole. I felt like I'm skinny however I had some meat in areas of my ribs and well proportioned in

93

the butt & legs. In Zoey's case it became so much talk that Mack had to let her go because she became skin and bones.

Chapter 10

Surprise, Surprise!

*A*nother month had past another year at last I hoped for better day's I continued to pray. No word from Javontae but word got back to me that I'm no longer engage. It took some classmates to tell me the scoop. Instantly on the phone I knew I made a terrible mistake in taking a chance of letting go of a good man. My mouth dropped but I picked it up with a rapid reflex. "*I can't believe the nerve of him*," I thought in my conscious.

As soon as I got off the phone with them I sat and contemplated. The call I got was one of his closest female confidants so I knew that that's want he wanted. I'm going to wait before I did a mistake and went off. I knew this is something I could handle. I see he's trying to play our situation like the movie Two Can Play This Game.

After two days I called Javontae. With the phone ringing for a long time he didn't answer. I got his phony recording but didn't want to leave a message. With me calling two more times I figured that's what he wanted. So I just fell in the trapped of calling him first when he's in the wrong in my eyes. With me I feel I have to know an answer right this instant. Tomorrow being Tuesday I planned to make a trip to the N.Y. to give him a big surprise. I got a map and the estimated driving time is three hours. I got in my car on the highway 95 at ten in the morning.

I've never been to his dormitory or suite however I knew it's in the graduate housing. In good timing I got there I didn't want to alarm him of my presence. I got in to the building and asked the front desk for a Javontae Howard's room number and told them that I've been directed to leave a note on his door from a professor. With no problems, it's given to me and I went directly there taking the stairs. Getting closer and closer I had thought over what I'm going to say: Ask him how could he do me this way?

I got to the door and hesitated to knock but did it anyway because I came too far. I knocked on the door three times paused a minute and knocked again a recognizable voice said: "Who is it?" I thought about putting my finger on the peek hole but it's no reason to hide. So I stood there with pride still wondering why. It took him ten minutes I know before he opened the door. To my surprise and shock he's standing there. First thing I notice the bed fixed however very messy sheets. And books and paper's on the bed.

He said: "Why didn't you call?"

"I did. So were not engaged anymore?"

He said giving me this crazy ignorant look full of Drama: "You made it that way. I CAN'T BELIEVE You Didn't Come Pick Me UP After I Waited For YOU…On Christmas…. I Was All By Myself on Christmas… NO WE'RE NOT ENGAGED ANY MORE. I CAN'T

BELIEVE YOU."

Giving the same crazy expression back saying: "Believe ME. I CAN'T BELIEVE YOU! I WAS BY MYSELF ON CHRISTMAS TOO. After all that money I spent on tickets, food, gifts, decorating, you name it and you'd rather go see their PARENT'S. I DON"T know D.C. like that and I TOLD You That. What was wrong with you saying to them: Let's go meet her somewhere, she's lost."

"I WASN'T Going To DARE ask them to do that after all that driving," he said making an even crazier face.

I'm in total shock of how he's making it all my fault. I kept making the point of the initial plans we had and that was with them dropping him off at my place. The discussion turned into an argument resolving into canceling the engagement for real. I felt like it's a release off my shoulders and a blessing in disguise. Yet in still I'm heart broken from the stupid mistake of letting Aaron go. At the end of Javontae's arguing point he tried to be an ass by saying: "Go on with your life you'll be okay. Don't stress yourself out about it." By this time I walked off with him continuing: "Don't lose any sleep or stop eating because of this."

"Trust me… you're not worth losing my rest or eating less wit chore` bitch ass." By this time I'm at the door to the stair's he's saying something that I didn't take the time to hear.

The ride back to B-More seemed long I just kept thinking how I lost Aaron over Javontae. I can't believe it, what a lost. I knew I still had hope Aaron is going to call me and I'm going to have my sob story down for him to come back to me and I know he would come back because he never wanted to leave me. I couldn't cry because I knew it's my fault.

I worked hard at putting that aside and focused on

my school work and enjoy my Clothing Construction class Part 2. With every body's mind made up on what they were going to design for the fashion show. I'm proud of myself because I'm ahead of everyone and I'm making a three piece Capri suit, most of my other classmates where either making a top or bottom.

Dawn's showing up half the time for class. She's sticking in there with Norma Jeans. I got my insight from her on what it's really like. She said it stays pack with nothing but niggas all around standing up, playing pool. When I asked her does she make money and on an average how much, her body and face adjusted thinking. When she said three hundred to sometimes five hundred a night, I said really. She shook her head for yes.

It made me wonder if she exaggerated in how much. I made it seem like it's believable by nodding my head yes with a frown. I knew how she worked at Oasis being very inexperienced. Then again some guys like that. She gave me the low down. It started to sound cool learning they had big tipper's there, plus all the Hip-Hop and R&B hits you could think of. Norma Jeans rules where set up differently. But hold up a sec... I'll tell you later bout that!

Dawn became hyped about it telling me after class of how she loved it. When I wanted to stay far away from it. Dawn made Norma Jeans seem like it's the place to be. But seeing the crowd during the aftermath, it seems to me like too many niggas in one closed spot also knowing the place could get HOT, especially mixing liquor with half naked female bodies prancing around and they didn't have a bouncer if anything goes down.

All in all I'm hoping it wasn't consuming her because she's slacking behind everybody in class. Professor Celeste is impressed with me and my work. Dawn's the only one looking like she wasn't going to finish her bubbled skirt. She's still cutting her fabric for her designed pattern. My project is going very well having some pieces already together.

Our instructor said she had a surprise for us at the fashion show. I decided that I'm going to invest in this nine hundred something dollar sewing machine that does leather and jean. That's my late Christmas present to myself. Also start taking sometime to go out and have real fun.

Chapter 11

Something NEW

*A*t the Oasis club there were two bouncers. Two big Black dudes, Big John and Spider. We had a doorman. Louie, the door man is a short Italian guy that knew what to say to get you in Oasis. They all wore a Tuxedo shirt and a black vest with a bow tie. Spider's full time and Big John worked on the weekends. We stayed crazy busy on weekends to where we needed them both. Spider would always make passes at me that made me throw up inside but he's a funny guy. Spider also did some side jobs doing security for night clubs as well.

One special night Spider is doing security for a Kevin Lyles birthday party at Hammer Jacks and he called me on my home phone to invite me to go. Kevin Lyles is with Def Jam. I went just to get out and socialize in the night life. I'm not going to fully describe what I had on but its simple dark grey metallic looking dress pants and a black tank. An Express outfit with cute mary-jane pumps. What made the outfit.... is the V-neck black tank that had

Marabou hair around the V shaped tank. I took it further than that by rocking my leopard blazer. I'm a little outdated with the jacket however I looked good. My hair is down in soft curls with some of it up in the front. Even though it's last minute I got in V.I.P status walking in front of the extremely long line and stepped right into the place with Spider unlatching the red velvet rope. I felt like a star.

I'm smart though, quickly doing a coat check. I'm by myself walking around but... so. That place was packed. A whole new experience for me. Since it's the winter season people were dressed in much style, Coogi outfits, Armani suits, nice designer outfit's males and females. There were plenty of designer fur's worn by males and females. I'm feeling like I'm in a zoo with all kinds of fur coats around me everywhere. Much bling...
DAIMONDS.... The ones that be bright shining. It made me think I need to get with the program because it's a beautiful site. I should have known the party was going to be like that by the way girl's dressed at Morgan State.

I'm still content with my setting at the Oasis. India and I are close especially outside the club, Donia (India) would come by and I would curl or crimp her long hair that's down her back. We liked the idea that we both just started working around the same time. Times were slow after the holiday's, just taking care of my major responsibilities. The majority of the girl's had warmed up to me. Even Gi Gi and I smiled at each other in passing.

Alexis and Ice, the loud mouth chicks with no manners, no class, just White trash that looked high class. Even though Ice is a dark long haired White chick that tried to sound all Itailianish or act like she's from New York knowing she's from Baltimore. Talking big sh*t in the locker room on how much of a hustler she is but just imagine it every day how drunk they could get. It didn't have to be on the weekends, everyday well at least the times I worked. I wasn't naïve I knew they dibble and dabbled in coke.

One time at work Gi Gi walked pass me looking straight ahead not doing her usual fake innocent smile to me. Instead she walked down the bar to have this big conversation with Ice. Then she came back and did her smile she usually gives me. Right then and there I knew she's a fake that could never be trusted. They all seemed so cool with Nicole and on the low she kept me informed about their character.

Sometimes when I took Nicole home she would give me the inside on everybody that's staff there. Nicole is a veteran that knew it all. Most of the dancers needed a cab but some started asking me for favor's to take them home for gas. I'm down for that, gas money. I started my own cab service. Devine, Bonnie, Nicole and Zoey I took home. But only people that I'm mad cool with and really spoke to.

I scheduled my off day's at the club two days out the week. I always made time out for me. Whether it's take out at a nice restaurant or a good meal cooked watching a movie. I also did my hair and cleaned. I'm basically a home body.

I decided to invite Jamonos over to chill sometimes. I know it might have been a bad move on an exotic entertainer's part however I thought we were way past that, becoming friends. He's cool and I figured knowing each other for a good five months. I got to know him and didn't think he's psycho. First time he came over I'm washing and folding clothes.

He's a retired drug hustler that dabbled in the high end type products however made so much profit he cashed out to start a legit business. Jamonos didn't boast and brag but I could tell he's smart with his money.

He would bring the finest kind of lime green marijuana over I had ever seen and so good I couldn't finish the whole blunt. Which seemed like a nationwide no no rule: you have to finish the whole blunt, he joked but not in my case when I'm done I'm done. I don't deeply indulge in getting high nowadays I just do it sometimes to maintain.

We had a cool understanding. We shared with each other some things. I told him about my recent situation. He told me about his situation just getting out of this crazy long relationship. Were his girl broke a house window out to get to him and another girl getting it on.

I told him how I ended up in Baltimore and the drama with my ex – best friends back home. With us, we weren't trying to mess around with one another. We both understood we were trying to cool out from previous relationships. We really got to know one another. He would even mysteriously leave me some bags when he came over on the week end. I lived right on Moravia Street in east Baltimore, apartments on the ongoing busy driving street. So as he left I would watch him get in his black Acura.

A few weeks had past and one particular night at work this guy came in. He's tall, brown skin and cute in the face. I'm instantly attracted to him but knew how to hide it and keep it business. I went up to him and I'm always nervous on this part approaching the guy. I like to add how I want him to have a good time and casually got into asking if I could join him. He gave me an up and down look and nodded his head for a yes to the bartender. At all times I kept a scarf with me I took my scarf and put it on my seat. I had my cowboy's cheerleading outfit on with two long ponytails. This guy looked like an athlete, so I started the conversation off with asking did he like sports. He's flirtatious and I'm blushing like a school girl. We introduced ourselves, his name is Garland. He's cute with a smile like Denzel Washington, a body like a retired football player. He had an attitude that he knew he had it going on. My type of man but not too cocky, he looked like an average guy that pays his bills. He wore a simple black t-shirt with a gold cross pendant around his neck. He impressed me by pulling out a big wad of money that I tried to front like I didn't see. Garland bought me two twenty's. Then we had a funny conversation especially after a big bottle of Moet. All I told him was that's my choice of drink. At the end of our time being last call he got too comfortable and asked if he could sleep with me. I gave him a smirk with a polite no. He asked if I could at least go to breakfast with him.

"No thanks…Well I hope to see you again," I sat up straight to get up from the bar stool I got closer to tell him how much I appreciated him with a sincere look, he nodded down. As I walked away he watched.

Garland came in a week later and sat with me on one twenty he asked the same thing wanting to take me to breakfast. I told him that I couldn't and that I had to go straight home. The next good Friday night business is booming. Garland came in and this time he bought me a small bottle of Moet since he knew that's my choice of drink. We had more great conversation and when my time was up. I told him thanks and I would see him later. As I begin to walk off Garland asked again if he could take me to breakfast. I stopped and slowly turned back around taking ten seconds to think about it. I answered saying: "Why not I'll follow you."

So that's what we did. At the restaurant not once did he ask if he could sleep with me… I'm very pleased, but he did flirt. When he asked things most of my answers were maybe, especially the ones of us seeing each other again.

He mentioned this is not the last of us seeing each other. I thought in my mind hold up pump your breaks. Then responded with saying: "I'm always at the Oasis, that's where I'll be." After breakfast I paid for it and said goodnight. He caught up with me to walk me to my car. He knew I was playing hard to get.

Why wouldn't I. I pay my own bills having everything I needed with a bunny vibrator that kept me satisfied as long as I kept up with good batteries and condoms. The best thing it didn't play games/Garland looked like a game player.

When I came in on Thursday, there's a new girl on stage with an exotic look with a nice toned shape in all the right spots. She's definitely a threat to all the dancer's. When I got on the floor most of the girl's were trying to be her friend and tell her the rule's. I ignored it all and would introduce myself later too many girls were jocking her. The night's at a cool pace with me only having six drinks at 12:15 a.m.

Even the cast from The Wire would come in and sit with some of the Diva's. They had their pick. Even tough I wasn't part of Gi Gi's diva crew I always sat with the actor Wood Harris. How I strike'd up a conversation is complementing him on his role in "Remember the Titans." Every since then every time he came in I sat with him. We would do nothing but talk. I never asked him for a lap dance I enjoyed the talks. He wasn't trying to flirt or get at me in bed. When I asked about involvements, he was straight up and told me he had a girlfriend back in L.A. We always talked on general topics.

I sat with this Black man that seemed to be in his early fifties. One night he's having a mental conflict. He gave me a little bio on himself that was extremely long – good looking☺ He's a professor at Howard University. We were perfect to talk too. He's very sad because he was having marital problems with his wife. She's cheating on him. He's so broken and hurting. He wasn't even drinking any alcohol just needed someone to talk to. I was glad it was the weekend, his problems had me drinking.

By this time in my career I could put on a counseling role. See it wasn't always about showing your body and dancing. Sometimes on a lap dance guy's just wanted to talk. Spend that time talking on a range of topics. That's when you know they have a genuine respect for you. It's mostly about showing your personality to get drinks anyway. I'm very intellectual and it's easy for me to talk to guys. Show empathy if they're going through something. I have to say I've been told many times in the club that I was the most intelligent female there.

The same night the new girl is standing two seats down from me. So I introduced myself and she did the same. Her stage name is Selena. Selena is Israeli and Russian combination. So that should explain her personality trait. She's very demanding and her opinion was always right. She's very pretty and was new to the stripping business. She picked up this business very quickly in one night. I told her just months ago I was in her shoes but I told her she would do great at Oasis.

India and her shared small talk as well. A White girl name Asia that thought she's Black put Selena up under her wings. Nicole is there too, Selena mostly went to Nicole to talk or get information.

Selena looked just like the actress that played on "A Time to Kill" Sandra Bullock that dark hair, exotic look and her body is curvy shaped with perfect grape shaped sized breast. She played her clueless ancient very well and had that attitude of every man in here wants me. On stage she reminded me of me dancing for the first time with a sexy smile and eye contact. Never had done this before but looked like a natural, a true entertainer. I mean this girl could move to where most of the girl's doubted that this is her first time stripping. She played Sade and Michael Jackson's "Liberian Girl" and rocked it.

After a while of dancing so in to it Selena even hopped onto the bar at a customer. Ms. Kim and the bartender had to grab her and pull her back on stage. But Ms. Kim knew she was going to be a cash cow. Ms. Kim pulled Selena to the side and explained how it works when performing.

Selena's Mack's pride and joy he found working at Outline clothing store in Towson. Outline is a high end boutique that sold popular high end name brands. At the store he told her she could be making more money working for him. He never yelled at her either. When she's dancing most of the girl's where whispering among cliques. Gi Gi wasn't threatened and was disinterested since she's the main attraction amongst us.

Gi Gi kept that nonchalant expression on her face most of the time. But that night was all Selena's, she racked in all kind of money from guy's and other dancer's regular's. Some of those same girls that were smiling in her face were going to be her mortal enemy. Soon I knew those girl's would become jealous of her. Not me, I don't have a jealous bone in my body however I knew money is getting ready to go slim for a lot of dancer's because of her.

India sat with this cute Black guy that wore fly suits all the time. He's a regular and would sit with three to four girls at a time. But he started to just come in and sit with India for some weeks then she started seeing him outside the club. He's cute and was an attorney at law.

India and I bonded having the same thought process. We wanted to have a man so with guy's we sat with at work we could tell them that we're not available, the real truth. Garland would come see me often and he's definitely my type however I knew I'm going to take it slow like a moving turtle.

I told India about Garland. When he came in I showed her who I'd been talking about. She thought he's so cute. Garland worked for the husband of the singer Lil' Mo managing the tours or something.

He would always show how much money he had and I would make sure I didn't make it obvious that I'm paying attention. It's an out of this world roll of money, huge, I mean ignorant huge and neat too. Right there I knew I'm going to take it slow but considered seeing him outside of there.

Sometimes this beautiful reddish blond head woman with long kissy curl hair that came down her back came in. She wore a beautiful brown thick fur. She looked like a porcelain doll that's high maintenance. She looked like a classic beauty back in the Marilyn Monroe days, standing up most of the time while her company sat. She was a former dancer that's buddies with Nicole. She came in with her rich nerdy looking boyfriend that looked exactly like Austin Powers's, teeth and all. He's even shorter than her. But she didn't care I could tell she loved him. The red head just carried her self in a way of luxurious confidence loving life. Well that's what I read on her face. She would buy a drink to every girl she knew. Just a selected few and take time out to talk to each individual girl. She spent the most time with Nicole and Gi Gi. India and I just admired her beauty from afar.

A dancer named Niya started working nights. She usually worked the day shift but apparently needed more money. She's tall; my height however wore those thigh high platform boots that made her taller. She had a body like Tyra Banks and sported micro braids that she loved to flip. She's cool but had an attitude. She's definitely a hustler with a good game. She's a loner but cool with Ice's team.

Egypt and Mia also came over to nights and had good height on them as well just more competition for me. Egypt and I were cool to converse with each about attending our classes. She's tall fair skinned biracial dancer of Asian and African American descent.

Mia's a white girl trapped in a Black girl body. Tall, dark chocolate tone, skinnier than me but with some more ump in her breast area. She hung tough with ghetto Fab gold tooth Isis.

Getting home from work the first thing I did when I got in the door is thanked Jesus. Sit down and breathe. With the same routine of eating, counting my money and take a long bath listening to Alicia Key's album "Song's of a Minor" thinking about Aaron.

I met up with Garland on some Monday night's. We met at Jillian's in Arundel mall mostly. That's an outlet shopping place and Jillian's is attached to it and a movie theatre. Jillian's is a spot that you could eat fine gourmet or bistro meals that had big screen televisions all around with basketball games or other sport's shown. Then they have this massive room with cool games, a place to play pool and a bowling area. Very cool place to meet and date someone, my kind of spot.

The Great Outdoors is attached to Arundel Mills, a popular place for hunting gear and many other things. We'd go there to shoot at fake ducks and other hunting games they had in the store. One thing about Garland he's extremely funny and a big kid. And I used laughter as an essence of medicine for me.

Once we walked the shops, I made sure I bought something just to show I could. So I went to the Kenneth Cole shoe outlet to buy a nice pair of walking shoes. Our meeting each other is going on a strong two months. I'm taking it very slow but was beginning to like his company. He didn't even know where I stayed yet. And every night I would give him a renowned kiss good night. That would drive him nuts of curiosity. But I've learned that patience is a virtue. The Maryland and D.C. area is full of single women and he's too sexy to be single. But see I liked him to the point I'm willing to go there. Put my bunny rabbit up to see what he's working with. He had to show me more.... where he stayed, me to meet some of his family or friends. So I could really get to know him. I'm still feeling out his personality and spirit. Garland had just the right height and nice body with his designer jeans and crisp clean white T-shirts plus blinging ear to ear. I like that........ real simple however enough bling to make you double check... that would make me extremely wet. Okay.... then I finally gave in because I was turned on.

Chapter 12

Where does Beef Start?

Back at work as I predicted to India by this time the other girls are treating Selena mean, especially Alexis's team, like being behind Selena making her race up or down that skinny stairway to the dressing room. Acting as if they're in a rush screaming at her to move. If you're not careful you could fall down the steep wooden stairs. Alexis was the first one to start bullying Selena. One thing that got on my nerves about Alexis is that she would take over the dressing room when she entered, being obnoxiously loud with her crowd. She would deem the lights down for everyone in the room doing there make up. It didn't matter if we're right in the middle of something that takes a lot of concentrating. She had been there longer. It's really not much we can say to a wild child like Alexis. Then I started to understand why she did that. She's helping us with the lighting that's downstairs.

Alexis and I tried not to have beef however keep it cool and socially spoke. Her clique alienated Selena some nights. Going down the long strip bar Alexis would look at Selena mean with her eyes full of hate. Selena just ignored it and made money. Selena and I kept it cool to speak about general life things. She went ahead and complemented me on my body first. I gave the same complement back. I could tell she's analyzing me when I danced seeing her competition. She had confidence in herself to feel I wasn't a threat however when I backed it up with my educational background she knew I'm twice the beauty and a true threat. But she competed with all the other dancer's too.

Selena is hip to the game herself and didn't need anybodies help now. She stayed busy. Taking other dancer's distant customers, you know the one's that sit with other dancer's and not the loyal customer that come in and sits with you only. She wouldn't plug girls in like they were helping her when she first arrived. So the other girl's stopped plugging her in only Nicole would. Selena knew who was who by now. The one's that were professional and then the one's that put on a mask smiling in her face then talking behind her back, a façade.

Isis and Selena got into an argument one night but I wasn't there. India told me Selena didn't back down scared or timid however standing up for herself.

"So she bucked up to Isis?" I said looking amazed at India at lunch. That shocked India and me. We laughed about it with India adding in her Caribbean accent:

"She's tired of their sh*t plus she works out you know."

I guess Selena did get tired of them bumping into her and their intimidating looks. Selena mostly stayed to herself but talk to Nicole, India or me. She finally confessed she had been in a group as a dancer back in Israel.

When it's on the weekdays, not busy, just us in the club Selena would sit at the middle of the long bar and study Gi Gi looking dead at her. Selena emulated all of Gi Gi's pole tricks, even her red lighting and her distant sexy spaced out look. Guy's loved it. I'm amazed that she learned them so quickly. India and I would crack up laughing about that. How she caught up with Gi Gi. Gi Gi

112

had been doing it for years. Gi Gi and Jewel started dancing when they were sixteen.

Jewel started to miss work a lot some rumors where spreading that she's getting brand new boobies. India played it cool with Gi Gi. That's how I got the inside scoop of learning their clique too. Turns out Gi Gi is a big coke head. According to India majority of the dancer's in there did coke, Alexis, Ice, Melissa and more. I told India she needs to watch out from hanging too close to them she had been hanging with Melissa outside the club too.

One night Garland came in for me but I'm on stage. He looked cute as usual however rocking some designer indoor shades and a nice diamond piece around his neck not the gold medallion he usually sports. I mean he's blinging enough to get money hungry Selena's attention. She's talking to him for a minute but he kept his eyes on me and I kept my eyes on them. He knew what was up however still conversing with her never really taking his eyes off of me. She stayed there for a minute looking at me twice then back at him saying something and walked off. I got off stage and went to change into something else. I didn't even stop to get any tips just went straight to him saying what's up smiling. We took a seat at the end of the bar and he bought me a bottle of Moet. I felt all eye's on me in a GREAT way. We then sat in the back lap dance area and talked for a good five minutes about Selena. He laughed shaking his head saying: "That girl is crazy. She gotta be new," he asked

I explained that she was.

"She was asking me if I was a rapper or a football player. I told her no and that I'm waiting for you. She said waiting for her I look better than her."

"Talking about me?" I said pointing to myself.

113

Nuff said I got straight up to check her on that. I've been nothing but nice to her. I walked right up to her and tapped her on the shoulder getting everyone's attention however not letting them see what I'm saying: "Hey Selena... Listen never Hate on the girl do what you gotta do to make you're money but never hate on the girl." Looking at Alexis's group I added: "Because some of these girl's would whoop your ass for that okay," I said mugging the sh*t out of her.

She tried to play that dumb accent role.

I interrupted her and said: "Hey just don't do it. He told me what you said."

I had to get back to my company but she said her apologies. As I walk away the only ones that heard it good and clear is Devine's team which I'm cool with. Through them it spread amongst cliques. Some of the girl's started coming up to me about not liking Selena. I didn't respond to it I just didn't appreciate that one from Selena however kept my cool about it. She already had enough heat on her for taking other dancer's customers. I knew that if it was Alexis's clique they would have had a serious problem with it.

After the holiday's work is getting difficult. Mack even hired back old dancers. In this business you have to understand rejection. I'm dealing with it and didn't take it personal when guy's rejected to sit with me. I'm just not his type. I didn't get offended or upset by that. It could be difficult for me since I'm scarred but it was on how I took it. It's always best to ask the customer instead of having the bartender pull out a napkin and ask for you, a quick no from the guy so it wouldn't be obvious to everyone else. A lot of girl's couldn't take rejection very well and they cried like Alexis would in the dressing room. Asking us is she pretty enough or what's wrong with her- drunk azz can be.

114

Money was still fast and I didn't know why these bitches were complaining.

India and I ranked in the same, average drink getter now because money's getting slim. Some girl's would even go home without base pay if they weren't making money. I notice even the number one girl's had their bad nights. Ms. Kim even told me *I was riding on thin ice*, I just shook my head yes to understand with a slight frown. It's better on the weekends. But if you think how I think that's still a fast come up especially since I'm smart with my savings.

Tips always came in handy I would look guys straight in the guy's eye and thank them. Some guy's didn't like to tip, when the Raven player's use to come in girl's wouldn't even approach them because the answer would be no. They stopped coming in for some reason before I even got to Oasis. I couldn't believe the nerve of some guy's when they would say no just for a tip, which is very rare. But if they did I didn't take it personal a lot of guys did that to other girl's too. I would ask them to give me another kind of tip…. some advice which I thought was clever and would get them to laughing or joking with me.

I still had my faith and knew God had my back. Things still worked out where I'm still getting paid on time. I had me an extra account at the bank to where I couldn't withdraw money out until a certain date. It's money for something special. Having a scholarship is a plus to where I didn't pay for my courses or books and that's a blessing.

One particular night it's this very attractive petite Black female in regular clothes sitting at the beginning of the bar where the veteran's sit usually. I'm sitting in the middle of the bar on a few drinks. She's sitting all alone wearing a bad Fendi bucket hat to where you could barely see her eyes. Her hair is long past her shoulders, my length. The girl in the Fendi hat checked everybody out on their turn to dance, even me. I'm busy however kept occasionally checking out if she's still peeping the scene, just so happened that Selena's up on stage getting everyone's attention like Gi Gi did.

Gi Gi would always make a means to be up in the locker room on Selena's turn. Gi Gi came down and sat at Ms. Kim's usual spot, the first bar stool facing the crowd. The well dressed Black girl said something to Gi Gi being two seats over from her. Did she know Gi Gi? But I had to stop peeping from in the mirrors and play it with no concern. After a while I didn't see the female in the Fendi hat anymore.

Chapter 13

Game

The next night at work I'm already dress for the night shift, early. When I got to the bar and sat the same Black girl with the Fendi hat came in Oasis going to the back. So apparently she going to be dancing because I seen a bag with her. She came back down and had this black and white referee top on that's fitted showing her flat stomach with some cute black spandex short shorts. I thought it was cute because I rock different outfits that are role play style. She's very attractive looking like two singers, a Janet Jackson and Ashanti combination with a coffee with cream brown tone. She had a cute coca cola bottle 5 foot 4 thick toned shape. Picture Free from BET the VJ on 106th and Park's body, exactly but her stomach was even tinier. They even favored plus the onion shape booty. With a lot of sex appeal and could dance but very seductively not doing too much just wynding slow. She's definitely eye candy for the guy's.

After the night passed a little she's leaning on the stool two seats down from me. I leaned over and said: "O My God you look like two of my friends from back home, Laila and Carmen." Having a body like Laila's and a face like Carmen.

She smiled and said: "Really... Are they here?

"No. Back Home."

"Where are you from?"

"Texas."

"Wow! What are you doing here in Baltimore?"

"Going to school," I said.

Her stage name is Mocha and she's from Maryland as she unfortunately put it and going to school at another University called Coppin not too far from Morgan. I complemented her on her outfit and told her I wear role play styles too. We didn't have much time to talk because of business moving in. But later we sat by each other. She complemented me on my gorgeous hair as she called it. I asked her does she know of any good hair salons. I'm tired of doing it because the thickness and length. She recommended Starz Stage Michelle or Calvin. We converse every so often that night. She said while sitting once: "Girl... if my family only knew what I was doing. If one of them came through that door I would run to the dressing room."

"Girl…. me… I would run through those walls to get away from my father or brother's seeing me," I said pointing at the brick wall. We both laughed. Mocha also worked over at Norma Jeans for a little while. Mocha also converse with India too, what a coincidence that Mocha knew Misty. Which Misty would still come in every now and then. After I got paid at the bar at the end of the night I noticed that I didn't see India which is odd. We always walk together. No big deal I just walked out with Nicole. As she got a cab I hurried to the garage away from the outside nonsense by Norma Jeans.

India and I parked in the same garage. When I'm getting in my car India's Land Cruiser rolled up with her and Mocha in it. She's taking Mocha to her car where I use to park. I thought that's nice and cool. I thought Mocha was too. We all were fairly new to Oasis.

I also still had Nicole as a friend encouraging me. She spent the night with me on Friday. We went to pick up her puppy Tasha that had cancer however acted healthy coal black dog and cute. Nicole is like a bag lady with all kinds of bags as she's getting out of my car dropping some makeup, brushes and even a short straw. I wondered for a split second: "Why is she keeping up with straws?" I didn't think anything of it however she hurried to pick up her things.

Saturday day India called me and wanted us all to meet to go shop with Mocha to get some new outfits to wear to work. Since I didn't have a cell phone it's hard to meet up with them. We were all going to meet at a library. I got lost and couldn't find it or them. When I finally got to the library they had already left. I'm so frustrated that I went to purchase me a cell phone.

I didn't know anything about updated cell phones really. Later that evening I meet up with them at work. That night a mysterious guy came in the club he's sporting a brown coat with dark Burberry plaid on the inside. I approached him and talked a few minutes. He's Jamaican with a strong sexy West Indian accent. He bought me a drink. He's very clean looking from his fingernails to curly hair. His name is Bean. One thing he liked to do is drink. Crown's his choice of drink. He came in when we were almost letting out so we didn't visit that long. Since I got a new phone I could start keeping up with people that come and see me. I gave Bean my number and wanted to see him again.

Waiting to get paid Mocha showed me some features on my phone. We all had a good night of making money. To celebrate we went to breakfast. As we were walking to our cars a guy Mocha was sitting with a quarter of the night stopped her to talk. India kept walking however I thought we should stop and wait to ensure everything was safe.

At breakfast she told us her name is Iesha and we told her our real names. Iesha is very intelligent with good high end fashion sense. I'm surprised that she didn't hang with Gi Gi. It's cool because I felt like I'm in a team now with them.

One thing India and I said about Mocha amongst just us two is: Mocha knows what she's doing. With a beautiful face and killer body to match. She's always dress with the latest trends and her hair stayed in different styles.

The three of us met up at Towson mall to shop. Mocha had a sense of humor like Laila (back home in Tulsa) goofy plus her body. She also knew how to strike up real talk conversation Mocha introduced us to the Mac make – up line. In Nordstrom's we got to the MAC station it's a line all around the counter full of women wanting to get service like it's the last day of selling it but Mocha got 1st class treatment with a lady servicing her immediately. India and I both smiled at each other nodding our heads in agreement. India and I had to kind of wait a good twenty minutes until Mocha asked for more help on our products. I got a powder to fill in my eyebrows better with a brush. India and Mocha gave me advice on how to manage my makeup since I'm halfway clueless when it came to it. Any suggestions are helpful.

At lunch Mocha and I discussed what we wanted to pursue in life. Mocha had applied for a Delta Airline's International stewardess position. I could see her doing that. Mocha sounded well educated. We all had a lot in common. India being around two aspiring young ladies inspired her to pursue her education as well.

120

We decided to go out to the party for a new singer to the R&B scene. So we went shopping for the event. We all went our different ways leaving the mall. India and Mocha stayed together only to meet back up with me at my place in a couple of hours. I already planned to cook but I also cooked something special for Mocha since she's a vegetarian. My place is fully decorated by this time and when they got there they're both impressed by my place. We had so much fun getting ready. Oddly Mocha asked if the dude she met could come over. His name was Taz. I asked is he cool she said yes that she knew him. Taz even knew Jamonos so I said it's cool.

That next week one night at work Jamonos came in upstairs with Taz. First they sat then I came up the stairs and happened to see them. So I automatically sat down to talk to see what's up with Jamonos. I said what's up to Taz. Jamonos and I converse for a good five minutes. Him beginning another conversation while we watched a dancer entertaining he said: "We need to talk. Not here but soon about something…aaight. I got something you might be interested in."

"What's up?" I said interested.

As he's getting in to almost telling me Mocha sat with Taz or T for short. I smiled at her and she said so properly: "It's so crowded down there."

"O… Really." I responded back.

She then started talking to T.

"You know her?" Jamonos said to me strangely.

"Yeah… What's up?" I said in response to his tone.

"Don't trust her. Whatever you do," Jamonos said taking a sip of his drink.

"Why? She's cool…… What's up?"

He didn't say anymore but told me he would talk to me later on the other thing. It made me wonder on Mocha.

121

Made me take watchful steps on our friendship, but she seemed so much fun. But could she be trusted?

Garland and I were still in our just dating stage transitioning to girl-friend & boyfriend. I liked him because he made me smile and laugh. He started to come in females respected me and didn't talk to him. But he's becoming popular to know he's paid. Something he hasn't done in along time is get a Moet bottle; it was the smaller bottle this time but hey. We sat at the end of the bar upstairs and I drunk it while we talk. Out of no where Mocha came up from downstairs to dance. I just knew that he's going to draw his attention all to her but he didn't he drew more into talking to me not even paying attention to her. She had a cute construction worker's outfit on. I thought it's so cute that when she was coming down from her set I said to Garland how cute her outfit is. He looked quick but as soon as he did she said very quickly: "Don't look at me look at her," with an attitude.

I sensed something was up. Did they know each other? So I asked him what was up with that, he had no idea. I had about five to seven faithful regular's weekly. I got a huge surprise on a weekday at work my good friend came to see me, Matt. I'm so shocked, he came in drunk as all get out however I'm happy to see him. We only got to talk for one drink which is very odd for Matt. We sat right in the center of the bar when Selena's doing her set getting mad attention from the other spectator's. I gave her respect and watch a bit but nothing made my day like Matthew's visit. Grinning ear to ear I gave him all my attention catching up he gave his however suddenly looked at Selena and said she has no comparison to who he's sitting with right at that moment. I blushed and thanked him. Matt had a way of boosting my confidence with complements but not in a flirtatious way. He looked at Selena again and said it's something about her eyes, she has eyes of greed. Not knowing anything about her. He told me that I had beautiful eyes and an out of this World body. But he thought my eyes were the most beautiful body part on me that grew on him. At first it was my perfect plump rear, we laughed.

After that comment Selena made she became cooler with me. I didn't go off the handle like some of these girls have done to her. She even took me upstairs and showed me some pole moves she learned off Gi Gi. It's no one up there but us on the weekday. She would show me until I perfected it. I'm now well learned on pole tricks becoming a true entertainer that master the climbing, flipping up side down one's and the twirling my body around the pole ones.

My game face on stage is a sexy look almost mean and sometimes I would smile on a Janet or Mariah happy song. I danced to everything now a lot of Sade'…some of rock a lot of Hip Hop and R&B songs. The juke box didn't have too much rap. It had to be censored, no cussing. I could move to what ever is played really well as I entertained. India is my greatest fan to watch me dance on my turn. I too was an attention getter in the same category as Gi Gi now. Mack is letting me be the last girl to end the last dance of the night on extremely packed nights. He even asked when I would be on a big drink.

Mocha started to cool out on really showing up for work only Friday's and Saturday's. She wanted to talk to Mack into giving her a bartending position. Mocha's real life as Iesha is just going to school, working out and resting. She had received a letter of her application going through with the position as an airline stewardess. The only thing is she had to go to the airline school for three months to train outside of Chicago. She was so happy to get the news. Mocha's leaving in a month. We hated to see her go.

India, me and Mocha had bonded very quickly with only a month. After work India had brought to our attention how we bonded so quickly at our high end breakfast spot that stayed open in the late hours.

Our friendship went on for two months. I invited them to go home with me to Texas and Tulsa. It's so spontaneous that I took care of the tickets. Mocha is definitely down. India had too many responsibilities back here in Maryland, sending money back to her home in Ghana to her daughter, so she had to work. I made plans for the next weekend which is spring break to go. Mocha and I were going to spend the night in Texas for a day to shop then go to Tulsa. At DFW airport we were waiting on our flight to Tulsa. We really got a chance to get to know one another. Talking about our family and our background, Iesha is part Jamaican (West Indian) however she didn't have the strong accent.

We both shared a tragedy in our lives. I'm very opened and comfortable to talk about my car accident and scars. Explaining how devastating for something to happen to your face the first thing that people notice when they meet you is your face. I explained: "*Women and Men invest so much money in our bodies, face and hair so for something to happen to it...it's devastating.*" She told me something that's on her heart to say about how she suffered a lost with a child she miscarried. She planned an awaited son. He came in this world but died in her arms while she was crying holding him. She explained how her whole family was in there. Mocha said she was eating right, living healthy and made all her doctor's visits. That's touching to my heart because I didn't know how that felt and she's strong to put it behind her and move forward. I even spilled out how I was going to have a baby but I choose to have an abortion. Then the crushing end of how I lost him. I told

124

her I couldn't imagine any of those girls at work going through what I've been through and try to dance on top of that. I'm still standing…a beautiful being. She agreed that they couldn't. We connected that whole trip.

When we got to Tulsa Iesha met my family and called me Lonnie by accident. Close call my parent's didn't think anything of it. For some reason Iesha started calling me J. Lo. I asked her - why are you calling me that. She said: "You know Jordyn and Lonnie." I smiled and said: Okay. We went out that night with a guy friend of mine named Carlos. We were the main attraction when we got up in club Goodfellas. I had on a country pink dress from Arden B and Mocha had on an off white Dolce and Gabbana outfit. And I knew the Tulsa local guy's where going to be hounding my girl Iesha and to her this is a country ass piece of cake. Leaving me she disappeared to the bathroom. I had to watch her because even Tulsa has hating ass bitches. We were side by side having funny topics to talk about. Peeping out the scene and feeling the music. The looks of people staring at us you would have thought we were movie stars. I even hinted to her that a local NFL player is in the club that I know and wanted her to meet. Iesha seemed uninterested but had her eye on this guy in a white velour suit.

I kicked it with him on a New Year's Eve night out with friends in Dallas and he was cool. I knew of him I said to her: "He's about something." I didn't want her to get mixed up with some fake guy fronting like he wasn't accomplished but I knew the girl needed no help she knows what she's doing. Somehow the guy in the velour suit got her attention buying a bottle of Moet and sending her a glass. She accepted and they exchanged digits.

I also met up with my girl Yolanda and introduced Mocha to her. With Mocha's bubbly personality she just

125

hugged Yolanda from hearing about her threw me. Yolanda didn't know what to do so she just stood there having an odd expression on her face.

After we left Goodfellas we drove past the Chicken shack, a hot spot back in the day. The velour suit guy called and took us to breakfast. He bought a friend that I could converse with.

The next day is Sunday and I took her around my way showing her Tulsa mainly north Tulsa. They don't kick it like they use to. Ol' boy from last night called Iesha. He took me and her out to eat at Red Lobster. I hated that I was the third wheel but hey it's a meal.

Some girl with a guy came in and sat next to us acting ill. Well the girl started talking loud and holding a baby looking ignorant. I didn't know what the deal was. The guy with us stopped eating his meal and he lost his appetite. Something wasn't right. The girl is loud enough to where she's talking about a no good nigga. Iesha and I gave each other the eye and knew that she's talking about this guy. We left early and I wasn't ashamed to take my meal with me.

He's going back to Oklahoma City and wanted Iesha to come visit. So that meant I would have to drive her. He wanted to see more of Iesha. So much that he rented her a nice size car for us to meet him in Oklahoma City. He lived close to Norman where OU is located. Iesha wanted to go to Oklahoma University anyway to see it and pick up Taz an authentic OU jersey. Plus Carlos my friend she just met goes to school at OU.

Mocha and the guy were meeting up at the mall. Carlos and I took her to the mall and went back to his house to eat. Two and half hours later she called ready to be picked up from the Olive Garden. When I got there she had at least ten shopping bags around her side as she sat.

126

Mocha or Iesha is acting dominant in her tone as she talked to him. He's acting real strange. Iesha said: "Lonnie I want you to meet Keith, Keith I want you to meet Lonnie. It's like the dude is hypnotized he slowly looked at me with a duh da duh look like Scooby doo then said "O Yeah…." I looked at him and then looked at her then looked back at him.

Then I wondered why she introduced me again when I already knew him before she even met him. It took me back to what Jamonos said: "Don't trust her." I thought she's acting weird for some odd reason. That guy looked hypnotized and she had this mean look on her face staring directly at him. I wondered what's wrong. She said my real name lots of times around him. I had even discussed with her that I didn't want to be called Lonnie in my home town. It wasn't that hard to remember. I helped her pack her shopping bags to the car and left to get back to Tulsa to a sports bar called Majestic's to see a band called Full Flava Kings play which always attracts a crowd to hear this good music.

Got there getting great seats in the center of the balcony, it's packed. I saw my good friend named Daryl. I went to dance with Daryl. I didn't have to see him but saw the body image of my first love interest, Wanya. Surprised he's there in the back lounge area where the couches are located. I couldn't believe that the bad memories I have with him didn't even surface to my mind which is a great thing I'm happy and feeling my apple martini's with my homeboy Daryl from way back. Mocha stayed in her place the whole night and didn't drink anything but water. She had to drive back home because I kept getting apple martini's after another that made me tipsy but maintaining.

When we got to the guest room Mocha and I had a good laugh about everything. All in all it was a good trip.

We went back on Wednesday. We got some favor on our tickets and got upgraded to first class. I've been in first class before but Mocha showed me really how to do it. When we got our meal on the plane she ordered Moet for her choice of drink. I never knew I could do that, so I had the same.

Iesha (Mocha) talked about that Taz guy and expressed that she really has a lot of feelings for him. She said it's starting to get serious. He's street thug looking however cute. T didn't seem like her type. Her type seemed like a business man that's a millionaire.

As far as my interest I mentioned Garland but that wasn't serious like how Mocha talked of T. She really liked him. Mocha and I also talked more about our friendship the three of us connected. India, me and Mocha just started around the same time and how we all had something going on.

Back at work Garland came by thirty minutes before it's time to close. I'm happy to see him since I hadn't in a long time. I'm sitting with someone but he waited standing along side the mirrored wall. Ice approached him in a flirtatious way getting too close. I saw from the mirrors on the stage. I knew she's doing her job but still too close as she talked to him. Even though she knew he came in to see only me. After my drink I quickly got up in my army fatigue tube dress and said good bye to the guy I had a good talk with. I started approaching Garland and that's when Ice started switching to the dressing room to get dress. I said a few words to him and he wanted to stop by my place to catch up with each other. I told him just for a little bit because I had to go to school. He told me he would be right behind me. As everybody got dressed Ice and her crew were doing there usual, being loud and obnoxious over the loud Hip Hop radio station that's playing.

When I got home I warmed up the rotisserie chicken and rice with asparagus I had for dinner before work. Garland and I weren't seriously involved even though he told a few of the girl's I'm his girlfriend. Garland and I really started out as good friends. We had each other's back. At my place I waited and waited too long. A good forty-five minutes and Garland had not arrived. My instincts felt something was up with that. Where was he? Did Ice have something up her sleeve in the talk she had with him? As that popped in my head I got a call on my cell. It's Garland and he said he's on his way. It ended up being another hour. By the time he came buzzing to enter I had changed into my night clothes. I made up my mind I wasn't going to answer the door. So when he buzzed up and called both numbers I didn't even answer.

The next morning he called - still- I ignored the phone and got ready to go to class. Since Garland knew my Wednesday schedule at school he drove up there looking for me. He found my car and parked by it until I came out. When I noticed him my expression immediately changed shaking my head no grinning saying: "Look at chu. You must feel guilty. You did something with Ice, didn't you?"

He walked with a grin on his face saying: "Mann….naw…naw it wasn't like that."

I grabbed for my keys out my purse to get away from hearing unnecessary lies. He blocked my way by his arms and body.

"Now come on…. Are you mad?"

"Why would I be mad.? What… What was that all about last night? Why did you take so long, you hooked up with Ice?"

"I didn't do nothing with that girl. That girl is crazy."

"Who?" I said to him.

129

"Ice."

I rolled my eye's walking off disgusted. He grabbed my arm to try to explain: "The other night I forgot you were out of town still. I came to the club looking for you. She approached me talking and I told her you were my girl."

As he explained I'm making slight gestures saying "mmuh" as I listened.

"Well last night she approached me and said I want to dance for you. I told her that I'm cool not wanting one. It just so happened that my partner was looking for a girl to do a private party. I called my partner and took her."

That's when I gave him a crazy look and said his name: "GARLAND!"

"Wait let me finish. Nothing happened." He said with his Denzel smile.

So I let him finish the story having an expressionless look on my face.

"When we got to my boys spot she's like I don't want to do it unless I get to fv<k you."

"I told her how I'm seeing you and I just brought her to dance for them then be out because I'm meeting up with you. She said if you're not going to fv<k me I'm not dancing for them. And I told her I guess you're not. She cussed me out and told me to take her back to get her car." Getting out of the car she cussed him out even more amazed he didn't want to sleep with her.

Giving him my evil look I said: "You're lying?" He swore up and down that's exactly how it went down. I asked "Why you didn't call me to tell me you were going to be late?"

"I didn't want to call you when I had her cussing in the car," he responded saying.

For Garland this is only more reason not to trust him to take it further.

I knew Ice is a cut throat snake but now I'm going to give her a peace of my mind.

So the next time Ice and I both worked was a Tuesday night. It's slow with just one or two girls having some business. It's my turn to dance and I picked a song that no one had played before. The R&B group 702, "Where My Girl's At" Just so happened Ice is one of the girls having business in the back lap dance area. She knew what I was insinuating by the chorus of the song: "Where my girls at from the front to back. So are you feeling that put one hand up could you repeat that trying to take my man see I don't need that so don't play yourself."

Egypt walked by after her drink looking up at me smiling nodding her head feeling the song too but Ice was in the back and I could see the steam coming out from her ears. As I walked off the stage and the song's ending she shouted out: "WHATEVER!" I knew I had cooked up some beef that was bound to happen. That song started it all.

She called all her regulars in that night. She was the top girl that night in making money but so what. I had to watch my back Ice is a big rough tough talking chick. That night getting dressed her clique is doing their regular ignorant cussing conversation. I had moved my locker next to India's away from Ice's along time ago, our locker's use to be right next to each other. So it's no tension there. India and me did our regular thing getting dress fast to get paid quickly and be out.

That weekend Ice tried to compete with me on gaining drinks and money. We both were staying busy getting them. On a time out that we were both having. I'm sitting on first bar stool close to the mirrored wall, the first seat where Ms. Kay sits - toward the crowd entering the bar. She came to stand by my side where I sat to fix her dress in the mirror looking at her body. What she didn't know is that I have special X-Ray powers to make her disappear. I made it seem like she's invisible to me looking straight ahead then sometimes glancing at the dancer on stage doing there set. She stayed for a good five minutes trying to be funny. I acted like it didn't faze me. What these bitches fail to realize that I don't make a means to compete I just do me.

When it's her time to dance I'm on a sixty however sitting at the bar talking. Ice was more up on the latest craze of new CD's we had in the juke box. Surprisingly she played the rapper Tupac's song called "How Do You Want It?" Ice got the majority of the clubs attention. She's doing her thing but it only hyped me up anticipating the time for me to dance to it. As soon as it's my go round to dance I went up to the juke box cheesing with the biggest smile to find the new cuts. Yeap! Tupac with only three songs to the CD: "How do you want it?" "California Love" and "Gangsta Party." I'm not biting but of course I played my favorite two "Gangsta Party" and "How do you want it?" I had literally all eyes on me moving so good even the bartender's watched. Later that night I had Garland come in and top it off with a bottle. Another good night… I don't know what Ice did but I topped it off with almost five hundred dollar's. But no doubt in my mind that Ice did well. I heard she tricked sometimes and had her clients or whatever she called them come in that night.

After work that night India's going to hang out with Melissa. We had learned all the different clique's habits. And one of the habits Melissa had is snorting coke. India made it seem like Melissa was cool. Melissa and India had similar Indian features and Melissa put India up under her

132

wing because they're the same kind. India explained to me that's what Melissa said. I told her to be careful around them and don't be foolish.

That night Nicole stayed over my house but first we went to get her puppy Tasha.

The next day which is a Saturday I just chilled and cleaned up. Pick some movies up and visited with Jamonos. I finished cooking my dinner/ studying. Folding my clothes and pulling out what I'm wearing that night.

Later that day India called me very excited to say that she did coke with Gi Gi. I shut the mood and her high down saying: "Are You F<CKING NUTS? ARE You CRAZY?"

"Can You Believe…GI GI DOES IT…. Can you believe It?" India said.

"SO… if Gi Gi is going to jump off the Brooklyn Bridge you'll do it too?"

She laughed and said in her accent: "LONNIE… its just coke you smoke weed,"

"SO…. that comes from the Earth… God put that there as a plant, HINT Get IT."

That shut her argument down. I warned her that she's playing with fire and pleaded for her not to do it again.

She even told Mocha. Mocha flipped out on her too. Mocha is getting ready to move to start her stewardess training. She came in on the weekends to work and stack even more money that she already has. I let Mocha know I'm worried about India.

That night at work I watched India like an eagle even when I was on stage, who she talked to and even who she went upstairs to the dressing room with. I'm worried about the person that I called my friend.

A handsome man walked in and sat in the center of the bar. I'm on my last set on stage. Usually I sit until the next song comes on. And as always I'm nervous before I danced having all eyes on me as I show my dancing technique. I'm always a sight to see grinding slow to the beat. See it wasn't always fast with me. Since my girl Selena showed me a thing or two on the pole. I had mastered some things. When Gi Gi wasn't there I used the red lights she puts on. I always watched myself in the mirror and knew I had it going on.

This guy is watching me and I'm watching him through the mirrors. He's a chocolate tone and had a face like Pharrell Williams with high cheek bones. He had those slanted eyes. I don't really be checking for the dark chocolate kind but the brotha is fine with a close hair cut to top it off. As I got on the floor to collect my tips I went up to him and introduced myself. He had this intelligent street sound with a high education in his background. It's something about him that lit a strike within. It wasn't all sexual even though we were both sex objects, him having a body like a star quarter back and me having a life size Barbie doll bodies to match. I sat and he bought a twenty. I was content with that and built up a strong conversation to match his high education. His name is Barron being in his early forties. He had to run an errand to the downtown of Baltimore and just stop in but he resides in D.C. He's drinking on a Coca Cola. I just drunk that tiny drink slowly and it was plenty of time for us to think and explore a little bit of our minds. He told me he would come again if he could considering his busy schedule. To you all I have to admit I was hoping he could.

At this point in this business I checked female's hard on dumb questions. Not ignorant like cussing out however checking educationally while in a calm state. Once, a certain female (Isis) tried to get a guy to have a drink and they turned the her down. She came back to where we usually sit and said Lonnie you go try him.

"Ut…. Ugh. Don't try to help me make my move." I let them know I'm not here trying to intentionally compete with them; I make my money my way and Do Me.

Or once a dancer said to me that I looked like a certain female on T.V. and I disagreed I let her know something. It was never something way out of disrespect from the girl's, never, just minor issues. When I make a point I get it across with much tude in a smart elick educated way, give them a smirk to wait for they're reaction. Mostly making girls walk on and let it register. Me clowning in a sort of nice way, let's just say I got comfortable or let's just say I had a certain look to insinuate I'm not to be F'd with but I seem to still have a cool, peaceful sweet side about me. I almost check'd the most popular dancing diva in the house, Yes Gi Gi. She played dumb one day talking to me acting like she didn't know what this stuff was that holds your hair with a shine that she tried once, "It's like this gushy… Ugggh….It keeps the hair together uummmm" She said as she thought.

I answered for her by saying: "Gel?" Looking in an odd way.

This bitch smiled and said: "Yeah…."

"*Whatever bitch*," I'm thinking but I just smiled.

As we got dressed from the night we talked amongst each others clique. Ice is the only one I had a problem with. And we both just avoided each other however I knew the beef was cooking. It was just a matter of it getting done. India and I during work spread out from showing our closeness but when we get dress we talk. She wanted me to go out with Melissa and some more other girl's. They usually go out and have a real drink at this strobe light club. And when they invite me I always said no

135

thanks. I dislike strobe lights they make me get a head ache. India told me they think I'm a snob for never taking up the offer to join them. So tonight I decided to go. For some reason India wanted me to go, *probably for her to watch so she didn't snort no blow*, I thought. Since my girl's Divine and Bonnie were going I thought this might be fun. I like Divine she's cool. She kind of reminded me of my old friend Mia's attitude, but she's white. Divine knew she was beautiful in looks but is real cool on acting like it. To me she had become the top girl after a blond haired bombshell named Diamond stop working.

When we walked up to the spot we look like an entourage, me and India really being the only coloreds in the bunch. It's mostly White people in this club and that's when I felt uncomfortable playing nothing but rock however understandable. It looked like a three story basement party. We split up when we got in. I just went and sat in a corner not trying to let these lights effect me. While half of the people where stuck on E. I went to the bar after fifteen minutes to get two coronas with lemon and India met me there.

"What's up? You having fun?" India said.

"It's not my kinda club but I'm cool. What's up? I said giving her a deep look with a grin." Something within her felt self conscious.

"LONNIE… What?" India said grabbing on my arm.

"Nothing…What?   That's you… Where you been?"

"Just walking around come on lets dance." She said.

"Really India I don't feel like it."

India left when I was ready to leave after another fifteen minutes with no problems. It's just that my body is adjusted to getting home at a certain time, eating and

counting my money for the night. Then my pampering
routine soaking listening to track number five "Troubles"
Alicia Key's first album. I would sometimes cry thinking of
my situation or Aaron, what we had and I lost. I wondered:
What is he doing? Is he okay?

I started to go to the baddest hair salon with the
phenomenal hair stylist in the northeast of Baltimore, Starz
Stage was the place. It's decorated very hip modern.
What's bad about this salon it had a wooden basketball
court runway floor when you walk through the door. Every
hair stylist, I mean every last one could jam on any grade.
They'd make you leave out of there like a class Act. I went
to Cal and I mean WOW! He made my hair bone straight
but a little bit past the shoulder from cutting it. Iesha had
recommended me to go I had to call Iesha and tell her good
looking and thanks. Cal cut my ends and I wore a bone
straight look with so much body. Everybody there loved
my new hair look.

I went to the mall by myself to pick up some
fragrances. I thought back to my professor, Dr. Merrell
saying to have different kinds of books to read. She said
you should read different things at the same time to
enlighten your mind like an educational one to a self help
book, to a novel. She had personally recommended Iyanla
Vanzant's book "Value in the Valley" to me. I stop by the
book store in the mall. As I passed this hat store I notice
this huge poster taking up one of the store's window with a
man in Kangol ball cap that looked just like Aaron. He had
on a Kangol ball cap that's black with his shirt off flexing
his muscles with his hand on the back of his head. A real
sexy look, this guy had the same everything of Aaron then I
looked closer the guy in the picture had Aaron's body
frame. I looked closer he even had a body mark like
Aaron's. I notice Aaron had a dark dot on his biceps. *Wait*

137

a minute that's Aaron, I thought. I saw the speck on the model's arm that identified to me that's Aaron. I smiled but the next second I wanted to cry. I even dropped my jaw but quickly pick'd it up. I stood outside that store for a good ten minutes I went in there and ask if I could please have the picture when there done. The manager didn't see it being a problem when their finished. I went home and cried with the thoughts of: *I wasn't thinking, how foolish of me. I lied to myself in thinking it would be easy to get over him and the baby we could've had.* It literally made me determined to find him. I'm building up some nerve to go back to his mother's place. Matter a fact I plan to call Sunday. I'm happy that he's having success. California is where Aaron needed to be. Once I get in contact with him. Would he take me back?

Chapter 14

In the Game

The next day I called Aaron's mother and no one answered the phone. Since she's a nurse aiding people in their homes Ms. Carla stayed busy. I didn't know his moms work schedule. That big picture is a sign in seeing that fine man of mine. All I needed to say is come back; I'm Sorry and I knew I could have him back because I had it like that. All I needed is to get in contact. I did want to stay in touch because I loved him so much. I do know the true meaning of real love.

It's something that Garland didn't have that Aaron did. I'm glad I filled Garland out. He didn't share enough for me to put all the way out. Garland and I started spending less time outside and more of him showing up at the club with pride. He's now acting like he had ran into some money blinging like crazy. Garland would only sit with me on one drink constantly flirting. It's cool cause I like to rub it in Ice's face somehow he's still sitting with me fronting like I was with him. She was pissed every time. That's how I knew it's half and half. Either she's pissed that he didn't F- her or the other half he F- her and then played her. I don't know folks.

Later one night in the dressing room alone India and I got a chance to talk. We were discussing if something went on with Ice and Garland.

"I don't know India....I think something went down with Garland and Ice. You see how mad she gets when he comes in," I said to her.

India responded in her Jamaican sounding accent: "Lonnie he doesn't like that girl he likes you. I over heard her say: "He didn't want to f<ck because he's with Lonnie,"

"What... You heard this?"

"Yes...She was on the opposite side of me talking to her friends. Lonnie he really likes you."

That's some assurance that he wasn't lying. India is trying to convince me to go ahead further with my relationship with Garland. I would just roll my eyes because I'm convinced to put a halt on the relationship.

Sunday I usually stay home however the Orioles were playing. That meant the club tonight... was going to be tight... to capacity meaning more cheese.

The next Saturday India and I had a farewell dinner for Iesha (Mocha) at the Olive Garden just us three then we did some shoe shopping. One thing I'm going to miss with Iesha is her bubbly personality. She's always in a good positive mood, living an absolutely healthy life. You need people around like that in your life. What I liked about us is that we were independents, all reaching for something going to the next level, even in Donia (India). Some of Iesha and my motivation rubbed off into Donia's contemplation. Iesha left that Tuesday and said she'd keep in touch.

My hours and the money I'm satisfied with. I loved what I'm doing still with my schooling. I was even Dawn's alarm clock to show up for our morning clothing construction course. I had part of my pieces sewn up. I would try to motivate Dawn… if I can do it she could do it. Make school first I didn't work every night I didn't have to work every night. I wouldn't allow my self to get behind in school. I'm determined thinking in my mind.

See working is like going out… its fun however there should be a balance. The only thing that wasn't healthy is half way lying to my parent's. They were so proud that I was sticking in with Baltimore. They didn't know anything about what I'm doing…. successfully pursuing. It's eating at me feeling the guilt as I talked to them weekly.

But this week….this week coming up… a millionaire is coming to the club to spend mad bricks of money. He comes in every year. Last year he spent 25,000 dollars in just five hours. Everyone is looking forward to him coming and bringing some other men that worked for him. So I prepared ensuring everything is right for me, getting my hair, nails, feet done having the best scent ready for them.

The millionaire man is coming in tonight. That night everyone is anticipating the man and his guest. The place is spotless, staffed groomed up and Mack even had on one of his best suits. All of the upstairs is reserved for the million dollar man and his crew. I have to say all of the A list Diva's had it going on, we all looked beautiful, new outfits and new make up. Even the B's and C's stepped up their look. I bought this eighty dollar outfit that's a bright yellow, an exotic Tarzan/Jane look. A four hour phases of white outfit's. It's something about white that fit my body just right. I'm obsessed with looking in the mirror at it.

It's a regular night being around eleven o'clock I started to feel like he wasn't coming in. By this time the staff is sweating bricks especially Mack who stocked up on liquor. Still making money and making moves the female's

141

that danced wondered too of their arrival. A half after the hour it became suddenly slow to make money. I'm cool on having eight drinks almost nine with a hundred dollar's in tips.

Sitting in the far back of the bar on a double drink with a regular, India and I are talking about how they hyped this man up to be this big spender that would be there the whole night throwing out cash. *O well....* I thought. As we watched the crowd and other's making their moves suddenly Frank the bartender said: "They're HERE"

New rookies and every money hungry gal took off running for the front door steps. Just leaving the guy their talking to in their dust... not trying to wrap the conversation up instead they got in on the race. India and I busted out with laughter at seeing all these girls stampeding to the steps to get up stairs. Getting a good laugh we took our time hugged our company good bye thanking them. With a smooth pace like the other divas in the club taking our time going the back steps to get up stairs. Once we got upstairs it's funny how the corporate looking men pick the money maker's. The girl's with that exotic and very taking care of look got chose. Some of the ones that ran up first didn't. I had two regular twenty's casually talking amongst them all. Nicole is all in the mix making the guys have fun and get loose. One guy chose Selena and me to sit with telling us their enjoying different clubs on Baltimore Street having fun. Selena and I spent most of our time with him gaining three non- alcoholic 60's and one Moet bottle that I only drunk half with Selena pretending to take lil' bitty sips. He gave us each one hundred dollar's. All in all we all had a good night, even funnier with them staying only two hours. It was a good money making night.

Garland came in at the last fifteen minute's wanting a favor. He wanted to stay at my place. Even to the point of

142

begging me. I didn't know for what reason however he needed somewhere to stay. Since Garland had been over before. Plus he's my friend by now that needed a favor. I let him stay but he wasn't getting any play. I gave him my key and told him something is in the refrigerator to eat. I made my best cooked spaghetti I told him to save me some of my spaghetti.

When I got to my place he's eating a plate full of spaghetti in my living room and was almost finished. I instantaneously cop'd an attitude. I went straight to the refrigerator then looked in my sink and saw my empty container of my bomb spaghetti.

He didn't even leave me some and that right there is a sign. I flipped out right then and there telling him to leave repeating: "Ut Ugh....GET OUT....Get Out Right NOW."

He's asking why a bunch of times: "Why? What did I do?" He said trying to hide a smirk on his face.

"No YOU Didn't... Just Eat Up All My Spaghetti. I TOLD You To Save Me Some," I said standing there looking serious. He stood up trying to embrace me.

"Ut Ugh...No YOU Gotta Go. Leave." I started gathering his velour jumpsuit jacket guiding him to the door. My door is right behind his heels as he left not understanding why I'm mad. It was enough for two grown people to eat. First the suspicion's with Ice now this. I planned to leave him alone.

At work Garland sent me some red roses in the club by a runner. It's a beautiful arrangement in a vase. I thought how beautiful and impressive it was. But still I had made a decision and stuck with it. I didn't have time for his tricks even though he's fun to be with. What made me be this way really started on Valentine's Day. He made me pay for half the meal that day. I let it slide because we didn't have any soul ties. Plus he bought me a big oversized card with chocolates and roses.

At the dinner table eating at the fine dining seafood restaurant Garland explained he spent all his money. He had only sixty dollar's and our meal was $120 dollar's. I paid the rest of the bill but was feeling ill. So I called it a night declining the thought of giving him some of this tight-tight. Low and behold a blessing in disguise of not giving him all my treasures I had inside.

By this time India had become involved with her lawyer friend that comes in with the fly suits. She let me know what was going on. His name is Robert and he's a flirt however very low key. He's very sexy looking, with a studious look with glasses plus having muscles. A bald head brown skinned milk dud. India sat next to him while he bought two or more other girl's drinks, but you could tell India's his main squeeze.

She had to put up with annoying Ali. Sometimes when I walked past I caught Robert looking at me. India finally introduced me and I got in where I fit in sitting with them getting to know him. India sat on the other side. Robert and I had a lot in common we both attended Morgan. And he once entertained. He's very intelligent, ambitious and knew how to have a good time. He didn't like to get lap dances just talk after a long day at work. Robert is a regular almost once or twice a week and he would spend good money. We all had to take turns in talking to him while he continued to buy us all drinks. Almost the end of his visit he would just visit with India.

On Wednesday its pumping full capacity with mostly White customer's partying hard. I notice that most of the brown skin girls weren't doing so well except Nicole and Isis. India and I both had less than five drinks, I only had three. And the whole night Ice is racking in bank and rubbing it in as she sat with them, dancing on stage, staring all in my way. It would make the next person mad however I just used my secret powers and made her disappear. I would make them all disappear. It would work, everyone would disappear and it would be an empty bar with just me in it. Sometimes even the music I would zone out and not hear anything. I never took anything personal but this bitch is starting to get on my nerves. It was all mental to where we would act like theirs no beef however its tension between us two. Instead of duking it out we'd send messages through songs because we didn't really have a reason to fight. Trust me I got her attention and she got mine. She played this one rock song that got on my last nerve, Disturbed: Down with the Sickness.

Gangsta Party was the official battle song in the Oasis. But it wasn't only played by me all the time but I played Tupac, like "Temptations" that was only played by me because no one could get with me on dancing exotically to that song. Also Jon B "Are you still Down."

I didn't have any problems with the other females. Ice and I had a silent beef. Even Gi Gi started playing this song from Janet Jackson's album Rhythm Nation. The song basically was talking about a female getting beat by her man and done wrong. The whole time this bitch it staring at me as she danced, the whole time. It's so obvious to me that it made me wonder.

Once up stair's I sat with hardly any body up there. She played Cypress Hill "Rock Super Star…. *Is she trying to test me?* What is she trying to say but I blew her smooth the f--- off too, I didn't have time and I wasn't going to make time. I started to make her disappear too. When I wasn't sitting with a guy I would read my small poetry books, it was for a class. The white pages reflected really

145

bright making the black ink stand out. So my attention was focused on something positive. These girls were silly.

Niya is a dancer that came over from days. She was always in her grown up making mad bank. Niya mainly sat with a lot of white guys especially older ones. She stood about 5'10 rocking the high thigh platform stilettos boots making her an Amazon proportion just right. Brown skin like me wearing some long micro-braids down to her back that she loved to flip. She's cool… we spoke and kept it social. And she too kept it solo. Yeap she played Gangsta Party too. She had no beef that I could think of however, one night she's giving hard salty looks popping her gum while we sat. I didn't notice it until India came up stairs. I was up there in the dressing room for a five minute chill time talking. In my robe alone fixing our hair and make up she came and sat by me worried saying:

"I think Niya has a problem with me."

"Why…why do you think that?" I responded saying.

"I don't know she keeps staring at me looking mean," India said with a sad frown   on her face.

"I don't know I haven't heard anything."

The rest of the night we started making some green I mean MONEY! Once again it's on…. shaking for that cash. Everybody, up stair's and down stairs. I didn't keep my mind on India's issue too much cause of how busy we got however it's in the back of my mind. I kept my eyes on things but never detected any problem's Niya might have. She seemed cool making her money too. A real crunked night. It was so much fun and I'm enjoying it. Keeping my mind occupied from the thought of losing my guy. Because it constantly ran through my mind. Aaron's one of a kind.

The night had a real good end making those dividends. In the dressing room, everybody is cheesing with big smiles as we got dress talking amongst each other's crews. The radio down low, I notice it but at the same time seeing Niya walk in with no grin not even a smile from the night. She got to her locker and opened it then became loud saying:

"WHOEVER THE FUCK GOT SOMETHING TO SAY ABOUT ME LET IT BE MUTHA FUCKING KNOWN. I'm Getting Real Tired of BITCHES Having My $*d DAM Name In There Mouth Talking About Me. I Keep TO MY SELF ...AND I Always HAVE New BITCHES HATING."

She's going off loudly pointing her finger in the air talking to Ice and other old veterans standing around as they instigated saying "Yeah. I KNOW..... Mmmugh... DON'T You Hate That Sh*t, Mmm uh."??(Etc, etc and other things.)

Got some like Divine even saying: "Who is she talking about?" It got everyone's attention even ours, India's and mine. I'm trying not to pay too much attention to her because I've never said anything about her. I'm almost dressed but India wasn't just having on her jeans and a bra.

Mugging and rolling her neck: "Yeah MUTHA FUCKER's ARE Gonna Learn ABOUT FUCK-ing with ME. WE NEED TO GET THIS SH*T OUT IN THE OPEN CAUSE THIS BITCH GOT IT ALL WRONG," Niya said starting to get rowed up.

With Ice keeping her hyped up instigating saying loud: "Yeah I KNOW (laughing & dapping each other's hand)Uuun UGH....Niya let me know...What's up.........."

147

I stood there thinking: *Whatever bitch, if any thing goes down I'm rushing into you. I'm ready to throw some bows with her, for real ready.*

It's so loud getting everyone's attention on both sides with everyone on just our side. Niya is mean mugging looking in our site in the far back right corner. I finally said: "Who are you talking about… Me?" Pointing to myself.

"NO…" Niya said not meaning an attitude but she had one.

India quickly said: "Is it me?"

"YEAH it's you… BITCH… Got… MY Name ALL In Your Mutha-FUCKING Mouth." Ignorantly Niya is going off as India tried to explain her self repeating: "WHAT…NO" throwing her hands to her side approaching Niya. I didn't like how the scene is going so I walk over there with her.

India said in her West Indian accent pleading: "UT…UGH… NO! NO NOT ATAll… I Have NOT Been Talking About You… NO…No Niya I love you. I think you're beautifall."

Niya said close to her: "YES… YOU HAVE."

Niya's heated really not trying to hear anything India said. As I stood there it felt like a fight coming on. Not a fair one. India being 5'4 I planned to take Niya but I had Ice looking over her shoulder at what's going down. Ice is looking like when it pop off I got Lonnie. Ice looked away however gave me quick glances every now and then. *Okay*…I had my serious look on for whateva.

I said: "Niya….. She hasn't said anything about you to me and we talk about everything inside and outside of this club. And nothing has ever come up about you." I said with a sincere look.

Niya looked and said: "All I Know is that someone told me she WAS."

"No... Niya I Promise I haven't," India said looking apologetic.

"I KNOW People Need to keep my name out there mouth," Niya said turning to her locker. She calmed down.

We went back to ours continuing to get ready to go home. I'm too grown for the B- S I knew that fight would've been a mess. As we got paid walking to India's Land Cruiser we talk about it all the way home. It made India stress about why Niya thought that. I started questioning India about what she says to that other clique when she gets high on that sh*t. Was she talking too much because India could talk? She was proud to know I had her back. I just wasn't going to let that fight go down. Even if it meant trying to fight the both of them, Niya and Ice until they broke it up because they were looking ready and I was ready too.

At home I did my usual cooking, studying and cleaning on my Tuesday off of everything. I decided to go to Aaron's mom's house. When I got there, no one was there so I left a note for her saying who I was and giving my number to please call me. I'm determined now to get Aaron back I knew I could get him back. I kept putting in words how I'm going to convince him to come back to me, he could even stay with me and I would even give him gas money for his traveling. His love is what I need.

Chapter 15

What Kind of Games Are We Playing?

This dancer named Sierra needed to talk to me at work one night. So we went to the dressing room. Sierra came up close to me looking concern saying: "Lonnie…What's going on with you? People are talking about how skinny you're getting.

"You're getting very thin. What are you doing?" Sierra said with her face all dramatized faking like she's concerned.

"What…What do you mean…What am I doing?

"Well I just want to let you know people are talking and when it get's Mack's attention he usually fire's girl's for that. That's how Zoey got fired."

With a crazy look I said "ZOEY…WHAT…I'm not ZOEY's size. I'm not that skinny." I said with an attitude Zoey's skin and bones skinny. I had some meat and most of it is in my rear.

Sierra said very low: "Doing that stuff will make you lose."

"I know you're not assuming I do drugs… That's what ya'll DO around here… NO…I Don't do avy kind of drug but weed. Other drugs that's y'alls shit. I've always been this size," I said with an attitude and very insulted knowing she snorts coke. And she's coming at me with it.

I wasn't skin and bones like how she's trying to put it. I'm 5'9 weighing 142 pounds wearing a size 5/6 that I've been in since I can remember. Plus I'm only twenty-two. I knew if any loss weight is from stress of this lifestyle. I knew it's something I'm handling. I put myself into this stripping business I can get through this. My attitude is f - you bitch's talking about me I wasn't here for them to be concerned about me. I had an attitude all night. It had me stressing so hard that I told my regular's…that I knew would give me an honest opinion and they all said: "Lonnie you look fine."

Right then and there I knew its just hater's everywhere. And what better place for that to occur than a titty bar with cut throats (vultures) everywhere. It disturbed me so much that I finally went to Mack with it. He didn't see anything wrong with my size and told me not to worry about it. He thought it's nothing to be concerned about.

Gangsta party got played out. I mean everyone played it. From Isis, Justice, me, Niya, Ice and some more other's. I never got tired of it tough. I would always bob my head to the beat. That night of Sierra telling me the word that's been spread about me pissed me off. I started to get pissed seeing the Alexis crew, Ice, Melissa and Isis talking and looking at me as I danced. They knew I had the best body in there. When it's my turn on stage I played DMX-"Ain't No Sunshine" to really kill the noise and to tell them that's really how I feel adding a lil' sexy mean mug to it. And I freaked it having everyone's attention silent not

151

holding any conversations. It's rarely played only by me and Lady.

The game will never stop in strip clubs…from the brain games of the girl's playa hating. That will never stop. From the mind games girls were playing on the customers will never stop. From the games the girls played on themselves will never stop…using mind altering substances will it stop?

I started to realize that Nicole is hiding something from me. Her nose continued to stay wet in her nostrils all the time. My nose ran too sometimes after I got off the stage however her nose would be runny and also a little red at the bar just talking. That's what made me wonder. I didn't want to think she's doing coke or anything like that. I just didn't want to believe that she use such a dangerous drug. Not Nicole she had it going on and always looked together.

How she explained to me different signs of someone doing coke I'm getting the same signs of her doing it. I gave her the benefit of doubt. Until one day I went in the dressing room, saw her and Gi Gi on one side together, rarely seen on the main floor talking.

Gi Gi is putting something back in her locker and Nicole is sitting there but when she saw me she quickly got up. I'm concerned however knew that Nicole is a grown woman and could take care of her self. Her and India were my best friends in the club but knew they would have the mind to eventually stop. India is still trying to get me to try ol' china white almost every other time we worked and my reply would be the same cussing her out: "Hell NO…Why are you doing it?" India would just roll her eyes.

One time after work, just Selena, India and me in the dressing room, India just pulled out her neatly folded dollar bill that had some coke in it and just snorted away with her cut off straw. It freaked me out blowing up the spot saying to her: "What THE FUCK Are You DOING?" I said looking at Selena's reaction. Selena looked at the situation like... *So it's not me*, not having an expression of concern fixing her lashes.

"INDIA... WHAT are you thinking? Why Are You Doing That?" I said pleading with her. India had never done that in front of us. India wouldn't have a valid reason making up excuses why she liked it. Then she would bring up the weed issue that I have. I would reply: "I only do that on the weekends and SO What? That comes from the earth. Man didn't touch that plant. I balanced my indulgence strictly for the weekends...after work or my days off of school." I hated to see my friends going down that destructive path.

With Nicole being the number one oldest working Vet entertainer in the club stacking paper each night, I mean hundreds of dollars. Always having two rolls of money leaving out she kept in a real secret place. I just didn't know how to approach her if that's what helped her make an end.

After work one weekend Nicole came back to my place to spend the night. We got a light bite to eat. Our usual is becoming clean and washing our facing clear of make up becoming natural, feeling natural. We sat up and talk on a deep level. I shared some things on the reason I left home. How my heart is mending from my second heartbreak and the past. She looked upon my old issues as if that's nothing.

Then she shared the biggest secret she had been keeping her whole life. Nicole had been working on the block for years when Baltimore Street had ten blocks of nothing but strip clubs. One night she got a ride with one of her loyal client's and they tried to take advantage of her.

The guy pulled over in a dark alley way and tried to rape her. By violently hitting her and holding her down so she could not scream.

By the time he had her down he then was taking time to pull down his pants, he didn't know she had something to defend herself, a knife. She pulled it out with her moving and squirming around and it went into his body killing him right there with it. She left his body in the dark alley and ran never reporting it. As she explained sitting up ventilating with her voice raised yelling: "LONNIE……. DO YOU REALIZE HIS BLOOD WAS ALL OVER ME…….. DO YOU KNOW HOW IT FEELS TO HAVE ANOTHER… PERSONS… BLOOD… ON YOU? DO YOU UNDERSTAND HOW IT FEELS TO SEE SOMEONE DYING…….I DIDN"T MEAN………I DIDN'T MEAN TO."

Tension rose with Nicole looking very hysterical screaming out with her hands raised up with a slight tremble in them. I just remained calmed shaking my head yes to let her know I understood looking at my carpet. Then I look at her and said calmly: "Nicole… Girl… right now you're scaring me. Nicole it's over. You survived."

I then gave her a long huge. I finally got her to go to sleep on my couch. We tried to go to bed. I couldn't help but to think what I'd heard. No one has ever told me that they've killed someone else. I didn't lose any respect or treated her differently. It was just too much for the brain.

I stayed in constant contact with Jamonos, he's my friend now. He's very cool… plus only staying at my house just enough time to chill then bounced back to his business. It's nothing lovey Dovee. However each conversation was good with us never getting into what I might be interested in. I would always send him on his way with a hug. Once on our recent visit he wanted me to ride some where with him. Funny thing he's in a black navigator with cool tint, so it's a joy ride for me. Going past a golf course I recognized the area. It's just through these row houses close to Ty's on York road. He slowed down when we got to the back of the row houses in the gated back area.

After we left out the neighborhood it was a big steep hill that stood out with this area. I didn't ask any questions however he asked how long until my lease was up to my apartment. I told him I have about three months. He nodded his head and said he's going to need a favor something simple but sort of over the edge. He told me he would meet me tonight. Since he knew I was going into work I assumed there. It made me wonder, what's the favor?

Saturday night is live and direct. Guy's coming in knowing exactly who they wanted. No dancer is sitting at the beginning of the bar, we were all working. Some just sitting at the bar talking to their customer's. Some giving lap dances in the back area, one girl dancing to two songs, plus you got up top. The top floor same thing. With thirty girl's usually working on that night fifteen up top and fifteen down on the 1st level. And we switch in the mid-hour of work. Dancer's where even in the dressing room freshening up taking a quick change. I have to be honest (stripper's) dancers or entertainer's what eva you want to call it keeps a good hygiene going… well at least the girl's here. I know I did. Coming to work showered up. With each outfit in a zip lock bag. Wipes, lotion, perfume, bacterial hand sanitizer, had to keep that on deck at all times. Also just in case I break out in a sweat a hand cloth and mad beauty care products up top… in my locker. I kept a neat locker…. I can't say the same for India next to me. Some girl's like her freshen up with other things but did it on the low low. Because Mack didn't allow that.

155

Once he sees a girl snorted some blow they gots to go. No matter the seniority their fired. When the clique of girl's who smoked marijuana twos and threes, you could kind of tell someone was chiefing. In the closed two stalled bathroom up stairs. With that group of girl's he let slide only the ones that have been there for along time however he'd cuss and fussed loudly at them.

With me I did that solo with air freshener and once he caught me. He opened up the door quick with a mean look on his face. It made me even jump from being caught. He looked then quickly shut the door with out fussing at me. That made me know I had some kind of pull.

My regular for going on three months named Gary came in. The one that talks too much when he's drunk however when I spotted him Lady's talking to him. And to add to that he bought her lap dance and they went up stairs. In the club that would of caused friction with a lot of these chicks. I wasn't mad at her but *damn dude bet not stop sitting with me.* I didn't have a problem sharing on getting money.

Finally ol' boy came back in…. Barron. The sexy chocolate guy that had that football player's body but standing at 5'10. He sat downstairs and I was coming from upstairs. Approaching him on sight with perfect timing. When I sat and we were approached by the bartender he ordered a sixty dollar lap dance.

Like last time he ordered a coca cola and we went right upstairs. We first chilled out and I sat to talk to him. He's interesting and mature. He had a great job in D.C. as a camera man for a major news station. It's something very sexy about him. He's also impressed with my drive in educating my self. He's someone I could talk to. Then I got up and did my little twirl in a seductive manner. Me taking

156

my time leaning up against him smelling my Escada, moving with a slow wynd that got them going all the time.

The same night Jamonos came through the doors and we got a chance to talk. He needed to use someone's address to get something very important delivered. He didn't say in so many words but referred to it as work but he offered giving me a large amount of money, were talking G's. I'm semi down with it as long as it's when I'm moving out. He said okay it will work. I can't believe he's putting faith in me. I can't believe I'm down. When he told me a ball park figure of how much I get... I was with it. Just a down payment for my Benz I had already started pricing in the newspaper. Jamonos and I started taking drives out to Columbia, Maryland to these fairly new warehouses. It's close to Arundel Mall.

I got out with him once and inside they had new furniture pieces, leather clothes, and furs. All different kinds you name it. I had to stop at this beautiful black and white chinchilla it was just my size. Jamonos started talking to the Iranian looking gentleman and I seen Jamonos give him an envelope. The guy took it and Jamonos came back to where I was standing and said: "You like this?" I shook my head yes touching it "I love it," I said smiling at him.

As we left and during our ride I got a call from Iesha… (Mocha). She loves Illinois and wanted me to come there to hang in Chicago. I made it my plans at the end of the semester's get away. She's head over hills in love with Taz. She constantly shared how she felt. He's even planning to move there if she decided to stay.

Jamonos and I after a drive to the warehouses stopped into Jillian's to grab a bite to eat. Jamonos is also meeting with Taz to talk some things over. Taz seemed laid back and was always making moves. I still didn't see why Iesha was head over heels for him. He dressed street with urban designer wear. He looked like he needed to shave his beard. He's fair skinned biracial of Iranian and Black culture, cute however a little husky and short.

At work that night I almost racked in my goal for the night. As usual we all got dressed listening to the radio. Since the bartender and bar maid is counting tonight's make we have to sit and wait. So after we get dress the pot head group like Devine, Bonnie, me, Justice, Isis and sometimes Kiwi would go chief out. I worked with Kiwi at Diamonds. Kiwi is a dark chocolate Jamaican chick that had a real petite body that could really talk the hustle. See Mack didn't care about after work smoking marijuana. It's just that during the night the police walk through the club. Mack didn't want them to smell it.

Chapter 16

The Brain Games

$School$ is going well. I kept supplying my brain
with knowledge. My art class stayed interesting learning all
cultures of art visiting museums for projects. The semester
was almost over having two months to go. I'm in a
marketing class as well that kept me busy with group
projects. Mr. Jackson always kept us interested in
marketing ideas. I'm in a new computer tech course. A real
husky looking thug guy use to help me with my computer
problems in that class. It amazed me he knew so much
about technology. I always sat close by him to ask for help.
I associated with a few classmates at school however they
never knew what I do for dough.

 My clothing construction project was in place and
almost ready to wear. With the other girl's behind tasting
my wind of how quick I'm finishing. Professor Celeste was
very impressed giving a big grin when she passed my work
area.

 I went to talk to Professor Celeste, like how I did
with all my professor's to see how I'm doing. Find out
where I'm at in my grade. Professor Celeste's expression
looked so excited holding in the big surprise that she was

going to announce at the fashion show that's two weeks away. She mentioned to me the designer school in New York called FIT. I told her that I wanted to go into design work. She smiled and told me that I had so much potential to go so far. She was convinced that I could do anything. She also gave me a hint telling me to impress them at the fashion show. So I took her advice under consideration. I bought some nice shiny silk fabric. I'm going to design a half shirt that had a pirate feel to it.

I talk to my parent's weekly sharing my accomplishments. As always they're proud, also missing me, especially my Dad. He still hadn't found a job but was cleaning this elementary school at night. He would go in the library were they had a big map of the U.S. on the wall. He would locate how far Oklahoma is to Maryland. They missed me very much. My Mama was holding it down. She even helped me on the car insurance. It continued to eat at me the fact I was living a lie.

Finally I got a call from Aaron's mom. She explained how she was terribly busy. Ms. Carla seemed distant over the phone I understood why. My mind zoomed into her knowing that we did have the abortion, plus Aaron telling me she thought I was ghetto. I couldn't believe it, she hasn't seen real ghetto. Ms. Carla said she had not talked to Aaron since he got to California which was four months ago. That's the same time I had spoken to him. Mrs. Carla and I agreed to keep in touch.

Iesha and I kept in contact, she wrote me and I wrote her back. On the weekends we called each other. I'm on the phone with Iesha one weekend. We were having a good conversation. She's doing well with her training. We were also making plans to meet in Chicago. I already had two girlfriends there, Carmen and Natalie. It's the noon hour and I expressed to her that I needed to go to Towson's

160

Nordstrom's MAC counter and Victoria's Secret's for some smell goods for tonight. When I got to the mall I did what I needed to do and came right out. I'm walking to my car in my orange and white J.Lo velour get up suit. Putting my keys in the door I heard some one saying something manner-able however trying to get someone's attention by saying: "excuse me." I didn't pay it too much mind but heard it again however this time I looked over and saw this guy's head hanging out this gold bubbled eyed Lexus GS 300 that's shining in the dark garage.... wheels and all. Seeing that.... this guy had potential enough that I guess I could walk back over there and see what he's talking about. He stunned me with his finest features looking like the big brother to Chris Brown the R&B singer, but brown skin. L.L. Cool J's lips with a Pharrell Williams face bone structure. He had a look to him that would remind you of Shyne, the rapper but finer. Licking his lips he asked my name and I almost said Lonnie but said:

"....Jordyn.........and yours?"

"Lucky" He said.

With a straight face I said:

"So Lucky.......What's your real name?"

He gave me his government.

"Kejaun......So you got any kids?" He said with an east coast accent and attitude that turned me on but feeling like I'm on an interview with his ran down list of questions. With every question he asked I asked the same of him. I'm impressed that he didn't have kids. He even asked about my tag being Oklahoma plated.

"O...I'm here for school studying at Morgan."

He shut down everything by pointing to his face asking me: "What Happen?"

With confidence I told him about my accident and how I almost had a modeling career. As I told him my back

161

bone straightened up as I spoke. By the looks on his face he was impressed.

"Confidence …….I like that." he said.

"See you been shopping…whatcha get me?" looking down at my bags. I laughed then said sarcastically:

"MMmmuh….You know what… we left it in the store (giggle)."

He said: "Awwwh…I can't get out," looking down at some crutches in his passenger seat.

"My man went in…. getting something real quick."

He's fine I mean real fine….sexy enough to be Mr. Right. He wanted my number and I gladly gave it to him wondering what was next. He had game, originality and a smooth operator. I left Towson SO EXCITED!

When I got home I called Iesha and Donia on 3 – way telling them about this guy saying: "O MY GOD! He might be the one ya'll."

I had to slow my feelings down. I knew that I had to be a challenge, all guys like challenges.

I knew I wanted to take this slow however knew he's husband material. I started to panic wondering how I was going to explain I'm a Dancer.

"I'm going to be straight up with this dude and tell him what I do"

"You really want to tell him…. No…Don't do it" Iesha said

"Yeah don't get into that right now. You're serious ugh?" Donia added.

He called me that night but I had to race off the phone from being at work. I didn't want him to hear the loud mouth Alexis crew. Barron came in that night. After I got down I sat with him. I told him about the Lucky guy I met. Barron was a good listener from the start.

162

The next day which is a Saturday I got up and did my regular Saturday morning thing. I made my big breakfast. After I ate I got a call from Lucky. Instantaneously grew happier getting goose bumps and chills all over my body from the excitement in being on the phone with him. I sat on my couch to listen to his smooth sexy voice. It's so streetwise with intelligence and mannerisms. He asked what my plans were for the day. He asked me to stop by where he was. He gave me direction but I got lost anyway. It was close by Towson off of York road, some aaight apartments. When I reach the apartment he took his time to answer but I forgot he's on crutches. We sat on the couch and were having a good conversation leaving this new flat screen 50'inch off, with lots of eye contact and Lucky licking his lips constantly. In the apartment it's a cool set up he had going on looking like Pier One. He's a magnet and I felt like I'm the metal drawing close to him too quickly. I complemented him on his apartment. Lucky told me honestly that it's not his apartment but a friend's.

A friend….it had a woman's touch so automatically knew a female friend's apartment. So that became a subject to talk about. On that subject…… he explained how there's nothing between them so smoothly. Saying how they were involved in the past but are strictly friends. What steered him off of her is that she had a child. I felt a little at ease not blowing up the issue to make it seem like I wanted to be argumentative. I didn't want it to seem like I haven't got any trust to give if the relationship furthers. To Lucky, I still speculated that something was going on with the two in a joking way. He's leading off that subject so smoothly on to something else. He was in the military. We were the same age and he's a Pisces. I told him about my goals what I wanted to do. I wanted to impress and put my best me

163

forward proving to him I still had that confidence. I still had my brain. During that talk showing much confidence he came closer to me. Out of no where he reached over and smoothly pulled my hair over my back and started in to kiss me like L.L. would, soft and slow. Then kissing on my neck and hitting that spot on my collar bone. Female's out there do you know what that did to me. It made me extremely aroused to the highest extreme. Do anybody know what I mean?

I had to take a set back and sit back. He asked so sexy: "What's wrong?"

"Uhmmm…..I think we should slow down,"

He told me: "Why…were both adults…we can handle this and whatever comes our way." He sounded so sexy that in his voice made me want to climax. He's so good to look at.

"Can I use your bathroom?" I said.

"Yeah…" he nodded straight ahead.

As I got up I saw a quick glimpse of a picture in the living room of a female holding a toddler. She was on the chubby side but cute.

With thoughts of that running through my mind and how sexy he was going through it, no way was I going to go ahead and be blind. I had to think deeper. What this brother might have on the side. I had to be sex patient to impress this kind of guy. And when the truth is revealed that I take off my clothes to provide a meal. I didn't give it up so easily for a cheap thrill? I knew this brother could be with any woman he pleased just in the way he looks and I didn't even know what he's packing.

Okay too much time in the bathroom I flushed the toilet. He's still on the couch with his bottom lips all wet. I didn't want to sit back down but I did any way hoping he's not in the same mood but he was. Lucky coming in closer. I

abruptly said: "Why don't you come over to my house I don't feel safe with this set up...you know with this being your friend's place... okay," then I got up.
"Alright."

He slowly got up too. I walked over to the door and said: "What do you like to eat," he responded with shrimp. "I know just what to cook for you," with me thinking I know just the right spot. Red Lobster is making the meal for tonight.

He told me he would call me. I stop by the mall at Victoria's Secrets to pick up some fancy house shoes, went grocery shopping, and picked up Red Lobster carryout, plus a bottle of Moet. All of my errands took two hours. As soon as I got home put down the items I went to shop for, the phone started ringing. I'm smiling through the phone when I answered it. Perfect timing, it's Lucky. He told me he would be over in a minute. I knew in guy timing that meant 1 to 2 hours. I started to prepare in pampering myself.

He got over there late around 9:30 p.m. I had put on my Victoria's Secret. It was the white one with the thigh high and guarder belt. I looked like a sexy heavenly Angel. I put on the television after three knocks - I went to the door with my robe on. He came in looking so good. We sat on my couch and he talked about how good I look wanting me to model my outfit by turning around. I did and accepted the complements with a thank you. I already had the bottle of Moet on ice in the living room I just needed to get the glasses. I sat our Waterford flute glasses on the table. I already ate the shrimp scampi. We sipped a little on the champagne. I had made these chocolate strawberries that I had sat out. We had that for dessert. I took the lead and grabbed his arm leading him to my well design bedroom and I climbed up on my bed un-strapping one of the guarder straps and played a game with him finding the rest to get out of these stocking quickly I was feeling him bad.

We started to passionately kiss on one another then kissing each other's shoulders. It felt so good to be with a man and he knew exactly how to touch me. Old feeling appeared, feelings I haven't felt since Wanya, my first, the feeling of pure excitement throughout my body, what a feeling. He dropped his baggy pants to the floor. He climbed in the bed. I asked did he have a trojan. He said: "I don't use that." He got out the bed and pulled out a gold and black wrapper from his jeans. He pulled off his boxer's and I thought *"O MY GOD. HE HAS THE BIGGEST "D/(k" (PENIS) I HAVE EVER SEEN."* It's so big I'm almost to a point of saying no thanks however…. I am no punk I had to experience how this felt. I haven't had that many but his D/(k needed to be in an Art Gallery in statue form as an example. It was over nine inches long and when I held it…it was the roundness of my fingers connecting in a circle shape (soda can size), it was beautiful. We got our groove on and he had a magic stick that worked so well.

Chapter 17

Friends....How many of us have them?

*B*ack at work Devine is set on getting some breast, she's a nice small b cup. She already had her money for the ten thousand dollar something job. She's the coolest female at Oasis. Devine that night asked where's Mocha been hiding. Then she started expressing how beautiful she thought Mocha is.

"I'm telling you if I had the choice to be Black that's how I would want to look... she's so pretty (giggle). She looks like Janet Jackson." Devine said cheesing. Mocha well Iesha is pretty. To me she looked like Ashanti, the R&B singer.

As beautiful as Devine is she even had insecurities, one being her breast. Devine was gone for about two weeks. When she came back its vava voom Devine. Her breasts are a perfect C cup. She even let me feel them and they felt so real. They even drooped like natural breast would. They felt totally natural and whoever did her job was the bomb, a master at breast sculpture. They didn't have the wedges on the side either.

Devine is so happy with them her confidence sprouted up to the roof. Devine was already a money maker however became one of the top girl's every night, even

Monday and Tuesday. It made me think about using my measly G's on some new titties.

Bonnie too, she's flat as a board but thick toned with long brown hair going down the middle of her back. Devine and Bonnie are real good friends. They lived right next to each other. They both had one child. I would take them home sometimes, each giving me gas money. Devine's very generous with gas money because she made bank each night. We would chill sometimes in Devine's lavish blue, cream and grey house. It was nicely decorated with her big fat grey cat that was beautiful. I've always been afraid of cats my whole life. It's the first cat I got comfortable around.

Bonnie and Devine were tight just like how I was tight with India. All four of us were cool to kick it with during work and after. Sometimes we would all be in the locker room together. Once India and Devine both pulled out some coke and just snorted away. Bonnie and I looked at each other with crazy odd looks. In my mind, *O.M.G...* I'm totally shocked at Devine. Is that what's been keeping her so bubbly all this time?

They usually get it from a white guy. He sat with India religiously. That was money India could count on plus him giving plenty of free coke. India was so careless on doing that. Go head if you want to... I thought she's being a fool. Our friendship was straight up, telling each other like it is, friendly but kept it real. And when I brought up the coke issue it's like she wasn't listening, in one ear and out the other.

Barron is a good person to talk to. He came to see me at work one day but I was not there so he sat with this Jamaican chick named Kiwi. When he did visit with me we always had a good conversation. It's like I could tell him anything and I didn't feel judged. We became friends instantly. One night he came in and I'm on stage. "Are You Still Down" by Jon B. is going off. Gi Gi is working that night and came from upstairs. As soon as she saw sight of Barron she approached him as if she knew him.

They talked and it made me realize that Gi Gi hardly ever approaches someone so I knew that there was a chemistry between the two. On my third song I played "No Diggidy" by Blackstreet. I knew that she had asked to sit with him but he turned her down. She walked away before the bartender's asked. In her seat she looked red hot with her arms folded up like a five year old. But cooled down not trying to show her emotions when I came to sit with him, I only wondered: *what's that about?*

There was a new girl by the name of Fox. Fox is very pretty. She's West Indian and Black, golden caramel skin tone. She had a track stars body, lean with muscles in her legs, she's flat chest with gorgeous dark golden brown hair down to her back. I could tell she's a tomboy. She had a cool personality that everybody welcomed. She's openly gay and proud. She moved well to Jamaican music and played rock also. She's an average money maker. In having more business I'm one step behind her. The same with India, Fox was one step down from India in ranking.

Nobody was more of a money maker than Selena, she still kept racking in, her and Devine are neck to neck. What most girl's hated is that Selena did this work sober not needing anything to help her have a good time. I even wondered what keeps her cute personality going. I didn't drink heavy on weekdays only a V8 splash juice or beer but the weekends I drunk liquor.

What I realized Selena was high off life and being a foreigner on vacation in the states. That's what made her work hard keeping her act going plus coffee to keep her

169

perky and not drowsy. When she took breaks a runner would go get her coffee.

She could be the role model for Dancer's around America. But still a Good Girl Gone Bad.

One night I was making money awfully slow. I hardly had any drinks only three with twenty- three dollar's in tips and it was 12:45 a.m. India wasn't doing good either until Tom came in after she called him. I sat with them on a twenty. After that I was walking around desperate needing more drinks. It was like I was the only girl not doing well for it to be a Thursday night. Every girl was busy except me it seemed. I had some nights like that but other pretty girl's had their bad nights too. I went up stairs and seen high maintenance girls like Tonya jacking off some guys in the lap dance area. They're trying to play it off hiding it with their backs but I saw how their arms were moving fast. I was not that desperate.

It's disappointing to see some girl's have no morality and respect for themselves. Doing things like that you start to pick up a bad reputation but seeing these supposedly high class dancers' do that made me sick to know that's the reputation we had throughout the whole world.

What girls would do when they're desperate just to get a good tip, a bottle or that big number of drinks. It was all about the C.R.E.A.M. **Cash Rules Everything Around Me** theme in their minds.

I wasn't going to allow them to touch on me in some places and I'm not going touch on their private area or mine. I kept it strict with the house rules and everyone that got a lap dance from me enjoyed to the highest pleasure. I never wanted to be caught up in just trying to get the money… hundred dollar bills ya'll. So I didn't knock the girl's however it made our negative reputation to be truthful.

But getting cream kept on our lights, rent and fashionable clothes on our back. Especially if you didn't have kids, it's lovely. Sure some females have better days than other's on getting that cream.

Coke…well "Goodies" as they called it was some high priced stuff. Some high maintenance girl's like Tonya was hustling with it. So hustling for that change was important to get all our needs and wants met. Doing coke supported a lot of girl's livelihoods. I didn't do coke but a lot of the High Stake Diva's did, excluding a few. Sure I loved money however it wasn't that serious I've already lowered my morals by even being in here. If that's what it took to keep a roof over my head then that's what I'm going to do for the time being. I'm not selling my body for sex or having intercourse.

Don't forget I got trapped however I wasn't going to act like a tramp jacking someone off or doing anything sexually with the guys. No…No…that's not me I had to be a lady. I felt like I was the most highly educated female there at night which they knew by the way I talk and my mannerisms. Girl's that weren't too proud inquired about my studies. I would tell them Design and Marketing.

Once a square White dancer commented that if I had a clothing line, they would wear my clothes just by the way I dress coming to work. I'm glad she said it in front of everyone including Gi Gi in the locker room. I smiled and thanked her heartedly.

I always had to keep it fresh, hot and different going or coming. At work I had a plan to switch up my style so I started wearing my Victoria's Secret lingerie especially the white guarder belt one that looked good with the fluorescent light. I bought a pink & green fatigue chaps outfit from Devine. Girl's where so jealous of my sense of creativity.

Usually I get to work thirty minutes before it's eight. I started coming in even earlier. The daytime girl's started coming up from their shift. It was two new brown colored girls. The thick one sounded country and speaking to everyone as they passed, hardly getting responses. I thought she's overly friendly too early. Why is she being all nice… this wasn't a nice place to be that friendly. I spoke to her and she started complementing me on my hair and outfit. I thanked her nonchalantly. She asked was it all my hair. That's something that I get asked in Baltimore all the time. I kept my hair, nails and feet done every two weeks, for my feet every week. In this business you had to keep your feet up. I asked her did she like the club. She responded with a big smile saying yes nodding her head excitedly.

The next time I worked the excited chick worked that night. I'm busy that night and when I was on stage she's admiring me with two Black guys I know. Craig came in and sat with me sometimes. Craig is a banker. His partner is talking to the new friendly female. She's also smoking a gold black n mild.

I got down to get my tips and came along to them. I got a drink by Craig after I go down the long bar. I took my self up to the dressing room to freshen up because I gave them a show so much the temperature rose sweating all good. When I got back down there I greeted Craig first and the new girl is giving me rave complements. She had this young exciting smile starting this stripping game. Kind of like how I was excited to be trying something new.

We introduced ourselves. Her name is Suga and she had a swang in her talk like she's country too. So I asked her… where is she from? She said Florida then

172

Miami. She thought I had a beautiful body. I gave her the cold shoulder however thanked the friendly female. I started my conversation off with Craig trying to get that lap dance. I got it. But with Anthony his friend, it was a little different for the Suga girl. He had his eye on India who's busy at the moment. Later that night Suga came and sat by me. She's asking insight on the club. I told her this is the best club on the block to work for. She also asked about Norma Jeans which I knew only a little info.

I found out we had something in common she went to Morgan as well. She's on the dance team in the band. Since its spring semester she had a break to do this. Stripping is something she said she always wanted to do. She's young, not even old enough to order liquor. I started to feel like maybe I should take her up under my wing because she looked like she could be persuaded to do anything.

She's almost my height but I'm taller, her tone is light butter brown like Beyonce. Suga had meat to her bones in the right places cute wide hips, a butt but not as juicy as mine. She's not busty but had something to grab on to. She wore long blond extensions down past her shoulders.

I introduced her to India who is stand offish to get to know her as well as Nicole. She welcomed her however didn't really vibe with her. After work Suga parked in the old parking lot I use to park in away from everything. We walked out together and I gave her a lift to the parking lot, since it's a block up. When she got out the car I asked what her real name was. She smiled and said Kysha. Suga's sweet as can be almost as sweet as me. She needed to work on her game. I started to get the impression Suga is fake because of her smile she portrayed being too nice. But she continued to stay as sweet as Sugar. India didn't want to get to know her, I didn't expect her to react that way. India even showed it by saying: "Why are you hanging with her, she's young." I sensed her big sister role come out. I explained no one showed me the ropes and she's new. India just rolled her eyes very skeptical of Suga.

Working over a week Suga is below average however still trying to make Oasis work for her. Mrs. Kim the owner watched her like a hawk. I was attending the last bit of school and worked during the week because I was planning for the trip to Chicago to have fun with my girl friends after finals.

Suga didn't mind coming to pick me up for work on weekends. Riding in her car I got calls from Lucky. So she heard things that made her want to inquire about the guy in my life. I told her very little however I did impart to her his nick name. She responded as if she didn't know him but knew I liked him a lot.

Chapter 18

Keeping it Real

Going on two weeks it seemed like Lucky would call on bad timing when I'm in class or at work. I would leave class or at work I'd go to a secluded area to briefly talk. When I was at work I didn't want to answer it but I didn't want to avoid his call. I didn't want this guy to think I'm seeing someone or had a different life, which I did. I wasn't ready to tell him about it. Plus every time he called I was looking forward to it. I wanted to be honest and tell him because it's already bugging me. I talk to India for advice.

"If it's on your heart to tell him then you should," she said.

In the exchange of calling each other I called Lucky when I wasn't at work. On the weekends he started calling right in the middle of work. I would ignore some calls. That Saturday he questioned what was up: I never answer my phone and I'm always out this time of night. I didn't want to lie but I told him I was out with some girl friends.

He became skeptical. Every weekend the same ol thing. Playing phone tag for hours. At work when I think it's a good time to call him I mean no ones in the quiet dressing room…silence…. Ice and Alexis's big mouths would come up. It never failed some loud mouth's coming upstairs. I would always get caught up in telling him I'm with friends. With me dancing having a schedule like that is hard to manage I started ignoring his phone calls more. It started to get old.

When we spent time with each other it's various days out the week. Lucky would just pop up over my place but always perfect timing. If I happen to be getting ready to go to work, he knock on the door, all my plans are cancelled.

On the weekend after work I got a call from him just as I'm leaving. He figured something is up. Calling me at 1:45 a.m asking where I was… then quickly saying: "Don't Lie." Again I said with friends.

"Be at your place when I get there aaight." I heard authority in his voice, and I liked it.

Soft and sexy I said: "okay."

Chop- Chop…. I'm not keeping this man waiting. I get an adrenaline rush when I see him. I was always excited for him. It felt like Christmas and I was getting a present. My body responded well with Lucky. I got there and took a shower getting my body oiled and ready for him. When he came to my door with a precipitated knock, I quickly answered. He came walking in right towards me. I started to back up because I didn't know what he's going to do. He looked frustrated however sexy asking all kinds of where I been questions. With one of the questions I answered him scared like he was my daddy "I was with my friend Donia…." He finally sat down blowing out steam through his nose. I sat beside him. "I thought you where starting to look like wifey. You the kind of girl that likes to be out?" Lucky said.

176

"No baby it's not like that. I don't be all out partying just hanging with friends."

On my couch I sat like a trained puppy looking at him up and down from his side view. Then I said: "Let's go, I want to take a trip. Like on an island or something." He gave me a smirk.

We had a good talk about me being up and out in the late hour I told him: "Since I don't have any family here I hang tough with my friend Donia and her family. There from Ghana and so they haven't got any family here, we got that in common. We work together. We also hang outside of our job."

I didn't want to lie however I'm really feeling this guy. And my job is not a normal job. It's going on week five and I soon needed to come up with my plea. That night while sleeping very lightly I heard Lucky in the living room talking to someone that had been texting all night. He told them not to call him anymore. Saying that he'd found someone else referring to me.

An hour later after he left I got a call on my home line from some female asking for a Teron. "Teron… there's no Teron here." I told her. *MMmmm*…I thought that's sort of suspicious and tied it with Lucky.

Suga is sweet. I even saw her on campus finally. She came up to me grinning all hard. Seeing her also proved to me she wasn't lying about going to Morgan some girls do. She lived in Towson… so for lunch we picked up subway and went to her IKEA decorated apartment. It's cute for her to be a freshman. She's an army brat and was basically spoiled having her mother pay her bills. Suga is a youngin that started to look up to me analyzing every word I spoke. We even got on a real name basis.

177

Because she asked I let her know the ropes on how to score those drinks and some examples on what to say that may work. Always go for the highest drink.

"I know it's scary to approach a guy…a stranger you don't even know. But remember to be yourself and have fun and want them to have fun. Most importantly have confidence in yourself." I asked at the end of us talking about the club life did she smoked marijuana. I warned Suga to stay away from hard stuff.

I asked what her religious base was as well. I'm glad to find out she's a believer in Christ. I shared my beliefs on how God might view this. "God understands everybody's life. With this work be honest with what you do. Never degrade yourself in a low standard with working in this kind of environment. Do things that only make you comfortable. Never do anything you can't look at yourself in the mirror and be content with the choices you make."

I even mention how it's a dirty business especially with the females… be careful. And that's that. That's all I really had to share for right now and let her ask whatever she wanted. I wasn't too shy to tell.

At work, just how Nicole did for me I did for Suga putting her up under my wing telling her good approaches. Some of my guaranteed regular's I sat with I plugged her in. By this time poll tricks are simple to me. I even tried to go over some with her. I let her know some hygiene rules: Always spray a paper towel and wipe the polls preferably with alcohol. Never, I mean never put on body oil. Getting on the pole or laying on the stage can make things very greasy and slick to where someone could fall. Suga is into that fast booty shaking and I was past that. She's at a steady pace of making money but not as much as India or me. Then again her parent's pay her bills so she's set. I had to think about all my bills now that I took back over paying

178

the car note I wanted to also go live in the suburbs when my lease was up.

YES! The end of the Semester only having a month and four days away and today is the day I'm showing off my three piece Capri suit. It was nice fitting just right for me, tailor made. I invited Suga to the fashion show since the class promoted so much around campus with posters and flyers. With twelve girls in the class just two girls finished their whole project. I was one of them but I half way finished the half silk pirate shirt but ready to wear.

Flame/ Dawn is upset for many reason but played it cool. She didn't finish her skirt all the way and she just wore a shirt out of her own closet. Her father is late running on C-P time and her mother is there bright and early on W-P time. We watch from the back I'm so excited because Professor Celeste told us she had a surprise at the end of the fashion show. I loved surprises. The professor's assistant made us stop looking through the curtain. Its show time I planned to work it. It's slightly packed however amongst the crowd I saw Suga and her immature looking friends.

With fashion I had a rush. I'm second to the last person since I completed a whole outfit. I'm the best feature. When it's my turn I even took the blazer off for people to see my halter top blouse I created. Getting down to the end of the mini runway Professor Celeste is accompanied by a beautiful looking Asian and Black woman. She had real high cheek bones with bronze color hair to go with her butter brown complexion. I have seen her face before but I'm working the run way focused. It was so quick. When I got to the back that's what everyone is discussing. Who was that?

Professor Celeste said I could show the other shirt but with the jacket on since it showed my stomach. I planned to take it off as I'm leaving the stage. I walked

179

back out there to rock my shirt and get a double take. I made sure I showed how it gathered at the chest. Her face has been on T.V. I had to think and let it register: "Yeah she's the mother of P. Diddy's oldest son. Yeah I knew it with those slanted eyes I just thought about Biggies video "I Love It When You Call Me Big Papa," she was in the video. Then it occurred to me that her name was Misa and she was a stylist for major hip hop/ R&B artist like Mary J. Blige. I'm hoping it was her because she's the surprise. My heart began to race when Professor Celeste came back to the dressing room.

First thing Professor Celeste did is tell us how we did as a whole in production, then she intelligently introduced her to us and it was Misa Hylton. Misa had a beautiful grin on her face but wasn't looking at me but glancing around at us. Professor Celeste said that Misa is willing to let one of us come and intern with her for a week in New York – however, explaining in so many hidden words they would have to get there on accommodations. We all got excited however not as much as me because I knew and they knew it was mine. I had it in the bag. After Professor Celeste spoke Misa began to speak on what she had in mind, a creative eye that's willing to take chances in putting an ensemble together. She chose me… on the time and effort I spent and was impressed with the little silk pirate shirt. I took off my jacket to show the whole shirt again jumping for joy. I'm grinning ear to ear with a bright smile thanking her.

Everybody in the class congratulated me on the opportunity. Expressing in different ways that they wished they had stepped their game up. I got Misa Hylton's information from her assistant… office address and a date that works for her. I thanked Ms. Hylton sincerely on the opportunity. Things where looking good for me. This was

180

going to be easy take the train up to New York and stay with my cousins.

(Dawn)Flame is nonchalantly excited for me however I knew that that's her persona. I introduced Flame to Suga. Told them they work in the same kind of field they both smiled at each other understanding what I meant. Flame invited us back to her house to eat. Dawn could be a master chief, her cooking looked restaurant ready. I added that Flame works at Norma Jeans. Suga wanted to learn about Norma Jeans and more curious about the club.

I could see a little bit of me in Suga, just a little bit. She played that deep south country role talk, also grinning looking like a little girl. Suga told us she had been to some Miami clubs to watch but never worked in one. That was a place I wanted to hit up. I showed Suga my place and she's very impressed at my furnished apartment. She had two girl friends that lived in my apartment complex.

I had much to think about. I'm leaving next week to go spend a week interning with Misa Hylton. I met Jamonos at Jillian's to discuss the package getting shipped to my house. We just needed to do some research on who does the route, what kind of guy. Also making sure that my information like name is false on the shipping. We got it set up to where they left a medium sized box at my door step. Jamonos let me know this is the dangerous part – if the package was being tailed.

What's good about my parking area, you could see who's parked on the main road. I told India I needed a favor if she could stop by my apartment to just put something up. India had an edge so I told her the deal. Only telling her it's risky but adding: "But do as I say and there will be no problem."

She looked at me with a slick grin.

"1st make sure no one is in their cars which there could be only seven parked. 2nd no police cars in sight…alright…forget it and leave."

"Alright…what else… What's important is making sure you watch your surroundings."

I told her don't make it obvious that your looking around also stay in your car when you check to see if anyone's in their car.

"You're coming to visit they don't know you're coming to visit this particular apartment. Make sure no one is in the inside stairway so take your time going up the steps if so." I gave her an extra set of keys to get in and she could put it in my apartment until I get back. (For my knowledge) Jamonos is coming to pick it up.

All India had to do is say she's checking the apartment if someone outside in the hall questioned her. I prayed everything would go smoothly. I'd take my chances just another come up. Jamonos had planned to give me two grand. I could make that in a good two weeks however I appreciated Jamonos for trusting in me. I also talked to him about flipping half of my money. I had to stack plus we had the plan intact. India didn't ask that many questions and she felt cool about it. Which I thought is a good sign knowing she's down with me.

I planned to give her two hundred. I hoped it would fall threw. You know it's always good to have a plan A and plan B. If someone keeps snooping around abort the mission. Play it off like your knocking on the opposite door across from me on the third floor.

To impress Misa Hylton I needed to dress to impress. I went shopping at LV XI and Forever 21 having the high end looked for a low price. I'm now on a budget. I'm moving in a month and what a busy month I had. I'm so blessed to have friends like India. She's letting me stay with her until my two bedroom condo is ready at Century Condominiums.

The 40 hour internship is next week and that's when the package for Jamonos is being shipped just a day before I get back. India's going to put it in my apartment the evening of getting delivered. After doing the intern, finishing the business with Jamonos, I'm visiting Chicago to have fun. I had planned the whole thing out for a few months plus getting something delivered twice and it's the same cool around the way dude. I felt safe and felt like things were going to go smoothly, Lord willing. Then go visit my girl's in the Chi, and then come back from that. Then moving my things to a near by nice storage. I had my things boxed up besides clothes and kitchen wear.

Lucky's happy for my accomplishments on my intern and for that he took me up to New York. It's a real nice road trip talking about goals in life and where were trying to stand. He's so my type, Mr. Right. We ended the trip very nicely by going to a Ruth Crisp. He dropped me over my cousin's in Harlem. He parked by the fire zone, its cool because my cousin's own the apartment complex. I left fifty dollars for gas money in his change slot without him noticing it. I thanked him and gave him a long kiss good night. With him I'm now digging a love life but still hiding something deep down on the inside. We're in his ride while looking fly in a gold bubbled eyed GS3 Hun. His kisses made me so aroused but all in all I had to focus. I'm in the NYC for a purpose Misa Hylton is a well known fashion stylist for major artist.

Cousin Bethany is so happy and proud that I had accomplished an intern like that. As always Jorge her husband and she welcomes me with open arms. Already knowing the guest room is mine. Lucky called me as I'm laying everything out to wear for tomorrow. He told me he got back. I'm beginning to like that, hearing his sexy voice. I have never heard so much hood however with mannerisms out of this world nice. It was too good to be true… when I felt I'm living untrue. The next morning I had to be there at eight.

Chapter 19

MAKE YOUR DREAM A REALITY

That morning at 6 o' clock a.m., I took a revitalizing shower in the guest bathroom so excited about my week. It's a sunny spring day. I got dressed and wore a black Limited suit. With this black and white top from LVXI. With Bethany home is home and I'm welcomed however during the week day you're on your own. I called a cab at 6:40a.m. No telling when it will arrive and the unfamiliar New York traffic time. It's always amazing to see all those yellow cab drivers taking people to their destination. I'm so excited at the same time crossing Manhattan bumping right into traffic. I'm still cool because the cab driver obviously knew where he's going. I stepped out of the cab at 7:42. I got to the building that Misa's office is on the 3rd floor. An ebony colored young lady assumed to be the receptionist/assistant sat at the desk I approached her with a greeting telling her my name. I came there meaning business, having with me a portfolio of some things that I made around my house. In the picture's I had them on Professor Celeste's Mannequin. It's two garments but at least I showed effort with adding my resume' I got there fifteen minutes early.

"Yes Ms. Brown have a sit and Misa will be with you." I could hear a real East coast in her accent.

185

My style is real different very Midwestern with prep and spunk. I hope I could contribute. I knew I was blessed and this is major. I started to walk around. When I got in the office it's like a magnet drawing me near to Misa's pictures on the wall of famous artist she's worked with. One picture with Mary J. Blige made me stand in complete halt to stare at them. I gave a big grin realizing Mary has step foot in here. I finally sat in the sitting area. I looked over my things and wondered what this week was going to be like. I planned to write in my journal the whole experience. After another thirty to forty five minutes Misa came walking through the front door on a cell phone saying some things about a meeting and what she would gather naming these big name brand designer's: "That would be great for me. Email her shoe and fitting size to Denise." She's dressed in turquoise and had a huge brown big name designer's bag, I bet. I sat up straight grinning excited inside.

"Okay, thank you… bye," Misa said ending her call. I stood up smiling ready to shake her hand. She looked at me deep and focused in on me. "Okay… Jordyn right?" Misa said shaking my hand.

"Yes…How are you today?"

"Doing well thanks and you?"

"Doing Great! I want to first say I really appreciate this opportunity and your time this week. I'm feeling really blessed right now."

"Great…I'm happy about doing this…first I have to show you around and then we can sit in my office discuss how things are going to go. Misa was a cute five foot four. She explained she had a project. Also each day I had eight hours with her to total up to my forty hour intern. I listened intently, writing it all in my brain. It's for a female news anchor just starting at NBC3 CBS5 station. Yes!

Project…this was a dream come true. What an opportunity just what I dreamed. Misa was having a meeting with Ms. Kim Sui finding out her colors, size, and style made to fit in her appearance. I'm going to sit in on the meeting – I planned to take notes.

What a great opportunity. I always wanted to work around the T.V. industry. After we toured the five roomed office that had a safari feel like my apartment but with more expensive taste, gold and animal prints all over. I asked questions about the fashion industry. The only celebrity I asked her about is Mary. Not personal questions but how awesome it was for her to work with such a great artist I looked up to. I started realizing along time ago that every song that Mary J. Blige has sung intertwined with my life some how. I wanted to meet her; I sort of hinted to Misa but didn't want to be pushy about it. Misa smiled and said: "O Mary…she's overseas but maybe."

I got to work… note taking…answering the phone…going to get lunch and thank you cards from a Fifth avenue Hallmark card shop. It was easy I just took a cab paid by Madison Star to get the bistro type of lunches. When I go make runs for her I take her petty cash for transportation to get there. It's so cool. After lunch Misa met with Ms. Kim Sui and I sat in. The test is taking notes on what Ms. Sui was looking for. Second day was exciting Misa reviewed over mine and her notes from the meeting. We looked on line and were discovering Ms. Sui's taste, sizes, jewelry pieces…etc. Misa is handling a 7,000 dollar budget. Doing this made me picture what I'm going to do in the future, a fashion stylist hey…then even a designer…then maybe hired on a video director's staff team the sky is the limit. While I was in New York I went to Fashion Institute of Technology, toured then bought a designing guide book from their book store.

Misa receptionist/ assistant is nice to be a New Yorker. Denise is her name. I would ask her about FIT. Denise filled me in the best she could. Even Misa thought it's an excellent move and I could always use her for a reference. I thought it's a plan to think about because this is a fashion capital, one of the biggest.

With Bethany in my corner, she owned two apartment buildings in Harlem so I could do the move and have some place to live. But New York is too big of a city for me. This week flew by fast. I gave Misa an eighty dollar Cheesecake factory gift card and a thank you card. I didn't want her to forget about me.

On Friday I'm nervous as hell because I would either be getting a call from India (Donia) she had to walk away or she put it in my apartment. As planned I talked to Donia before she left her place. At Misa's office my hands where sweating, having my cell phone near to me at all times. I couldn't keep it off my mind and couldn't believe I'm taking this stake to get on the grind. I went to pick up some Ellen Tracy suits, Chloe blouses, 3 Behnaz Sarafpour outfits, tops from BCBG for Ms. Sui.

In these high end fashion boutiques like Asprey & Garrard I couldn't keep my mind off it going over and over how India is suppose to do it. Once I heard from India I could signal Jamonos everything is cool so far.

Riding in a cab that seemed like a long trip because of traffic I wanted my cell phone to ring so badly. I didn't want to call until she was back on the road to her place. I thought about text messaging her so I did saying: "*What's up? Is everything alright?*"

I'm beginning to get tears in my eyes thinking the worst. Thinking of plan C to use the money I saved up to bail India out if she's in any…… ring ring…My phone started ringing I answered so quickly I forgot to look to see whose calling… it's Iesha. She needed a favor bad. I asked what kind. "Well I want to go out but I haven't received my money in the bank. I wanted to see if I could borrow fifty dollars."

I thought with my mind racked on other things, like Donia. But my first thought: *Why is she asking me for money not Ms. Esha that gets the job done. By her appearance she looked like she had boo coo money stashed away… Ask one of your baller friends. Why ask me? I trust too easy. Could I trust in Iesha?* I knew she was good to repay.

"Remember I'm in New York interning for Misa Hylton." Excitedly she said: "O Yeah that's right. How's it going?" "Great!" All the while I'm thinking of Donia. *Is everything okay? Did it all take place?*

Taking five minutes to talk then using the excuse I didn't have any cash on me. Plus I asked how will she get to it.

Iesha said: "O you can western union it."

I had to think about this one suddenly a beep on my phone. "Let me call you back Esha."

"OK! Bye!"

"Bye," I clicked over.

"What's up?"

Donia said: "It's in there."

"Alright…You leaving?"

"Yeap… I'm in my truck going back home now."

I sincerely said: "Thank you."

She said: "Alright…" I could see and hear in her voice a sly grin through the phone.

Right when I got off the phone I called Jamonos and told him it's alright. Time for part two him getting it out of my crib. Everything went as planned thank the man that has always carried me through the sands, trying to come up with this master plan.

I called Iesha back willing to do the favor. It seemed like in New York they have a Money Trans fund on every corner.

Okay so I got home from taking a three hour train ride on Saturday. Suga offered to pick me up. We were becoming personal and I was afraid of that. I like that she would listen to every word I said carefully. We even shared beauty tips. She invited me to go to her church. I had met her mother being over her house once before. I thought it's cool that her mother knew what she does…dancing. I felt her mother is very understanding. I didn't know how my mother would react. I thought about that and Lucky…how I felt I'm deceiving them.

After Sunday service we went to the grocery store. During the visit I got a call from Iesha excited about her night out. Saying how she met Ashanti, the R&B singer. Iesha is excited and I'm excited for her to have met a celebrity she favors a lot. I kept the call short and sweet, she thanked me.

Back over to Kysha's mother's home. I got comfortable taking my shoes off. A young male, a next door neighbor that's Kysha's age came over to watch some movies with us. Being childish Kysha played and danced in there family room while I helped her mother with the smothered chicken. Now her mother I liked. She's very attractive with golden hair and on the voluptuous plus size. She's sweet, so I realized Kysha could really be a sweet person. I couldn't believe Suga would rather shake her tail then help her mother. I had a week to regroup myself, pack and also go to work.

I told Mack about my absence - doing an intern however ready to get back at it. Plus I loved dancing. Once again it's an intense moment for us in the club. Trying to make them dubs keeping the number of drinks coming when I'm averaging seven to ten of them. Average however okay by me, I'm guaranteed one hundred and fifty. I'm getting it plus I'm gaining tips to equal out on the transactions I did in New York. I shopped for shoes. Over all it was a great experience. The rest of the Sunday night I just lay'd around my place.

Later that night I'm up folding some clothes. I got a call from Barron. Some how he had a problem with Kiwi, he needed my help. Out the kindness of his heart he loan the girl four hundred dollars for a bill. It's going on the third month and she hadn't paid him back. We called the club to see if she was there and she was. After work we planned to put a little fear in her to pay up. I'm down with Barron and if he needed me as back I was there because we connected like that. I didn't want him to have to check slap her I would do it. I met him up to the block. He was standing near the Chey Joey's were she's working now. I had on a black and white striped tank with some sporty black short shorts. We plan to be by the corner when she came out – talk to her then demanding for the money tonight.

My mindset is: *This man gotta come down here all the way from D.C. to collect his money. I wasn't having it.* Kiwi came out and we both got on the side of her. Barron drove his GL320 SUV 4 Matic Mercedes and we lead her to it. We got in and drove off. She's claiming she didn't have it. "O…YOU GON HAVE It," I said.

She paused for a minute and looked in both of our eyes that meant business. She told him to take her some where. I drove my car. They stopped and I got out of it to get in his vehicle.

"I Don't have it. A lot of things have been going on, a whole lot of sh*t, man. But I promise I will give it back to you," Kiwi said. Talking about her finances pleading for him to give her a few more days right now she only had two hundred dollars. He explain to her that he's not coming back up here for this…today…right now…all of it. We took another drive some where she thought she could find some other funds.

We pulled up across from these row houses. She said: "Can't we just do this another time. I TOLD You I Didn't Have It," Kiwi said with an attitude.

"O…You trying to get smart. This man went out his way for you, slick talk him again and see whata happen," I said getting on the side of her face with an attitude. I knew she got scared a little because she fletched.

Kiwi and I were cool, we didn't have any problems but when it came to Barron I had his back more. I'm willing to bang her on the top of her head if he wanted me to do it, Donkey Kong style, I wasn't playing.

She went in this house fifteen minutes then came out with the money. I got back in my car and went home. After that Barron and I became even tighter.

Got back home and of course I called Lucky to see where he was. Lucky had started going back and forth to New Jersey. He told me he would be back on Wednesday and he would stop by. Yes, I awaited Wednesday's arrival I thirst for more. I felt that I was going to tell him the truth. I wanted to be real and keep it real of why I was up odd hours of the night.

When it came to those funds I had love for this life style and it wasn't that bad. I just wondered so much on how Lucky is going to react. Would he stop seeing me? Would he think I was a whore?

Chapter 20

Lucky Charm's

𝒲ednesday came and I had my place spotless with a new bra set to wear his favorite color purple. My reaction was as if I missed him when he came through my door. We embraced and he held me by the waist as I hugged him. We gave each other good kisses all the way to my bedroom. That night we held each other for a long time. I was laying on his chest and something in my heart is saying tell him…tell him…go ahead tell him. I was falling for this guy and I wanted to be real.

In my sweetest softest voice I said resting on his chest. "Look Lucky there's something I want to share with you and I don't want you to judge me for it."

With that said I took a nose dive at it and came straight out with it. "Lucky I'm a dancer at a club." I'm so scared to look up that I just started talking from the beginning of the idea. I took him back all the way to me living with Lauryn and the situation of having to find a place. I also said how I refused to go back to my home town because of some bad memories there. I planned to do this only a month to come up with money. I told him that my parent's couldn't afford to help me any more. I told him my dad got laid off then how I got trapped. Explaining how I had to stay with it. As I'm explaining I finally look up from his chest... the look on his face is expressionless but listening looking straight up at my ceiling. *Did I make the wrong choice by telling him? Was it too soon? Does he think differently of me now?* Are just some thoughts going threw my mind. I explained how I work at a classy place with strict rules to where the guys can't touch us. I told him how it works with making money. We don't even have to take off our thongs.

"For real...So you strip ugh?"

"Yeah...But Please don't think differently of me now," I said sitting up.

"I know a few females that strip," he said with a change in his voice.

"I'm not like those other females. I'm different."

He kinda sat up on the pillow saying: "Yeah I heard that before."

"It's a temporary thing. I'm not doing this my whole life"

So he ran down a bunch of questions. Lucky likes to ask questions like how long have I stripped. After the second question he asked abruptly: "You sell your pu((y?"

I looked him dead in the eyes with the sincerest look saying: "No I don't."

"Yeah you probably work at Norma Jeans or Foxy Lady."

"NOoo..." I said insulted that he would think I worked at Foxy Lady. I heard dreadful stories about that club, it's a trashy club to work in where guy's get their you know what sucked and occasional sex, plus it's a club with mostly Black ignorant ghetto girls, big thick girls. Oasis is nothing like that. I explained how Oasis has class, one of the best clubs there. It's a white collar gentleman's club no

195

riff raff aloud. He took it well. We fell asleep in each other's arms but after I told him I still didn't know how he felt. *Was it ok?* He left me early that morning when the blue black night is getting just a taste of white and orange. He's so quiet I didn't feel him leave. As I woke up I wondered did I change things.

On the weekends after work Suga always wanted to hang and go over Flame's, I wasn't with that. I had to go home to wait on Lucky to call me or call him which where usually Friday and Saturday nights. The way Lucky talked to me gradually changed. He didn't sound suave and a gentlemen to me but hard with a cold tone now that he knows what I do, referring to it as "Stripping." He believed the stereotypes of a stripper and believes that all females that take off their clothes acts the same. Stripper this and stripper's that. Questions back to back: "You work at a how many strip clubs…you be getting hit on all the time ugh? You go out with those guy's you see there? How long are you going to be doing this? Just when I'm thinking you're wifey I find out you work in a club," Lucky would said.

He would throw all kinds of stuff in my face on how it goes down over there at Foxy Lady. He wanted to know everything about my job in a militant tone. In a way that turned me on his aggressive nature had it going on. I would tell him the differences in a dancer, entertainer and a stripper. I told him that I'm an entertainer that could dance her ass off and didn't need to sleep around or sell my body to no one. I told him I'm different, I just dance.

Coincidently he came over once when I was watching "Player's Club." I would cancel out in going to work when he called me or stop by during the weekday now. He would say no go to work…go ahead and go… so he didn't knock it so much. I started to believe he didn't want our relationship to grow. When he came over instead

196

of making out with me he would want me to dance for him then he would fall asleep or get a call and then he's out. He would tease me knowing I wanted more. One Friday he wanted me to go buy two specific DVD's to watch. I rushed over to Best Buy to purchase the movies. I took off from work and got Olive Garden take out. He even fell asleep on that. He's taking advantage of how I catered to him now.

Every opportunity I'm trying to get him home with me every night. He would laugh at my suggestive mack. I got everything I'm looking for in a man when I think of him however I didn't have his heart yet. He didn't have my heart either but I'm feeling this guy. My heart is still attached to Aaron's however I never spoke about it to Lucky. Even though he asked me deep thought questions which I liked him to… getting to know Jordyn…. but in a demanding way, his tone of authority while always rocking that Encye. He did have a way to keep me going. Racing around my house making sure everything was tight. Getting hype when he came around ready for whatever to go down I mean contagious. "Contagious," sung by Truth Hurt's just came out and I'm truly what that song was saying anxious of what I've been waiting for.

I was almost at a point to where I would do anything for this man. I would bark like a little dog for this man. I was sprung, so sprung that this man is precisely right ensuring I kept my sh*t right, hair, nails and pedi foot down every time he came around. I cooled out in catering food every time he came over because he never ate. I did…I ate every thing even the ordered dessert. But sometimes he would share that. I would be soiling and thumping my kitty kat crazy then he would get a phone call. I would hear it's a dude on the other end saying meet me at the spot. He would bounce and leave me all hot.

Really teasing me…I'm telling you it's happens occasionally thinking what a tease.

I started sharing that with regulars that came in how I liked someone very much. On thoughts that I might even have to quit dancing, my talk about quitting over some guy is serious business. They all knew I was excited and had a thing for this guy. Barron is someone that I could talk to like a brother. Share my inner most thoughts with him and it was mostly Lucky. He's my mission to keep.

See Barron is a little bit too old for me, in his early forties. Already having did the family thing, now divorce with a kid. He explained how he lived that family life that I'm going to get for the future. Even Bean is married and had on a nice gold wedding ring that had four nice sized diamonds in it. He's also good to talk to when I spoke on Lucky, India as well. Every body started to learn about this "Lucky" character. They all just sat there and basically listened.

By this time I'm receiving real tough love from Barron. I could always count on him to give me a male's perspective, which is tough and came be deep. Barron made a good point that I'm letting Lucky have all the control. I wanted to have some control. But Lucky took control, he's a control freak. However I like how Lucky took charge. Barron always had a way to enlighten me and give me knowledge, like a brother is supposed to do. He's a good listener. Bean too…he was the type that listened until he thought he had enough to drink and remember he could drink. Just sitting at the bar drink after drink. But I only shared to a few about Lucky. Some of my other regulars might get jealous.

After my hair appointment I got a call from Lucky saying he would be over my place in about an hour or two. As soon as I got off the phone with him I started cleaning up my place well what was left of it my sofa, glass coffee table and dining room set. I started to move all the boxes neatly stack ready to go. Fifteen minutes later I got a buzz on my door. Could it be Lucky well no… he never buzzed up to be let in. I answered it and it's Suga to my surprise she did a pop up.

She said she's visiting her two girl friends that live in my complex so she just wanted to stop by. Plus she had a surprise some green. That made up for her unannounced visit I wanted to make it quick so I could blow out the smoke in my balcony. I'm a prissy smoker so I wrapped my hair because I wouldn't dare have Lucky smell smoke in my hair. So we chilled with that and I let her know I'm getting ready for some company. Being nosy she said "Oooo is it that guy Lucky?" "Yeah…"

I tried to play off the subject of Lucky and try to hurry up, finish doing what we were doing. I'm excited about my getaway trip to visit my girls after next weeks finals are up. "I'm leaving next week end," I said to Suga in our conversation.

Suga offered to take me to the BWI airport and Arundel mall that's close to the airport. With that said I got a knock on my door.

My thought: *"O NO HE GOT HERE EARLY…"* It was Lucky and I knew it. I jumped up and started running around to find my brush. I wanted to answer the door however not in my scarf. I didn't want to keep him waiting and I sure as hell didn't want her to answer it. I'm embarrass that he caught us still smoking. I ran to the bathroom to pull down my long thick hair. His knocks became louder and more anxious to get in. Suga asked: "Do you want me to answer it."
"Uuugh…"

His knocks grew louder to where I could tell he's frustrated.

"Yeah…go ahead," I said still having my hair all over my head. When Lucky entered he looked at Suga expecting me. I didn't leave them much time to talk by the time he stepped in my apartment I'm in the room combing my hair in place from my wrap. I introduced Suga by her real name Kysha. "This is Kysha, Kysha this is Lucky." They said what's up and hi as I watched them like a hawk.

We sat while he sat at the table. Suga still had the cigar in her hand and she passed it to me. I shook my head telling her I didn't want any more. Lucky said: "Go ahead do what you where doing before I got here." I'm too embarrassed to inhale on it anymore and told her to go ahead.

"So you STRIP too?" He asked in a rude way. My eyes got big as a warning to Lucky to lay off. Comfortably Suga answered back: "Yes."

"Where you STRIP at?"

"Oasis"

"O Oasis with Lonnie….You be getting naked too?" Lucky said harshly.

"Kysha you don't have to answer that if you don't want to. He acts this way sometimes," watching them both closely as he talked to her in his authoritative way waiting for an answer. Me not liking it however played it cool.

"It's okay," She answered liking it with a smile.

"So you want to strip? You can't find anything else to do?

I looked at him like I'm irritated.

"Naw it's alright. I like to dance," Suga said answering him.

I felt funny so I hurried Suga up to leave. She finally got the picture.

Since finals were upon us I worked very little during the week. I decided that I would take the weekend off to study for a final I had on Monday, scheduled at 10 o'clock. One evening Suga changed plans and needed me to pick her up. Since we usually car pool and she mostly drives I told her I would pick her up. Being last minute I picked her up at 7:30. I already had my make up on and was ready to go. We got there at 7:50 rushing up to get dress fast to make it down by eight. It's dead and everybody is sitting around looking at each other in the front of the bar. I had a final two days away and I could be home studying for it.

An hour later I'm telling Suga how I could be using this time studying, she agreed. We came up with a plan to tell Mack we were leaving. When I got up to go to him India looked at me like what are you doing. He's at the far end of the bar. I told him that I wasn't feeling well to stay plus I had a final in two days since I drove Suga had to come with me. Mack gave me a straight faced look and said alright go home. I have asked to go home two to three times before but this time seemed different. Mack seemed frustrated however acting cool about it. When Suga went to see if it's alright for her to go he got irritated.

The day after my final I went to work that night to keep up with my attendance. When I walk in Oasis early at 7:20 p.m. Frank, the head bartender told me to go talk to Mack. Mack is at the end of the bar. I walk back there and sat on the bar stool next to Mack, he said: "Lonnie I have to let you go."
"Why?"
"I really needed you the other night and when you left you took another person too."

I laughed a little like he's joking and said: "Are you serious?"

"Yeah…On a night like that I needed you and then you come down late I just can't allow that right now."

Enough said… I said okay. I went up stairs to grab my things out my locker. As I finished India came in the door and knew something was up. I talk to her briefly to tell her what was up. The locker room is starting to get crowded so I left. I had been there a good twelve months and was pretty good at making money. I'm shock but was not about to beg for a job like this, that's not my style. I packed my stuff wondering what I was going to do now. Sure I had a plan B, go into my sayings but at the bank in my one large account I couldn't touch until the end of the summer. I had to keep working to keep everything like my bills maintained. Suga came up the steps and just learned she's fired as well. We both knew it's because of the other day. Plus Suga was already in hot water. Not having too much to pack Suga caught up with me leaving out. We walked past Norma Jeans going back to our cars.

"I don't know what I'm going to do now? I guess I'm going to try Norma Jeans out. What about you?" Suga said excited.

"I don't know that is one club I'm trying to avoid."

"I'm going in there to see if I can work you want to come?"

"Naw…that's cool I'm going home I have to think about this.

I knew I could get my job back, this is only a test and Mack is testing me.

I went home got comfortable with a glass of wine. I knew working at Norma Jeans is going to one ignorant experience. I hope there would be no drama. Norma Jeans looked like a live club. I called Flame and she's excited about me coming over to the club. I'm nervous of the thought however ready to take a holiday off but first just concentrate on the finals. Getting laid off of my job kind of paid off to focus in on doing a good job on my exams, then go to Chicago and have a good time, worry about that later.

Arundel mall is close to the BWI airport. Suga took me there to get some jeans to wear and a top. I shopped in the LVXI store for a top. As I shopped Suga just browsed. Suga picked up a shirt exactly like one of the shirts I had. It's the same pattern but I had a different color. When I went to pay for my things I bought her the shirt she picked up for taking me to the airport. I found these hot boot cut jeans that fit just right. They were different, being a dark stone wash with just strings by the side hips.

Chapter 21

The CHI Time

My flight is leaving the BWI airport at 11:15 a.m. and my fight got in at O'Hare airport at 2:35 p.m. My home girl Carmen is picking me up. Carmen and I were cool from high school and we were in the band together. Natalie too, we were on the majorette squad. They both were going to the Art Institute of Chicago. I love both of their artistic ways. When Carmen picked me up from the airport we got caught in the Chi's break on breaks traffic.

Carmen is someone I could talk to about what I do. When I express what I did she didn't look down upon me at all but asking how was it. I knew that I could count on her not judging me. She's the third person I told that I danced. Iesha is coming down from Peoria, Illinois from flight school. Iesha manage to come since the next week is testing time. I connected Iesha and Carmen too to hang they practically looked a like.

Iesha had a blast with Carmen when she came down before to hang with her. Iesha and I were staying with Carmen in her cute loft that's decorated with her art. At 5 o'clock we were picking up Iesha at the Chicago Union Station. Carmen stayed in her car and I went to greet Iesha inside. I couldn't wait to see my new friend. I knew she would look her glamorous beautiful self. Her train had announced their arrival and I looked at everyone that came off the train but didn't see Iesha coming forth. I looked and looked then suddenly someone jumped up around my neck hugging me. At first I thought it's a little boy in a white and orange jogging suit... no its Iesha excited to see me. She's wearing a short cropped look with hardly any hair on her head. It's a cute cut I just didn't recognize her. I'm so happy to see her.

We went out to a nice restaurant and got back acquainted with what's going on in our lives. Iesha socialized however brought along with her some note cards. Her new look I had to get use to. I'm use to her wearing her hair in all kinds of cute styles. This lady kept her hair done every week but since she's in that small town she had to manage her own hair. I thought she had just cut it off but she had been wearing extensions the whole time.

When we got back to Carmen's we watched Sex in the City marathon DVD and called Natalie. She's going out with us tonight. I'm excited to see her. As we waited until it's time for the night life, were talking to each other about being in the minor situations these ladies encounter on Sex in the City. I took a closer looked at Iesha and her features came out more. Some recognizable features from someone else I knew. Someone I knew that's close to my heart. In my mind all I kept thinking of was Lucky. *She looks like Lucky.* She looked like him... same color and smile with high cheek bones. It's hard to believe since I had described Lucky to a T to her. I blew that thought off. We took a trip with Carmen to get some money out the ATM. While she's at her bank I got a call from Suga.
"Hey girl"
"Hey Kysha"
"I don't want to disturb your trip but...Girl guess what?"

"What?"

"Lucky called me and was trying to talk to me."

"How…What was he saying?"

"Well he asked did you make it to the airport and then he asked what area I stayed in and if he could come over."

"….What did you say?"

"I told him no you were my friend and I don't think you would appreciate that."

"What else?"

"That was it."

"…..Okay…"

"How is your trip?"

I said with a smile: "O the trip is going great were actually headed to the mall to shop."

"O……Well I'm working at Norma Jeans tonight. I'm nervous….."

"Don't be. I hope you do well"

We got off the phone and it pissed me off however I wasn't going to let it disturb my fun. I shared the news with Iesha and told her I couldn't trust Lucky or Suga.

We stopped by Michigan Avenue to go to Nordstrom's. I had to pick up some make up and Carmen needed something from the MAC counter too. In my thoughts I keep thinking how Lucky is being sneaky behind my back getting her number out my phone and calling her. I tried to put it all together of how he got my phone and got her number.

That night we met up with Natalie and went to this club that had an urban style that's diversified with different types of cultural music mostly Neo soul. I picked just the right outfit to wear. I had on a white earthy linen shirt that I wore some light color jeans that fit my hips and the length of the jeans dropped to the floor literally dragging over my heels. It's a Black, White, and other race kind of club that had a nice vibe.

One room had a stage with a band and the other room is a lounge. In the lounge area it's cool having the floor covered with white foamy bubbles. It's neat because the bubbles didn't stick to you getting your clothes all wet. We sat and chilled in there. I had an apple martini and the girls had their favorite cocktails. Natalie and I caught up with what was current and we missed each other.

As we were leaving out the band started playing this African beat on the drums- that's a fast pace. The area had cleared by now half closed with hardly any one there. As we walk by shaking it up, twisting our hips with each other to the fast beat. Its fun and we planned to have some more tomorrow. Natalie took the sub way train back to her place and we went back to Carmen's. Iesha and I crashed on the living room couches talking before we went to sleep. I mostly talked about the move to Norma Jeans and that call from Suga. That morning we slept in and had breakfast. I talked more to them about this Lucky dude and my move to Norma Jeans. I knew I could handle it… but what to handle I didn't know. What kind of crowd does Norma Jeans bring?

That night we club hopped. The first spot you had to go up some stairs that looped around the building. As we got in the line that had formed down the steps, a big guy walking by recognized we were dimes and told us to follow him to the front. I knew a big percentage had to do with Iesha she's badd long or short hair. She could work it…. her personality, pose, style and body. On top of all that she is beautiful. An all around package, she looked like she should be the number one video girl in America. But I have never seen her on any. We got in the front of the line. Not only those steps outside but inside as well there were more steps with a line full of people. That night I wore my black see threw shirt & black bra I picked up in New York with those hot jeans I picked up with Suga that had my side hips showing. My shirt covered my skin that showed out the jeans. I had some stiletto sandals from Aldo. We all looked cute but who looked the cutest were Carmen and Iesha, they look like twins. Being the same height and Carmen wore a paper boy hat putting all her hair in it. We got in and did a lap around the club- stayed there for a good hour to have a drink then left to go to Red Bull. Now that place is on and cracking. It's so krunk off in there. Carmen, Natalie and I danced. Iesha just played the back scene finding a seat by the wall viewing the whole dance floor. It's so packed off in there. I had a real good time that night not having any worries on the brain, not Lucky, Suga, or not having a job. At the end of the night we had to wait on Iesha because the club owner was trying to get to know her. Natalie is showing she's ready to go while Carmen and I kept coming up with conversation. We had a fun weekend and it's good to see some people from my home town.

The next morning is our last day. Iesha and I both were leaving out before five. Since we had a late night we all took our time getting dress for the day. We had planned to go to this famous shoe store that had all kinds of different looking shoes in price range that go for two hundred to the thousands. Iesha's train is leaving at 2:45 p.m. On the way to the train station we planned to go to the shoe boutique. Iesha got in Carmen's long big bathroom to take a shower first. It's a good thirty minutes and the water is still going. We did need some of the hot water too. I'm next up to take a shower but the water is still running. I started doing other things. Since Carmen's shower had a glass door I wanted to go in and get my tooth brush to continue to get ready in other ways besides my shower.

Carmen came out of her room seeing if the bathroom is vacant. No Iesha is still in there taking a shower. Ten minutes later I went ahead and knock on the door to tell her I'm coming in to grab something but when I opened it Iesha is standing in the mirror in her robe not even looking like she had been in the shower and the water had been running a good forty minutes now. She looked at me and I looked at her then got what I needed and close the door back. She finally came out but it was just enough time to get her to the train station. The shower incident I thought was weird and strange of Iesha.

When I got back Suga picked me up. I made her tell me word for word what was said on the phone with Lucky. She also said he had called again asking was she picking me up from the airport and could he come over.

She filled me in on how it is at Norma Jeans too. She said she made money but heard the weekends are better. I asked about the girl's working there. She said that some had attitudes. She said some where friendly as well. When you're dealing with females in this kind of business you will sometimes get the stares, looking at what you got on, who you talk to and how you work. I gave it some thought to just try it. Suga is happy that I had considered it now by saying: "We can start off at a club together."

Around six, I went to Norma Jeans to see if I could get hired. When I went into the front door they had nothing but Marilyn Monroe pictures. Not until I step inside of Norma Jeans did connect the two. The manager gave me the run down on how it works. It's basically set up with the twenty, sixty, hundreds and they also have bottles of champagne. Just like Flame said you have to make four drinks to even get a base pay. For some reason I knew its hard work to get a drink up in here. Brother's like to give you a hard time and really make you work hard just to get a

209

twenty dollar drink. The money I could make is mainly made by the tips I would receive. I took a good look at the club. It's set up just like a night club, the bar went in an oval circle and the pole looked like a jungle gym. It's a skinny black stage in the middle with two poles vertical at the end of it and a pole up horizontal.

During the day shift, its live pack with guy's getting off of work with suits and ties. Lots of Black men even the rugged ones. Some where even eyeing me and I'm dressed in my Roca Wear velour suit. The dancer's were majority Black. I saw two Hispanic dancers and one White girl. I believe the White girl had a lot of heart and streets. I saw girls getting on the bar to get there tips. The lap dance area is on the back wall with individual booths with the lady of choice. The metallic looking club is classy I wondered where the girl's trashy acting. I nodded my head yes thinking to myself I can do it.

I went home and sat on my balcony to contemplate the whole thing. I really didn't know what to expect however knew that it's going to turn out for the best. I knew I was one of the best. Because I made sure I had the best, best clothes, my shoes clean, nails, hair and definitely feet check every week. I'm happy that it's the summertime.

Every weekend I would try to call Yvonne, my play cousin. She's my friend and confidant someone that knows me. I kept her highly informed and yes she knew about the Lucky situation. I told her I'm going out on the limb for this guy. I also told her I'm going to start working at an all Black club. Her first reaction is: "Awe Sh*t."

I told her mainly everything that's goes down with me. One cool thing about Yvonne she listened and never knocked me, having a way to make things come across clearly in giving advice so smoothly. She ain't been through the things I have but she has a way to feel what I'm

210

saying. She was always keeping me enlighten about not sweating the small stuff.

It never failed after I got my hair done. I get a call from Lucky saying he's coming over. I told him not to bother. He asked with an attitude: "Why"

"If you want to go visit someone why don't you go to Kysha's house or better yet call her?"

"So she told you…"

I responded with nothing

"I was just asking her when you where coming back,"

I knew he was playing games but for some reason I knew he's a pro. Still for me, it sent fireworks throughout my body, so electric.

He came over and got violent acting grabbing on to me asking repeatedly why I didn't believe him. Confessing he doesn't like Kysha. Then trying to flip it questioning who else have I been with, wanting to know if I sleep with customers that came in. It would work and I would plead with him that I was not involved with no one but him. Then the stripping issue would always come up. Once he found out I dance he acted so dominating.

Lucky started doing some crazy things like showing up at my place two to three in the morning like a thief in the night only he made his presence known by beating on my door alarming me even shaking the door. I would be scared to open it however didn't want to disturb my next door neighbors. At first I hesitated to answer his loud knock but because of the noise I would. He'd burst in grabbing me down to the couch kissing all on my neck to make out then stop abruptly. Making me want to beg for more but instead I got pissed and frustrated. I started to express my feeling to Iesha and tell her what he would do to me.

She became upset going on about it. Then adding: "When I get there we're going to f*<- his car up. What kind of car does he have?"

I stood there on the phone in my kitchen and paused then said: "Naw...I don't want to do that, I don't mess with people's property."

"No you're a sweet person. He shouldn't treat you like that," Iesha said.

I couldn't understand why he's treating me like this. I hated to think that it's because I'm a dancer. Sometimes he could be so charming in the same breath he could be a dog in heat. Every time I thought about what he's packing I got goose bumps all over. It's one good feeling. He had an anaconda size penis, it was perfect. It made me so upbeat and happy all the time that I found a nice piece.

It started to be every time we met up it would be on his time. When Lucky came to my spot, day or night he never had to buzz up. He would just show up at my door. Every time, which is spooky to me because the front door stays locked at all times. And when it was time spent... he would do nothing but talk about me stripping. I told him: "I could quit it's just that I have goals plus I loved dancing, it's not all about the money, it goes with my schedule. Also the attention is an adrenaline rush. But for him and his heart I would stop. I would quit." I said looking him into his eyes.

Yeah that saying: nobody wants to turn a hoe into a house wife.... Well excuse me I'm not a whore or a ho-e. I don't sell my body...I don't run off a price for my pu((y but dancing is my survival kit and I ain't been doing it long enough to forget...it is just a come up so those people that believe in that saying can shut the F^<- up.

Suga started to hang with me 24/7 coming over. I wouldn't dare mention to Suga how big his thing was no…no…NO. That is a new girlfriend rule. Now India or Iesha I knew I could slightly trust them. I told Iesha she's right I should have took her advice by not telling him. I couldn't keep riding a lie with someone I wanted to build with.

Lucky's charms were gone… he didn't have that any more. His romance was just too good to be true. He was treating me like a lady and now he's treating me like a stripper.

Chapter 22

The Challenge

My first night I rode with Flame and was meeting
Suga up to Norma Jeans. When we got there at 7:30 its
crazy packed.... niggas every where. Being a Wednesday
night it's getting packed with thugs, thugs and more thugs.
Rocking their clothes in that urban street style surrounding
the bar, rocking the b boy hats, jerseys, name brands and
Jewelry. Norma Jeans had a second level up three flights of
stairs, where there's a pool table. Surrounding the pool
table is bar stools for the guys to sit. Two televisions in that
area, and it stayed packed. This is a real popular club. Real
live with Mirrors and silver as the theme setting.

You had to pair up on this skinny long shaped shiny
black run way stage. I'm on the nervous side in new
surroundings. What would you expect? There were black
curtains leading to the dressing room. It's a hall way with a
big size mirror. Inside the hall way were two locker rooms,
the big one is mostly pack with female's ignant talking.
Then the other side is a long small locker room that had
two girls in it getting dress quietly. Flame and I went in
there. That locker room was fine by me because the other
locker room was as loud as can be. Unfortunately they're

no seats; no vanity mirrors, only mini lockers that were all full. It's just enough of a mirror to see from the chest up. I gotten use to the luxuries I had at the Oasis. I had to put my bag on top of the locker. I have to make sure I bought my luggage lock the next time I work, I had expensive outfits. I'm excited because I'm going to give them my badd outfits on the top of every hour. I had them plus the other different outfit ideas like just a white business shirt and a tie. I knew being a new girl I'm going to get checked up and down. But by no means am I going to be intimidated by their stares. I knew females could get jealous too. Especially a beautiful scar faced female that could make money just like them. Someone like me that had a fierce body and clever style is a plus. And butt to back it up. Most important out of all that I had intelligence.

In Norma Jeans on stage you had to go with a partner so Suga and I teamed up. We were a good looking match being almost the same height. Flame had been teaming up with a dancer named Kiari that was one of the quiet girls leaving out the skinny locker room. She's a Puerto Rican / Black combo. Her body is built like a track star with real killer legs and fine curly hair. She's five foot five with muscle bound legs and thighs. She's attractive and I could see her tomboyish ways. She did these poll tricks that where amazing, some I had never seen before. She would crawl up the poll and then go down like a snake or better yet a caterpillar. It's so tight how she did it.

The thing about Norma Jeans the more you do on stage the more tips you get. In this club it's an all nude bar if you wanted to make money. My thoughts: *O No...I'm not doing it.* You could keep your thongs on but if you took them off the money would flow...over flow. For a Black female to make her money, this is the club. These girls were getting paid. These brothers would make it rain on the stage with dollar bills, especially for girl on girl action.

I got out the locker room and sat at the bar to peep the atmosphere. I'm above everyone plotting my approaches. Two girls got up on stage and played Mary J's song "Steal Away." Slightly grooving to the beat I got all kind of girl's looking at me while they still tried to work. I zoned them all out and knowing without a doubt that is a part of the routine.

Getting up on stage was a very nervous time for me. Suga and I pick two songs to play. We both picked one each. I played a rock song just to be different. She asked:
"Are you taking off your thongs?"
"NO!" I said with a screwed up face. "Are you?"
"Not if you're not," Suga said.

When I got up there I'm calm and collected however I had everyone's attention looking at me with bushels of money around the bar waiting to see a show. I mean all eyes on me even some of the girly's. They wanted me to shake my ass more and take my thong off but I'm doing my regular seductive movement with a slow wynd holding the pole then dipping low. We got some bills dropped however none that made it rain with dollars bills like the other girls showing their vulvas.

Enough to put in the bucket to gather the dollars up off the stage. It's about sixty-seven dollars… could have been more because the way the girl's be racking those dollars making the whole stage literally covered with dollars because of one thing taking off your thongs. After we danced we got up on the bar to receive our tips. One thing I didn't want to do is fall so I held on the bars. Some guys had the nerve to say that I cheated them by not getting a peak.

With the other dancers I showed I was friendly by a grin but also showed that I could stand alone. I spoke when spoken to even complementing some of the girls to make small talk. Later that night of making my rounds standing by the bar scooping other girl's technique. For some odd reason I felt some dancer's staring at me, kinda on my blind side. I looked out the corner of my eye not surprised to see a blond haired Luscious with those hateful eyes. What do you know she's not at Diamonds any mo? Here we go… the drama…working with a drama queen. I paid it no mind and acted like I knew of her but didn't know her.

Around 10:30 a beautiful voluptuous Spanish chick came walking through the door. I mean she's beautiful smiling like Janet Jackson. She had a black velour jump suit on carrying a bag. I knew she had big special privileges to come walking in at 10:30 acting like she didn't have a care in the world. When she got dressed a guy is already waiting with a sixty dollar drink. She sat there the whole night drinking nothing but sixty's. She got up and danced. She had a body like Nicole's but she didn't have Nicole's butt. But what this girl did have was perfect shape double D's that where so perky and they're hers. On stage she partnered with a Hispanic and Black chick that's cool. She didn't take her bottoms off either she even kept her skirt on. And just because Janet Jackson look a like showed her titty's the fellas would make it rain on the stage.

I gradually started asking the other dancer's: What is a good night to make money? They'd report three hundred to thousands of dollars some nights, especially the weekends. I wanted to stay away from Saturday's. That's when it's crazy packed. With the girl's some where checking me and sizing me up. On the low, I did them the same way knowing my beauty could hang. Some where high sidity wannabe bourgeois, some where around the way

217

girls, lots of ghetto girls. To them you would have thought I was a known informant for other clubs.

A few asked what club I came from. Some had curious eyes wondering what happened, *was she in a fight*? They couldn't knock my beauty because it's there yet and still I'm keeping up making money just as well as the next girl. I'm waiting for somebody to ask me what happen to my face. But no one ever said anything. It's lit up in the club so my scars were more noticeable. Bright enough so they could play pool. Which I thought is definitely a distraction from us making money. I started to walk around after I got off the bar. Boy was that an experience. I could tell that the guy's had their favorites. I made my rounds however... not any one bought me a drink. *Okay...that's cool. That's the first.... Being a new face in the club guys are usually really checking for me.*

Flame is telling me that I should work on the weekends and see a dancer name "Body" she goes up top of the vertical poll and drops down into a spit. Flame said it's amazing to see.

After my night I called India. She said loud and excited: "OOOOOoooo....You're WORKING AT Norma Jeans. "O you're going to do GOOD Girl, they're going to love your ass," smiling through the phone.

"I don't know...Its thug'd out over there," I said to her.

"I told you...I told you not to hang with that girl Suga. She's the reason you got fired. You know how Mack is. He's trying to teach you a lesson. Nicole and I have been trying to get your job back."

"Awe...Thank you...girl that place is ghetto fabulous. It's too thugged out for me. I'm making money but I have to put up with this shit."

218

I still couldn't believe I'm working at Norma Jeans. A club I wanted to stay out of. But hey... I had to stay paid. I'm so use to class in clubs which is definitely the Oasis.

That night I did alright racking in two hundred something dollar's. I thought that's below average. I'm steering away from the weekends because I knew it was chaotic. Just by walking past it when I use to leave Oasis, it was lots of people in front of this club. Just seeing how it is on that Wednesday was ludicrous.

If it gets this packed during the week it got to be ignorant on weekends. I went in Friday and that's going to be it for me, no Saturdays. Even on Friday it's bananas hardly any room to walk around. Working on Friday's compensated for the slow days, better money was made.

More than anything I loved the music. They had all kinds of Hip Hop and R&B songs. Even a little rock which I played to let them know I can dance flow off anything.

At Norma Jeans there's no schedule like Oasis. You could come and go as you pleased. If dancer's wanted that real fast money you could get it at Norma Jeans. Norma Jeans didn't have any security so if something popped off, there would be no one to break it up for a while. When you get a lot of young Colored people together that's what you get.... so if you like that kind of drama come to Norma Jeans. If you want to her loud ignorant talking people come to Norma Jeans.

There's this one guy you would have thought he lived at Norma Jeans. He's always there definitely a regular. I never got his name but he looked like a black crow. He would always be shooting pool. He knew I had skills because every time I'm up on stage I saw him looking at me on the slick side. I noticed he's very popular with the females that worked there too. He would always try to talk to me however... he never wanted to have a drink. He spoke in a rude way but still ask for my number... *yeah right*. After then I started ignoring him.

A couple of weeks of not giving him any play he got mad. I came from the dressing room just getting on the floor looking lavish and hoping for a good night. I passed crow face with a straight face looking ahead not speaking to him. He said to me: "COME HERE AND LET ME RAPE YOUR FACE."

I immediately stopped turned around and said: "WHAT?" stepping closer to make sure I heard what I heard.

He hesitated then said it again but this time acting like he was grinding somebody very fast holding them at the hip.

I stepped closure to him with the meanest look I could try to give saying for us to hear: "DON'T YOU EVER SAY THAT SHIT TO ME AGAIN…. **YOU HEAR ME**," Then nodded my head. I stared him down and he said nothing but went up stairs to play pool.

Yeah… it was a lot of rude ones. Once a nigga just grabbed my ass as I walked through the crowd, that's so elementary. Of course I stopped and brought it to his attention.

"DON'T touch me. Don't YOU ever touch me like that…THAT's NOT How You Get My Attention…." And so on.

"UUUuugh sorry bout that lil' mama," he said

"Well Look… but DON'T touch," I said rolling my eyes. With no security or bouncer's I see I had to get some M- F-ing respect around here and I had to do it on my own. It's ridiculous. I had to find the right time to get at Mack to get my job back. I don't think I can handle this.

This stripping thing slowly but surely became a bitter sweet. The money is good and fast for sure. But I

220

couldn't put up with this bull (**sh!t**) any more. Because of so call men like that not giving respect and plus not acknowledging I'm Black. A Black strong sister at that. Now… the well educated brother's that came in… they knew I'm a fine piece of art work. All of them loving my set as a new comer keeping up with the rest.

It's a job you had to step out on faith or luck. I started to see closure to the weekend I made more money. It's that type of crowd that made me scared and shy to go around speaking and socializing. I only knew if a guy wanted to have a drink with me when I went crawling around the bar to get my extra tips.

Because of not showing my kitty k, they would give me a hard time more than Suga. Since I'm refusing to show my kitty k I wasn't accumulating tips like the other girls. It's definitely show boating, tossing up dollars to see whose clique could to do it the best making it rain money, only when girls would show there P Val or was well known. I just couldn't do it. Hovering over the bar holding up their money they would say things like: "Come on… show us something." "Awe… ma you can do better than that." Really getting on my nerves because they knew I could entertain and I really didn't need to show any thing. Enough dollars were thrown to bend down a grab a few stacks of new crisp dollars.

The bartender's kept new clean dollars I notice. It started to get the impression Suga wanted more money. But she didn't want to be the only one taking her thongs off. I had to stand for something and to me that's a set up to trip and maybe fall. I didn't have to do it at Oasis. Girls like Jewel and Alexis did. There wasn't a big difference in the tips they got. Flame did it with no problem but got aaight tips because she danced more like her other half. Only her regulars tossed up money for her. I wasn't ashamed to show my kitty k in fact it's pretty. But the idea of showing my Va J J on this stage…this close compact stage. It's a nice set up but this club's stage is so close to the people sitting right at the bar.

Someone that loved it was Chocolate; yes Chocolate the chocolate Puerto Rican Chick. Miss DRAMA queen from Diamond's work there too. She's faking like she's glad that I came aboard at Norma Jeans predicting I would make money. I kept a smile with her remembering how she couldn't hold liquor. She hung tough with Luscious. They mainly partnered together.

The girl's were hating, grilling me up and down because of my style. Just because I wouldn't convert over to their style. Norma Jean's apparently had there own designer. The outfits were cute but I've never been in to looking like everybody else. I had my own way of doing it white business shirt, my role playing outfits. All my outfits were totally badd, hot and sexy. Real Playboyish. I even thought to start wearing my Victoria's Secret white outfit with the guarder belt. I stepped out and all eyes were on me. I walked around and bumped right in to some familiar eyes, Garland. He's blinging every where that made me not even want to look at him because he's shining hard. He looked at me shaking his head and said: "Why are you here with all these vultures, these hounds and money hungry bitches?"

"I got fired from Oasis." For some reason I'm nervous to hug him because his Baby's mother supposedly worked here. So I asked: "Is it okay if I hug you?"

"YEAH," he said pulling my forearm to hug him. We were hugged up for a minute getting these females attention to start some potential drama. It got Suga's attention to ask about him later. I told her nosy self he's just a friend.

I started to gain regulars, like this White guy name Michael. Michael who you would not ever expect in a Black strip club, he looked like a total square, very geeky looking but loved being there. He would wear these plaid long sleeved shirts with his crisp clean jeans. He's sweet and kept the drinks coming.

Later that night after I got about seven drinks off of Michael. I appreciated him so much for that because sometimes I didn't want to bother with my own kind. He always leaves when it starts to get too pack. I'm standing there after walking him to the door peeping the scene. Luscious stepped up to me looking me down and up saying in a ghettofied way with an attitude: "Uuuh UT Ugh…. This ain't Oasis. We don't dress like that…. Take that sh!t back to Oasis," she said talking about my white Victoria's Secret outfit.

"This ain't Oasis. This is me," I said looking her up and down like she did me.

"MMMmmmm…." she said mumbling something duck walking off switching her high tail.

Later that night after I got off the stage I went around getting my tips in my nurse's outfit. When I got over to the corner a group of husky girl's crowded around and sitting with this one guy that had a drink with Luscious. I'm not scarred but went to receive my tip from the guy since he's watching me. He tipped me. The big girl's didn't say much however they did look at me up and down with intimidating stares. But one of them is bold and so ignorant loud saying: "Uuuuh…YOU NEED TO TAKE THAT SH!T OFF. They all laughed. I just smiled as he's still putting dollars in my garter belt. All of a sudden she just grabbed my nurse's hat off my head. I said calmly with a serious look: "Don't do that. Give me my hat back."

She gave it back and they all watched me take my time to put it back on. I roll my eyes at her for doing that then I kept moving.

When I started feeling down about the move and also wanting it to rain on my dance set not those sprays of money tossed here and there. I finally got the guts to work on a Saturday night. Norma Jeans is picking up with guys early. I'm on stage and Bean came in having on a white linen shirt. He got some ones and started making it rain for me. I became so happy. My sexy look turned into a smile. I simply felt joy inside seeing him.

While getting my tips on the bar he got a seat in the back by the front door. A table with two bar stools he ordered his drink while standing and he got approached by Kiari. He bought her a drink automatically. I knew they had chemistry. I knew he's with someone but I'm going to be polite and say excuse me to her first to hug him and thank him because I was happy to see him. He offered me to sit while he bought me a drink too. Kiari looked in a sincere skeptical way.

When I worked on a double drink with a guy I always keep the other female included. But still I knew she's checking me out and I felt Bean had a place in her heart. To me Bean is my home boy. Someone I could be 100 percent real with. I kept him inform with my current endeavors with my intern with Misa Hylton, why I got fired, sometimes I would plug things in to talk about. I loved to talk to get Bean's feedback, most of the time he just listened with his expressionless face.

Getting up on the bar I dreaded but that's a big way to gain tips. Walking on it, having to watch peoples drinks and swat down to let them put money in my garter belt and the side of my g-strings. I always did it classy turning to the side way not having my legs gapped all open in their front

224

view unless I knew them and sat with them. I felt like an Amazon, too tall going past the top bar to hold on to keep my balance. I started to just crawl. Girls that work there would give off intimidating stares watching every move new girl's made. I'm trying to take it all in and work with it. With guy's I sometimes like the attention. I never cared about getting attention from the females. The round bar sitting at least fifty or more people, the club it self could have at least one hundred in there.

Some guy's would give more than ones sometimes fives. I would even go around the sitting area by the pool table. They had a T.V. distracting us from more tips some guy's around there were rude not wanting to tip because they were watching the game however when I'm on stage their watching me.

I'm discovering songs every time I work there. Everything you could think of is on this juke box. I had been working two weeks now and I hadn't worn my Dallas cowgirl outfit. It looked just like what the real Dallas Cheerleader's wear. It was hot.... I waited to almost the end of the night, my last time going up there. My first song I played is Babyface "There She Goes." For my second song is my ultimate dance tune J-D and Mariah Carey's "Sweetheart." It's the first time I felt the whole room watching me like how it felt at Oasis. All eyes on me and a little for Suga. But still no raining getting less than ninety dollars a dance set when other girls where racking in the hundreds of dollars a set. The other girls would do the same routine girl on girl and let them see their stuff to make them toss money up in the air.

Suga started to take her bottoms off. I thought that my dancing is enough to show case, remember it's too many niggaz in the place. I still did my same routine with that slow sensual wynd I shook my ass (butt) but it's with class.

See I had enough money stashed. I wasn't hurting for money, I saved. It's for a brand new whip. I put myself on a schedule to work Wednesdays, Thursdays and Fridays. That's as close to the weekend I'm getting to. I wasn't making boo coo money just enough to keep my cycle bills current and hair, nails, feet done along with grocery shopping.

I enjoyed my five regulars so far in the club on Friday's a rich African guy would spend lap dance after lap dance for me two to three sixty's. Michael, Craig the banker started coming in for me. Just two of my regulars over at Oasis came in Norma Jeans. Robert, the lawyer came in buying a few girls drinks including me. With Bean I looked forward to visiting with him but it would always be with Kiari. Not just us one on one. Kiari worked the weekday like me. I knew I'm tailing in after her. We all talked however when I was talking she would pay close attention. Most of the conversation would be them talking. I still made sure they knew I was present.

Kiari mostly partnered up with Flame. If Kiari wasn't there I also started dancing with Flame. Flame was progressing. She's starting to like a certain guy that's her regular since she started Norma Jeans. The progress was she liked guys now.

Suga would go in on the weekends. That's when she started mingling with Chocolate. As Suga took me home we got to talk. "You hanging with Chocolate kind of tough," I said to her after a week of notice.

"Yeah she's cool. She said she worked with you at another club."

"Yeah Diamonds. You know… do your thing but she really lives in the fast lane. Watch that."

226

Suga nodded her head as if she understood.

What the guy's mainly wanted to see is the action of two girls just pretending to get it on. For instance one girl in the other girl's crouch area with her hair all in the way. They absolutely would go crazy to see any show like that. That's the thing guy's come to see bodies with a particular dancer named Body, cute faces and girl on girl action. It's ridiculous how those guys would throw money in the air like that, hundreds of ones. Two females partnered up and they would always play Rob Bass "It Takes Two."

I finally saw the female named Body performed. What she did by climbing all the way up and dropping down into a split was amazing. I what more amazing than that was seeing the flying dollar's every where. Once I was in the smaller dressing room fixing my hair in the mirror and Body came in. I complemented her on her performance saying that the crowd loved it. She was very approachable and we became cool to talk to. Surprisingly she's a loner and one of the most popular females there.

We needed something else to attract us. Suga and I decided to do a routine. We got together and had practice at her place. Slowly but surely during breaks she would ask had I talk to Lucky. I told her: "Yeah we talk," shutting down that conversation on to how we were going to do the routine. Yeah I still had feelings for Lucky but he's crazy and the sooner the better for me to move from my place.

He became jealous of my time spent at my job and not enough time with him. Don't let him get on the fact that I work at Norma Jeans now. My regulars would call my cell phone he would answer it telling them not to call anymore. I tried not to get upset but explain to him that's how I keep up with regulars at the club. That's a business phone they don't have my home number like he had. He became mean and too aggressive. I'm through trying to figure him out. I wanted it to work however knew I had to stop dancing for it to. That's a big negative for him.

When I finally got the nerve and we've practiced for so long Suga and I finally did our thing, our routine went exactly like we practiced. On one part I got behind Suga and we dipped low and slow. The last song I took my thongs off. They threw money everywhere on the stage most I had seen on a set any where. It was a beautiful experience. That one set we made two hundred and seventy something dollars not including going around the bar.

Surprisingly I didn't have any beef with any girls, even though one girl tried to claim Mariah and JD's song "Sweetheart." She tried to cop an attitude but she just didn't know that's my song. O well I paid it no mind. The girls really weren't approachable at all. I just adapted to the people I already knew just the two, Flame and Suga.

With Suga, what I thought wasn't cool is every freaking moment she would want to do stuff with my friends after work. "*Naw... GO HOME*" is what I would think but I would come up with a nicer excuse of not wanting to chill and have fun with just the girls, yuck. I couldn't risk not being there if Lucky showed up. I don't care.... Call me whipped or better yet dickmatized and I liked it.

Dee my long time dancer friend would do pop ups by the club needing a place for the night. One thing about Dee she stayed positive in her situation. One night Suga followed me back to my house that night. Suga wanted to go over Flames and sit up to chill. She felt like the night wasn't over yet. It was almost two in the morning. My thoughts where: *it would be nice to catch up with Dee*. Just when I'm getting my car door open to go around the corner to Flames. I looked and saw bubbled eyed lights going west. Upp…its Lucky he stopped as soon as he saw me. Out of all nights he came flying by.

I got in to his car to talk to him for only a few minutes. He seemed to be in a rush. He had the 3rd degree questions going on. Who was in the car? Where you been? He's heading over to his partner's house.

Dee and I had to catch up one on one. I shared everything about Lucky. She joked around saying that I was happy Go Lucky. She saw the glow in me when I talked about him.

Chapter 23

God Please make me Better

Lucky started beating around the bush about trying something new. "New. What do you want to try new," I said while we sat on my couch.

"Have you ever been with a girl?"

"No," I said knowing what he's going to lead up to.

"What's up with your home girl? You think she would be down."

On the inside I'm steaming, hotter than coal in fire. On the outside I played the cool, calm and collect but said:

"I knew you liked her. You called her trying to talk to her."

"Naw...I was calling to find out was she gonna pick you up."

Like he does me I got in his face and said don't lie. He started playing rough hemming me down to the couch. I like it but didn't like the fact that he wanted to do a threesome with Suga. Well then again she's not that close to me like India. "She's kinda young and I don't know if I could trust her or you. Ya'll might start seeing each other on the side."

He's trying to convince me that he wouldn't. I had never thought about doing something like that. He had a smooth way of getting things across like a smooth operator. To top it off he looks good. I'm curious but didn't feel gay or like a dike. Suga's cute and had a nice body if I was a guy I might try to get with her.

I grew up some nerves to ask her and to see what she thinks about it. She told me she has never done that before. But without hesitation she's down, just like that. I told her: "Girl trust me you won't be disappointed." In the far back of my mind hidden, I knew she would be after him.

So I planned it for Friday night. Lucky would be there at 9 o'clock I went shopping for the experience. A new panty and bra set that was black and white. Ingredients for chocolate covered strawberries, fresh cut pineapples and grapes. My favorite champagne, Moet, all kind of beverage's and orange juice. If they're hungry I bought a platter of Chick Fil lay chicken nuggets with side dipping. Suga got to my house with her bags and her game face on excited to see what I'm getting. Since she came early we sat and chatted. She asked had I ever tried Xstasy or some call it E.

Suga had been on E a few of times, more than three. She told me her experience of making her feel aroused and good too. We knew a guy that comes in Norma Jeans named Mikal. Suga called him and we got two of them. So Suga and I wanted to try a threesome on E. We took one half at 8:30. After leaving a meeting spot we went back to my house and got pampered up. I washed every inch of me. Then I put on my best smell goods & oil. At this time it's Escada. Suga and I were having a real slumber party with every kind of muchie food and lots of orange juice too.

231

I called Lucky because he's planning to be here at 9 o'clock p.m. It's now ten. He didn't answer: *Muhmmmm...something is up*, I thought. Suga and I were sitting there talking starting to go on and on getting deep.

She also mention to me how her and Chocolate got together to go to a private party and dance for these guy's. They danced but did not get their money. I didn't fully understand why they didn't get their money. I told her to never do that: "Always get your money up front." I explained to her that she should be careful of doing private parties I heard they can be dangerous.

Suga became too talkative going on and on trying to talk I didn't want to get personal with her so I kept leaving the living room to avoid the talks. Then I put on the radio to hear some tunes and try to tune out of the talking. 10:30 became 11:30 then twelve I'm boiling on the inside thinking: "This nigga has the audacity to stand me up and I got this girl all in it." I became embarrassed with nothing to say. We had finished the bottle and were half asleep on my couches. At 12:30a.m. my phone rung on the house line in my bedroom. I got up off the sofa to get it. I knew it was him. In my sleepy voice I said: "Hello..."
"Wass up," Lucky said in his sexy voice.

In a threatening sound I said: "Where are you? I mean were waiting on you.... I'm going to take her home,"
"You GON Do What?   So ya'll waiting on me?"
"Yes and if you don't hurry up I'm taking her home."

He started describing all the stuff he's going to do to me only me and let her watch. I swear it got me so hot. And I'm already waiting on him getting steaming hot. "Where Are You?" I said to him irritated because I couldn't take it any more.
"At the hospital"

232

My conversation is shut down after he said that. Showing nothing but concern I said: "Is everything okay?"

"My sister had a miscarriage."

"Is she okay?"

"Yeah…"

My anger towards him not being there had disappeared and I wasn't mad any more. Everything was dropped however I'm still curious to know: "Are you still coming over?"

"Naw I can't"

I became silent but thinking: *Dam I got all this shit together for nothing… I understood it was his sister but you're going to be there the whole night.*

Quickly my mind thought to say: "Let me speak to the front desk."

"What?"

"Let me speak to the front desk or security in the hospital."

He paused not having anything to say and then the phone hung up. Did Lucky just get caught up in a lie? Why would he lie about something like that? Why did he want to miss out on having two beautiful women at the same time?

I went back into the living room. Suga was half sleep watching T.V. I gave her a pillow and my extra comforter. I told her something serious came up and he was at the hospital. Suga sat up showing much concern. I told her everything is alright. I went in my room pissed. We went to sleep that night and the next morning I took her to her place. I'm kinda glad we didn't do anything last night. Suga and I were becoming friends.

In the back of my mind that whole Saturday I thought about Lucky. That is it… that was the last straw I'm not dealing with his sh*t any more. I couldn't understand him. It's igging me out that he showed he liked me however he's very distant. I'm caught up and didn't want to be there anymore. I had feelings for him like my first, Wanya. I didn't want to feel that way anymore. That same Saturday Lucky came over. I explained to him that I understood but wondering why he hung up on me. He couldn't give me an explanation. I asked him was he lying he told me no. He had some kind of magic going on and I'm under a spell. Even though I wanted to let him go something lured me back.

I started sitting with this business guy name Otto at the club. He's well rounded in various business functions. He's a sincere fellow that would come to Norma Jeans just to see beautiful women to talk to. He saw interest in me and sat with me regularly in the early part of the shift. Surprisingly I discovered he's a Christian, a believer in Jesus. He told me he attends Bethel A.M.E and that I should visit. Every often he would mention it and how to get there. It's like a light bulb switch went on inside my head. That's a sign to get back closure to God in a sanctuary, no matter what my circumstance might be. Our talk's where simply about what's going on here at the club and current news around the world.

I started going back to the church I knew. I sat in the balcony where my spirit felt like its sweating. No matter how you look at it I never stop having a relationship with Jesus. He is and will always be my friend, I'm in his family.

I got back to my business, working. I went shopping at the best Dancer's boutique. Before I moved to Norma Jeans I had lost my French maid outfit. I ordered another one and picked up this red outfit. A week later it's shipped in. That night at work I planned to whip it out and see how it works with this unpredictable crowd. Getting dress I noticed Suga trying to have extra shine on her legs by putting baby oil on. I paid it little mind but remembered how I told her that's a no no. Hopefully it would absorb into her skin before we went up.

It's a busy night that the time flew by. We danced one set and the next set I planned to put my French maid outfit on. I sensed Suga is trying to be competitive with me all night. Watching my moves on getting drinks I kept catching her starring at me. She started acting funny, hanging with Chocolates crew. Next thing I knew after getting off a sixty dollar drink I had four minutes to go change into my French maid outfit. Before I rushed back there to change I told Suga to play 112's song "Anywhere" because I thought the song went with my outfit. I asked her what she's playing she said Tweet's song "Call Me." I smiled excited saying: "Perfect…"

I went to the back to change and powder my face with my MAC studio fix. I heard the other dancer's song going off about to play ours. I pulled the curtain back and walked out there with my strut to meet Suga at the steps with all eyes on me. I'm nervous however shield it with my confidence. We stepped up on the dance floor. Suga is in front of me getting on stage first.

The first thing Suga did was get on the floor to gyrate and rump shake real fast. I thought instantly it's weird to just get on the stage and do that especially on this song: "Call me" sung by the R&B singer Tweet. After seven seconds of pumping real fast Suga got up making room for me to walk through. I'm trying to be smooth and seductive. We have to cross each other to change spots. I got in the front for a minute then changed back.

During that same song I forgot the spot where she got on the floor. I walk on the spot and as quick as it happens I felt myself slipping and I quickly balanced myself to stand straight up. I didn't try to play it off. I had to stop to get a good look at the floor and my shoes because it's obvious I almost fell. I wasn't embarrassed because I didn't fall however I slipped having all the attention on me, even before I slipped from this hot looking outfit. Then I had to go and almost fall. Then I started thinking right there on the dance floor. *Did she do that on purpose? Was she intentionally trying to make me fall because it's so obvious to what she's doing?* She got on the floor that one time and that's it. She left oil all in that spot. I have never seen her put oil on, ever.

The next thing that left me stunned is the last song she played. It's Amerie "Why Don't We Fall in Love." She and Barron only knew I disliked that song. For me it would bring up wounds of dealing with Lucky. That's what I wanted so badly for us to do fall in love. Also memories with Aaron, I believed if we would have had our baby and if it would have been a girl. She would have looked like the R&B singer Amerie. Watching videos at home, when that song came on I would turn it. It would hurt if I watched. So try to imagine me dancing to it. Plus it's not a good song to dance to. The rest of that night Suga and I had very little to say. I'm glad we didn't drive together tonight because I was heated and she knew it.

The next time we worked once again she's trying to compete with me. Plus trying to make me jealous by hanging with Chocolate and her girl's. Little did Suga know I don't get jealous.

It's so packed off in Norma Jeans and when it gets like this I chill and don't move around so much, let the money come to me. I just stayed in one spot where my back is to a wall not where the crowd is walking behind me. I had to watch my own back. I didn't have the mirrors any more like the other clubs.

With Suga I didn't understand why she's acting weird like this. I've been nothing but nice to her. Sharing the game with her and this is how she repays me. This girl is supposed to be my home girl and now she wants to act shady. I didn't have time for this I couldn't take Norma Jeans anymore. I couldn't work around these evil eyeing bitches anymore. I got really sick and tired of how Norma Jeans system is set up to make money. Even though I made better tips over at Norma Jeans now I'd rather be back over to Oasis where the respectful guys where. Even the drama at Oasis I could handle. Here I had to watch my back at all times and I didn't want to be in that thug environment any more.

My apartment is totally cleared only having my sofas and bed. A guy from the furniture place is coming by to help take my bed down. I didn't want to go to Norma Jeans anymore. I planned to get my job back at Oasis.

I put on Faith Evan's CD Faithfully, the song "I Love you" on repeat and became very aroused. I pulled my old rabbit out climaxing back to back several times. On one of them the home phone rung suddenly. It's Lucky. He's outside. He told me to come out. I washed my hands slipped on a cute plain dress from Banana Republic and met him down stairs. I got in his Lexus and he said: "You've been playing this." He turned his volume up and was playing Faith's "I Love you." It startled me and I wondered how did he know that? He said: "Look there's something I got to talk to you about." I said with so much concern plus still shocked: "What is it?"

He pulled out this picture and gave it to me. It's a couple. I looked closure it's him and this heavy set female. I mean a real big girl.

"I have to break off what we got because this is my girl and where getting back together."

I wasn't smiling but inside I thought it was a joke. I gave the picture back not needing to take a double look. He told me how he felt for me but said I'm not the one. It saddened me and I didn't understand. I took the rejection well however shocked.

"I want you to ride with me. Did you lock up your apartment?"
"Yes"
"Alright…ride with me."
"Okay."

I slowly came to see all the things that Lucky was made of. *Did he have secret powers? Did he bug my place?* I still wondered how he knew what I was playing and what else did he know. I asked again and he ignored me. *O My God…Can he read my mind?* I didn't know what to think. We went around the way to a neighborhood I had been to. It's by Morgan. We drove through and he told me to get in the back. This guy is coming to talk to him. The guy came out from one of the row houses. They talked for a good fifteen minutes while I sat in the back wanting to cry. Lucky took me back to my place. It's final, the end of that.

Depressed, stressed however getting plenty of rest. Lounging around in my bed clothes. I either got things delivered or ordered something to go from a restaurant. I completely stopped working for a good week. I had to pack all my things anyway in to storage. My lease is up in a week.

The next chapter in my life and new slate. Barron helped me put all my stuff in storage. After we got everything out the apartment I treated him to breakfast. That's where I shared my deepest secret. How I fell in love with my first Wanya and how he broke my heart. I went into how we had a fight and what caused it. With Barron I could share with him my deepest secret and that was it.

Now it felt like I'm reliving that same feeling with Lucky. Barron had a way in making me feel okay with myself to accept things and move on keeping God first. I also shared how I couldn't take Norma Jeans anymore.

I met with India and we planned to go talk to Mack to get my job back. When most of the girls where out and paid. I'm waiting outside in my car. India flags me to come in. I walked in and the door man Louie and the bouncer Spider were happy to see me. Mack is all the way in the back of the bar sitting with his suit on. He started shaking his head no saying: "It's too ghetto for you...ugh?"

I gave him a hug and said yes. I sat down and explained my faults like hanging with that young girl. Coming in late then trying to leave early. I didn't even want to beat around the bush so I said: "Mack can I have my job back. It's too thugged out over there at Norma Jeans." He laughed and asked when did I want to start back I told him next Thursday when I get back from going home. I thanked him and India gave me a hug excited.

Suga and I kept our distance however she called me my last weekend in my apartment to go out. I'm waiting for a good time to ask her had she been with Lucky because I had that feeling. I told her that I needed to speak to her in person. Just so happened, my good friend Carlos is in D.C. doing an intern with BET. He wanted to go out too.

I didn't have a beef with Suga I still kept her close because I felt I still needed her. I'm with us going out. Dawn took me to get my hair braided in skinny long braids that took for ever. Carlos and I drove his rental jeep following behind Suga and her clique she hangs with at school. They were all her age. When we got to D.C. we got out. Suga and I had on the same pants. The same ones I bought when she took me to the airport. I thought its funny look at baby girl trying to dress like me. We got in line and I said to her: "Hey Twin."

Thinking in my head: "Okay this is going to be a competitive night out." I knew I looked better than her in them. To prove this I'm going to see how many times she's approached versus how many times I'm approached. That will determine who looked the best in those jeans. During the night as I predicted I'm getting attention left and right. Getting drinks left and right. Suga is actually sharing drinks with her friends trying to keep up with me. I'm getting asked to dance she's dancing all night with her friends and never once got asked to dance. She danced as if she's a stripper getting all on the clubs floor gyrating. I'm also embarrassed by the way she's dancing because we had the same jeans on. I didn't want people to think it's me.

The rest of the night I slowed down on getting more drinks however it left me at the end of the night tipsy as can be. Instead of riding in her friend's car Suga and one of her girlfriends wanted to ride with us. Carlos had this special mix tape that's playing some hip hop cuts. One song after another, I'm feeling good flowing or singing right on point. Tupac's cut "I Ain't Mad at Cha" came on. I flowed precisely to that. I just started thinking about all the people who have done me wrong like my ex best friends from back home. I guess I sounded too much like the artist. Suga said: "Dang Lonnie…You sound so serious. I'm starting to take it personal?"
"Well then if that's how you feel…… I'm just flowing to the song."

After that night I stopped being in contact with Suga. I knew how smooth Lucky was and I wouldn't put it past Suga to slide with him. That's what I get for dealing with fake bitches. India and Nicole was right, she's too young. I was just trying to help her.

Chapter 24

Bitter Sweet

I went back home for a few days. Summertime in Tulsa is always popping. I rented a yellow convertible mustang. I caught back up with my family first. My only good standing friend in Tulsa is Yolanda. She's still having man problems with Bear her boyfriend. I listened to her and filling her in a little about Lucky. In the back of my mind I thought about everything Lucky had done and said, even the lie about his sister's miscarriage. It's on my mind and I tried to stop thinking about it and have a good time.

I looked good with my hair done and rocking new styles for Tulsa with the J.Lo wear. I had on my pink and white stripe halter shirt with kool lock pants and some white keds. We went riding on Sunday. That's a day everybody is out at the car wash. We rode on motorcycles with some guy's I held everyone up trying to find my glasses. After we got off we walked around. I instantaneously zoomed in to spotting my 1st Wanya. My eyes were like a radar. We spoke to each other with our eyes then a nod. Please don't let me get on the way I use to love him. Later that night Yolanda got a call at her furnished house at Bear's.

It was Bear he told her to tell me to come out side. I'm nervous wondering why: *What does Bear want with me?* So I asked Yolanda. Her eyes grew big and said: "Wanya wants you," It's awkward because the last encounter we had with each other was the night of our fight. When I got outside I got in to the truck. First thing we did was apologize to each other. It felt good to release the tension and let it go. With the thought we're cool, on good terms.

That night I went out to an after party they had after the skate jam. I only changed my undy's and pants. We met up with Yolanda's hood home girls. I mingled around by myself. When I came back all the seats were taken at the table where Yolanda sat with her crew. So I stayed by the dance floor. One older female is so loud at the table, so loud that I didn't even want to be around her. So I stood by the dance floor. A guy started a conversation with me.

Then the loud mouth female noticed me and started saying in a negative way repeatedly: "Uuhm...WHO IS THAT? WHO DO SHE Thinks SHE Is?"

From where I'm standing I heard however looked out the corner of my eye to see Yolanda's reaction. Not once did Yolanda come to my defense to say to the ignorant female that I'm with them. That was a sign that Yolanda had some shady ways about her. The rest of the night I had little to say. Yolanda probably wondered but she didn't care. When people are down they want to bring you down and every time I'm in Tulsa I felt down. But when I left I'm up and feeling positive. A week later that loud mouth female that tried to front me out at the club died from a rare sickness suddenly.

242

When I got back I settled in and went to give my key back to my first apartment. The place where I started from nothing and gain all the finer things I had. Looking in the empty apartment made me remember where I came from. I took only two suit cases over to India's.

I got to Oasis early ready to work. I had my sports bag with all my outfits clean and pressed. I got on the floor early showing Mack I'm focused. Nicole came late as usual but she didn't know I was there. I wanted to surprise her. Approaching me like I'm a new girl she's excited to see me back giving me an extremely long hug. She hugged my neck and pointed up to the female's that where in the portraits on the top wall. She said: "Remember you look better than all these girls on here and have the best body I've ever seen. You're beautiful. I wanted to tell you that." She gave me hugs all night.

I was back. I even brought more clientele to Oasis. I didn't even announce that I was going back over to Oasis to the people I sat with at Norma Jeans. I just told them that this was the original club I worked at before Norma Jeans. I also had some of my regular's phone numbers. One of my White regular's became stalker type wanting to tattoo my real name on his arm.

One giving me any order drink I desired. I'm loving it back in that cool low key environment. Back to where I could see everything. I felt like a new girl again making new girl money.

I became cooler again with some dancer's excluding Ice. The same dancer's where there except Selena and Jewel. Jewel still wasn't back from her operations. Selena was trying to work at this club call The Gold Club outside the Baltimore County and on the block at Oasis. Mack soon found out about it. Went and saw her perform at the Gold club. He gave her an ultimatum, Oasis

243

or there. She can't work both. She chose the Gold club and I didn't blame her. She didn't want to put up with Alexis and Ice's mess however I would take it over Norma Jeans any night. I'd rather be in a club where there White girls, Black girls and other nationalities so the guy's had a variety to pick from. An all Black strip club is too much drama and you always had to be alert.

I'm all moved out of Moravia Parks apartment. I'm glad away from Lucky knowing where I stayed. I gave up loving Lucky. I couldn't take that being controlled any more. I'm proud of myself for moving on, no more coming over my place at 3 in the morning acting a nut.

I stayed with India. India is my home girl, down. She let me stay with her in her two bedroom apartment shared by her sister Diamoni. Donia didn't even want to accept money for my stay which I thought was love. Diamoni and I hung out before. India use to bring her to the mall. Diamoni is beautiful same height as Donia. She looks Blacker with her features but West Indian with gorgeous curly hair like Aaron's.

It really looked like Diamoni and I were related, our wide noses. She is on the laid back side not having a crazy wild side like her sister. Diamoni is cool along with her Jamaican boyfriend that stayed there too. They met on the internet and fell madly in love. To help support, Diamoni worked at a grocery store in our neighborhood as a manager. I'm planning to stay a couple of weeks until my condo is ready. We were going to live right down the street from each other in the suburbs.

Every day before work India, Diamoni and I would go to this Chinese food buffet that's the bomb with everything you could think of Asian like. I loved to eat especially all you can eat places being that Chinese food is my favorite. In Donia and Diamoni's food tradition they eat everything with rice. Every day that summer we ate there…everyday.

Leaving work the downtown area of Baltimore gets crowed, from night clubs to goers on the block. Everyone tries to get on the 83 expressway it gets congested. India is driving her boyfriend's car. It's a fly 535i BMW. With us being slightly tipsy India drove towards Yorktown and Cockeysville. We're having a good time talking about the night. It's heavy traffic going full speed of 75 to 80 miles per hour. India accelerated with short notice changing in the middle lane. At the same time the person in the fast lane next to us wanted to change in the middle too, going the same speed we were. The cars almost touched each other with India jumping back in our lane. The other car did the same, changing back in the fast lane but steered too hard and hit the guard rail making a full spin hitting other cars. It's a big crash. It was a nasty one that we know left some injured. We kept going however India became hysterical amazed that we almost got into a wreck. India became very emotional. She cried out saying that she's sorry for putting me through that… knowing that we both were in bad car accidents in the past. Calmly, I let her know that its okay we were safe now. But honestly I didn't feel safe until I got in the house.

There's a new Black girl that started to work. She's very personable. Fair skinned with a short shag. It looked like she worked out on her body. Her name is Asia. She worked going on a week and already got into an argument with gold tooth wearing Isis. I wasn't there but the next day she's talking to me in the locker room when Isis walked in. Asia turned the conversation into talking about bald headed females from Baltimore. To her it seemed like every girl from Baltimore had weaves. I'm not an instigator so I said nothing but knew where she's going with it by having a smirk. Isis never said anything.

Asia thought I had a beautiful body. She mentioned The Gold Club to me. Asia said they all look like super models and cheerleaders. She added that I would fit right in over there. I heard from Selena that the club is very nice. On the weekends I started to see Asia sitting with Gi Gi or leaving out the dressing room sniffing her noise with Gi Gi. I already knew something was up.

Now that I'm back at Oasis. Bean would come in and I had him all to myself. *No more sharing him with Kiari.* For the first time he bought me a bottle of Moet to celebrate my move back. All the girls took notice to that, him buying a large bottle. Bean and I talked but he was never on a personal level with me. Mainly hearing what's going on with me and my life, giving him the inside scoop of what's going on in the club. He mainly teased me about Lucky saying how much I loved the guy. I respected Bean and loved his accent. Bean was a real Rasta. Tall, dark ebony color he had a face that shined like a wise owl. His hair is always groomed but curly. I had already started looking forward to him coming in. A month later, what a coincidence that Kiari moved over to Oasis.

I'm stacking my money. My goal is to get a 320 Mercedes Benz. It was almost time to buy. I started looking in the Sunday paper. I knew I could handle the payments. I had a pretty nice down payment. I calculated all my bills to come with the rent on my condo to utility bills. I probably couldn't shop anymore like I use to.

With perfect timing Jamonos started coming back into Oasis. I sat with him once or twice at Norma Jeans. He had a new favor however this time me going to Philly. He said he would give me the details later. I'm with that. We met up at Jillian's restaurant. He gave me the details. I'm going to give eighty thousand dollar's to some cats out there in exchange for some work. I'm taking Jamonos's Louis Vuitton backpack where the money is stored. I'm going to get in the guy's Lincoln SUV to go to a near by garage. It's close to the train station. The guy's name is going to be Ramone. Ramone is going to count the money with his money machine in the car. Jamonos looked me in the eye saying he wanted me to know this is very important: "For doing this I'm giving you five thousand dollars. The scary part is bringing it back but once you're at the train station and get in my car you're straight. I'll take you to another garage where your car will be. Do you think you can handle it?"

"Yes...I can do it," I said looking him in the eye.

"Okay. Can you do it Wednesday?"

"Wednesday is perfect. What time?"

"Your train will get in Philly at 4:30 p.m. That's one of the busiest times."

"You depart at 6 o'clock and you will be back in Baltimore at 7:45... Cool?"

"Alright," I said confirming that I'm down.

On the train I looked cute as if I'm going to see a guy. I had white fitted business shirt and jeans with stiletto sandals. My sandals went with the back pack I had on my back. I'm nervous and kept my eagle eyes watching, especially watching for potential undercover agents. I wanted to just get it over with. Jamonos had a way of planning with précised timing. Everything is going as planned. Going back is the scariest ride ever. I felt like I'm sweating bullets however it didn't show. I got to Union station in B-More and Jamonos is waiting right outside the door in his Acura. When we got to my car and nobody is around that's when I felt safe. Jamonos gave me the money in a smaller version of the Louis Vuitton back pack. It's so cute how he just tossed it to me and said count it at home it's all there.

"Awwwwwwh….Thank you very much OOOOoo….I appreciate this," I said giving him a hug so excited about the money and the bag. I knew it's real that's the only way Jamonos knew how to roll.

I had now saved and gained over seventeen thousand dollar's and had my ten thousand dollar down payment for my car. I knew I needed to get a co signer for a car like that. I also had a regular that ran his own business and he could put me on his payroll. I wrote down a list of people I could ask to co sign for me.

I could ask Barron for this favor of co- signing. I would not let him down. If he would do it I had it all in the bag. I looked in the automobile section every Sunday. I called Barron and asked if we could go to lunch. I meet him up at the Olive Garden. I'm with a full smile he knew something was up. I didn't come out and say it but my conversation was leading around to asking.

I'd told him that I've saved up ten thousand dollars for a down payment on Mercedes Benz. He had a Mercedes. I just needed a co signer. I felt a little comfortable and I asked would he co sign for me. I explain that I would not let him down. He looked at me and said he would have to think about it.

I loved my new place. I got moved in on a Saturday. My good friend Reggie and a male friend of his moved me in. That night I had to go to work and keep up my schedule appearances at the club. I knew that Mack was watching me like a hawk.

All Monday thru Wednesday I set up everything in my place. It's a two–bedroom condo that had stairs. It also had a patio in the back. The kitchen, a bathroom, living room and dining room is down stairs. My master bed, bathroom and study room is upstairs. I loved it and I made it home. I even planned to buy a toy yorkie terrier.

I kept up with Yvonne and Iesha updating them on my change back to Oasis. Yvonne's glad for me on the move back. Iesha is through with her training and she planned to come back for a week or so until she gets assigned a city to be an International airline stewardess. She needed a favor again for her to come stay with me for a week or two. I'm with it; Iesha is one of my new best friends. She also wanted her job back at Oasis for a while so she could stack her money.

It's not a hidden thing that India is out there still snorting coke and still trying to make me try it. I told her I didn't have time for it and was not going to waste my time doing it. But yet and still I became curious wondering what's the big deal. After work we went by Melissa's. I had no choice on the days I rode with India. Even Gi Gi stopped through and since I didn't snort coke they would go in a secluded room and do it. India would come back and be worried about me, checking on me saying: "You alright Baby Girl? You ready to go...... Will go... come on Baby Girl." I tried not to show it but every time India would know I was ready to go.

Every now and then I would get a call from Lucky. I would shut the conversation off when he tried to control it by hanging up. He would want to see me. I would tell him that I've moved on. He didn't believe it. I'm glad he didn't know where I stayed because I didn't need to add to the drama in my life.

Bad enough I'm still stripping. The lifestyle is a bitter sweet. It's fun, making money and the days where it wasn't busy just dancing on stage. Sometimes you had to deal with obnoxious guys in the club and the cut throat girl's that made it a mission to get your money too.

The Oasis club never changed it's the same old thing. One good thing about it I loved to dance. It's a passion and I knew I could do it well. I attracted all kinds of attention and I have to say I liked it. But the lifestyle was getting pretty old. Working at a strip bar had its good days and its bad ones. I realized it still equated out to a regular entry level job.

That's why I didn't go out to dance clubs often because I worked in a strip club where I could dance and get paid while having fun doing it. Plus it's the summer time and it's always money to be made in the club.

We had the same old music a few new CD's. I played Tupac all the time "Temptations" was my favorite. A thought came to me one day concerning the song. Playing his song Temptation back in my mind I knew right then and there in my life that I was a temptation to everybody watching or also the ones who got lap dances from me, all the entertainers - Temptation.

We got new music in the juke box and one of the CD's is Faithfully by Faith Evans. I fell in love with the CD so much because I had it. That became my CD to play forget all the stupid stuff I started with the song messages because it became a battle. I still played battle beef songs however it's mainly for the beat not the beef. One of my forever favorite songs to dance to: Usher "I Don't Know" It was amazing to see me my ego move on that song whipping my hair around. I got attention all the time on that song having some of the girl's heated. Even on that song I sent a message. Not for more beef but that's how I felt. It's something I couldn't end since I started so I started to play positive music all the time- Faithfully – track number 11 is my song because I use my secret weapon – in the love songs I reference my love for Jesus Christ. If you can understand I put Jesus in that place of whatever love song I

250

played, R&B especially. It's my number one secret. And "Faithfully" is my first feature song when I did my set.

I also played relaxing things like Sade – Black Paradise and Kiss of Life.

Gi Gi's still playing that Janet Jackson song every now and then however wouldn't make it obvious with starring at me.

Iesha's guy friend Taz would come and sit with me. We would converse over the latest Hip-Hop news and when Iesha is coming back. I kept the conversation on general subjects. I let Iesha know that he came in and sat with me too. She thought it's cool.

Chapter 25

Out of Control

Jewel is back and I mean Jewel was back looking beautiful as ever. With a new body, she had been off for a few months healing from new C cups. Her baby's daddy wanted her all to himself apparently. India became very jealous of her instantly talking about nothing but Jewel's body. Going on and on not even on the low... in the dressing room she talked about Jewel while sitting at the bar. "O my God she looks beautiful.... She picked up some weight.... Look how her face is even fuller. She looks younger.... Look... she even got her teeth fixed."

"What was wrong with her teeth?" I asked.

"You know... her teeth were crooked," India said smiling then we laughed out loud. I realized that Jewel did have flaws even though she acted like she didn't. The kind of girl that knows their all that but tries to stay down for the dudes. Really hiding her stuck up side, when the guy's leave it comes out. I recall now that her teeth where crooked, but she's straight now and stunning. Jewel even had a Marilyn Monroe white halter swimsuit on that's hugging her hips, with her hair blow dried straight not curly. India kept ringing in my ear until I brought it to her attention saying: "Aaight…she looks good… gosh." I still remember what the other Jewel looked like…. Jewel was more flat chest than me, she just got an enhancement, I thought just sitting there not sharing that with India. India is steaming on broil, hot… knowing that Jewel was her biggest competition. Jewel was everybody's competition. The girl is very pretty with beautiful hair, beautiful skin. I complemented her and asked how was the procedure when we got a chance to talk. I tried not to make it a big deal. It's a busy busy night and after a lap dance I went into the dressing room seeing ghetto fab Isis with her head down on our big trash can in the locker room. I didn't pay it any mind until it was around 1:15 a.m. I walked back in the dressing room and she's still hanging on to the plastic trash barrel. Something wasn't right… I asked her was she alright? Does she need me to go get some water? For a minute I thought she's sleep or hanging over dead. I walked over to see if she's still breathing. She did respond shaking her head yes finally. Isis wasn't on my team however a sister needing help.

I went out on the floor to notify one of her friends. Mia… a girl she buddies up with to do double team games with their customers. Mia's also the one Isis walks out with. She was sitting with someone but I just tapped her on the shoulder and whispered in her ear. After I got her water we walked back in there and Mia slightly pushed Isis's arm. She fell over in her chair unconscious. Mia said that she had took lots of E but didn't know how many. They called EMSA to come and pick her up. I left out when I saw she's taking care of by Mia. After we got paid a lot of veterans went over to Mercy Hospital.

I considered my self one and went up there with India. I told myself I would never do E any more people where dying from that. Isis got her stomach pumped out but was going to be okay.

After a week at work it is becoming terribly slow, very little business on week days. The pressure is sort of on. How you could tell is Mack's short temper. The best time to work was on the weekends. I had enough money put up for each bill I had to put on.

India and I went to the dressing room one night. I'm fixing my hair close to the light bulb mirror. India is reaching in her purse for something. She pulled out that ol' dollar bill. India said: "Come on Lonnie just try it." "Girl…Why don't chu go on with that? Why you want me to try it? What could possibly be the big deal."

With no one in the dressing room I grabbed her dollar and her straw and took a snort of it and it's like: "BAM." It's definitely a hit that instantly gave me booming boost of energy. I could not believe I did it. It's better than E. I felt like here I AM – And I feel GREAT. I started working and made lots of money that night and it was on a slow weekday. That Friday I did it again on the low with just India to know. It was a clean quick high. I didn't want to make it a habit. I made a bunch of Dow cashing in that night a G.

Barron came in and I'm so scared to approach him because I didn't want him to suspect anything different about how I'm acting. I went to him and acted normal however hyper and bubbly on the inside. In the same breath scared. Tonight… I didn't want to drive alone and I wanted him to follow me. Since Lucky's been calling me after work saying that he's on the block looking for me. I had Barron there to protect me. He said sure no problem he would come stay. When he got into my place I felt safe. I got ready for bed while he's in the living room getting ready to eat a sandwich. We slept in the same bed but we didn't sleep together.

He knew that I didn't need another emotional attachment right now. That morning I started regretting what I had did these past two nights. I pulled up my eye mask and broke down crying. He reached out and held me in his arms... tighter and tighter. I did so much crying that my nose started running. I cried so hard but not too loud. Snot is all on his chest that I kept wiping off. Even when I tried to explain to Barron that I did something I never thought I would do. I couldn't get it out. He kept asking what's wrong. "I did.... coke and......... that's not me." I cried for the simple fact that I broke my vow to my friends back at Langston, Yvonne and Teresa. The vow was that we would never do any hard core drugs like that.

Two weeks had past and I'm up on doing the same thing. I never bought it however didn't want to get caught up. I threaten India not to tell anyone. I knew how all them bitches were gossip queens like Sierra. India promised she wouldn't. I'm steadily making a night five hundred to thousands of dollar's easy. Enough that I'm getting some money to put up for a bigger down payment on my car or better yet find one I could pay all up front.

On that weekend I only indulged in the goodies, well India goodies that she offered. When I did that I notice that's how I made more bank. I didn't want to put it on that but it's a big difference in money when I did it, great money. I didn't want any one to know. I told India when she hangs out with them don't even mention it. She can get crazy running off at the mouth. India tended to do that when she got loose I made her promise, she promised. India was caught up in this life style. That's what she worked off of. I didn't want to make it a habit and I had to break it.

Even Bonnie started doing it but to my knowledge she didn't know I did it. I told one other person and that's Nicole because I trusted her. She knew about the game and she did it on the low. She looked straight dead at me expressionless. She's stunned without anything to say not even confessing to me now that she did it. After that night I never saw Nicole again.

I'm cool and collected not acting wild & crazy, just chilling feeling like a million bucks sitting at the bar. I didn't change, but it was an intense high. I started to become overly self conscious of everything. Did I look like I'm on coke? Is my nose running? My nostrils felt clear however it had a burning sensation.

With my regulars I became self conscious. Could they tell? I didn't act too bubbly but myself.

Same night Jamonos came to the club to talk. He needed another favor after the incident a few weeks ago. He gave me the details, it's going to be the same thing only me giving Ramone forty G's that's it. Not with me bringing any kind of work back. Jamonos is going to give me fifteen hundred for doing it. I'm with that having that large amount is risky but since I'm a female I was low risk for any kind of danger like that. I'm a good girl and I look like one.

On weekends is when I really partied. An hour into the shift I got a Moet bottle, a hundred dollar drink and then I had one hundred and fifty dollars in tips. I'm heavily intoxicated, however maintaining. I had snorted coke in the middle of the shift. I got another hundred and two sixty dollar drinks, and five twenty's. I smoked half of a blunt with Justice during work. After work I smoked a whole blunt waiting to get paid having 46 drinks that night, after we got paid and full for our services. I walked to my car. India didn't work that Friday. Taz is in this new shiny red Porsche that sparkled for attention. He called me over to it.

He asked if I wanted to take a ride with him he had something he wanted to talk to me about. He's also dropping something off and he had a stick. Taz and I have never talked business but maybe it's something. I didn't see anything wrong with it I've rode with him before. Plus it's my first time in a Porsche. We dropped off my car at India's and before I got in the Porsche I said: "You're going to bring me back to my house right?" He said "Yeah, ride with me somewhere."

"Alright…" I said but thinking cool a favor. We drove all the way to Silver Springs Maryland. This chronic that we were smoking was out of this world. It made me so high. I never felt this high before in my life and I so badly wanted to come down. I knew my limit and I stopped on half of that blunt. Only to add to how I'm feeling before. O my…I'm now out of my mind high. When we got to this ritzy neighborhood we came to a big two story house with a front yard which is rare in these parts. It's a beautiful house that didn't have any lights on. "Come in with me."

"Naw……..naw go ahead go inside and get what you needed to get. I'll wait out here."

I felt so weak and couldn't move. I'm comfortable where I was but wanted this high to go down.

"Come on…will be in here just for a minute."

He came over to the passenger side door and insisted that I go in by opening the door and gently grabbing my arm. My arm dangled back to my side, because I couldn't move. I'm so weak. He insisted that I get out by using his weight and strength pulling me out the small compact car. He held me all the way to the door got me in the living room to a couch. He put on the T.V. and said he'll be back. At this time I'm weak and too intoxicated. I'm still conscious of my surrounding but wanted to go home. I kept fading in and out with my vision

257

as I dosed off to sleep. I got so sleepy. I laid my head down because the green had me gone. There for a good ten to fifteen minutes. I'm so intoxicated that I barely heard Taz jump on the couch. That's when I felt him come closer to me pulling up my shirt kissing my waist side. Then he started feeling up my skirt.

"Now wait a minute I didn't come here for this...Stop." I said sitting up. He pulled my thighs back down and that's when I started repeatedly: "NO...Don't DO this. What about Iesha? I'm not trying to DO this?"

Him being in a zone with his high he didn't even respond to what I said but with persistence of trying to get to my panties. I couldn't handle his strength so I guarded my private part with my hands screaming no.

"ARE YOU LISTENING TO ME? T PLEASE.....STOP... I'VE BEEN RAPE'D BEFORE DON'T DO This," I screamed out and to pout up a cry, again feeling so weak.

My Brazilian cut panties had elastic strap on the waist side. He started to pull at them and one side broke. I let go of my private area for a split second trying to pull it back together. Like a vulture Taz started going at it giving me oral sex. With me saying the same no and then all of a sudden giving him one sign of it feeling good he got on top of me penetrating. I was saying: "*O MY GOD...O NO.*" Then thinking: *How did he get his pants down so quickly.* "PLEASE...**NO**...UGGggghhhh STOP," I said repeatedly.

I tried with all my strength to get him off of me. Hearing me cry finally made him stop. I pushed him off of me and jumped up grabbing my purse as dizzy as can be. I wanted to get out of there and call a cab. I'm feeling blind trying to find the front door in this dark house. As soon as I found it Taz met me there to stop me.

"Lonnie I'll take you home. I'm sorry my fault. Come on"

"NO...I can't believe you wouldn't STOP. I'm telling Iesha about this. You raped me," I said pushing his arms away from me.

I finally unlocked all the locks on the door I pushed myself out the door and started calling a cab on my cell phone. He tackled me down on the ground trying to grab my mouth but I had enough strength to block him.

Repeating: "Who you calling?" He got on the crazy and paranoid side thinking I'm calling the cops. I kneed him in the stomach and took off down the street running out the neighborhood just trying to get away to the main streets.

I called a cab and they picked me up fifteen minutes later at a gas station. On the way back to my place Taz is calling trying to explain that he didn't rape me saying that I liked it. "NO I DID'NT. You're a fucking lie and a rapist. You're fucked up," I said hanging up in his face.

He called back a few times but I didn't answer. I'm feeling sick and everything in me started to settle in more to the highest intensity.

With me having all these drugs in my system. I'm heavily intoxicated. I'm scared to notify the police. I should have never went with him is what I kept repeating. Being ambitious thinking it's another come up.

I got home and started spitting up something white in the toilet which I knew I had too much. I started crying...crying hard and I cried out to God on my knees saying: "PLEASE................ TAKE ME...PLEASE...O GOD....PLEASE just take me Jesus...I can't.... I'm on my knees rocking by the toilet. And the first thing that came to my memory is how my Mother used to correct me by saying: "Stop saying I can't. You can do all things through

259

Jesus Christ who strengthens you," Quickly got up in my spirit. I got up and stood. I looked in my mirror as usual after a good cry. Looking over all my flaws inspecting them closely, trying to love and embrace my scars. Wondering why my life feels cursed. I was living a nightmare. I cried and cried again… and again. Where is my life heading? After that month I gave it up. No more coke for me. It wasn't my style.

I couldn't understand I had been sexually abused twice in my life. The second time I'm too scared to go to the hospital. I kept thinking they would examine me and see drugs in my system. Plus I had a business going with Taz's partner Jamonos. I didn't want Taz to get away with it. I'm in deep thought about it. I'm thinking: *How was I going to tell Iesha what happened*? I made up my mind that I'm going to be straight up and tell the truth." I spent a week and a half out of work which is cool for me. First half I went to the doctor to get a thorough check up from the GYN. I'm thankful that I had negative signs of all STD's and my HIV test. I never have and I plan that I never will.

I went up to New York for a holiday rented a room from Crowne Plaza, stayed in the room getting room service and shopped for a day. I relaxed that whole weekend. When I got back to work Taz would come in Oasis and I would sit with him just to get drinks while he explained himself.

I said to him: "I told you no. If you would've stopped that would have been respect but you didn't you kept going. And that's really fucked up. You're fucked up. You had something in that weed. I don't care what you say I have never felt that way before in my life." He constantly denied that he did. After that he had very little to say but kept apologizing.

260

I felt like when I told Iesha it should be face to face. She called me that Sunday and was going on and on how much she loved Taz and there thinking about getting engage. *Engage*: I thought to myself.

"Are you sure he's the right one for you?" I said to her. She believed he was. She's coming in on Friday. She needed me to come and pick her up from the airport. I'm nervous for some reason in telling her. I knew I wanted to because I had never done a female friend like this before.

One night after work we were getting dress. India's feeling weird. She told me she had some goodies with Melissa. India is quiet about it but was so shook up that she wanted me to drive her Land Cruiser. After getting paid she decided that she wanted to drive over Melissa's house and ask her why she's feeling this way. India started flipping out in the car. Slurring and talking crazy while her hands were shaking.

"What's wrong with you India? What did you take?" I said very concerned.

"I did some coke with Melissa but Lonnie it was something else. Devine said Melissa had special K."

"What's that?" She explained as we drove to Melissa's. We got over to Melissa's place. Melissa is just pulling into her garage.

"What the Fv<k did you give me?" India said walking up to Melissa.

"Nothing," Melissa said startled to how we approached her unexpectedly.

"Naw you gave her something different," I added.

"I swear Lonnie that's what I gave her. India I gave you regular coke. India what's wrong?"

India said sounding mad: "I feel funny alright."

"She told me you gave her something called special K," I said to Melissa.

261

"No I had that but it's not what I gave India."

We walked away but India was still shook up. "See…that's what I'm talking about you need to let some people loose Donia (India). She probably did give you that stuff. You need to give it up. Your daughter is here now. You need to stop. I'm not doing it anymore…"

India is scared to go to the hospital because of the substance that's in her system. She also didn't want to be alone while she slept so I spent the night with her. Donia's little girl is there now. She had been in Ghana with her mother. She's asleep when we got there in India king sized bed. The next morning her daughter Avie is up bright and early smiling under the covers at me. She's beautiful little girl with slanted eyes. She looked just like India but lighter skin.

I told India about my situation with Taz and how I'm going to tell Iesha. India believed that I should, she didn't want us to lose the friendship that us three had.

When Friday arrived I had plans to pick Iesha up at 2:35p.m. at the airport. I wasn't feeling well being my first day of my cycle. I'm hurting for many ways. My cramps and throwing up plus getting the strength to explain what happen. I got to arrivals and stayed in my car to pick her up. I called her on her phone twice she didn't answer. I waited and waited for a good hour. I didn't want to leave and then come back out there to get her. After another thirty minutes of circling around the airport I called her phone again. She answered saying she's upstairs. "Upstairs," I said after I got off the phone with her.

Upstairs is where you depart from the airport. That's another weird thing, why would she have me waiting all this time in arrivals where she should be. I planned to wait until we got to my place to tell her. We went to Panera's Bread to get lunch. She's now back to wearing her hair long. After we got to my place and we got back to conversing on the latest. I broke the news to her explaining every detail of how he abused me.

"O My God... Are you serious?"

"I'm very serious.......I kept saying no. It's so fuck'd up," I said about to cry.

I explained that I should not have been there but I thought it was dealing with business.

"Jordyn were going to get him...Okay," Iesha said looking me straight in the eye.

"Just wait..." She kept repeating. Iesha sort of knew the deals Jamonos and Taz ran in fact she knew more than I even imagined. She asked if I still hung with Jamonos. I told her yes but nothing serious.

Iesha needed to stay with me for a couple of weeks. She loved my new place. It's a cute home for me. Iesha became Mocha again getting a job back at Oasis. Another goal she set is to get her car from her step mom and step sister. She's going to try to steal it to take the car with her, whatever it took. She needed transportation where ever she was stationed at. Plan B is to make enough money dancing for the down payment on another car. The first two day's she's busy the next two days were slow for her, if I didn't hook her up with several drinks she wouldn't have made money.

The weekend I noticed how Mocha is taking all my money with the guy's that come see me. My banker, professor and a street hustler came in and she approached them never once pulling me in to win. Plus the guy's she knew. I felt it's shady however I didn't want to reveal my feelings. Iesha only worked a week. She made money which was good for her to stack but never once repaying me that fifty back.

Instead she went shopping with her anonymous friends to Towson, never once inviting me to go.

Sometimes she borrowed my car. It's alright though because I'm focused on my summer goal. By the end of the summer stack my money up so I can put an end to this sin. But something within is recalling me back when we were in Chicago. How she and Lucky looked so much alike. Same nose, skin tone and high cheek bones. For some odd reason I couldn't let it go or shake it that this girl might be faking it. I cut back telling her so much about Lucky.

Jamonos came in on a Thursday night. He had the plans hooked up tight. As always he runs down the plan. He makes sure I understand every move. We were going to congregate at that same house close to that hill and pick the money up from Taz. When he mentioned Taz's name I rolled my eyes and he immediately asked what's up. Looking dead into my eyes, he acted like he didn't know. I figured Taz was embarrassed by his actions and didn't tell Jamonos. Jamonos kept saying in due time I'll tell you when we're going to do it.

I played it off and told him Taz is acting up with Iesha. He went back into the plan. I was going to be transporting eighty thousand dollars to Philly to Ramone again this time we were going to a house and count the money there. And Ramone is going to bring me back to the Train Station. This was going down Sunday night. They would collect all the money they needed to get some work I'm bringing back. This time I'm nervous because it was going to be the big Louis Vuitton duffle bag full of his products packaged neatly. Do you know how many years I could get for this, even being involved with this, but I needed a route out and this is my ticket so I'm with it.

When Saturday came and I'm trying to think of smooth sailing, everything is going to sail through okay. I

264

got a call and a familiar intelligent voice answered me back. It's a voice I haven't heard in a while that brought a smile to my face. It's Dr. Roderick Boyd, the John Hopkins heart doctor. He wanted to meet at McCormick'& Schmicks. He stopped in to show some interns a little something at the hospital and had to return to D.C. He's been busy with his health clinic that finally came to life after a whole year. A brand new facility he showed me some pictures.

I'd told him about my accomplishments with my Misa Hylton intern. I told him how I'm doing well in school. I shared how I saved my money and was trying to get out of the entertainment business.

To make up for lost time we went shopping at the downtown Harbor and a trip to the Spa for me. He's a good friend that made me happy with no strings attached. He made me smile or be happy every time I'm with him. He dropped me back off to my place and headed back to D.C. That night we had summer shower's it rained the whole night.

The next day I took it easy and watched church on T.V. I turned to a minister by the name of Dr. Frank Reid preaching on renewing your mind set. I liked his style of ministry and it quickened my soul. At the end of his message I discovered it's the church a guy name Otto told me about. India and I were going to go next Sunday because we both were looking for a church home. I needed it for my soul.

I tuned everything out and took a nap. I woke up at 7:13 in the evening. I got out of bed dressed up in casual clothes. The sun sat in the middle. Jamonos and I had planned for him to pick me up at the club and we were going to ride out to do it. I told Jamonos that I still wasn't situated in a place, just in case he wondered why I didn't want to be picked up at home. On the inside I'm nervous shaking in my sneakers but was real chill about it on the outside.

I had one of my business savvy regular's print up a check close to the amount I had. The check looked endorsed. Jamonos thought I was clever chick he wondered why he didn't think of that. We got to the house around 8 o'clock. It's getting dark just a little light of the sun but gradually going down. We parked the truck in the back of the row houses. As always I check my surroundings. Taz is there inside counting the last of the money in the money machine.

Taz kept his head down not wanting to look at me. I couldn't stare at him either. He disgusted me to look at him. I wanted to get it over with. Jamonos and Emad started talking about picking a rental up for something next week. Emad is a part of the grinding division of their deals made.

Very neatly Taz put it in the bag stacks with a cardboard ban around the thousands of hundred dollars. I got use to holding that kind of money for Jamonos. I vowed that I would not let him down. I stood next to the door waiting on them to pass the back pack to me. "Check to see if it's heavy?" Jamonos said passing it to me. I put the bag on my shoulder and said: "No it's cool." But I'm thinking this thing is heavier than a mug but I didn't want to complain.

I glanced down at the designer rug. I started thinking: *The five thousand dollar's I'm getting sounded good. I wasn't going to play with this money. It's a come up to set me on getting a real j-o-b. For real... last time, time out for this. This ain't me, my family would be so hurt if I end up getting caught up and sentenced.* I got in my zone of positive thinking making sure I had my part of the plan

266

down. Jamonos wanted everything to look normal and
smooth. He's told me before when he has funny feelings he
drops everything and cancels it. This time he just wanted to
get it over with and move it. He had been holding out on
this deal for a month.

One time he told me that he had been noticing a
black Denali Yukon for two weeks. He didn't think much
of it because there's a lot of black Yukon's, not until this
same one with no front license plate was down on the block
of Baltimore Street in traffic six cars behind him one night.
Jamonos is always watching stuff like that. Little did I
know he had that same feeling right at this very moment.
Jamonos saw the same SUV coming down the hill in the
kitchen window. And instantly knew that it's an undercover
vehicle. Suddenly Jamonos pushed my arm and said:
"*RUN*…Don't Take The Car Just GO."

Two steps to the backyard I pushed myself out the
back screen door. Looking around nobody is in the back. I
secured the bag taking four sprints and took all my power
to leap my body over the gate, with all my strength. Thank
GOD we were behind some woods. I can see the dark
shadows of the trees.

Running in between trees I took off running like a
track star. I looked back once and saw from a far red and
blue flashing lights behind the back of York road. I'm
scared and didn't know what to do but save myself. In my
mind I kept picturing my family and how disappointed
they'd be so I ran even faster. I ran and ran through the
woods like a for real scary movie I even tripped in some
mud. Mud splashed all on my upper body and knees. I'm
glad I wore jeans. I took a deep breath. That's when I
listened just to hear if I'm being followed. No signs. My
heart is beating double time. I'm now by a golf course right
off of York road. I knew Ty my good friend lived off that

road. Since it's gated I called him on a pay phone at a
community shopping center. I hoped he's there because I
didn't want to be in these muddy clothes having a bag full
of money in this back pack. The phone rung and rung but
no answer, *F- it*. I called a cab at a Chinese food restaurant.
I'm scared, nervous and thankful to God. I mean I didn't
leave a trace but worried about Jamonos. I hope they didn't
have work in the house. And usually Taz and Jamonos are
smart about that. Jamonos and I had planned if anything
happens to him on what to do. With whatever work or
money I have to always give it to his sister Joy. I had her
number. I called a cab and went home and showered. In my
robe I sat in my bed and starred at the money. With
thoughts of: *Man that's a lot of money. If they go to jail
would it hurt them not to have the money?* But I wanted to
stay loyal to Jamonos because of our respect for each other.
We had gained almost a two year friendship. I couldn't take
his money but I'll take Taz's half for what he did. I hid the
money in a place no one could find it, over my cousin
Lauryn's, in her garage. Since I still had Iesha as a guess in
my home I had to be careful.

I couldn't go to sleep. Not a wink I tossed and
turned until finally I drifted off in the early morning. As
soon as I was comfortable in my sleep I heard the key
unlock my front doors. It's Iesha. She got dressed for bed
and climbed up in my huge bed. After she got comfortable
in her sleep I couldn't get back into mine. Something inside
of me a voice from within kept repeating: *"check on your
door, go see if it's locked, HURRY, Get up."* Finally I
listened and went to check my door. I grabbed the door
knob first and it opened right up. I'm amazed that my door
is unlocked. I listened to what I heard on the inside. I'm so
restless that I went back to bed. In a few hours of sleeping
Iesha is in a deep sleep but started to toss and turn so much

I started to wake up. All of a sudden she reached over and grabbed my neck. I quickly grabbed her forearm to move away and said "Esha." Still in her sleep she just she rolled over falling deeper in her sleep I thought: "This fool is crazy."

Something is up and the whole situation was weird. For one thing her leaving my door unlocked and then her reaching out in her sleep to grab my neck. I didn't sleep the rest of the night just pretended to. The next morning I planned to tell Iesha she had to go. It's going on the fourth week which equated out to a good full month. I felt used and unappreciated. She mainly stayed away but had her bags parked in my walk in closet. That morning she didn't slip out while I was still sleep. I got up and did my regular wash up things. I went to the living room where she ate her yogurt. "Iesha...Look we have to talk."

Iesha gave me her excited attentive look.

"Iesha...How much longer where you planning to stay? Don't you have somewhere else you can stay like with family?"

"No...I don't have a close family like you. I hadn't been assigned a city yet but I should know this week. I'm actually planning to move out Tuesday but I'm trying to get my car back."

"Well about last night. What was wrong? Did you have a bad dream?"

"What?   What are you talking about?" Iesha acted like she had no earthly idea of what I'm talking about.

"You don't remember grabbing my neck?"

"NO...Are You Serious..." Suddenly Iesha's cell phone started ringing. Well there's my ride." She grabbed her bag and grabbed the door handle but stopped and turned back to me and said: "Did you talk to Jamonos last night?"

I didn't know what to say and didn't know if she could be trusted. "Yeah we talked for a little bit. She nodded her head and said bye. I didn't know what was going on. What did she know? She had an ill side to her.

Chapter 26

Small Winnings

I wondered about the mysterious and furtive mannered Iesha. But it didn't stop my plans for the day. Barron knew of a place that had a nice selection of Mercedes to look at. We went to breakfast then the BMW of Towson and looked at a 2001 bubbled eyed 320 Mercedes Benz. I first admired the car while Barron watched with a smirk. He found out a woman sold cars here, she's really good with making deals. We went in there to meet the sales lady and get the keys to test drive. She's a beautiful woman with fair skin named Ms. Crawford. All three of us got in to drive it. It's a beautiful silver and black interior with wood grain. We went around a couple of blocks then caught 83 Parkway. Inside I loved it. I couldn't believe it; my goal of getting it is finally here. I loved Barron for this. I'm glad he put trust in me. I guess when we hemmed Kiwi up it showed how down I could be.

Barron co signed and I showed the information I had. We sat in her office for a good fifteen minutes she came back and asked what kind of a down payment. I told her its fifteen thousand she nodded her head down as she's writing. "You know this is going to bring your car note down," she said before walking away. We signed the papers and she had someone from detailing department detail it out.

"O...that's great," I said smiling.

With Barron I told him everything, well almost everything. You would have thought he's my live journal. I told him things that were occurring recently, the only thing is that I didn't tell him about the money but I told him how weird Iesha is acting. He asked: Did I want him to get her out of my place because to him that sounded dangerous.

They had my new baby Benz shined up. I couldn't help but to smile. The last thing Ms. Crawford did was put my tag on my new Benzy, small winning but in my big head a big win. I embraced Barron for a long time.

"Thank You. This means so much to me. I appreciate it a great deal," I said to him. "I know," Barron said looking into my eyes with his adorable smile.

I went to White Marsh Mall where they had Victoria's Secret. On my way there I got a call from Iesha asking me what I'm doing. I told her I'm in White Marsh. Then she asked did I want to go out to eat. I told her I already called in take out at the Olive Garden.

We got off the phone when I entered the mall. I did a walk around to my favorite shopping places extremely excited about my new car. After leaving out the mall walking to the parking lot I saw a gold bubble eyed Lexus rolling by but it had new spinning wheels. I played it off acting like I didn't see. What if it's Lucky's car? I hurried to get my keys to the car but it's too late I saw the Lexus do a double back down the one way.

Getting out of his car quickly to grab me by the arm asking where have I been and why come I haven't answered his calls. I didn't know he called because every

272

time he called it's private. And I shouted to him: "I Don't Answer Private Calls Anymore Especially NOT Yours," getting out from under him.

Reminiscing of all the things he did to me. I'm startled, a part of me wanted to get far away from him and a part of me wanted him again. We share something that's so rare. I wanted him to really see my pad. I don't know...It was just to show him my independence. I gave him up and now I wanted him to be mine.

He looked at what I'm riding in and was trying hard to not let me get away. "Did you get my letter," I said.

"What letter?" He said.

I rolled my eyes saying: I left a letter on your car on Cold Spring. I know it was your car. He acted as if he didn't know.

"Look I have to go," I said pushing away.

"No I'm going with you."

"No Lucky. We are through. You and Suga had something going on and then you have a girlfriend."

"No I don't.....Jordyn I swear I don't," he said grabbing my upper arms

"No... Lucky...I can't let you. It's OVER. Please don't follow me," I said to him snatching my arm away getting in my car.

He wasn't taking no for an answer. I got in my car and drove off. I'm watching my rearview hoping he wasn't following. Sure enough he was two cars behind me. I detoured all around White Marsh mall parking lot. I found another parking spot quickly to get into Olive Garden. I stayed there for an hour. I knew that Lucky had other business to attend to. When I walked back out to my car there's no sign of Lucky. I finally went to my suburbs of Cockeysville. When I got to my neighborhood there's a

273

park and I stopped to see if I could see a gold Lexus following me. The coast is clear and no sight of Lucky.

When I got settled and reality struck that I got my dream car I screamed as loud as I could. When I got home I parked it next to my Neon that I still planned to drive to work. My new car is a pride and Joy. I didn't want to tell Iesha that it's my car. Tuesday came and I'm almost relieved that she's leaving; the grabbing on my neck stunt was enough. We made it a pizza night with us ordering pepperoni for me and cheese for her. We watched the Queens of Comedy however Iesha is leaving, still on that mission to get her car back. When she's getting ready to go she stopped at the door strangely saying: "You know that's a whole lot of money. They're really not going to miss it."

"What do you mean?" I said not really having a clue of what she's talking about.

"What are you planning to do with the money?" She asked.

"How do you know about the money," I said to her.

"T told me some things too. With his side of it I'm going to need maybe for a down payment."

I wondered did she know how much money I'm hiding that I hadn't touched.

"I haven't touched that money. I'm not until I get in touch with Jamonos's sister. I've been calling. I even tried calling the jail and they say they don't have an inmate by that name. So I'm holding on to it," I said sitting on my couch.

She back closer to the living room area and said: "Do you think Jamonos is worried about that, he's not even concerned about the money. Do you know how many businesses they have?" Throwing her heads back like it's nothing.

I cut in and said: "With what he does... of course he's going to be tracking his money. I want to at least get word from him on want to do."

Iesha smiled nodding her head down then looking up saying: "Don't worry about him I'm telling you to keep it. They're going down."

"We don't know that," I said. Iesha is kind of pissed by her looks however playing it cool then she said: Have you ever run track?"

"Track...What makes you ask that?"

Iesha looked around with a clueless expression then said: "I don't know the way you leaped over the fence Wow, you ran like a track star." (With a low tone giggle)

She made my body shut down in my seat thinking: *How in the world does she know that. I never told her that. She wasn't in the house.* I kept a cool, calm and collected expression but I'm puzzled on how she knew.

She looked at me and said: "Keep some of T's part for the way he treated you. No one deserves to be done like that....But I do need some money from his thirty thousand," Iesha said gathering her stuff again.

I'm still hypnotized by her and her mysterious ways, I said: "How much?"

"O just twenty thousand." Her cell phone started ringing she said: "I gotta
go, Bye."

I slowly said: "Bye."

She left however I'm still nailed to my seat thinking what is she trying do? Wondering how she knew. Jamonos didn't want her to know any of the business he ran. The only person she could have gotten that from is Taz but I figured he's in jail. When they got hemmed up at the house how would she have seen how I leaped over that fence. How did she know?

275

When I think too much I want my favorite snack food, popcorn and rocky road ice cream. At the store I go in there to get one thing and come out leaving with bags of food to cook especially for my Sunday dinner. As I left I went to fill my gas tank up with premium. I got to my parking lot. As I gathered my groceries out of my new whip. I turned around Lucky is standing right there making me jump.

"O MY GOD. You scared me. How did you…."

"I was at the grocery store and I saw you," he said

I didn't see where he came from or what car he's in, he just appeared. I'm more watchful than that.

"What do you want Lucky?"

I wanted to see him but I didn't want him to know where I stayed just in case he starts to act crazy but it was something about him. Was it his lips giving me kisses? I could look past the Suga thing but I didn't know if I could trust him. I let him walk me to my place because I didn't want to get loud. Once again I amazed him on how lavish I'm living. I put my groceries away and questioned him about his involvement with Suga. He confessed that all she did was sucked his you know what. He promised me that he did nothing else. Which I knew is a lie that I didn't believe. It made us have an argument and I don't like to argue or raise my voice.

"I need you to leave Lucky."

He starts trying to reverse the argument into how I need to tell my parents what I've been doing, trying to make me feel guilty.

"Did you tell your parent's you've been stripping? You need to tell your mom."

I asked him again to leave. For some strange reason I couldn't make him leave. It's like he knew I wanted him to really stay. He got back to his cocky comfortable self

276

saying: "Come here," with his authoritative sexy voice. I walked over to the couch and sat with him. He started to peck my lips softly with his lips then to kissing passionately… so much that he grabbed me up and took me to my bedroom. Again my heart got wrapped with his magnetism. In my hallway I made him stop and told him to let me go. "I cannot sleep with you and I really mean it." He still wanted to stay the night. He just held me but I couldn't sleep, finally I did that early morning. He got dressed quietly getting ready to leave. As soon as the front door shut I got up. I waited thirty seconds to tip toe out to see what he's driving. I hide behind my complex building. Looking around for his shiny Lexus instead the brake lights of a new modeled black SUV

The next morning I got up and saw that Iesha didn't come in that night. I went to my cousin's to get twenty thousand but in my mind I'm shocked of how she knew I ran that hard. Was she there? Was she the police? And another thing I have to get the nerve to ask her is she related to Lucky. It's something in my heart that I already knew the answer to. When I got back Iesha is there gathering her stuff by the door. In my mind something is telling me to ask what I have been wanting to since the Chicago trip. She gave me a check for fifty dollar's for when I loaned her some money.

I put the twenty thou in a Victoria's Secret bag and gave it to her. I didn't want any problems. I just asked her what kind of car she's going to get. She said an E class Mercedes Benz. I nodded my head and smiled knowing that's our style. When we were saying our goodbyes and she thanked me. I said: "Iesha have a seat I need to talk to you about something real quick." She's very attentive with her bright glow on her face.

"Is Lucky your brother?"

"No…. my brother's name is Teron."

"Well….."

We heard a horn blow repeatedly and she said: "O that's my ride," giving me a hug around my neck saying bye and thank you. "Did you need any help with the bags," I said to her. I thought she would but she quickly said no she's got it.

"Okay… well call me when you settle in." I'm glad to see her go but wanted to be nosy and she how she's leaving. Since my condo is facing the back end of the complex I waited until she got down stairs. Then another twenty seconds so she didn't know I'm following her. I caught the tail end of a black Denali Yukon picking her up. The same one Lucky was driving, I was sure of it. The same one that Jamonos was suspicious about my heart dropped to my feet and I thought I was going too collapsed of being trick, bamboozled and at the same time grateful.

A week past and I hadn't heard from Iesha. I went to cash that check and it bounced. She left me puzzled with all the clues to answer their deceitful plan. Brother and Sister's, a double heart ache. I hadn't heard from Lucky either, when I called him it went right to his voicemail so again I said O Well. Leaving me with unanswered questions that I put the pieces of the puzzle together myself.

2002 Manolo Blanic came out with a timberland stiletto boot that were so hot every celebrity from Mariah Carey to Beyonce' is wearing them. They're hard to find and selling out all over. Everybody at work talked about how much they wanted them especially Gi Gi's high maintenance crew. I too wanted them badly.

At school I got on line to search to find these boots because I wanted to be the first to rock them at work. On the East they were sold out everywhere. The search was on and it didn't take me that long to locate them, well a day in a half. There at Dallas's Galleria mall at Nordstrom's. I guess in Dallas, Texas they weren't feeling them because I called New York, Chicago and California's Nordstrom stores. It took three days for them to make it on my door step. I'm so excited jumping with this white big box. That weekend I went to work showing off my new Manolo Blanic boots and 320 Mercedes Benz. I walked in the club Gi Gi and Autumn's eye were glued to my feet as I stepped to the locker. After work when we got dress Autumn and Gi Gi were both ashamed to pull out there knock off Man no no's.

The guy that runs to New York to get there Christian Dior and Louis Vuitton purses turned out to be giving them fakes like they're the real deal. I made their jaws dropped when they saw India and me get in my new silver whip. I even parked in the same parking lot as Gi Gi to let her know it's me.

Now at work everybody's on my team and half of them envied me. Yeah my life is going on and I had everything I could possibly need accept Aaron.

On the D.C. radio station they announced that the Roca Fella Family is going to perform at the MCI center and there's going to be an after party at the Insomia night club. "*YES! I'm going,*" I thought in my mind. I wasn't with going to the concert by myself. I just planned on going to the after party at the Insomia. I got dressed in my most expensive looking outfit from Arden B. The one they would notice me in. I had a lavender beaded top and some form fitting jeans with stiletto sandals. Very flashy but simple.

Went to Cal for him to whip my hair to make it shine and have krazy body. I traveled alone and got to the

279

Insomia club around 10: 30 p.m. To get in the ticket's where forty dollars that I happily paid because I wanted to kick it with the greatest updated rapper in the world, Jay-Z.

I stood around and people watched for a good hour and a half, had two Apple martinis. They had enough space with four levels however it's packed. I took one good look around and went to the main level to wait some more. Then suddenly the D.J. announced that Jay-Z is in the building. People went crazy. I'm at the corner of the bar standing trying to play it calm and cool. I zeroed my eyes in on a big crowd of females following apparently Jay-Z. I thought for a second and it came to me that I didn't want to go over there. If I did I would look like them. I backed up close by the door. I knew that the crowd is coming to the door for him to get into VIP. The crowd is guiding him closer to me. I took a few steps up to look and I saw him, its two big bald headed brown skin body guards. Memphis Bleek is right behind Jay-Z. I thought two more steps up and we were practically 5 steps away from each other.

They stopped, Jay-Z looked around at the crowd cheering him on then they took three more steps and we were literally across from each other with a big space in between. I could've reached out and touched him. My heart started beating fast. I wanted to squeal so bad for my favorite rapper but I remained calm and quiet. He had on a Redskins Jersey. I knew that it's my time to show my worth. I didn't want to come off as a groupie wanting to sleep with him but a woman he showed interest in. Jay-Z beings three steps away from me now, I just started smiling looking amazed that Jay- Z is so close. I shook my head in disbelief and then he looked right at me. He started scooping his surroundings; the unruly crowd is at Aaah. Looking stunned I said out loud: "…I can't believe Jay-Z…. HOV… Shawn Carter…Jigga Jay-Z is RIGHT here in

280

front of me; I gasped for breath and said softly: "O My God."

He looked at me up and down, that's a good sign. That meant he's checking me out. As they were getting ready to pass Memphis Bleek is following behind Jay-Z. Then they started walking towards me and my heart felt like it jumped a beat. It's now or never to say something. By this time Jay-Z is about to pass me. We spoke with our eyes as he passed, I said in my Midwestern accent: "I want to go wit cha'll," I said looking like a sad sexy kitten. Memphis Bleek responded nodding his head yes saying:

"…Alright Ma…"

That's enough for me that I got right behind Bleek and the body guard let me do it. I lightly grabbed a hold of Bleek's jersey. I felt like a winner, "YES." If I caught their attention I must be one fly female. My confidence level sky rocketed to the sky that night. I'm so happy that I felt like I'm in a dream. I wondered what would happen next. Taking deep breaths thinking: *What am I going to say?* I started mastering things to say in my mind to impress. Abruptly out of my dream world because I still couldn't believe I'm behind Memphis Bleek. We went into the clubs stair way headed toward the VIP room suddenly these guy's got rushed by overwhelming female fans that went crazy grabbing them at their sight.

They were about to rush into me if I didn't get pushed to the side, in the corner. All kind of females were trying to grab these men. The body guards had to intervene by taking Jay-Z and Memphis Bleek up stairs to VIP. I'm tossed in the corner and couldn't move. I'm trapped with females all over the place in this average sized area that's tight with female fans, including me. Thinking *"Fu<k."* *Now looking like them I didn't stand out like before.* I followed the crowd of other females trying to get to where

281

they went. When I reached the door that Jay-Z went into they asked for one hundred dollars to enter the VIP, which is cool because I had it and I went in there. They lead the guy's to an exclusive VIP that was not letting anyone in unless you were industry known. Flirting didn't even help with the man that guarded the door because another notch already tried. I saw Tigga from Rap City. I acted like we knew each other saying: "What's up Tigga?" He said what's up smiling from ear to ear speaking to other people too. He went into this clear glass door where Jay-Z and the others were chilling.

The one I'm in is for the local VIP's. I just sat by the door for a while. It made me pissed. The guards at the door would not let anyone pass unless you were a big shot somebody on T.V. I stayed for thirty minutes then went back down to the main level. By these steps is a balcony with Jay-Z and Ludacris leaning over it talking. Every now and then Jay-Z would pull out his two way and be playing with that. Then Ludacris and one of his boys are picking females out of the crowd to come up. The females had their hands up high as if their in the sea of love dying to get picked. I got as close to the steps as possible but I couldn't get in view. It's like trying to get in a popular club and there are so many people ahead of you. I'm too far from the steps. They were letting the females go up. Inside I finally thought: "forget it" plus I got sleepy wanting to go home. I almost had a chance to kick it or just to speak to the King MC and I wasn't aggressive enough. I got back in my Mercedes and headed to B- More. "O Well" I thought.

Chapter 27

Drama In the club

Since Jewel is back she got all her customer's business and then some with her new figure. When she left India had gained her clientele. Majority of the guy's didn't want to leave India high and dry because most of them had grown close with her. There's tension between India and Jewel now because of that.

They weren't chummy chums like they use to be. They would be on a drink with a guy that came in for both of them. Instead of sharing convo with India Jewel didn't speak at all. And India would initiate conversation but still Jewel remained silent. Then one night Jewel went into the bathroom and India is in there using it. After she got out of the stall Jewel asked if she'd been talking about her. India coping deuces saying: "No....Jewel I don't talk about you." As she said that India gave her the most sincere look. That's all that was said during the night.

After a busy night of making mula there was a big issue with Ice. Apparently close to the end of closing the club down Ice had to go. Really needing to go, I guess she couldn't make it to the bathroom and she peed in the trash barrel behind the upstairs bar. It's located by the stage were customers were watching. I didn't see her do it but I guess she showed her trash-ness to a few customers. Ron the new manager happened to be coming up the steps seeing the whole thing.

So at the end of the night Ron and Ice were sharing words down stairs when we were getting paid. Ice got loud he's getting loud right back. I've never seen this side of Ron. He's this short quiet man with Poindexter glasses on. It got so bad that he raised his voice ten times louder saying she's fired. She started cursing him out saying he can't fire her. Then she went on this trip about how much she's down and has been down for this club and bitches in the club can't fuck with the girls she hangs with. "I GO HARD..... I GO HARD FOR THE PEOPLE I FUCK WITH" she said repeating it loud gathering her stuff. She was mad. Everyone just sitting around waiting to get paid and to get away from the nonsense, she still stood there cursing out loud about no one can fuck with her. India and I both looked at each other and rolled our eyes ready to get paid and get away from her loud mouth. A lot of other girls were annoyed too. Ice wasn't talking about nothing she's just embarrassed she got caught p-ing in the trash. Finally Spider and Big John had to escort her out. "I DON"T NEED YA"LL FV<KING HELP LEAVING," she said in a gangsta way as she walked out the bar.

All of a sudden as she passed Big John trying to guide her out, she punched him in the face. She quickly ran out while Big John rushed after her. Most of the other females were saying how that wasn't right. It took all of Spider and Louie the doorman's strength to hold Big John down from not going after her. DRAMA!

284

After work of course India and I talked about everything that went on that night as we drove home in her Land Cruiser. It had her in deep thought about Jewel approaching her. I could see on her face that it worried her. That's all she talked about on our 15 to 20 minute drive.

"Are you sure you haven't said anything stupid while you be on that sh*t when you're around Melissa or Gi Gi?"

"No........I only talk about stuff with you...you know that. I don't know Lonnie something's up."

"MMMmm...Sounds like some bodies instigating....Just trying to start stuff,"
I replied.

India said in her Island accent. "But why.....I don't bother no body...and I'm nice to everyone ya know."

"I know....Their just jealous. Don't worry about it."
I know I wasn't. When I went there I went for one purpose: Get Money...That's it. I didn't have time to make friends that's going to eventually turn fake...I learned. I'm glad I had India to talk to in the club but I'm born to be a loner and a leader. Only a few females could relate that worked there like, Tiara in school, she quit after that night of Ice's little drama. I never saw her again.

When Friday night came, all the dancer's prepared to have a good night dressing to impress ensuring we looked and smelled good. India is home she felt sick and didn't feel like going.

Miss Diva herself was back, Niya flipping her long micro's. She went to California for two weeks out there making money. And boy did she put on to how much she made. To her Cali was the place. When we were getting dress she's going on and on about it... then abruptly she stopped in her loud conversation on the opposite side of me and yelled. **"O MY GOD... I FORGOT....**

285

GIRRRRRRL….. I Was At A Bank when It Got ROBBED…YES." That's when both sides of the dressing room got in it. Saying: "NO…You playing?" "Are you fu<king serious?" "O My God what happened?" Were things that some girl's where saying.

"Yes…No joke a real robbery and two people died Yo. You know that's real big there."

Even I got interested listening in I couldn't help but to she was loud enough.

"Well what happened… I'm going in to get big bills for my ones from my tips. I'm in line and I heard a gunshot someone yelled: "GET DOWN AND PUT YOUR FU<KING HEAD DOWN NOW."

"They shot the security guard in the head scaring the sh*t out of everyone making everyone scream, even me. I'm praying to God. Girl that's the scariest feeling…. I thought I was gonna die. They made every come into the main lobby room and sprayed the cameras. It was three men dressed in black. One was going for the money and the other two held us at gun point. They grabbed a female that was pregnant pulling her up putting the gun to her head telling the teller's to fill the bags. The pregnant woman is screaming out she's pregnant. Some guy got up and said: She's PREGNANT. Let HER GO. They shot him in the stomach. People were crying and sh*t."

Every now and then Niya exhales a deep breath then go back into talking about it saying: "They finally left. When the police arrived they gathered everyone for questioning. The ambulance made it but it was too late for the people they shot, they were dead by then. It was sad that the guy they shot wasn't even with her but still tried to protect her."

As Niya said her story she had everyone's attention to where our ear's where glued to listening. It's 7:59 p.m.

and most of the girl where upstairs until Mack came up cussing and fussing. Most of the girls rushed but the main stars took their time getting one more touch up. I still had to make sure my hair is right on both sides.

During work Niya's busy either with her customer's or girl's swarming her to hear more of the story. No doubt I wanted to hear more but wanted to get to talk to her by herself. I wanted to know what part of California she was at. Eventually before the night was over I asked. She told me L.A. That same night some major ballers came in. How did I know...they were blinging from ear to wrist... I mean shining. I was sitting with regulars but they're kicking it with Jewel and Niya. 1:15, almost at the end of the shift Niya walked up to me as I leaned back on the walls standing there scooping out my next move for the last drink or introduce myself for a maybe next time.

"Some guy's that we were sitting with earlier are having a bachelor's party for their man getting married. They're giving each dancer three hundred dollars."

I gave her a "so... whatever" look.

Niya understanding what that meant she said: "I know... but girl they got money. Trust me I'm telling you I know them. There big tipper's plus it's only for two hours after we get off. Getting dress includes the two hours so we will be only dancing an hour in a half. Easy money. Justice, Fox, and Jewel are going. Well... Jewel is trying to make up an excuse for her baby's daddy."

"I never did a bachelor's party before because they don't seem safe."

"O this one will be safe I don't play that sh*t," Niya said giving her attitude look then smiling saying: "Are you sure?"

"Where ya'll gonna dance at?"

287

"The Renaissance Hotel. At their top suite at the hotel downtown."

"I want to do it but I'm not with all that fv<king or sucking. I'm just there to dance," I said giving Niya a fierce look like I don't play that.

"Me too…Me too I'm not with that either."

I mean two hundred dollars for two hours ain't bad plus with tips being made for two hours. Plus they're having it at a high dollar hotel. I felt safe knowing it would be more than two girl's going. I'm doing aaight that night having nine drinks with hundred and seven dollar's in tips. I never complain when I made my change. But doing this bachelor's party would set my night off right. Those guys did look like they had money blinged out bright like the rapper's do.

"Alright I'm in."

"Is it okay if we ride with you," Niya said.

See I knew that most of these females didn't have a car and if they did I would make them drive themselves. They probably heard about my 320. I'm glad that I drove my neon. I don't want anyone in my new Benz except India, that's it, a two seat car for two people.

When she added gas money I'm with it saying: "Aaight cool."

Jewel's wasn't able to go. When we got there we pulled up and parked. The hotel looked nice and luxurious. They told Niya the suite number. Justice knocked on the door and when they opened it. They had a corner view of the Harbor. It's a beautiful sight. Big tall glass windows, 13 feet high ceiling in the living room. They had a bar on the other side, two big bathrooms and a master bedroom. Justice and Fox got dressed in the big bathroom. Niya and I got dressed in the Master bedroom. This suite was so fly I knew that we were not dealing with bull sh*t azz guys. This is a classy suite. Its eight guy's all black. The bachelor is a cute Spanish and Black guy. So it's on… they had a nice CD with nice tracks to dance to. The guy's had big wads of money. I'm going to enjoy this. With the lights deemed we got in the living room while they sat on the nice white leather couches. The bachelor grabbed a hold of my hand wanting me to give him a lap dance 1st because they're saying I had a body. All the guy's kept ooohing and aaaaahing when they were looking at me.

Sure the other girls were hot like Fox; she's very pretty with golden brown wavy long locks. Her hair is beautiful down to her back but she kept it in a pony tail. The four of us did our thing and the guy's loved it. We switched so each guy could test our lap dances out. The guy's tipped very well. Every time I moved they're stuffing my guarder belt with ones, fives and tens. Trust me it's a lot of money wrapping around both thighs and garments. So much we had to take breaks stashing ones, fives, tens and twenty's away. Then the guy's got turned on wanting some girl on girl action. I'm not gay and I'm certainly not going to volunteer myself. Fox is out there…. gay and proud. The three of us knew it. So Fox is stepping up to be one. Then Justice and Niya were saying: "Lonnie you. You do it." "Yeah you do it."

"Noooo…I'm not into that. No you do it."
"Go………..Go ahead Lonnie," Niya said.
"Ut ugh. I wouldn't know what I was doing…I don't know."
"Come on I'll do you," Fox said

With five seconds to think about it I got on my back on a soft rug and they crowded around us like they were about to play dice or watch a pit fight. Fox pulled on my tied to the side bottoms taking them off saying: "OK Lonnie just don't cum in my face," and then went at it.

289

Moving her tongue at a face pace. It felt good and it looked good to the guy's so much that they made it rain twenty's, fifty's, five's and one's all over us. The feeling and seeing money rain every where in that circle was a beautiful sight... that I put some of my concentration on grabbing money. I had a hand full of money and I know I grabbed about four fifty's too. Fox did her thing but money turned me on more. We both went away with two- fifty a piece.

I know I got a little bit more money in my top while she did her thing. Just for the show not including what we made for being there plus our stash away tips. We let the guy's know that they had about twenty more minutes and we were wrapping it up going home. Of course the guy's where trying to make passes on us to stay the night, however we were not having that. What a good night and it was safe I went home and stashed my G away in my black velvet circled shaped box. Saturday I planned to rest and pamper myself at a spa for a nails and pedicure. I treated myself to some shoes.

A whole week had past and still India worried about the tension between her and Jewel. On Friday the same old thing smell and look good to impress to make money. It's busy I mean real busy from the time I got on the floor. I got a chance to go to the locker room. To my surprise India is in there blowing on a cigarette. She looked worried. "What's wrong with you? I said to her.

"I don't know Jewel keeps starring at me looking mean and I don't know why."

"Don't worry about that. You making money?"

"A little I'm waiting on Tim to come in," she said.

"Well I have to go back and don't worry about that," I said leaving back to continue this drink.

Around 11:30 p.m. I got a drink with a Black guy up stairs and I'm trying to work on getting him to the

290

private lap dance area. Robert our lawyer friend came in to unwind after another hard day in court. He came up stairs.

When he comes in he just wants to chill. Of course the girls that usually sits with Robert sat with him for a drink like Ali and India. I'm still in the center of the bar with the same guy. We got into a conversation to why my lap dance would give him a natural high. Out the corner of my eye I saw Jewel step to India tapping her on the shoulder while India is sitting with Ali and Robert.

In a corny way Jewel said to India: "You're going to get your ass kick tonight."

"Why? What have I done to you?" India said raising her hands to her side.

Only thing I saw is Jewel reaching to deck India right in the face. That's when I jumped out from this guy's lap to run over there. I heard Robert yelling out: "I DON'T HAVE TIME FOR THIS SH*T," watching it go down.

By the time I got there saying: "What's up? Utt Ugh…Ya'll beta back up," to Jewel and Ali. I'm standing in a b girl stand ready to fight. Ali and Jewel just stood there cuz they didn't want none.

I glanced over at Jewel who's holding her head because blood is streaming down her forehead." I didn't see that India had thrown a half full bottle of beer right at Jewels head. India is cussing loud in her West Indian (Jamaican) talk. It got everybody's attention. I grabbed India to go in the dressing room. Isis had our back grabbing the other side of India. We're helping to sustain India from acting wild trying to explain her self. While Ali and Devine took Jewel in the bathroom. Blood is coming down India's nose so I went to get something to wipe her nose.
"Watch her for me," I said quickly to Isis.
"I gotch chu," Isis said holding India down. I took off my glass slippers because I thought it's about to go down. I

rushed to the bar to get a wet cloth and some ice. Everyone up stairs is still watching and talking about it. Spider the bouncer came up to see what's going on. Thank God Mack isn't there. I got back in the dressing room to care for India. We got dressed and got out of there. We drove to our suburban community pub and got a drink talking about the whole scene and wondering if Jewel was okay. I hoped she was. One thing we knew that it was either India or Jewel that's going to be fired. DRAMA!

Chapter 28

Stood Alone, Solo

The next night we went into work and they let India go. We heard that Jewel went to the emergency room that night and got stitches in her forehead. Something that India deeply regretted. India packed her things and left that night. We suspected that might happen so we came in separate cars. I hated that happened in the first place. Now that my only friend is gone I'm now left alone with no one to talk to and walk to the garage with.

Since India and I heard so much about the Gold club India decided to give that club a try. She went the very next day and they hired her on for day shift until she showed she could work night. It's a different set up than the block. You paid to work there and the rest of the money is yours. The fee's depended on if it's weekday or week nights. Weeknight's fees were seventy- five dollar's and you had to pay a fee to the bouncer's as well. But the key is making the money because it wasn't easy. The Gold club is an all White collared club with majority of the customer's and girls White.

Selena worked at the Gold club and she made money. Selena is a popular name, The Gold Club already had a Selena, making my friend change her name to Sasha, just an FYI (For Your Information) However we will continue to call her Selena☺

Selena is beautiful enough to make money anywhere, even Miami. Since she's on a vacation's pass as a foreigner she traveled the states. And being a stripper she had to go visit one of the best stripping capitals; Florida. She had been settled in Miami working at Tootsies for two weeks.

India was by herself too. She had to start over but she took a few of her regular's with her to the Gold club. She's amazed at the set up of the club. It's very high class. Oasis had nothing on this club fitting one-hundred and sixty people comfortably. India's nervous starting all over again. For her first week she did very well. She began to like the Gold club.

I missed her already. At work I stayed to my business only associating with Bonnie and Devine mostly. Not having my best friend. Girl's like Gi Gi and Alexis thought I would go under but I still stood alone. Girl's wondered: *"Could I make it without India?"* Yeap...I knew I could.

It's a new dancer there. She seemed real outgoing to all the dancers. She's pretty looking like an Audrey Hepbune. Her petite size and hair color too. It looked as if she had a little bit of Asian in here but White. She wore glasses and wore her hair pinned up like Audrey Hepbune. She mixed in with Gi Gi and a little bit of Melissa. It's her first time being a dancer. When she danced she danced like a ballerina with a little bit of jazz. To me it's so funny how she danced, dramatic however unique.

294

Bean is now into Gi Gi and didn't sit with me anymore, all of a sudden. It hurt my feeling for the first time. With other guy's it didn't bother me but not Bean. I grew too close to him and that's a rule, keep it business never personal. Bean and I never did anything outside the club but we had built on to know one another and I loved our visits. But it got at me the he completely shut me off and went on to the next big thing, Oasis's main feature. Now he's buying her bottles. Plus Gi Gi knew how to rub it in for me to get jealous but remember I don't have jealousy within me.

She would play love songs before Bean came to visit her like Brian McKnight "Do I Ever Cross Your Mind." In the locker room all Gi Gi's crew would ask her certain things about someone. However never saying his name but expressing how he made her feel. And it would be while I was in the dressing room too but I just zoned into what I was doing, my hair, make-up or getting dress.

For some reason Justin Timberlake's song "Cry Me A River" became a battle song. Yes something I started again because I walked in on Gi Gi boo oohing one night in the downstairs bathroom. It's funny to me and she knew just what I meant. So that song became heavily played.

With the ballerina stripper I didn't know her name but after a month she got too comfortable. After a good Friday with every one getting dress she told me I had something on my face saying: "O there's something on your face..." She started looking closer trying to tell me where it was. She pointed close to her jaw saying: "Right there.... right there." I looked in the mirror and then realize she's talking about my scars on my jaw. "O no this is a scar from a car accident," I said smiling.
She said loud and sweet: "O... O I'm sorry."
I smiled and said: "That's okay you didn't know."

Next week had past and I set out to start trying to go back to my original self. I still had it, meekness, humbleness, kindness and a beautiful spirit. But my bad side cursing and attitude that's not me. So I set out to not curse any more. I only cursed when I'm thinking out loud to myself or hanging with India anyway but that needed to stop. I wanted to cut that out completely.

The next Thursday at work it's a slow night. In the bar it's at a medium pace with guy's coming in. Every so often I would go to the locker room. By myself I'm on one side praying under my breath softly and meditating at the same time. Miss ballerina girl comes up. I finished on touching up my face and stood up.

She walked up to me and started pointing close to her forehead saying: "Uuugh you have something right......."

Before she could say any more I interrupted saying: "GIRL YOU BETA GET OUT OF HERE," in a ferocious tone bucking her way like I'm going to hit her. She kicked rocks trying to get out of there. It's funny and it made me laugh out loud.

I paused for some seconds looking in the mirror with a straight face with no smile and said: "Forgive them Jesus for they know not what they do," I said out loud and I'm proud that I didn't cuss her out. I slowly walked on the other side were my locker was and there's Gi Gi sitting there quietly patting her face with a pad. I got what I needed and left back down stairs I wasn't going to let these girls get to me. I even thought that Gi Gi might have put her up to it. They even told Mack that I'm bullying them. They thought they could bring me down but Lord knows they can't... I have him.

And speaking of him India and I started attending Bethel AME religiously on Sunday. Going there my

296

relationship increased with spending time and praying to the heavenly Father to take me out my situation. I'm sincere with my prayer. I think I had the answer. I'm still waiting on Jamonos. I kept calling the phone number that he gave me for his sister.

Friday night at work Jewel came back. I ignored her but she made it a means to stand next to me in the mirror so I could see her face. I didn't even pay attention. Close to the end of the night we talked and killed the animosity we might have towards each other. I let her know that was her and India. I made it clear that the rumors she heard were false and India had nothing but love towards her. It would have been better for her to pull India to the side and talk like adults. After work we even walk to our cars together. I acted like a phony just playing along like we were cool knowing things weren't.

On the other hand India is making new enemies at the Gold Club. She's a beautiful dark long haired woman with a B+ body. She should have expected for them to get jealous.

I got a call from my home girl from back home, Yolanda. She just had a big fight with her boyfriend Bear and she desperately wanted to get away. We both came to the conclusion that she should come up here and stay for a while to get away from Tulsa. After a week of thinking she decided to visit. She flew up on a Thursday and had a ticket to come back when she's ready to go home. We caught up and I filled her in on my drama.

I didn't tell her about the situation with Jamonos but the drama with Lucky and Iesha. She's amazed and couldn't believe what I had been through.

After we got back from a dinner we chilled in my living room watching T.V. I got a call from a hysterical

India saying some girls jumped her at the Gold club. She's talking so fast, I told her to slow down. When she got off of work she came over to meet Yolanda and tell me what happened.

At the Gold club they're two girl's dancing, one is on the main runway stage with the pole the other girl is on the small stages walking and dancing back and forth. When the song is over the girl on the main stage has to leave even if she has a line of tips waiting for her. But why would you want to walk away from money. So India's getting her tips this blond headed girl cussed India out saying get off the stage. India went back upstairs to the dressing room to freshen up.

When she left to go back down on the floor, the girl that cussed her out is coming behind her. When India went down the skinny spiral stairs the girl got behind her making India hurry down the steps. The blond headed girl's friend is coming up and they both started punching on India. The bouncer saw the whole thing and didn't stop them.

The next night India had a plan to get the blond headed girl back since they wanted to play that way. She wanted us both go there under disguise acting like we didn't know India. We got there and the Gold club is very classy with gold stars on the top of the ceiling. The club is huge. We stayed there until the end to have India's back if anything popped off. At the end of the night India got dress and we were going to meet her were the dancer's parked.

Apparently something set India off while they got paid because the door busted open with the bouncer making India leave. India is going off cussing them out. The White girl's were behind the bouncer. Yolanda and I got behind her ready to set it off.

The blond girl's friends were holding her back. The bouncer's made us leave but I remembered their faces.

298

After a week of getting away Yolanda left and went back home.

India had to come back on the block. She wasn't going to work at Norma Jeans without me. So she went to a new club called Tiffany's. It was owned by the same owner of Norma Jeans however this club is lower key and laid back. The club is just starting out with a few dancers and India became one of them.

It's slow all over the block. If Oasis didn't pull in customer's no other club did excluding Norma Jean's. I'm having my slow days again. Where I'm getting a few drinks are none just my hundred and fifty dollar base pay and tips. I tipped out the bartender's and bouncer's that night. And a bunch of dancers were doing the same. Jewel and her crew were going out the same time that I was. Loud enough so I could hear a little of her conversation saying: "Can't ball go home."

I was about to let her young, little ass have it but I remained cool ignoring them. At least I remembered Jewel when she was still flat chest having her bad days. Not wanting to go in but since I had that Benz. I had to keep paying my note and my insurance plan. I still had money in the bank however it's to help when I lacked on the block I still kept up with my bills. That's why every time I make a means to work I go to keep up with my cash flow.

So now India and I are back car pooling again. After work one night India and I are walking to her truck. She had a lot of things that were heavy on the brain. I just listened not giving any advice on what to do because it's heavy. I told her I would be there for her. India parked in the parking garage a block up from the block so it's a walk. When you get to the glass door of the garage you have to swipe your ticket. This is a nice secure garage you had to pay a little bit more.

The only thing is that they didn't have cameras scanning the parked cars. We got to her Land Cruiser that's totally trashed. Scratched, windows busted out and eggs on her paint. We both stopped in our tracks stunned at what we were seeing. I looked over at India and tears started streaming down her face. She started going off wondering who did this. It didn't take us long to figure out Jewel was up to this. I noticed Jewel didn't even come to work that night. We went down to the garage keeper to report it. We went back up there to see if it would start. Luckily it did. I had a towel in my bag with a bottle of water. We cleaned it the best we could.

Yeah…Jewel did it, we already knew. India had no other enemies. Jewel wanted to let it die down then strike back. The same night India wasn't thinking and left her work clothes in her truck. Someone came by and stole them. India also let Gi Gi know where she stayed.

But I had India's back and we were not going to let Jewel get away with that. The next few days India rode with me to work but on the weekend got a Pontiac Grand AM.

So the next few days at work Gi Gi and Jewel were getting together doing kiddy sh*t like sitting across from me talking and starring at me. Plus Garland started to come in and have big drinks with Gi Gi.

Before he walked in once I had already put in the songs that I'm going to play. He picked Gi Gi to hug up with at the bar to make me jealous. The songs I played were Musiq's "Girl Next Door" and "Breakdown" sung by Mariah Carey. I hesitated to play the second song once I got every one's attention including there's. But I went ahead boldly and dance to it making them two disappear.

Also Jewel did the worst thing you can do as a stripper… she slept with one of my customers to stop sitting with me. When I would walk in the dressing room they would burst out laughing all of a sudden. When I'm using the rest room and having a smoke break they'd walk in coughing like the smoke bothered them.

To add insult to injury with Bean sitting with Gi Gi now... I would stomach it by sitting at the bar while they're in the back popping bottles open. It would be on a weekday when it's only one level so I couldn't go up stairs to work and try not to see it. Some girl's like her wouldn't take it and go upstairs in the dressing room to avoid it. But when Bean comes in he stays for a while. I just tried not to think about it and be a soldier about it. But still I wondered: *What did I do?* Gi Gi and Jewel knew how to rub it in. I started to get real sick of them. Jewel had it coming too.

One night I'm sitting at the end of the bar all the way in the back. The last seat by the stage. I'm reading because we didn't have hardly any one there. All the guys watching were with someone. Gi Gi comes and stands right in front of me having her back toward me facing the stage. My legs are not under the bar, they're on the right side of the chair where she stood. If I wanted to get up and move around I couldn't. She stood there with her hands on her hip for a good ten seconds waiting on her turn to go up.

I mean what's up; *What was that for?* I thought. I got upset with her invading my space like that. When she got off the stage she went up stairs. After a while I went up there too.

When I entered the empty locker room I approached her to say: "What's up?   Do we have a problem?"

She looked strange and said: "No... what are you talking about?"

"Just before you danced you stood by my chair as if there's a problem. If I wanted to get up out my chair I couldn't because you're there. ALL I'm asking is there a problem because to me you're trying to make it personal."

"NO… YOU'RE MAKING IT PERSONAL."

"NO YOU'RE MAKING IT PERSONAL WHEN YOU GET IN MY PERSONAL SPACE. Where I'm FROM GIRLS WILL WHOOP YOUR HEAD IN FOR STUFF LIKE THAT Okay." When she got loud I got loud to finish what I'm saying. I walked away because I would have broke her.

Wednesday I went to the club when it first opened around twelve. My goal is to not let any one see me enter the club. When I first walk in just go up to the second level steps to get to the dressing room. I saw our new manager Ron and spoke to him. Thinking: *Dam someone saw me-O Well I'm still doing it*" I had a back pack on my back. What's important is what I had in the back pack. You know the bottles that stylist use to put perms or dye on peoples hair. I had about five of them with a little spout. I found Jewel's locker that was lock. I unloaded my bags of bottles filled with bleach, yes bleach.

I took the spout and screwed it together with the first bottle, poured down the open way at the top of her locker. See I knew that her locker stayed messy with her clothes down at the bottom. She should have been like me only leaving my locker with my shoes and care products. I bought in my outfits every night.

I had four more bottles to go I wanted to make sure I destroyed some of her money making outfits. I used every drop I had in each bottle and no one came up the stairs to witness what I'm doing.

The same Wednesday night I came in early and got dressed and wanted to see how Jewel was going to react. She went up the stairs to get dress but never came back down stairs. The other dancer's talked amongst themselves about what had occurred. At the end of the night a dancer named Destiny asked if she could borrow one of my outfits, this tropical looking get up. She should have known better than that. I played dumb and acted like I'm taking it home to wash. I knew if I gave her that bad outfit I would never see it again. The next night Jewel worked and she wore a white tank top and some white panty shorts. To me that's a sign that I had messed some of her things up. I smiled. I'm itching wanting her to say something. She never approached me however had a new CD in the juke box and played Missy Elliot's song "Gossip Folks." In return I played the song too. Then she returned with Christina Aguilera's song "Can't Hold Me Down." I played it as well cause I felt the same way then played DMX "Ain't No Sun Shine then a triple dose with Method Man "Your All I need." (Referencing her cheating on her boyfriend with s guy that comes to see me.) At the end of the night nothing is said.

Saturday when I got there the manager Ron called me into the office. He had to let me go. He didn't want to tell me why but they had to let a few other girls go too. I already knew the real reason why, Jewel had big favoritism with Mack. I left holding my head up with pride. Not that many girls were there when I left but I'm sure that I was talked about that night. I will always remain a legend at the Oasis club in that game I made it far. I left holding no grudges.

I'm out of work again and refused to go back to Norma Jeans. Tiffany's they didn't make that much money over there. I decided to get away from it all so I call my girl Selena. She's down in Miami having fun making money at Tootsies. I told her that I wanted to visit and she's excited. She told me that she would ask the manager's if I could work as well. That's one thing I planned to do is go to Miami and work.

Chapter 29

M.I.A.

I landed at Miami International Airport Sunday around 3o'clock p.m. I just wanted to get a feel of one of the capitals of live entertainment. Selena showed me a little bit of the town in her beautiful convertible car. Its so many high rise apartment places on her street she lived that I thought Selena's doing it big. Then we turn into her parking lot to her two story ran down beach front apartment complex.

Selena is a smart spender. She budgets the g's she made. Once we got into her place she gave me a key that opened the front entrance to her apartment and a key for the apartment. Her place is a room and a bathroom, that's it with a microwave and a refrigerator. A twin bed and a futon couch that lets out as a bed, the futon is what I'm sleeping on. Since I'm staying a week she asked for the money up front to stay, its four hundred dollars. It's almost half of what she's renting the place out for a week. I gave it to her with no problem but thinking: "Damn...I thought we were friends." I knew that Selena is about her money, friends or no friends. We sat and caught up in the car while driving to get something to eat. Selena well her real name

Diana, just got a lipo procedure done a month ago. She's obsessed with her body. Before she had a beautiful one with all the right full curves. Instead of working out she did lipo. She spent ten thousand dollars on it. I'm thinking "Dumb broad, this is what she invests her money in." We got on cosmetic surgeries. She suggested having plastic surgery to me 1st my breast and then wondering why I won't fix my eye. She asked sounding dumbfounded in her Russian and Iranian accent: "Why come." I explained. "Because each surgery it takes time, little by little." She still couldn't understand why it couldn't be fixed right away. "I dunno.... that's just the way it goes."

We went to El Pollo Loco, my first time going. I had grilled chicken and rice dinner that's the bomb. We were going into Tootsies tonight to work. I asked her did she tell the manager's about me and she said yes they knew I was coming. I'm excited and pumped up. I went on a vacation three months ago in Miami and went into Tootsies to see Selena dance. So I'm already familiar with the set up.

When we got to the club we went into the back room. The back door leads to the locker room. It's nothing but lockers and benches to sit. Oasis's dressing room is the best I've seen so far in my stripping lifetime. This dressing room had no comparison. In Tootsie's dressing room you had to go to this one big mirror to sit down and do your make up. How the girl's made themselves up is dramatic. It's so many blonds and boob jobs I lost count. Tootsies had lots of school girl looks and the dominatrix looks. All kinds of body shapes but no one had my body.

The manager isn't there yet. I started putting on my eye shadow nervous wondering how they're going to accept me. I don't know what Selena told them. I still wondered would I be working there. A guy walked by and he looked like the manager dressed up nicely.

"O look Selena is he a manager?" I asked.

She looked kind of nervous looking at me. She played dumbfounded and didn't move. I got up and walked over to him to introduce myself.

"Hello...My name is Lonnie and I'm here with Selena. She told me she talked to a manger about me coming for a week to get a feel of the club, because I'm interested in moving here to Miami." I said that just to get the job for the week I had no intentions on moving to Miami.

Giving me all his attention he said quick as a flash: "O were not hiring right now. But what you can do is fill out an application and it takes about one to two weeks to evaluate and then will call you. Have you danced before?"

"Yes...currently I live in Maryland and I dance at a club called Oasis."

"O...Ok Oasis."

He nodded his head suggesting that I fill out an application and walked off. I didn't try to beg for a job or say that Selena told me I was hired. I walked back over to Selena and she inquired saying in her Russian accent: "What did he say?"

"He said their not hiring... Selena...I thought you said I was hired?"

"That's what they told me...What are you going to do now?"

"I don't know...." I looked around for a phone book to check out some listing of gentlemen's clubs. Called a few to see if they're hiring. Most clubs here are set up on a fee to dance and the rest you pocket and to me that's a win situation however I had to find a club to work at. The clubs don't close down here until four in the morning. I couldn't believe that. I still had my confidence that I'm going to make my money. I gathered myself and things to leave. I had a week which is all good to me. I just wanted to test the M.I.A. out... see... what it's about I'm never scared to go anywhere.

I called one of my regular's from Oasis and he comes down to Miami a bit. Just so happened he's there on a business trip here in Miami. Originally he's from London. He volunteered to pick me up; I have some trust in Neal. Neal is an auctioneer that sold hundreds of thousand dollar sculptures. In the back of his rental Mercedes he had these valuable small figurines that where ten to twenty thousands of dollars.

When he visits Maryland he visits me at the club, very intelligent guy. He spends big money. He picked me up from the Tootsie's club and took me to a restaurant called Houston's. I knew he knew of some Black classy clubs. He took me to one I didn't like. Then he told me about the Black and Gold club. I called them and they're hiring telling me the fee to dance, which was fifty-five dollar's on the weekday and weekends seventy-five. We went by there and it's an old movie theatre turn Strip Club. This club had so much potential than what appeared outside. It was nice on the inside. There were big black curtains all around. It's a nice set up with this royalty theme in the lap dance area. The club had three big stages. One is the main stage, that's the main big room that they only used closer to the weekend. I went just to check it out. Since it's a long day I decided to go back to Selena's place.

By the time she made it in I'm knocked out sleeping. The next morning we sat up and ate bagels with coffee. I wanted to go to the mall for lunch. I came down with enough cash however wanted the money I made to stack up to see how much money I could make in Miami.

308

Since Selena and I weren't working in the same club she offered me to borrow some of her clothes. Like me she had expensive taste. She had a black dress, at the neck expensive looking rhinestones, like a choker.

I went to the Black and Gold club around 9 o'clock that night. When I got there someone is standing in a booth but he's helping another female out. I stood there and waited. He looks so familiar I said: "You look familiar........................ You've been on some videos?"

He smiled and said yeah I'm partners with a lot of Miami rapper's.

He broke down the game that someone had already told me on the phone. I asked as I paid: "Do you think I'll make money here?"

"O yeah you'll make money," He said.

He led me to the back in the decent looking dressing room. Some Miami girls were getting dressed slightly checking me out. Me being me I said an all around "Hello" then got to getting dress then be social later to let them know I wasn't stuck up just getting in my zone. That night all the girls seemed cool. They asked where I was from. I told them Baltimore and they had heard of the block. They weren't haters but congratulators telling me the guy's were going to love me and plus you're a new girl too. So they let me have my own lane to gain most of the guy's money that came. I introduced myself to some of the girl's just to ask how much they make a night here. In this club they had a D.J. that called your name when it's your time to go and dance. They already had a Loni, so I went by Gia. In this club they played nothing but hip-hop and a little bit of R&B. The majority of the customer's where Black dudes. They love some me. For a lap dance it cost a guy only ten dollar's and I thought that's cool compared to the block.

The guy's only had one song with us. It's fast paced money to be made and its guy's waiting for me all night. On a Monday I made seven hundred dollar's leaving at 3 o'clock in the morning. I got a cab back safely to Selena's place.

Tuesday we stayed around her apartment and lounge around resting during the day. Selena went to go work out. What became a routine is going to eat at El Polo Loco's before work which I didn't mind, I loved it. We went back to her place and Selena got ready to go. I stayed around, went and sat on the beach to read until the sun's going down. That's when I started to prepare and go.

So far I'm making money and it's just Wednesday. That night one of those females stole my phone. It's alright though because I just found another Sprint store and bought another one.

Closure to the weekend Neal is coming in to see me. It's Thursday so I wore the black dress that fits me with the rhinestone around the neck. It looked gorgeous on me. With the girls I sensed jealous looks you know the screw face kind pressing down on there lips. I'm working around the Black and Gold club. I met this dude….O My God…he looked like Aaron. He was almost the same color but lighter complexion, height and had hair just like him. He wore it in a pony tail too. I asked if he wanted a lap dance. He said no and he doesn't get lap dances. He just comes in and cased the talent. With that said I became uninterested walking off because I'm about money. He grabbed my hand and asked if he could talk to me later about it. "If you want a lap dance or even time to talk on a lap dance okay" I said to him then walking off.

Later that night I got a lap dance in the VIP section which is up stairs. It's with this bald headed brown skin guy that had a body builder's body.

In this area the guy pays two hundred dollars for you to dance for an hour. This looked like a pimped out royal looking room with gold and red king chairs they could sit in. We had our own individual open booth.

I'm shaking it up looking over the whole club. I'm amazed feeling on top of this Stripper world. I could see everything. I even saw Neal waiting on me. I was aaaah feeling the hip hop music. He got another lap dance up there. When I got back down stairs I didn't see Neal but I saw the guy that looked like Aaron. He got a lap dance on the floor but just wanted to talk with that time.

"What's up…Why you don't want me to give you a lap dance?"

"I don't need a lap dance I got girls for that."

"Girl's... as in plural. So what? Are you a pimp?"

He smiled and said: "Yeah…."

"A Pimp," I said cracking up laughing. "So you're a pimp for real. For real? I said looking around cheesing. Where your girl's at?"

"One is on her way," He said. I'm amazed because I had never met a man whose real occupation is pimping. I'm so curious asking all kinds of questions. First getting his code name: Frisco, I made him describe his occupation to me.

Shortly after I got up after the song because who wasn't getting pimped… is me. Later on after four songs of dances, I went into the front entrance bathroom. A female came out the stall. She's very attractive having a black dress on like me but its v neck with the rhinestones in between her chest. She wasn't a dancer. I spoke to her she spoke back. When she came close to the mirror O My God she looked familiar, like someone from back home in Oklahoma, Jailah's friend Kalon, the one that was staring at me while I was dancing at a night club once.

Instantly the thought came to me: *What is she doing here?* I knew without a shadow of doubt in my mind that's her. I never forget faces. I played it off like I didn't know her. She asked was I making any money tonight. With my face bright I said "Yeah." I told her I'm just in town for a week trying out different clubs.

"That's cool, she said walking out of the bathroom. I sat in there for a minute, stunned. I continued to work and at the same time calling Neal to come back. I ensured that every girl that worked saw me using my new phone. Around 12 a.m. two Gucci girl's came in, I call them that because that's what they were sporting, from their bags to glasses. Well I guess they're the star divas in the club.

I could tell they made money but they didn't look like nothing but some old veteran dancer's in the game looking like they had a hard life in the face. They came in quite late but right when the club is jammed packed. I'm in the dressing room as they got dress; the big balky one is checking me out. Even when we got out on the floor she's checking me out. I started to think: "What was this all about. Okay is she gay?" I didn't know and I tried to ignore it. She's watching every move I made seeing how I got paid. Watching the guys loving how I'm dancing.

Later that night I'm in the dressing room refreshing up and the dancer that kept starring came in and sat in the chair next to me. I kept focusing on what I was doing in the mirror but I could feel her stares.

She said suddenly in her most ghetto tone: "What happen to yo face?"

I stopped what I was doing and looked at her to say: "O… I was in an accident. It was in 96 though." Then I looked back in the mirror to continue.

"So you make money?"

312

I smiled saying: "Yeah… I make money. I worked at a club called Oasis in Baltimore, Maryland."

She stared amazed then said: "I feel sorry for you."

I stopped what I was doing and shook my head no looking dead at her saying: "Ut Ugh…Don't feel sorry for me. Please…Don't feel sorry for me," rolling my neck as I said that for the first time in my life to someone.

It pissed me off but I kept my cool I'm not in my territory. I do well just as good as a girl with no scars. I just kept doing what I was doing, fixing my hair. Almost at the end of the night the pimp guy named Frisco ask could he take me home. I said no thank you. He offered to take me to get a bite at this nice after hour's restaurant. I gave it some thought and told him I'm leaving out at 3a.m. I thought he's cute but I let it be known that I don't get pimped if anything I pimp myself. He understood saying: "No I just want to take you out to eat."

So we left together. We went to this eatery that sold grilled chicken and rice wraps that were so good. An outside place we ate in the car while we talked a little bit about Miami. He got a call on his cell and he had to go pick up one of his girl's. Apparently she scored and needed to be picked up. On our way I asked more insight about pimping. "Does he hit the girls? Do they all live together? How much do they charge?" He told me they charge three hundred dollars. I couldn't believe it. He even tells me that his girl's steal from the guy's they had sex with.

"Yeah she'll go in and take watches or other jewelry, watch this," He said as he spotted her coming out of the building.

I couldn't believe I'm getting ready to experience how pimping really works. He picked up the same girl that's in the bathroom with the black dress. She got in the back. I'm silent as a mouse until he introduced me as Lonnie.

"So what did you get?"

She gave him a watch and I couldn't believe that this beautiful girl is doing this. I'm itching to ask her is she from Tulsa. This girl looked exactly like Kalon. After that, we went back through this ritzy area to take me back to Selena's. I remember seeing the most beautiful houses that I dreamed to have. When we got back to Selena's street I didn't want them to see where I'm staying. There were these high rise sky scrapper condominiums all up and down that street even right next to Selena's place.

The blue Skyscraper next door: I told him that's where I'm staying. Frisco is shock saying: "Right here?"

"Yeap," I said laughing on the inside. I slowly walked to the glass door of the building with a man standing behind the desk looking skeptical of me. I played it off asking him different questions about the condos. I waited until they pulled off. Then I walked back out to go next door to Selena's place.

Friday night Selena wanted to go out but as for me I'm on a paper chase and I didn't have time for real clubbing. I'm on a mission to reach 5 G's. I went into my bank account to sponsor this trip never touching Jamonos's money. I'm leaving Saturday.

I went to this other club for half the night called Legends and the Black and Gold club for my last night on a mission. I apologized to Neal and slightly begged him to come in. He did and we spent three hours together talking giving him two lap dances in VIP. Being a Friday the club stayed packed making the time go by fast. I made enough money to reach my goal and three-hundred more. I took a cab safely back to Selena's. Saturday I took Selena to lunch and she took me to the mall to shop. I even had some

314

money that I came down there with. She took me to the airport and I'm B-More bound. India picked me up from the airport so I could tell her about my adventure in the M.I.A.

Chapter 30

SWEET Memories

I always feel bless. Even my trip to Miami I felt blessed and enjoyed myself. I came back safe. I made some money, just feeling blessed. At church I even gave a full amount of my ten percent. Feeling the favor on my life even in this circumstance; it's okay. It was a documentary hand's on experience. The path that I chose, sustaining, trying to let the Lord God All Mighty have full control. Not a man or a so called pimp, O No.

When I got back to my place I needed to go grocery shopping. I like to keep my cabinets stock with up to date food and ingredients I might need. As always getting more than what I even had on my list. Walking out feeling excellent and planning what to cook for this week an old frail White lady approached me. She had on worn looking clothes however clean looking. She looked poor but had beautiful blue eyes. She said her greeting in a sweet way: "Hello… Pretty Girl. O My"

"Hello" I responded but with a side grin continuing to walk to my car. I wasn't scared or nervous just knew that Baltimore is full of cons. She didn't beg for money but wanted me to listen to her. She kept repeating how special I am in so many different ways and how I had a gift that has not fully been revealed. I'm not the one that likes to brag on my self but love to get complements and revelations of how there is a purpose for me. What she said was so interesting and got my full attention I didn't pay attention to what she asked next.

She said in her sweetest voice: "Let me see your hand sweet child, don't be afraid, I want harm you. I'm one of Gods people."

Very hesitant however I wanted to know what she was going to do. I gave her my hand she flipped to the side of my palms.

"You have lost someone very special to your heart that you met here and now he went away to uughhh…. California ……. You're very dear to his heart….."

I moved my hand back not wanting to believe in it and what a coincidence she knew that.

"But through what happened he still loves you," she added.

"Okay….Thanks," I said acting in disbelief but shocked.

"I wanted to tell you that. I am one of God's people sweet heart but I am awfully hungry do you have any change?" The old lady said closer to me to hear her better. She looked so sincere.

See *I knew it. Just a game and a hustle for her. Making me feel she's helpless. But in the back of my mind I knew she was slight accurate with her tale and had one of God's gifts. O well* I thought. It was good. I gave her the first five dollar bill I saw. With appreciation in her eyes she thanked me. I got in my car and drove to my place. Thinking deep of Aaron.

The next Day I called his mother's house, the phone rung and rung. When I felt the answering machine is about to pick up I heard a deep voice of a man saying *Hello.*

317

Having a bright smile on my face I said:
"Hello...may I speak to Mrs. Carla Coasta."

He asked in a dull and saddened voice: "Who's speaking?"

"Jordyn, one of Aaron's friends," I said bright and energetic.

"Okay.... hold on," he said dropping the phone.

Within ten seconds Mrs. Carla came to the phone.

"Yes..." Mrs. Carla said in a sweet concerned voice.

"Mrs. Carla...Hi...This is Jordyn Braun. How are you?"

"Ugh...Not so well Jordyn...My husband is sick."
"O...I'm sorry to hear that. I wish there was something I could do," I said sweetly with sincerity.
"How is Aaron? Have you heard from him?" On my end I anticipated for his number to contact him to let him know I care for him.

With a long pause of Ms. Carla in deep thought she said: "Jordyn...After I say this I have to get off the phone with you. So when I tell you this I will just hang up the phone."

With so much concern in my voice of wondering why I said: "Okay."

"Some one shot Aaron and killed him in a bank robbery click Duuuuuuuuuuuuuuuuunnnnnnnnnnnnnn, the sound of the dial tone in my ear.

I dropped the phone and dropped to the floor screaming, I cried until my lungs got sore. My face was on the floor crying my heart out. I couldn't get a word out, not even "Why" because of holding in my breath for the longest until it hurt my vocal cords, then grasping for air crying. I cried until my heart felt it because my mind hadn't and I was frantic. After and hour my heart is in pain in fact

I stayed in the same place all night not even sleeping just thinking about my lost, crying every now and then.

The next morning I got up from the floor to at least get on my couch to be motionless. If any moving, it was in slow motion. Slow tears would fall. The phone ringing at a constant, I couldn't sleep and I couldn't eat. For a whole week. My good friend Donia/ (India) got concerned from not hearing from me for a whole week and then not answering any of her calls. She came over knocking on my door. Moving motionless it took me forever to answer the door.

As I opened it her first reaction was going off in a play-full way then she saw the look on my face.

"What's wrong?" She said.

We sat on my couch and I cried and couldn't tell her why. Donia just held me as I cried my way into telling her Aaron died. And she knew plenty about my long lost love Aaron. She just held me patting my back saying: "It's going to be okay Baby Girl."

For a whole month I stayed home. India was a big help to me in this time of need, bringing me food making sure I ate. She would stay and make sure I ate everything on my plate. She even came on the weekends and got me out my place for walks in our neighborhood park and shopping at Towson's four floored mall. We couldn't go out to eat because on two occasions I tried to sit there but I would breakdown and cry. Making me not want to stay there and just get my food to carry it out. I was a mess. I started to blame myself.

I knew that God had prepared me for the news of his death. The same bank robbery incident that Niya was talking about in California. Aaron was the one trying to help save the women. He died helping to protect her. In my book that makes him a hero. To stand up and be brave when you have an opportunity of death pointing right at you. He stood up and knew it wasn't right to have a woman at gunpoint. A Brave Heart.

The void in my life had died and I didn't know what to do. Could I handle this? Will I be able to make it? My Grandma said I would. I've been through many storms. I needed some strength so I started watching Preacher's, Pastor's, Bishop's and Doctor's who preached and taught the good word of Jesus Christ to lift my spirit up. I kept praying I gotta get through this.

It took me a whole month to recover from the news. Now I had to regroup and try to move forward in my life. That's what Aaron would want me to do. I had so much on my brain. I still hadn't heard from Joy, Jamonos's sister. I didn't want to start going into his stash with paying for things. With all the stuff on my mind I had to get back on the grind. Just until I found a real job.

Right when I'm feeling blessed, it never fails. My mind is strong and I knew eventually my heart would get back strong and mend. I believe because I am born with faith.

Chapter 31

GO GETTA

*I*ndia, her sister Diamoni and I started going to Bethel. Not missing a Sunday service. Dr. Reid had so much anointing that it spread throughout his huge congregation. It's spiritual nutrition that built my spirit back up. I had faith. I knew that I could get out the situation I'm in. I just needed to go fill out applications for a better job. I had no job.

Now that I didn't work at Oasis I tried out Tiffany's. The club India worked at, the most recent new club on the block with only two months of being open. The same owner's of Norma Jeans, so the same system. However they didn't have the massive clientele so that's how I was down to work there. I automatically became a top money maker along side India however the club would have crowds sporadically. I mean no fast pace of guy's coming in at all. When we did, we made money, not the money I'm use too. So I knew soon I would be making new moves plus India started acting kind of shady.

After working there two weeks and making the club money I thought I would have earned the respect of the female bartender's. One dark haired female that bar tends at Norma Jeans and a red head that I've never seen. The dark haired one is okay in personality. The red head is a bitch.

One night after work I'm the first girl down to get paid. All the very young dancer's where still up stairs acting there age, obnoxious and loud. India being amongst it all, I got dressed quick to get my money and be out. I'm there sitting and waiting at the bar. The two bartenders are calculating everything up, that's fine I know that takes time. Another fifteen minutes and all the other girls are gradually coming down to get paid. The bar maids are wrapping things up with about fifteen female's to pay. They waited for me to be the last one.

Now in the clubs I worked at before when you're one of the money maker's you're serviced first and better. However this red head distributing the money is taking her time that I finally stood up as if I need to really go. As I watched her pay all the other's even India left with her new young friends. Afterwards I let the red head know: "You know I was the first female down and I waited over thirty minutes and I'm the last one paid...I mean damn... I made this club money tonight and I'm the last one paid..." I had a slight attitude.

She looked at me with an attitude too. She didn't say anything however tossed my money on the bar. It didn't go all over the place. I looked down at my money and I literally wanted to jump over the bar to start choking and pounding my fist in her face with a good grip of her hair.

"Okay...okay...it's like THAT. You didn't have to throw my money and act like a Bitch about me asking why I'm the last to get paid." As I said that I'm gathering my stuff, walking to the steps to go down to leave this club. She's talking sh*t saying: "O GET OUT OF Here with THAT." Repeating: "You're a BITCH"

"I'm the Bitch... OKAY we'll see who the bitch is."

I'm proud that I walked away from the situation.
Nonsense, just evil non sense. No more going to that club.
However the next night I went to talk to the owner and tell
him how I was treated. He knew I was a money maker and
didn't want to see me go however was upset of how I was
treated. Who knows if he said something but let me know
he would.

I decided for the meantime for money give the Gold
Club a try. I went during the day. India told me to get any
shift they're hiring for, if they say only day take day and
work up to night. She had to start during the day. India told
me night is where the money is.

I told the bouncer at the door that I'm looking for a
job to dance. He asked for my ID to see how old I was. He
told me he'll be back walking away. He brought back this
handsome man wearing glasses with a dark suit looking
like Clark Kent. He introduced him self as the Manager
Jeff. I introduce myself. Jeff asked a few question's like:
Did I work somewhere before? I told him Oasis. He looked
impressed by nodding his head. He told me to change into
something where he could see my body since I had on
baggy jeans. The stage in the Gold club is huge. I'm a little
bit nervous.

I went up to the dressing room which is beautiful
Oasis had nothing on the Gold's clubs. The locker room is
separate from the two big dressing rooms with vanity
mirrors and comfortable seats. It's so high class, marble
showers. I put on my netted dress that had a Jamaican look
with the colored tie die yellow and green. I looked like one
of the chicks from Dancing with the Stars after I made my
self up. I went down the glass steps to the stage to perform.
The steps were steep and I took my time down them. By
Jeff eyes... he looked like one of those spectator guys not
at work... dying wanting to flirt. After I got down and got

dress back in my street clothes to go back and talk to the manager. He said he would hire me for day time. I told him: "Sure that's fine." He wanted to see if I could work first. I'm going to give it a try. I wasn't hurting for the money just wanted to keep it going.

I loved the rules for the lap dance. Like Oasis the guy's could not touch and the lap dance area had a bouncer just for that area to make sure everything is alright. The hustle game is set up like Miami, pay a fee to work and the rest you pocket. One thing they had about the block is that we get something off the twenty dollar drink too.

The best thing to go for is the lap dances that were twenty-five dollars. In the separate room is luxury lap dance area that went from a hundred to three hundred dollars. Girls could go topless in that room. All that money you keep. After paying the dancer's fee and the bouncer's fee, the rest of the money I made I pocketed.

It's a very classy club, my first week I learned the club. The pole went all the way up the high rise ceiling with streaming stars that look like real stars. Like the stars on the ceiling… the chicks looked like stars on T.V in this place, meaning more competition. I got drinks but I wasn't making a big profit because I'm still at day shift. Less people but a lunch crowd. Guy's mainly wanted to talk. Guy's would come into eat lunch and leave. They had a nice kitchen and a full menu.

In order for me to make money I had to get lap dances and get to nights. It's a majority White club however they played all kinds of Hip-Hop. When it was my turn to dance the D.J. gave me out dated songs that I really couldn't dance to. Sometimes even rock that I didn't know which I thought was real shady. I already told him my request: Hip-Hop and R&B. During the day ten to twelve females work. At night its thirty to forty more female's, all competing for money. I got an adrenaline rush every time I danced on that stage. I got along with most of the females. They're professional at what they do. Sure there were loud mouth wild ones however adult acting.

I spoke however kept to myself. The dancer's were very professional approaching me introducing them selves. Lots of them complemented me on my body. Some of the females were considerate sharing some of the rules, like the one about the tips on stage, the same issue that India had.

One blond haired White chick kept it cool with me during the day to converse. She was outrageously thick but toned with all the right curves a sista would have. She's a mad money maker with Black and White guys.

I fell in love with the big runway stage that had a long stair way to get to it. The club is the size of a gymnasium. With the stage being in the center for all the attention is such a rush, lights, music and action. This is such a classy place. The guys had these nice comfortable chairs to sit in. It got better closer to the weekend. But it had one down fall, racism. One female bartender kept ignoring me and this Black guy wanting a drink. She kept passing us up. I have never experience racism not even in my home state of Oklahoma. I'm trying to gain drinks. But she kept ignoring me. I finally said "HELLO," loud enough to get her attention. She got an attitude not wanting to serve us, haters.

I worked for a week hardly making ends. I range for that whole week working four days with just five hundred and twenty-two dollars. I know that's not much but it was during the day. My regulars at Oasis work during the day, so when I called for a visit they couldn't come in. Daytime few men stopped in. But I was one of the top Black females making money day. There's this Black females that had a

White girl trapped in her. She talked beginning everything with: "Like… O My God," you know the type.

Remember this is an all White club. Hardly any Black guys come in. I did good enough to impress the sharp dressing manager Jeff. He's cute. I continued to ask him about nights until he finally said alright.

I called my regulars on my first night at the Gold club and let them know I'm working nights now. Getting dress the girl's were more loud and rowdy. I tuned them out. As always I keep to myself, but looked approachable and I'm saying hello to some. Nights were even better however I had to work extra harder than these White females just because being Black. The pressure is on but guess who wasn't gonna step back, me Lonnie. Got some acceptance and some rejection I kept on stepping until I found the one that showed any interest in me.

Bean and I got back in touch with each other. Since I'm working nights so he finally came in. As always making it rain dollar bills. I wondered did the girl working those nights he did that get jealous because no one does that for them. Bean always gets the best of what ever. He took me in the lavish lap dance room. It's like being in a fancy magazine layout living room with a fire place but nothing was burning.

After a while Jeff the manager is impressed and I caught his eye. I would sense the attraction however avoided it for professional reasons. He bought me a couple of drinks to talk. After my second week there he took me out to eat. We had a good chat just for him to see where my head was. He's very impress to learn that I'm in school. I told him I'm getting ready to retire on being a dancer and focus on getting my degree. In his eyes he wanted to say no but responded with: "Wait until we have the contest."

"What contest?" I asked.

"We have a contest called Miss Maryland's Best Body."

"It's happening in a couple of weeks just wait... you'll start to hear the girls talking about it."

In a couple of weeks school is starting back and I had a goal of cutting this lifestyle out.

One night at work I just got threw with my dance set. I went to my locker to freshen up before I went back down stairs. As I'm leaving a red curly headed White girl is leaving the stage. She rushed down the steps so quickly and we bumped right into each other. I didn't know whose fault it was but my first reaction is to say sorry sweetly. This cocky White girl says: "Yeah...........yeah" with an attitude walking to her locker.

That made me get an attitude back following her to the locker room saying: "Whoa...wait a minute you really bumped into me. You should be saying excuse me. Where's your manners?" She didn't want any problems when she saw me step up to her. She finally cop deuces saying: "It's cool...It's cool." I wasn't a punk I had to stand up for myself.

After that it was tension. I thought it would be something after the night. What if her loud mouth clique tries to jump me? I knew I was by myself. I called Barron up to tell him what's up. He told me to blow that sh*t off. I'm getting tired of those night girls trying to test me.

I had a particular incident a long wavy haired blond female like India's issue. Her friend is dancing and would get her tips slowly on her song, even after her song is off. Seemed like every time she did it I'm after her. And that's a no no. Girls didn't play that. After a while of her still doing it I just started doing my set and she'd get bumped by one of my poll moves of me lifting up my body. It happened twice and finally she said something to me. I

327

acted as if I didn't know saying "O… I bumped you I didn't even feel you…sorry." Then later I told her about the rule and how she needed to really be off the stage. She went to go get this short petite brown haired girl. After a while the little brown haired girl came up to me saying with an attitude: "Excuse me…The girl that you said something to that's my friend.

"SO…AND." I said to her.

"SO…That's my girl and she's new."

"I don't care…Ya'll make a big deal out of people taking a long time with tips…. but when one of ya'll girl's do it… it's cool. No it's not cool. So whatever…It can be whatever."

She got upset far away talking big noise to where the bouncer came up the spiral stairs. When they came that's when she's really trying to act like she wanted to do something and step up to me. He's holding her back while I stood there.

I said loudly: "Yeah BOUNCER GET THE DANCER BEFORE WE BE BOUNCING UP IN HERE."

That's when she went off jumping up and down. Finally they calmed her down. After the club was over she's in the bathroom getting dress talking loud with her friends but never stepped up or got out of bounds. I began to realize that these girl's where just a bunch of talk.

I'm going to do the contest just for fun to see where I would place. It's happening in two weeks. Like Jeff said everybody started talking about it, asking each other where they going to run. I told no one that I was running just pretending to not really know too much about it.

Selena had heard about the contest way in Miami and came back to Maryland for a while to work there and be Sasha. She had her bordered room paid up for a year. Now Selena is hard competition I mean she thought my body was more beautiful than hers and I thought the same of her. What she did on the poles were amazing by now, she's the one that really taught me the really dangerous looking poll tricks. A lot of females from other clubs came to compete. Like this Black chick from Norma Jeans. Short and petite muscle frame name Te-Ra. We exchange some conversation once at Norma Jeans about liking to dance to some rock. It's another Black girl there that's competed three times and lost all. No Black girl has ever won. Jeff really thought I had potential to win. Cherry this reddish wavy long haired White female is running. She's pretty and had a cool personality, easy to get along with. We were cool in the club. She had a body with all the right curves with small breast. She's into a little bit of Hip Hop. Everybody is secretive about their outfits but she's excited letting me in on seeing her opening outfit that's a Fifty cent theme with the Gucci gun holster with red trim and boots. It's cute but I had something better.

It's this White girl that started the same time I did. She had long thick brown hair. Long, I mean down her back all the way to her butt. And one thing this White girl loved to do is swing her hair everywhere and it would fall back in place. Her name is Porsche. Then it's four more other White girls. We had a meeting the night before the contest

In the contest I'm definitely representing Hip-Hop music. I'm going to bring it. None of my regulars were coming, potientially two. Most didn't believe the contest is fair to the Black females. And weren't even sure they're coming because of the expensive cover charge. A lot of my regulars didn't want me to go through with the contest. I'm simply doing it to see how far I would get however put my all in to it. I spent well over five hundred dollars on expenses for this four day event. From outfits, accessories, props, make up, and I even got long extensions in my hair. Plan B backups like safety pins, grip for shoes, etc.

During the contest they wanted to do a bathing suit scene – that wasn't part of the itinerary. It's something last minute. This is very important for the judges to score on different semi title categories like best body, face, legs and butt. I wasn't prepared with a bathing suit but I had this zebra print top and bottoms outfit I wore. They just wanted us to prance around and dance a little to half a song and come back up the stairs. It's going to be quick, quick, quick next girl after the next. The D.J. with eagerness got every ones songs. I had a second to think and the first song that came up in my mind is Chingy's song: "Right Thurr." I rushed to put the last minute outfit on. We all lined up to get ready to go out there. The MC is going into the prizes were competing for. I'm going to be the fifth contestant that went out there. They're starting the show in five minutes. With that known I had to go to the bath room.

I guess you can say I'm nervous and excited all wrapped in one. I told Selena to call me if they called my name. When I got out the bathroom there was a problem. The MC is in the middle of the girls acting frantic calling for my name. "LONNIE….Where's Lonnie. JESUS CHRIST YOU MISSED YOUR CHANCE TO BE JUDGE." He was acting like an ass.

I became a nervous wreck saying: I'm HERE…I'm right HERE…what's going on?

"I CALLED YOUR NAME YOU WERE SUPPOSED TO COME UP."

"I'm SORRY…I'm supposed to be the fifth girl going up."

He's still going off on me. And I finally said: "FORGET IT…. I don't have to go. You're making a big deal about it."

"O sweetheart this is the part you want to do OKAY…
they're judging you on this part for the semi titles," he said.
I felt bad, embarrassed and at the same time set up because
I went to the bathroom as he walked down to the stage start
the show. The five minute introduction and then the four
girls before me something didn't add up.

"You have one more chance to go out there. Let's
go…I'll call your name again," he said giving me a
frustrated look.

The bathroom is just around the corner. I didn't
understand why I was called out so quickly. I blew it off
but knew its competition time. And Selena had her game
face on. But I thought we were better than that. The least
thing Selena could have done was call my name, nada
nothing from her. I put my game face on and I went down
the stairs feeling the music. When I focused down on the
ten judges its one Black guy. *O Well.*

I brought my CD player to listen to as I got
prepared for Showtime. I practiced my routine in my mind.
After a while the girl from Norma Jeans asked to see my
CD player to listen to her music too. When it's my time to
perform I danced to three songs. The first night I had a red
dress on dancing to Lumee D - "Never Leave You" then
R.Kelly's song "Move Your Body Like a Snake, then JD's
and Mariah's cut "Sweetheart."

Selena did a one act show that she planned to do
every night. Great idea, I didn't think about that. She came
out looking like a little girl with pig tails saying she had
been drinking her milk and one day this guy is going to
want her. Then she went back behind the stage to transform
into a woman. Her routine is dynamic with all these high
pole tricks in the air barely hanging on. I didn't see it
however saw it later. The Black girl from Norma Jeans Te-

331

Ra is dancing a one routine act too Michael Jackson's "Smooth Criminal."

Cherry did different acts in the competition. Cherry did her thing in her red Gucci holster get up playing 50 cents "In the Club." Then in other songs she mostly played alternative punk rock. After Porsche that swings her hair is dressing up as a tiger, similar theme I'm doing my final night.

Chapter 32

The Moment You've Been Waiting For

The second night I rushed because I had to go pick up my CD from my friend Reggie at his studio way in the suburbs of Maryland. He made two and one was marked to be the right one because the other skipped. The first song is going to be Floetry's song "Sunshine." I did an arrhythmic dance to it with a flowing white ribbon." The second song is Ashanti "Rock with You." The third song is going to be The Best of Both World's CD: "Body." Then I gave them just a little taste of LSG's song "Body." I'm wearing white. It was a one piece tub top swimsuit but I added a boa around my chest. And I wore my glass slippers with the silver heel. I'm late getting there and I'm trying to rush to get ready and organized. 1st thought on my mind I need to listen to the right CD. I asked Te Ra for my CD player and she said she forgot it. I looked at her crazy and said: "Where is it?"

"OOoh I left it at home but I'll bring it tomorrow," she said finishing her makeup sitting down.

I wanted to snatch her right out the chair. I'm running around trying to find someone with a CD player. Luckily Cherry had a music box. I wanted to hear the song at least one good time. I went to the body mirror in the back and once again the D.J. is in a rush to get all the CD's. Without thinking about the two CD's I had I gave him the one in the CD case ready to go with my real name on it.

So when I got out there they played "Sunshine." I interpreted the song through dance. I did the arrhythmic dance with a flowing ribbon which flowed beautifully. The song meant so much to me, it hit home. It's basically saying how I felt. It was beautiful. The ribbon did all the right moves flying in the air. Ashanti's song came on and I'm going along with my performance and then all of a sudden she started to re-sing the verse. With the thoughts of *O MY GOD. I gave him the wrong CD.* I couldn't believe this is happening. It kept repeating and repeating. I finally got the D.J's attention to shut the song off by slicing of the neck sign. He finally got it and went into the next song which is Jay-Z and R- Kelly "Body"

Inside I'm so upset. I didn't show it just went along with my show like nothing wrong happened. Wondering did I lose points for that? Did I lose out on my chances of winning? I keep forgetting it's just for fun but I love to compete in things like this.

We all were wondering who's going to win. Cherry thought it's between us three Selena, me and her. We all had eye catching performances. I thought the same but there could be only one Miss Body Maryland and Miss Body Baltimore.

That night I went home and improvised my plan of the last two nights I had to really bring it to pull my score up which I didn't know.

Tomorrow I knew I had a huge surprise for them that would bring my score back up. I planned to wear my Carnival parade outfit that Donia and I wore to the parade in Ghana. It's red and gold with beautiful colorful gems on the boustia and gem belted skirt. The part I loved about it, it had arm sequence bracelets that had a flowing sheer cloth for both arms. I'm going to look exotic because red is one color that looks good on my skin. I had gold platforms already that went perfect with this ensemble. I'm going to win mad points back from the music messing up the other night.

The only thing about the outfit I lost the feathered hat you wear in the parade. I made a long feathered piece that tied around my head. The piece I made in the middle of my forehead had colorful gems. I even had face gems to stick on my face. I planned not to put too much just one jewel piece on both sides of my high cheek bone. In the parade we wore tennis shoes in the competition I was wearing my gold platforms. Since I had them almost two years the grip on the bottom of the platforms came off. So I bought new grip for the shoes. They stick and stayed. I even practice at home on my kitchen floor to make sure they would be ready.

Friday and Saturday night is bringing a big audience so we had to park around the corner to give space to the spectators. A mini shuttle took us back and forth. The crowd is coming for us but also some featured Entertainers from Las Vegas that our like celebrities in the Stripper world. They got ready in a private dressing room just for them that had floral arrangements and water with finger foods for refreshments. What a rampant night. With the regular girls scheduled to work and the contestants of the competition getting ready for the big event. I started pulling out my secret weapon outfit from the Carnival. All the girl's at work that night gave me complements and knew I was in it to win it. They couldn't hate and felt that if they didn't complement... they're hating. I even made confident Selena look.

In support Donia (India) and one of her long time regular's Tim came to see my performance that night. None of my regulars had showed up so far. I wasn't worried about it. Donia's support that night is all I needed. Having someone else I knew in the crowd always hyped me up even more. My songs where "Contagious" by Truth Hurts. Walking down the steps my movement is slow. One thing I didn't do is test the grip on my gold platforms with this stage. When I got out there I had to do my whole routine being cautious not to slip. I couldn't believe how slippery it was and still I did my routine.

2nd track is "Big Pimpin" by Jay-Z featuring Bun B and Pimp C. I felt both songs went with the outfit. Truth Hurts "Contagious" is a belly dance tune. "Big Pimpin," If you've seen the video it shows them at a similar parade we attended in 2002. The girl's are dancing around in the parade with the same outfit I'm wearing that night, mine is unique and beautiful. I took my gemmed bra off to the last song. The last song is slow something for them to learn Christina Milian's "Dip it Low" and I rocked it like a pro, just keeping on the belted skirt.

During my whole performance Donia is out in the crowd rocking her body. When I got back up to the dressing room a dancer working that night said: "O My God, Girl you ROCK IT! You're going to win it."

I smiled saying: "Awe...Thank you......Thank you for that."

"Have you ever seen Queen of the Dam on Aaliyah's introduction part?"
She asked.
"No... I haven't."
"O My God...The part when you came out you did exactly what she did walking out."

336

"Really... I'm going to have to watch it," I said to her curious to know how it looked. Well I guess that's a good thing. I went home being confident that tonight's performance helped my points from last nights.

That next morning Selena called me needing me. Her only outfit she's wearing had ripped and she needed a sewing machine. She knew I sewed and asked did I have one. I had invested in this expensive sewing machine. Someone else competing with her may have said no but since she was still my girl I said sure come on over.

Her eyes I detected jealousy at my styled up place. I could see the envy in her eyes knowing that most of her money is spent on her getting citizenship here. She sewed her things and gladly appreciated it. We didn't talk about the last night of us competing against each other however both of us in our own right wanted the title.

The last night of judging which is on a Saturday, as usual I'm running behind and nervous. They wanted us to bring a nice dress for when where getting the results of who won. I had this black and white dress that had a small Hawaiian pattern that I got from Be Be's. Not the tropical leaves but small Hawaiian flowers. The outfit for my last performance in the competition I saved to be the best.

I'm not nervous at all with none of my performances I shield that with my confidence and sexiness. I'm going to play Cat Woman. I had these Patton leather cat ears this Patton leather halter cat suit that fit tight. It looked tailor maid to fit me. What I loved about this suit – it was for dancer's to take off easy. The inside is like a vinyl feel but cloth.

I got it back home in Tulsa shopping for the event. When I took the cat suit off I had on these black Patton leather thongs. Fish net thigh high's with some ankle Patton leather sandaled platforms. Looking like the same shoes the

R&B singer Monica had on in the Video "So Gone." I had this big thick rhinestone choker on my neck that blinged and a bracelet to match. I looked like a high maintenance black cat. I stepped out on the Pink Panther's theme music and stood there looking out binoculars acting like I'm looking for someone. Bending all down looking to play it off to put the binoculars down, then I played several seconds of Monica's song "Like This and Like That" on her Miss Thang CD. It started off like: "I just can't keep from going… I'm falling in love with you. I need to know if you want me for sure…" I was on the steps on the part throwing my legs up like I'm falling when she sung: "I'm falling in love with you." It looked hot and it was a sudden move. Then after those two minutes it went into her latest single, "Gone." My good friend Reggie and I put me in rhyming on the CD in the part she raps on. I got out my jumpsuit and I played a remix with the "In Da Club" beat with Beyonce' singing a verse that started out with she's the hot chick with the Manolo Blanic's. It's so tight and I had my super ego going on. Then I mixed that with her song "Crazy." If you've seen the video I did exactly want she did but in my own style. I had every step down packed even the ones I made up. You would have thought she taught me herself. I even acted to trip and fall gracefully like she did only in stiletto platforms tell me that ain't working it. Jay-Z's part I Roc'd it, with the crowd stunned at my movements. The third song I'm pumped. My last song I gave the White audience something to really feel by playing "Lose Yourself" by Eminem and that's exactly what I did swinging my hair around like a rock star, going up to the top of the pole losing it, swinging around then dropping down the pole fast.. It's outstanding, as normal having all eyes on me. I got everyone's attention interpreting that massage through a dance. I only danced

338

three minutes of the song. It's a certain length of time per entertainer. That whole performance is a female that got gone scooping out her man with these binoculars and she explained how crazy she got and at the end lost herself in the music.

When it's time for the judging for some odd reason I'm nervous because I wanted to win it all of a sudden. Everyone in the contest is made up and ready in their dresses. Selena wore her black dress with the thick rhinestone neck piece. My dress is the same cut form fitting, my whole back is out with a circle. I made myself look Hawaiian because of the print in the dress. We all were supposed to walk out together down the steps and stand mid way on the steps. It's almost time for judging. Out of the whole competition I did an outstanding job. We all did.

The crowd's favorites were Selena, Cherry, Me, and Porsche that swings her hair. The moment for judging, going into the different semi title categories like Best legs of Baltimore and Maryland, Best face in Baltimore and Maryland, Best body, Best Ass, Best Creativity in Baltimore and Maryland. I'm not going to go into what everybody won. Selena did win Maryland's best face. I won Baltimore's best legs and Porsche won Maryland's best legs which I should've been Maryland's since it's the best trophy to win. Then I won Maryland's best body and Selena won best body Baltimore. And I won Maryland best ass hands down, everybody in the crowd clap and cheered for me going down to get my trophy. But overall the title of Miss Maryland's Best Body winner was..................
When they were doing the drum roll I held my breath in. The drum roll seemed so long. They finally called out Cherry. They put a big crown on her head, the tassel and gave her a bouquet of roses. I clapped for her because deep

down inside I knew she's going to win it. Then they had to quiet the crowd down to announce Miss Baltimore's Best Body. I wore my grin the whole the time, being confident. It's a feeling that beauty contestants should understand. The announcer said: "This was a hard one folks but the winner is," The MC started tearing the envelope up to get inside to announce the winner while the drum roll had started for him, Bthrrrrrrrrrrrrrrrrrrrrrrrrrrrrrrrrrrrrrrrrrrrrrrrrrrrrrrr.......... I'm so nervous of the outcome thinking: *Who would it be? O My God. What if I win "I know I'm not going all the way to Vegas if I do win the title.*

Both winners had to attend another contest in Las Vegas. I wasn't sweating it win or lose, it's just fun. I'm just doing it for a challenge to myself. Then I thought what I long drum roll with all those thoughts they stop and the MC said: "Miss Baltimore's Best Body is...Again I took a deep breath: "Cherry." That's when I exhaled. She's shock. I'm behind her and I patted her on the back saying congratulations still smiling and clapping for them. Inside, my bets were on them. I was taking my chances. My attitude is this: I was shooting to win…. my goals were to win the whole title but if I didn't so what. I wanted to see how far I could go. But I didn't understand why I won the category of Maryland's best body semi title and Selena won Baltimore best body. I still didn't place? I blew it off. Selena is so excited. Cherry is too, still surprised. They made them go down to the center stage and get totally naked taking pictures. That's why I knew it wasn't meant for me to win. I would have felt uncomfortable but they didn't. When it's time for us to walk back up the dressing rooms I'm glad because I'm ready to go home. I got dress

340

but when Selena and Cherry came up I gave them hugs. Selena is so excited however getting dress the same time I am…early being 1:25 a.m.

"O" I didn't forget. Te Ra is down stairs mingling with some of the other performer's like crowned Cherry. I went down stairs in my warm up suit asking Te Ra for my CD player. "OOoo girl I'm sorry I forgot it again."

"You forgot it again ugh," I said looking deep into her eyes. "Okay…." I said walking off. I went right back up stairs to her stashed away bag sitting under the vanity. I looked through her bag just to see if I saw my CD player. Nothing. *Okay*, I thought *I'm getting something*. I grabbed her fake knock off Man no no boots and took them right outside to the garbage, hiding them in two different spots. I went back up stairs to gather all my things from my locker playing it off and walked out with the winner of the contest Selena (Sasha). Te Ra had suspected that I had done something as I walked out not retaliating on her head for not bringing my things back but smiled. She ran up stairs as we were going down. As soon as we got to the bottom floor that bitch is screaming my name: "LONNIE…..LONNIE You Need To STOP Playing. Where's My Shoes? I ignored her and continued talking to Selena about her winning and continuing to the Vegas competition. When we got outside Selena got a phone call. At first she's going to take me to my car. I grabbed on to her new sporty red Viper to get in the passenger's side. She got off the phone and switched up on me saying in her Russian/ Iranian accent: "O honey I'm sorry I'm meeting someone and I got to go."

"Selena…You can't take me around the corner."

She said in a pitiful sounding tone: "Baby I'm sorry."

I had already got cozy in the seat but got back out to catch the Shuttle van. As I got on the bus to go to the other

341

parking lot, Selena reverse her car out of her parking spot too fast and hit someone from behind. We all got out and it's a fender bender to her brand new whip. See if I was in there I would have been looking out to help her.
"O Well."

I went home and warmed up some Pizza Hut and balanced it with salad. I'm happy and content with my awards. I'm glad I didn't win. I didn't have to take pictures with my clothes all off pretending to like it. That's it for me what a challenge.

The next day I got a call from Jeff, the manager. And he didn't understand the results he just knew I was going to win it. I told him its okay but didn't understand how I won Maryland's best body semi title and didn't place. I told him that my song that messed up might have knocked my points down too. But I'm cool and that was it for me. But he already knew from our nights eating breakfast I gave him my notice of leaving a long time ago. He said: "I know...I know but I want you to feature next weekend one good time showcasing your performance," he said in his sexy Italian tone. It convinced me and it did sound nice to have that private dressing room all to myself. He wanted each girl from the performance that worked in the Gold club to take out a weekend for them to feature. Jeff let me do the first weekend. Friday and Saturday I planned to do my Carnival outfit playing Truth Hurts and Jay-Z "Big Pimpin" routine. Saturday night the so "Gone" and "Crazy" routine.

In my whole career of dancing I never fell but when I was playing Beyonce's "Crazy" I stumbled not being nervous or walking down the steps. It's ironic I did because in the routine I'm just walking into doing this down South stomping on the floor. (It just looked like your tapping one foot on the floor while hopping.) After I stumbled it went perfect with what Beyonce said "And baby you're making a fool of me." So I played the stumble off perfect with doing that. I couldn't believe it…. my last time dancing. But at the end of the performance I change it a little not having my last song Eminem's "Losing Yourself." Giving myself another challenge of playing a song I couldn't bare to listen to. I had a breakdown of crying in my friend Simone's car once off the song "I Never Want To Live Without You," sung by Mary J. Blige. It was my sophomore year in college. Ever since then I couldn't listen to the song because of how hard I cried. So… on the last song I played it and nailed it even climbing all the way up to the top of the ceiling looking out into the crowd. On the part where she sung: "So I wish upon a star," I'm climbing up the pole to the stars on the clubs ceiling that literally gleamed, "I follow you where you are," I bent over the pole looking into the crowd. It was the most beautiful part of the whole routine. A routine that I put together in my head. What guy's always went crazy for is when I crawled my way back to the stage at the ending only to walk up the steps. When I got all the way up to the top of steps I said good bye to the game by giving them a princess bow because little did they know they watched a part of history of a true Entertainer. I really didn't work that night. I put on this short Zebra dress that tied on one shoulder, it's bad. I went out in the crowd and got mad offers for drinks. Drink number eight is with this Black guy and he loved my performance.

I told him this is my last night. I shared with him during the whole time I danced I did it honest and always respected myself. I had to earn respect in each club I worked at. I'm made the best out of it. And now I don't have to do this anymore. The whole time I'm working with females in the club with different disputes with girls never once did one of them call me scar face or some kind of name regarding my face trying to diss. It's like they knew better not to go there. He felt me totally one hundred percent. After a while I ate and had champagne with my favorite buddy Bean.

Chapter 33

From Rebellion to Redemption

My dream had finally come true. I got out the game. I waited by the phone and never got any calls from Jamonos or Joy. Jamonos is a good dude but I guess he wasn't too worried about the money. For what Taz did I took it as a settlement. Paid my condo up for a year, I paid my Mercedes Benz off. And I saved the rest just for a rainy day, got a job at New York and Company cool and legit to pay my miscellaneous bills.

Simply what it boils down to with that lifestyle it's just not healthy. Sure it gets females through their degrees; feed their kids, way of living and habits. It can be fun and glamorous at first getting all this attention. But it can turn into a bitter sweet nightmare. It's been a wonderful experience and then again it's been a heavy burden. I've been set free from that. I'm just a country girl missing the life of peace and quiet. I learned a lot in that game. Be careful who you call your friends. Never throw dirt on people that keep it 100% real with you. Don't trust anyone you don't really know, only family. Make the money don't let it make you and don't let a substance control you. For lust…control it. Give it up and turn it loose. Don't get caught up in anything negative, first positive thought that comes to your mind – think it through & go for it. For lost loves- You never know what you got until it's gone.

I'm content. Without Aaron my heart will slowly mend. It will take time and then I'll be fine. To fill that void I bought a Yorkie terrier to replace the child we never had. His name is Joey. I can't bear to go to the place Aaron is resting. I want to just remember the memories. He was my first real love and will never be forgotten.

I finally told my parents what I did as a living. It was bothering me too much. I apologized. They were just glad that I was safe now and they didn't want me doing that any more. I like my job at a simple clothing store. I'm in my last year of school making plans to graduate.

Some month's later India now became back to a house wife and mom. Her husband was out of jail back in his family's business. She's looking for a regular job and we still go to Bethel together.

Nicole became an instructor at an adult educational learning center teaching public relations. We talk every so often and go have lunch with Tasha and Joey, our dogs.

Flame well Dawn now likes guys. She still works at Norma Jeans and goes to school part time. We still talk on the phone.

Suga well that Kysha girl still strips and goes to school at Morgan. I have a class with her. I kept it professional by still keeping it social with her.

Iesha and Lucky were never heard from again. Still today that was an unsolved mystery. Did their plot fail?

Jamonos and Taz got fifteen years a piece. I finally got in touch with Joy, Jamonos's sister and gave her the rest of the money.

Barron and I still keep in touch. He's still a camera man for CBS. He found a woman and fell in love.

346

With the drugs substances and drinking I'm proud to say I took it one day at a time and gradually slowed down. After slowing down out of the fast lane I let go of all the people that stayed in the fast lane. After evaluating myself I stopped dibbling and dabbling in those things. Drinking I've never done heavily. Smoking I did when I was dancing in the strip club environment now I'm not in any dangerous surroundings.

I'm free... free as a bird this has been my Word. So despite what I did... you have to really look deep within. The whole reason why I wrote this is to get a clear understanding. So please don't judge a person for what they're doing or have done. You don't know where they've come from.

Repeat daily: I AM More Than a Conqueror

LaVergne, TN USA
29 July 2010
191366LV00003B/5/P